W9-BUV-440

MURDER
AT THE
CAPITOL

Books by C.M. Gleason

Murder in the Lincoln White House

Murder in the Oval Library

Murder at the Capitol

MURDER AT THE CAPITOL

A Lincoln's White House Mystery

C.M. GLEASON

KENSINGTON BOOKS
www.kensingtonbooks.com

KENSINGTON BOOKS are published by

Kensington Publishing Corp.
119 West 40th Street
New York, NY 10018

All Kensington titles, imprints, and distributed lines are available at special quantity discounts for bulk purchases for sales promotion, premiums, fund-raising, educational, or institutional use.

Special book excerpts or customized printings can also be created to fit specific needs. For details, write or phone the office of the Kensington Special Sales Manager: Attn. Special Sales Department. Kensington Publishing Corp., 119 West 40th Street, New York, NY 10018. Phone: 1-800-221-2647.

Kensington and the K logo Reg. U.S. Pat. & TM Off.

Library of Congress Card Catalogue Number: 2019950871

ISBN-13: 978-14967-2398-7
ISBN-10: 1-4967-2398-8
First Kensington Hardcover Edition: February 2020

ISBN-13: 978-1-4967-2400-7 (ebook)
ISBN-10: 1-4967-2400-3 (ebook)

10 9 8 7 6 5 4 3 2 1

Printed in the United States of America

To my dear friends
Erin and Devon Wolfe:
The two of you are an inspiration
in so many ways.

CHAPTER 1

*"Of soldiers the country is full.
Give us organizers and commanders.
We have men, let us have leaders.
We have confusion, let us have order."*
—*The Washington Star*, June 1861

*Thursday
July 4, 1861
Washington, D.C.*

*T*he country was at war.

Almost overnight, Washington, D.C., metamorphosed from a small, muddy town with pigs and goats wandering the streets into a city bursting with soldiers from all over the North—and with all the hangers-on that accompanied them: laundresses, cooks, wives, and prostitutes, along with marching bands, horses, and wagons.

Pennsylvania Avenue, which stretched at a dog's leg angle from the Capitol Building to the President's House, had gone from being merely busy to almost impassable during the day. If it wasn't one regiment of soldiers marching down the grand throughway, it was the marching band of a different one—not to mention all the other residential, supply, and visiting traffic that had swelled due to the sudden doubling of the city's population.

Everyone in the city—whether they be Southern sympathizers (of which many remained, despite Washington now being the center of the Union Army—or perhaps *because* it was) or Union patriots—was on pins and needles, waiting for the "big battle." Whenever that might come.

"Any day now," people would say, expecting news that General McDowell would begin to send his troops to Richmond, where the new Confederate capital had been established.

But nothing happened. The troops stayed, the residents waited, and people argued about when and how and where the war would be over.

This air of seeming inactivity battled with the wild patriotism of the soldiers who'd come from the North, on fire and ready to fight and "put down those Southern Rebels!" The city stirred with excitement and anticipation while at the same time, bemoaned the fact that the roads were jammed, that military parades happened every day, sometimes multiple times a day, that there were rifles blasting and cannons shooting at all hours of the night, that the once-sleepy city had been jolted into a waking nightmare of thousands of men who'd come to fight . . . but had nothing to do but cause havoc.

Today being Independence Day, the Avenue had been closed to all traffic for a grand military parade of twenty thousand troops that marched past the President's House. Mr. Lincoln himself stood on a small raised platform as the regiments from Pennsylvania clomped by under his watchful eye. Later, he went to the Capitol to speak to the newly-convened Congress.

The weather was perfect, neither hot nor humid as July in Washington often could be, but calm, warm, and sunny. Patriotic banners and flags hung and fluttered from poles, balconies, doorways, carriages, and horses. The celebrations had begun in the first hours of dawn with artillery salutes from locations all over the city and continued all day long with more dress parades and open houses at each regiment's encampment, as well as concerts, speeches, and picnics. After the sun went down, fireworks sparkled over the darkening city. Chinese lanterns hung from trees, and lighted paper balloons filtered into the sky.

If the sounds of those celebratory salvos echoed the reality of the war that simmered beyond their city limits, few would make comment. Instead, most Washingtonians preferred to focus on remembering the independence of their nation, rather than the Secessionists that threatened to destroy the very Union they celebrated.

Ignoring the colorful pyrotechnics bursting in the sky above, Piney Tufts hurried down Seventh Street. The Willard Hotel, where all the rich and powerful tended to stay, was just here, and the Capitol loomed in the distance, down Seventh and along Penn Avenue to the east. He didn't think he'd been followed from when he left home, but he needed to be certain, so he adjusted the hat down low over his brow and swerved toward the doorway of the fancy hotel to go around its block, just in case he was followed.

"Evening, sir," said the elderly doorman at the Willard as he did his job with a flourish. His gloves were startlingly white in the yellowish gaslight, and his posture was perfectly erect. He didn't even look up as one of the fireworks exploded above them with a loud boom.

Piney kept his face averted even as he waved to the doorman. He didn't want to take the chance of anyone noticing him—although the chances of that were slim, considering the wild revelry of the soldiers in the streets.

In the last two months, the confounded troops had taken over everything. They had been bunked in every government building—the Treasury, the Patent Office, the President's House, and even the Capitol. Their encampments took over every park and square, and the men were under little if any control by their superiors.

They conducted target practice wherever and whenever they

wanted, and the altercations between them and Southern sympathizers were growing more and more common. Piney did his best to stay out of the way of any troops he came in contact with, even when they had been barracked in his very place of work. He kept his head down and focused on his work at the Patent Office, and that kept him out of trouble.

Surely it was because of that circumspection—and the fact that he was a Southern sympathizer, although quiet about it—that his benefactor had originally contacted him. At first, Piney believed he was helping his rebellious brethren when the task had been set before him.

But then one of the deliveries he'd picked up had torn open and he saw what was inside . . .

And then everything changed. *He* decided everything would change.

And now, tonight, *he* was in charge. He was in control.

And soon, he'd be getting a share of it all instead of the pittance his benefactor had promised him.

He drew in a deep breath, stuffing down the nerves that threatened to upset his stomach. He was being *very* careful. He knew what he was doing.

Pinebar Tufts was no fool.

The white Capitol Building, which was his destination, reflected all the reds, blues, and greens from the fireworks dancing in the sky above it. The new dome was only half-finished, and the mast of the massive crane being used to hoist the pieces into place jutted straight into the sky from inside the circular structure, rising far above the height of the construction. The tallest part of the crane looked like a giant finger pointing up out of the building, with the scaffolding below, just inside the dome, resembling the fist and thumb of a colossal hand.

Piney expected the sprawling building would be empty, for Congress had met much earlier today and by now, everyone would have gone home—or to the streets to watch the celebrations. This was a risk he was willing to take, and late at night during the Independence Day revelry would find the building as deserted as it would ever be. Even the bakeries in the basement would be empty for another two hours or more. All he had to do was slip past the Capitol's night watchman, Billy Morris, and get inside.

As he approached the elegant white building, which had just been extended to twice its width by new wings on the south and north ends, Piney made his way around the massive pieces of steel and blocks of marble that sat on the grounds. They'd been untouched for months, right after the firing at Fort Sumter, but work had begun once more.

He paused at the top of the wide expanse of steps that led to the portico of the new Senate wing, using a shadow from the base of an unfinished column to hide. Had he heard something? It was difficult to tell, what with all the noise from fireworks and firearms. His palms were damp beneath their gloves and his heart thudded furiously, but after a moment, he slid from his dark hiding place and dashed up the stairs. The door he sought was a side door with an ill-fitting bolt that had not yet been replaced during the construction. It opened with a soft, low creak.

Only a month ago, it would have been impossible to gain entrance to the building unnoticed, for there'd been hundreds of soldiers barracked inside. Guards had protected every entrance, requiring a password to get through. Now, however, the seat of the United States government was quiet and still on the anniversary of its birth, waiting for Congress to reconvene tomorrow.

The only person inside the sprawling, unfinished complex was Piney, and he meant to retrieve the package that waited for him and quit the place as quickly as possible.

He hurried along on scuffed boots, relying on the moonlight and the flickering light from the waning fireworks, to find his way down the high-ceilinged corridors.

He never saw the figure that stepped from the shadows behind him.

An explosion crashed through his world—not from the celebratory pyrotechnics outside, but from the heavy blow that smashed into the back of his head.

Friday, July 5

Sophie Gates had been living in Washington, D.C., for nearly six months, and she'd yet to attend a live session of Congress. Not that she didn't have a good excuse—between writing twenty (and frustratingly so) unpublished stories for the *New York Times* and *New York Post,* assisting one Mr. Adam Quinn with two murder investigations, and then most recently working with her new friend Miss Clara Barton to help collect supplies for wounded Union soldiers, Sophie had been far more busy than she'd ever been while living in New York. And because yesterday was the first day Congress had been in session since the war officially commenced in April, there hadn't even been the opportunity to do so before now.

But it seemed Sophie was not the only female interested in watching the senators as they conducted the business of the fractured nation. As a woman who'd resorted to dressing as a man in order to gain access for her journalistic endeavors, she was pleasantly surprised to see a number of men *and* women approaching as she began to make her way up the broad marble steps to the East Portico of the Capitol.

She'd left her home in the Smithsonian Institute just after seven o'clock, planning to get inside and find a seat in the Senate gallery before the proceedings began—and before anyone tried to keep her out. She couldn't count the number of times people—mostly men, but sometimes well-meaning women like her mother—had told her she couldn't go there, or enter here, or see that or experience this.

"Miss Gates!" called a familiar southern voice. "Is that you? What a *treat* to see you so early this mornin'."

Sophie turned—she was several stairs above—to see Miss Constance Lemagne just beginning to start up the steps. As usual, the young woman was dressed in an abundance of flounces, lace, and ribbons. Her skirt projected hoops far wider than were practical for day-to-day wear, but Sophie reluctantly admitted that the matching bonnet—trimmed with yellow roses tucked inside the brim—was beautiful. In fact, the southern belle looked pretty as a picture in her fresh, sunny dress with its cheerful green trim.

"Good morning, Miss Lemagne." Sophie paused reluctantly for the other woman to catch up to her, for, however she might wish to, she couldn't continue on without seeming rude. She noticed the woman was carrying a cloth bag that was much larger than the small drawstring purse that dangled from her wrist. "What brings you here so early?"

"Why, I want to make certain I get a good seat in the gallery," she replied, drawing out her vowels. "It gets *so* crowded sometimes."

Sophie was certain the woman purposely thickened her accent on occasion, like now—but for what reason, she didn't know.

Yes, Sophie admitted privately—Miss Lemagne was a source of minor irritation to her, though she couldn't quite put her finger on why. Or perhaps she didn't particularly *want* to. It might have been the fact that the southerner was always dressed—*over-dressed*—so perfectly and fashionably, or that when she spoke with that drawling accent, she seemed to simper like an empty-headed hen . . . or perhaps it had to do with the way the genteel young lady seemed to show up whenever Sophie was doing something interesting—and thrust herself into the situation.

Aside from that, Sophie didn't really trust the woman. Miss Lemagne was, after all, the daughter of a plantation owner from Mobile, and she made no secret that her loyalties lay with Alabamians and the other states that had seceded. Sophie had recently tested out this theory by giving the other woman some information about the Union forces in Washington—exaggerated information—in hopes that it would somehow find its way to the Rebel army. Whether it did or didn't, Sophie didn't actually know. But Miss Lemagne had seemed particularly interested.

Sophie just didn't trust her.

"And I wanted to make certain to save a seat for my *dear* friend Mrs. Greenhow," Constance drawled as she joined Sophie on the top step. It was with no small bit of malice that Sophie realized the other woman was slightly out of breath from the ascent—likely due to the tightness of her stays. Surely no one's waist was truly that narrow.

"She told me she would be a bit late this morning," continued Constance. "I thought I would sit and make some drawings of the new Senate chamber while I waited for her to arrive." She gestured to the larger bag hanging from her arm.

"What a nice way to spend the morning," Sophie replied as they walked across the grand expanse of the portico toward the interior door. She kept just far enough away from Miss Lemagne so the other woman wouldn't attempt to take her arm as young ladies often did when walking companionably together.

The smell of fresh bread filled the air, along with thick smoke from a number of chimneys shooting up silt and soot. Sophie knew that was because the basement of the Capitol had been turned into bakeries in order to help feed the thousands of troops that had descended on the city. Until late May, soldiers had even lived inside the Capitol—turning the place into a messy, smelly, chaotic barracks.

She'd written a story about their antics and sent it to the *Post* (where it was summarily ignored *again*), describing the way the soldiers swung from brand-new chandeliers that had been installed in the Senate Chamber and how one regiment had actually sent a message to Mr. Lincoln asking for a bottle of his best rum (she didn't think the message had actually been delivered, thank Heaven). One day, another group of bored privates had attacked and nearly torn apart the chair that had belonged to Senator Jefferson Davis, who was now the commander in chief of the army they would soon face.

Sophie had walked through several times while the regiments were barracked there and saw and smelled things lining the beautiful marble corridors that belonged in a barnyard: food remnants, grease spills, even human waste. The place had reeked of odors and rot. Finally, the troops were kicked out so the newly renovated building could be put back to order before Congress convened on July 4 and so, hopefully, construction could be continued. Only the bakeries, which had taken over the entire cellar and pumped out silt and smoke nonstop throughout the day, remained as evidence of the influx of troops.

This morning, there were only two or three other people approaching the East Portico off Pennsylvania Avenue. The broad covered porch with its elegant columns had doors leading to the second floor and directly into the large circular room under the Capitol's dome, known as the Rotunda.

Sophie was trying to figure out how to politely extricate herself from Miss Lemagne—a difficult proposition when there was no one else around with which to speak or a crowd in which to get lost.

"I declare, Mrs. Greenhow gives the most *enticing* salons," Constance continued. She pronounced the word "*sal*-on" with an emphasis on the first syllable. "Everyone who's anyone—at least, in the social scene—in Washington is there, you know. Perhaps you would like to attend some evening, Miss Gates."

"That's very kind of you," Sophie said again, reaching for the heavy glass-and-brass door that led to the interior, for there didn't seem to be a doorman. "And please, call me Sophie," she added.

"Why, thank you. And you must call me Constance."

"Yes, thank you, I will. I—"

Her words were cut off by a shout that echoed inside the round marble room, followed by a startled male scream.

Sophie pushed her way inside, dimly aware that Miss Lemagne—drat her!—was close on her hems, and saw the crowd gathering in the center of the space. They were all looking up.

"Dear heavens," she breathed when she saw the man dangling from the huge crane that shot up into the dome.

"What is—oh my *stars!*" Constance was right at her elbow, and she sounded a little faint as she gripped Sophie's arm.

Sophie didn't pull away as she gaped up at the man hanging from a rope. She swallowed hard; she'd never seen a person who'd been hung before. She suspected the bloated, dead white face was a sight that would haunt her dreams.

"Who is it?"

"The poor fellow."

"We should cut down the poor sot!"

"What's that pinned on his coat? Is that a note?"

"I can't read what it says."

"Who do we send for?"

"Pinkerton?"

The small crowd was paralyzed by indecision, confusion, and morbid fascination. One of the men broke away and began to stride toward the base of the massive crane. He clearly intended to climb up and cut down the man, and that spurred Sophie into action.

"*No, wait,*" she said, then paused, shocked at how her shout reverberated so loudly within the round space. "Er—don't climb up there yet, please, sir. We must send for—"

"Adam Quinn," Constance said at the same time as Sophie uttered his name. "Send for Adam Quinn."

"At the President's House." Sophie spoke a little louder than was strictly necessary, considering that she now had everyone's attention. The group of people—all men—were staring at her. "He . . . he attends to things like this," she added, studiously ignoring Miss Lemagne, who'd released her arm at last. "For the president."

She heard some grumbling, but as no one else seemed to have a better idea, one of the bystanders was dispatched at a run to the Executive Mansion. Another individual, whom Sophie recognized by his uniform that he must be the doorman—he'd obviously been distracted from his duty—began to take control as even more people began to come in from the outside. He and two other men attempted to funnel the newcomers away from the scene. Sophie suspected this was simply so they wouldn't gawk, not because the doorman had any sense that there might be important information that could be disturbed in the area.

"Damned fellow," murmured a man at her elbow. "I say cut the

bast—er, the sot—down. Why would anyone want to hang themselves in the middle of the Capitol?"

"I have no idea if anyone would," Sophie said slowly, looking up
at the fellow once more. Her heart gave a little bump when she realized what she was seeing. "Because I don't think this man hung
himself. I think he was murdered."

CHAPTER 2

Adam Quinn loped from the President's House as fast as he could—which, in his case, was quite quickly for he'd been blessed with long and powerful legs that ate up distance with ease. In fact, the messenger who'd come from the Capitol with a garbled message about a hanging body had been left far behind him before Adam reached the Willard.

"Mornin', Mr. Quinn," called the hotel's doorman with a wave.

"Good morning, there, Birch." Even in his haste, Adam took note that the elderly black man seemed to have recovered fully from his injuries back in April, when he'd been attacked during Adam's investigation of a death in the oval library of the President's House.

"Guess there's a big ruckus up at the Cap'tol, and it ain't got nothing to do with that Congress for once," added Birch as Adam went on by. "Reckon you'll set it all to rights, sir."

"I reckon I'll try," he replied, wondering not for the first time how it had happened that he, Adam Quinn, a simple, one-armed frontiersman from Illinois by way of Wisconsin and Kansas, had found himself being the one that people—particularly Mr. Lincoln—called on to "set things to rights" nowadays.

Adam had only been inside the Capitol twice since he arrived in late February as part of the president-elect's security team, but both times he'd been slack-jaw impressed by the grandeur of the building. He'd never seen such a fine, white, imposing structure in his life. He might have seen pictures of what it had looked like before the additions of two new wings for the House and Senate, so he couldn't compare it with what it looked like now, with the Capitol Expansion being nearly finished—but the massive, fancy columns and impossibly wide steps that led up to the entrance made him proud to be an American and a Unionist.

Adam jogged up those broad steps to the center of the complex, where the dome was marred by the crane's mast jutting from its sliced-off top. His weather-beaten coat flapped around his thighs, and he'd barely remembered to shove a pair of gloves in his pockets—apparently, they were expected in society, but he never saw any reason for a man to wear gloves unless he was working or it was cold. His boots hadn't been polished in two weeks, but he'd bought a new hat that wasn't quite as battered as the wide-brimmed one he'd worn on the prairie. That was, he reckoned, an influence of living in the Executive Mansion where all sorts of dignitaries came and went, and where Mrs. Lincoln ruled the roost with a stylish, grandiose fist.

He really needed to find his own rooms, Adam thought as he pushed through the heavy glass door into the Rotunda. Somewhere with a little privacy—and a place that was near a barber, as he found it difficult to shave.

He strode into the large round space beneath the Capitol's dome, which served as a sort of entrance hub that connected the two wings of Congress. The wings contained their members' offices, which he'd learned were frequented by lobbyists, as well as the chambers where they met, argued, and created law.

"Over here, sir," said the doorman, gesturing for him to move sharply to the left and out of the round room. "Please move on."

"I'm here to examine the situation," Adam told him, and dug into his right pocket. He handed the heavy card to the doorman.

Along the top, words were embossed in fancy gold script: OFFICE OF ABRAHAM LINCOLN, PRESIDENT OF THE UNITED STATES.

Beneath the heading, Mr. Lincoln had scrawled in his own hand:

*Please note that Mr. Adam Speed Quinn acts with all the author-
ity of the Office of the President of the United States, and that all
due courtesies should be afforded to him in any request or action he
takes.*

Adam felt a slight riffle of guilt at employing the placard, for,
strictly speaking, Mr. Lincoln hadn't asked him to become involved in this instance. In fact, the President had been in a meeting all morning with Secretary Cameron and didn't even know
about the situation—whatever it exactly was.

Which brought the question that had nagged him all the way
from the White House: Who had sent for him?

"Mr. Quinn!"

He turned to see Miss Constance Lemagne pushing her way toward him, her pretty face framed by the arc of cheerful yellow
roses inside her bonnet brim.

"Oh, thank heavens you're here at last," she said, taking his
arm—his prosthetic arm, in fact—without hesitation. "Miss Gates
and I just *knew* you'd be the one to help. It's just terrible, Mr.
Quinn."

Adam blinked, instantly absorbing the information that the
only two young ladies he knew in Washington were both here, as
well as the answer to his internal question, and replied without
hesitation, "Miss Lemagne, what a pleasure to see you this morning—though I reckon I wish it weren't at such a difficult time."
These last words he added as he looked up to see a man dangling
from the heavy base of the crane.

Dear God.

He closed his eyes and offered a short prayer for the dead man.
Even if the poor sot had done it to himself, the man's soul needed
all the prayers it could get. *Especially* if he'd done it to himself.

"I suggested they wait to cut him down until you arrived," said
a brisk feminine voice behind him. "It was a difficult proposition,
for of course the sight is beyond tragic and the poor man should
be given his privacy as soon as possible, but I thought it prudent."

"Good morning, Miss Gates," he said automatically, even though his attention remained on the dead man. He'd seen plenty of men hung from trees during the Bloody Kansas conflict—including one of his friends, Johnny Brown, who'd been murdered by pro-slavers. He tamped down the flicker of rage before it distracted him.

"Oh yes, good morning, Mr. Quinn. Though not for him." Miss Gates's voice was sober as she looked up as well.

"No, I reckon not. Uh . . . thank you, Miss Gates and Miss Lemagne." Adam stepped away, closer to below the dead man, as the southerner released his arm.

As in the past when faced with similar situations, Adam had a glimmer of uncertainty as he stood beneath the scuffed and worn soles of the man's feet. Here he was again, with everyone in the room—literally—looking to him for answers.

"Does anyone know anything about what happened? Who found him?" he asked—then, catching himself, held up a hand to stop any response. "That can wait. All of that can wait. Let's get him down from there."

The base of the monstrous derrick filled the center of the Rotunda floor and was made with sturdy wooden beams that must have been cut from sky-high trees. Adam estimated the main mast was as much as eighty feet tall. It extruded beyond the top of a temporary roof made of canvas and wooden spokes in the shape of a gigantic parasol.

Adam clambered up the winding staircase built into the base and paused before stepping onto the beam from which the man had likely been standing when he threw himself off. The light was dim here beneath the oiled canvas ceiling and above the gaslights, but he could still make out disturbances in the layer of dust on the beam—footprints and other markings like scuffs.

Later, he would use a lantern to better illuminate the area so he could read the disruptions, but first the rope must be cut and the man lowered to the ground without adding to the disturbed dust. Adam looped his left arm—the one with a prosthetic that began a few inches past his elbow—around one of the beams that crisscrossed the side of the crane and, with his feet on the very edge of the beam and one foot curled around a crossbar bigger than a man's thigh, he angled out at his torso, partially hanging over the floor.

Below, someone gasped at the precarious position as he struggled to pull the knife from his right pocket. Adam gritted his teeth, hoping the buckles that strapped the prosthesis to his body would hold fast if he slipped. The edge of the squared-off wood dug into his flesh and blood elbow as he crimped his joint around it as tightly as possible. He could barely reach the rope; it required stretching his arm and body as far as possible in order to get a good reach.

Someone muttered below, "Why don't he just go closer to the damned thing? Gonna fall and split his head like a melon."

With the straps from his fake arm cutting mercilessly into his skin, the rough wood scraping through his coat and shirt, and the sawing actions causing him to grunt with effort, Adam reckoned it was very possible that would happen—but sincerely hoped the man was wrong.

"He doesn't want to step on any footprints up there." Miss Gates's pragmatic voice filtered up to him. "I'm certain there was a reason he didn't climb higher so he could cut the rope from above."

Adam heard this and grunted with effort and frustration. Well, damn. He certainly could have done that and saved himself a passel of trouble and a world of hurt, but he'd been distracted by the foot markings.

The rope had frayed considerably by now, and he gave a few more saws with his blade while his elbow groaned from pain and effort. Several men clustered below to catch and ease the body to the ground, and when the moorings finally gave way, there was a quiet exhale from the small crowd.

"Please just rest him on the floor," Adam called down, slightly out of breath from his exertions and still annoyed with himself for not thinking of climbing higher.

He was just maneuvering himself back onto the top step when

he realized someone was on the stairs just below him, and a pool of light had ascended as well.

"I've brought you a lantern." Miss Gates looked up at him, her face softened by the glow from the light she held. She'd removed her bonnet, and her gray eyes were sharp and curious as she handed her burden up to him. He reckoned if there'd been room on the narrow steps, she'd have pushed up to stand next to him.

"Thank you."

"I thought you'd need it to see—to be able to confirm my suspicions," she added, still looking as if she were going to climb up past him to see for herself.

Because he'd come to know Miss Gates and her determination, he gripped the beam next to him more tightly in case he had to keep her from falling when she attempted to push through. "Suspicions of what?"

"Murder."

Adam smothered his surprise—for he'd seen the note pinned to the man's coat—and turned to hold the lantern over the narrow beam. He heard the rustle of skirts behind him, but instead of coming closer, Miss Gates was descending.

With the new spill of light at hand, footprints and markings on the beam clearly showed the movements of someone's activity hanging the rope on the crossbar above. Whoever it was—and it appeared to be only one set of prints—had flung the rope up and around the upper beam once, then tied it to a second pole nearby to hold it in place. The excess rope was left in a messy, dangling heap on the beam next to the upright post.

What he didn't see was a set of footprints facing the edge of the beam where the man would have stood before throwing himself off.

Contemplating this, along with Miss Gates's interesting pronouncement, Adam left the remains of the rope and climbed back down the steps. He was ready to turn his attention to the body.

By now, only six people remained in the area—Miss Gates and

Miss Lemagne, of course, as well as two well-dressed men, another man in work clothes, and a fourth in a military uniform.

It was the latter person who spoke to Adam as he stepped onto the marble floor. "Mr. Quinn, I want to thank you for seeing to this matter."

"Commander Dahlgren," Adam said, shaking the man's hand. The officer had taken command of the naval yard when Commodore Buchanan defected to the south in April. Shortly after, Dahlgren had discovered that his predecessor had allowed the bombshells being manufactured there to be filled with sawdust instead of explosives. Since then, the new commander stayed on guard overnight at the naval yard—or had a trusted man in his place. Adam had met Dahlgren several times at the President's House and knew that Lincoln trusted and respected him. "I'll do whatever I can."

"I'm certain the president and Congress will appreciate being able to go about their business, knowing you've taken on the task. In the meantime, I've arranged for some of my men to stand guard in order to keep spectators—most of them, anyway," he added with a pointed glance at the two young ladies, "from bothering you. If you need any assistance, Private Belcher or Private Strongley will be happy to assist." This time he indicated two men standing at a distance from the group dressed in gray wool shirts and brogue shoes with dark blue coats.

"Much obliged, Commander." Adam shook the other man's hand again. "Does anyone know who this man is, or what he might be doing here? I reckon he was here pretty early this morning. Or late last night." An estimated time of death was a question his friend Dr. George Hilton could possibly answer, and he turned to Belcher. "Please fetch George Hilton. He lives in Ballard Alley—"

"Excuse me, Mr. Quinn, but I've already sent word to him to come."

Adam nodded at Miss Gates and smiled. He wasn't surprised that she'd anticipated his request. But he was startled when he noticed Miss Lemagne had a sketchbook in her hand and appeared to be drawing something—possibly a picture of the body. He considered making a comment, then thought better of it. Based on past experience with Miss Lemagne, he knew that suggesting she remove herself from such an unpleasant scene was a losing prospect. Aside from that, he reckoned he should begin to do his best for the man who lay dead on the floor of the Rotunda.

"His name is—was—Pinebar Tufts," said one of the well-dressed men. He was holding a short-brimmed hat in gloved hands and blindly turning it around in a circle. "Piney, we called him. I can't imagine why he'd do such a thing." He glanced up at what was left of the dangling rope.

"What's your name, sir? What can you tell me about Mr. Tufts?" Adam had already begun to form opinions based on the dead man's clothing and appearance, but it was important to understand how others perceived him.

"I'm Theodore Floke," he said. "I worked with him at the Patent Office. I'm a second examiner in the Agriculture Division. He's an assistant examiner with Mr. Taft in the Civil Engineering area, but Piney talked to everyone about everything."

"Do you have any reason to believe Mr. Tufts did this to himself?" Adam asked carefully. "Or why he would have?"

Mr. Floke shook his head, still turning the hat in his hands. "Not at all. In fact, lately Piney seemed happier than usual. He was always a pleasant man, but for the last week or more, he seemed to be particularly optimistic."

"Do you have any idea why he was so happy?"

Mr. Floke shook his head again. "Not really. In fact, work at the Patent Office has been slowing down so much because of the war that some of the assistant examiners are worried they're going to be released. No one's happy to give up a twelve-hundred-dollar-a-year job."

Adam leaned a little closer. "Was there anyone Mr. Tufts had a problem with? Anyone who might have wanted to harm him, or wanted ill to befall him?"

"Do you mean enemies?" Mr. Floke's eyes widened. "Are you suggesting someone did that to Piney? Why, there's a note pinned to his coat! It even says he did it!" When Adam didn't answer, after a moment, the other man drew his gaze from the dead man's body on the floor and spoke. "I can't think of anyone he didn't get along with. Piney was the sort of man who came to work, did his job, and then went home to his wife. He didn't drink or carouse, but he was the sort of man who was always open to take a chance on a new scheme or investment."

"Was he indebted to someone he might have invested in? Or borrowed from to invest? Or did he gamble?"

"I don't know of anyone Piney would have owed money to, Mr. Quinn. And he wasn't a gambler in that way. . . . Look, Mr. Quinn, working in the Patent Office, you get to see a lot of ideas and inventions come through. Some of them are nothing but fool's errands or junk, but some of the ideas—well, you could tell what had a chance of making a man some money. And Piney was the type of man who noticed things like that, and he'd say, 'If I had the money, I'd invest in this invention right here,' or 'This is a very useful tool that should be manufactured.' But as far as I know, he never followed through on something like that."

Adam nodded. That was interesting insight into the dead man and he appreciated Mr. Floke's candidness. "Where do he and his wife live?"

He made a note of Tufts's address as well as Floke's, then turned his attention at last to the body.

Someone had covered his face with a coat, and Adam lifted it as he settled in a crouch next to the body. Pinebar Tufts was in his forties, and the recent trimming of his beard and mustache, along with the cut of his clothing, suggested he lived a life of average comfort. Now he was close enough to easily be able to read the paper pinned to his coat. *For my sins*, it said.

Adam sighed and offered up another prayer for the poor man. Then he unpinned the note and tucked it into his own pocket and resumed the examination.

Having cut down more than one hanging victim in his life, Adam was accustomed to seeing the ugly way rope dug into the flesh of a man's neck and the horrible purplish coloring of his face—although Tufts's face wasn't purple or red, but was pale and gray, which he found interesting. And despite the fact that he'd seen hanged men before, that didn't make it pleasant for Adam to carefully examine the flesh at the collar of his shirt. A neckcloth sagged loosely from the opening, dangling over Tufts's waistcoat. Adam lifted the man's gloved hands to look for anything that might have adhered to his fingers, but they were clean.

Just then, a disturbance across the room caught his attention. "You cannot enter here," someone said angrily.

"I was sent for, sir." George Hilton's quiet words nonetheless reached Adam's ears.

Adam rose quickly and turned. "Dr. Hilton," he said in a voice that carried authority, "thank you for coming so quickly. Will you take a look at this?"

George met his eyes, giving him a brief nod of acknowledgment as he removed his hat and strode across the marble floor. He was only two years older than Adam, not nearly as tall, but strong and quick and very intelligent. His black hair was cut short to the scalp, and his mustache, sideburns, and beard were also trimmed closely. George Hilton was an excellent physician who'd been trained in Toronto and was someone Adam had come to think of as a friend during his short time in Washington.

However, since George was a black man, the very act of him assisting Adam with his murder investigations by performing autopsies on people—especially white people—was an incredibly risky proposition. Yet the man didn't hesitate to help, and it had been because of his careful examinations that Adam had been able to put the pieces together and catch two murderers.

Adam joined him, pitching his voice into a low murmur so that only George would hear. "Maybe it's best if you take him back to your office." When the doctor nodded, Adam looked over at the two soldiers. "Mr. Tufts's body needs to be transported to Dr. Hilton's place. Can you find something to wrap him in?"

That would give George a few minutes to look over the body, and then he could do the rest of his unpleasant work in the privacy of his cellar office.

"Can you tell how long ago he died?" Adam asked as he crouched once more. He knew the answer had something to do with how stiff the body was—or wasn't, or had been, or something along those lines.

"Between four and seven hours is my best estimate. Cause of death appears obvious," he added, but his eyes held curiosity when he looked up from his examination.

"It nearly always does. But there's usually something more for you to find." Adam gave a wry smile.

His eyes crinkling a bit at the corners, George rose to his feet and replaced the hat he'd been holding. "I'll send word when I have news."

"Thank you. Have you seen much of young Brian?" Adam felt a flicker of guilt that he hadn't spoken to the poor Irish boy for weeks.

"Oh yes." The crinkling at George's eyes grew more pronounced. "Nearly every day I can find something for him to do. He and his hen. The boy's a true scamp." He shook his head, but his lips twitched and affection danced in his eyes.

"I reckon Mrs. Mulcahey is appreciative," Adam said. And he knew it was a financial cost for George as well—for more often than not, Brian's small wages included "leftover" food that would help to feed his mother and younger siblings. "Send word with him and I'll make sure he returns with candles and kerosene for you." When George made as if to protest, he said, "The president will insist on paying for supplies."

"Very well."

By now the soldier had returned with a large canvas, and George assisted him with wrapping the body.

When they finally carried the corpse away, Adam turned his attention to Miss Lemagne and Miss Gates. "How did the two of you come to be here this morning?"

"Why, I was coming to listen in the Senate gallery with my dear friend Mrs. Greenhow," replied Miss Lemagne. She'd tucked the sketchbook under her arm but was still holding her pencil. "And when I saw Sophie—er, Miss Gates—I walked in with her. And then we saw it. Him, I mean. Just hanging there. We knew right away we should send for you, Mr. Quinn." Her dimples flashed briefly, but her voice was sober. "Is it another murder?" she asked, her voice dropping to a conspiratorial whisper.

"Yes," Miss Gates interjected firmly, but Miss Lemagne didn't even look at her. She'd rested her hand on Adam's forearm—his real one—and looked up at him, her eyes genuinely troubled.

"Why do you think he was murdered?" Adam asked Miss Gates, ignoring the warmth of Miss Lemagne's hand seeping through his coat. "He's wearing a note that says otherwise."

"He's still wearing his gloves," she replied.

"His gloves."

Adam turned that over in his mind as she explained. "I just don't see someone tossing a rope over a beam, tying a hangman's noose, then putting it over his neck and jumping—all while wearing his gloves. And where is his hat?" She looked around. "He's wearing a coat and gloves, but no hat? There wasn't one up on the crane, was there?"

"Sophie's right. I agree with her—it has to be murder," Miss Lemagne said suddenly. "One certainly couldn't tie a knot very well wearing gloves. And we should look for his hat. It must be around here—"

"And if it *isn't*, that means someone either took it or brought him here without it," said the other woman in a voice that was a little louder than necessary.

"I reckon you could be right," Adam replied, suddenly desperate to get away from the two pretty, charming, and exasperating young ladies. He wasn't certain he agreed with their assessment, for he could think of several reasons a man might not have his hat or not remove his gloves—but the pattern of footprints on the beam of the derrick made him wonder. No, he wouldn't dismiss the possibility that Piney Tufts didn't hang himself.

"I'll go look for the hat," Miss Gates said. She went off in a swirl of dove gray skirts, the pink ribbons from the bonnet she carried fluttering behind her.

"Miss Lemagne, if you wish, I can have Private Strongley escort you back to the St. Charles," Adam told her, referring to the hotel where she and her father had been living.

"Why, Mr. Quinn, you know Daddy and I aren't at the St. Charles anymore. Surely you remember that we moved in with Althea Billings—you saw us packing up the wagon back in April."

"Oh yes, I reckon I do recall that—"

"Why, if I were a sensitive sort of woman, I might be a trifle put off by the fact that you've so easily forgotten—and that it's been that long since I've seen you," she added, her southern drawl thickening as she drew out the syllables. Long lashes framed her cornflower blue eyes as she looked up at him. "Surely you haven't been avoiding me."

Adam resisted the urge to shift from one foot to the other. "Oh no, Miss Lemagne, I've just been—"

"But I'm sure you've been very busy, helping Mr. Lincoln," she said a little breathlessly. "And all of these soldiers in town—why, it's been *so* loud and crowded. Isn't General McDowell going to send them off soon? I declare, it's so one can't even walk down Penn Avenue without tripping over one of them Unionists." Her voice had gone a little hard at the end, and then she recovered. "Forgive me, Mr. Quinn. Here I am, prattling on when you've got work to do." She removed the sketchbook from under her arm and showed it to him. "I thought I might do some drawings of the scene, just as I did the last time. I've nearly got the first one done."

She demonstrated, opening the book to a page that showed Piney Tufts hanging from the wooden derrick. Adam managed to swallow his horrified exclamation, instead keeping his voice calm as he grasped the only straw available to him. "Miss Lemagne, I reckon I appreciate your offer for help, but—but what would your father say?"

He couldn't deny she was a talented illustrator, and the image was shocking in its accuracy and detail. But he simply couldn't condone a young woman being involved in such an inappropriate task. It was bad enough that she'd been here when the body was discovered.

"Oh, Daddy is far too occupied with Mrs. Billings," she replied with a wave of her hand. "They're going to be married, you know, once her year of mourning is over."

Adam hadn't known, but he wasn't surprised. Miss Lemagne's father had been a suspect in the death of Althea Billings's husband back in March, and apparently the two had known and loved each other years ago down in Alabama. "Miss Lemagne," he tried again, "your drawing of the—uh—last murder victim was very helpful, but I don't know that in this case it'll be—"

"I found it!"

Adam turned to see Miss Gates fairly running across the marble floor, ribbons streaming behind her, bonnet in one hand and a man's bowler hat in the other.

"It was down the hallway over there." She was hardly panting from her run as she thrust the bowler at Adam. "And look—there's blood on the inside of it!"

He examined the brown wool hat and saw that not only was there blood on the inside, but the outside was dented. The story seemed obvious: someone had hit whoever had been wearing the hat hard enough to crush the hat and break the skin. However, just as obvious was that the hat didn't necessarily belong to Pinebar Tufts. Adam hadn't seen any blood or wounds on the man; though, to be fair, he hadn't examined the back of his head. "Thank you, Miss Gates."

"I told you. It's murder," she said. Her eyes gleamed with relish. "Now, if you'd like my assistance with the interviews, as before, I can spare some time this morning before I'm due to report to the E Street Infirmary at half two. Miss Barton and I are meeting up to ask for donations from the people who live on Seventeenth Street."

Adam stifled a sigh. What had he ever done that sentenced him to have two lovely but stubborn and provoking women determined to interfere in his murder investigations? Somehow they'd each decided they were invaluable members of his team, and he could see no way to extricate either of them from such an unseemly situation.

He managed to nod. "That's very kind of you, Miss Gates. I

reckon I don't know enough about the situation to know who needs to be interviewed just yet."

"Very well, then, Mr. Quinn," she said in a suspiciously acquiescent tone. "I suppose I'll be on my way to listen to the Senate for a while. I believe they're going to be debating what to do about the senators who've joined the secessionists but haven't formally withdrawn from the Senate. Whether to expel them or not. Constance, we had best go and find a seat for your Mrs. Greenhow before the gallery is filled."

Adam was relieved and surprised—and, he had to admit, mistrustful—when both young ladies went off without further comment. But he couldn't concern himself with them any longer.

He had to do right for Piney Tufts, and his next order of business was to bring the sad news to Mrs. Tufts.

If he hadn't been set on such a difficult task, Adam would have enjoyed his walk from the Capitol northwest toward the neighborhood where Pinebar Tufts had lived. He followed Seventh Street north, passing the Patent Office, and noticed the motley array of buildings that acted as homes for Washington families. There were mansions next to boardinghouses, and redbrick row houses adjacent to wooden structures hardly larger than shacks, along with more spacious single-family homes made from brick as well. Empty lots hosted chickens, goats, and cows, and the sidewalks were narrow and rough. Black iron fences enclosed the narrow front yards of some of the houses, doing their part to keep random grazing animals out—or in, depending on the situation.

The beautiful weather from yesterday had continued, so the sky was blue and cloudless and the sun full and pleasantly warm without making the air sticky. Someone nearby was baking bread, and someone else had emptied a chamber pot behind their house, and the competing smells mingled with woodsmoke and blooming summer flowers. A huckster's cart rattled past, and Adam had to wait for a wagon overloaded with lumber before he could cross the street.

The dirt-packed street was soft but not messy. Every time it rained for more than a few hours, the swamp on which Washington City was built swelled, crept, and oozed up to create muddy, mucky streets and walkways. Adam watched a pig dart out of the path from an oncoming wagon filled with barrels, barely missing being someone's dinner, and he noticed a trio of goats grazing on a small patch of grass as he passed by the market on K Street. These were common sights in the capital city, and ones that still caused him bemusement when he saw chickens picking their way down a sidewalk.

Although the Independence Day celebrations were over, an air of patriotism remained in the red, white, and blue buntings and ribbons that fluttered from windows, and the many Stars and Stripes hanging from mailboxes, hitching posts, and windows. Despite the fact that Washington had always been a "southern" town—which accounted for the number of people who still wore the secessionist cockade ribbons and openly spoke of support for their rebellious brethren—an overwhelming sense of patriotism to the Union had overtaken the city with the arrival of tens of thousands of soldiers.

Adam had seen firsthand the wild chaos of the troops during the last two months: the drinking, brawling, whoring, and general raucousness had changed a quiet, genteel town into one that seemingly belonged in the Wild West. The troops, which had been whipped up into a patriotic frenzy in the North, had arrived in this small town and immediately discovered they had nothing to do but create havoc. It was an ongoing problem and a source of conflict between the city and the government's military. Once a month, the troops were paid, and things got even worse during the few days after. And with only twenty-five constables in the entire city, it was nearly impossible for them to keep the peace.

The address Adam had been given brought him to a small but neatly kept block of rowhouses on M Street. Made from the common pressed red brick as were most of the other homes that belonged to the working class, the line of four connected houses offered residences that were narrow on the street side. Two windows flanked each front door, and a second floor boasted two more windows above. One of them had a tiny black iron fence around its skinny front yard. He drew in a deep breath as he turned onto the abbreviated walk that led to the entrance and prepared to give Mrs. Tufts the sad news.

He removed his hat and, tucking it under his arm along with the bowler that Miss Gates had found, checked the time on his pocket watch. Half eight. Surely Mrs. Tufts would be dressed and about her chores by now. He rapped firmly with his false hand— there was no knocker—and waited.

After what seemed like forever, the door cracked open. "Yes?" The voice was female, but he couldn't see much of her. He did note a strong southern accent. "Who is it?"

"Ma'am, my name is Adam Quinn, and I'm here to speak with Mrs. Tufts." He hesitated to offer the card signed by Mr. Lincoln; it was just as likely to be torn up as it was to be revered, and he didn't see any reason to take the chance yet. The president had already replaced the card once.

"What do you want?" The door wavered a little, but the size of the crack didn't change. "I ain't letting strangers in my house."

"Are you Mrs. Tufts? Mrs. Pinebar Tufts? I need to speak to you about your husband, ma'am. You don't have to let me in if you don't want to."

"It's about Piney? What about him?" There was a tinge of fear in her voice now, and the door opened just far enough to reveal the woman he reckoned was Marybelle Tufts. She was in her late thirties and wore a clean apron over her dumpling-like figure. Her round cheeks were red from emotion, heat, or familial heritage, and her eyes were wary as they tracked to him. "Is he all right?"

Adam shifted the hat to his hand for something to do. "Ma'am, I'm very sorry to have to bring you this news, but your husband, Pinebar Tufts, is dead."

"*Dead?*" She emitted the single syllable, then simply stared at him, gaping.

"Yes, ma'am. May I come in?"

"Dead?"

"Yes, Mrs. Tufts. Your husband is dead."

"I . . ." She began to close the door, then appeared to catch herself and looked up at him. Her expression was one of confusion and shock, but no grief. At least not yet.

"Ma'am, if you'd allow me to come in, I can get you a cup of coffee or tea and tell you more about your husband."

"He didn't come home last night," she said, more to herself than to Adam. "He *always* comes home. He *can't* be dead." Her voice spiraled up a little as her southern accent became even more pronounced. "Mah Pahney *can't* be dead."

"Ma'am?" He didn't feel right about standing on her front stoop and telling her that her husband had been found hanging in the Capitol Rotunda. "Could I come in, Mrs. Tufts?"

She blinked up at him as if just seeing him for the first time. "What did you say was your name?"

"Adam Quinn."

"Do you know mah husband? Why are you here?"

"No, ma'am. I never met him." Despite his best efforts, the conversation was obviously going to continue here, practically on the street. "I was called to the Capitol Building this morning, which is where he was found."

"What happened to him?" Her voice was tight and unsteady and grief was beginning to build in her eyes.

"Mrs. Tufts, please. I reckon it would be better to tell you about this inside, in private. May I come in?"

She moved back wordlessly and he was finally able to step into the house. Though intent on the new widow, Adam noted the spare simplicity of the front room where he stood—for there was no grand entrance where a butler would greet a visitor as there had been at Custer Billings's house. Yet the furnishings in the Tufts home were comfortable and well-made, and the walls were covered with modern wallpapering. His impression was that the Tufts were neither wealthy nor struggling financially; they lived a modest but comfortable life.

He could see the kitchen and smelled meat roasting in the oven. The pungent scent of lye soap and the wet stains on her apron suggested Mrs. Tufts might have been doing laundry when he interrupted her—which probably meant no servants or slaves.

Mrs. Tufts had begun to sob silently, and she stood on the center of the rag rug looking lost. Her blond hair showed no signs of gray, and it was smoothed into a neat knot at the back of her head. Her face was round and firm with a myriad of dimples that appeared near her mouth whenever she spoke.

Still holding the two hats, Adam took her soft, pillowy arm and gently guided her to a walnut armchair upholstered in creamy brocade. "Is there someone I can send for to stay here with you, Mrs. Tufts? A friend, a family member? Does anyone else live here with you? Any children? Servants?"

"No, it's just me and Piney. Our children are grown. We used to have a housekeeper, but we sold her."

"Is there anyone I can send for, Mrs. Tufts?" Adam was a patient man under most circumstances, including this one, but he felt as if he'd been swimming upstream and going nowhere for quite a while. Still, the woman had just lost her husband. He allowed she had the right to dither and go absent.

"My—my daughter, Priscilla. She and her husband live on Fourteenth Street. Howard Melvis. But she's got the baby. Oh, what's Pris going to say? Her daddy's dead!" She burst into loud tears. Adam set the hats down on the table and fished a handkerchief out of his pocket.

He'd only recently begun to carry one he wouldn't be ashamed to offer a woman, instead of the raggedy cloth he'd previously tucked in his pocket. There weren't too many times he'd needed a fine handkerchief on the frontier, but things were different here. "Mrs. Tufts, I'm so sorry for your loss. I have more to tell you about Pinebar, but I'm going to find someone to fetch your daughter for you, all right, then? I'll be right back."

She sniffled and sobbed a response that he took as an affirmative, and Adam hurried out the front door. He reckoned he could ask one of the neighbors to send for Priscilla Melvis, but before he could decide which house to approach, he heard a familiar voice.

"Mr. Quinn! Mr. Quinn!"

What luck. Adam waved to the young boy who was running—as he often did—down the street toward him. Today he didn't have the hen Bessie tucked under his arm—which was unusual—and for once the child seemed to be wearing trousers that were neither too short nor too long for him.

Brian Mulcahey's boots slapped onto the ground as he roared to a halt next to Adam. The lanky twelve-year-old was barely breathing hard, though his milk-white cheeks were flushed pink beneath maple syrup freckles. His brown hair had a slight reddish hue in the July sun and, like Adam's, it needed a good trim. The boy reminded him so much of his younger brother Danny, though Danny was nearly eighteen by now and had gone off to California. Adam hadn't seen him for almost seven years.

"Dr. Hilton said as I should see if ye were needing any help, Mr. Quinn," Brian told him with an Irish lilt. His missing tooth had grown back in, eliminating most of the lisp he'd had previously. "He sent me off and I was about following you till you turned off by the market and got lost in the crowd. Then I been walking up and down the street lookin' for ye, and then here you were, coming on out of this house."

"It's good to see you, young Brian," Adam said, reaching out to tousle the mop of hair that was suddenly much closer to his chin than it had been two months ago. "I reckon if you keep growing as fast as you've been, you'll be taller than Mr. Lincoln by the time you're thirteen. And that'd make you the tallest man in Washington."

"Even taller than you?" Brian straightened up as much as he could.

"That'd be right."

The boy grinned, fairly dancing with glee. "*Gor!* Then I could maybe be meeting Mr. Lincoln sometime, then, couldn't I? And me mam says she can't keep me in trousers more'n a week at a time, I'm growin' so fast. It's a lucky thing Dr. Hilton's got some patients who were outgrowing their pants. He gave'em to me for doing some chores for him. *Gor* . . . Mr. Quinn, did you know he's got a *saw?* To cut *bones?*" His eyes were wide.

Despite the reminder of his own shattered bone being cut by a saw, Adam thought it was like a breath of fresh air to see the boy after the chore of giving Mrs. Tufts the bad news about her husband. Still, Adam's discussion with her wasn't finished and he didn't want to leave her alone any longer than necessary. "You can tell me all about it later, Brian. Right now I need you to go fetch a woman named Priscilla Melvis, over on North Fourteenth Street. Find her and tell her that her mama needs her and to come as quickly as possible."

"Yes, sir, Mr. Quinn!" The boy flew off as if he had wings on his feet, reminding Adam how energetic he himself had been at that age.

Back inside the house, Adam found Mrs. Tufts standing in the kitchen. "I wanted some coffee," she said, looking at him through eyes glassy with tears.

The kettle was on the stove and steam roared from its spout, but she didn't seem aware of it. This time, Adam helped her to one of the ladder-backed chairs at the eating table and set about pouring coffee into a pretty china cup she'd put out for that purpose. Without asking, he added a healthy dose of sugar to the drink—it was better than whiskey, at least this early in the day, he reckoned, though probably more expensive—and brought her the cup.

"Mrs. Tufts, are you ready to hear about what happened to your husband?" He considered pouring himself a coffee but didn't feel right about digging around for another cup. Instead, he pulled up another chair and sat across from her at the small round table.

"Yes, I-I think so. What was your name again? I'm sorry, I'm just so . . ." She sniffled and mopped her eyes with his handkerchief.

"My name is Adam Quinn, and you don't need to apologize. I'm so sorry to bring you such terrible news."

"What happened to my Piney? Please tell me." She sipped the coffee, her eyes widening perhaps because of the large amount of sugar. But she took another drink as if to fortify herself, and Adam began to speak.

"Your husband was found hanging from the crane in the middle of the Capitol Building Rotunda," he said, knowing it was best to speak quickly and plainly.

Mrs. Tufts gasped and the cup rattled onto the table, slopping coffee all over. "*Hanging?* By his—by his *neck?*"

"Yes, ma'am." Adam hesitated, unsure how to ask the next important question.

"But . . . how? Why?" Her eyes filled with tears again.

"That's what I'm going to try and figure out, Mrs. Tufts. So I need to ask you some questions—some difficult questions. Forgive me if they seem intrusive." He wished again for coffee, and, fleetingly, for the presence of Miss Gates and her pragmatic self. She'd know how to handle Mrs. Tufts sensitively. "How was your husband acting lately? Did he seem different? Or upset about anything? Sad?"

"No, no . . . not upset or—you're not suggesting Piney did that to *himself,* are you? Why, he would *never* do such a thing. Not my Piney. Why, that's an *awful* thing to suggest, Mr. Quinn." Her eyes flashed with hurt and fury. "Mah husband didn't do that to himself, Ah'll tell you plain as day."

"Yes, ma'am. I understand, and I apologize for upsetting you. I don't reckon he did that to himself either, Mrs. Tufts, and so now I want to find out who did. Is this your husband's hat?" He showed her the bowler that Miss Gates had found, but hesitated to hand it over in case she saw the blood on it.

Mrs. Tufts nodded immediately. "Y-yes. Yes, it is."

"All right. Thank you. I reckon I might need to keep it for a little while longer—but I'll get it back to you, along with—with everything else of his—as soon as I can." In order to forestall any questions she might have about why he needed it or why she couldn't have her husband's property right away, he continued. "Can you think of anyone who would want to hurt your husband, Mrs. Tufts? Anyone who had a grudge or any problems with him?"

He was watching her closely, and that was how he saw the flicker in her eyes—just a brief flash of something like fear or worry—before she looked down at her coffee. "I-I can't think of anyone who didn't like Piney. He was a good man, a hard worker, and he never bothered anyone."

"He worked at the Patent Office, I'm told. Four years now. Did he get along with the others there?"

"'S far as I know he did." She shifted restlessly in her chair and wouldn't meet his eyes. "He was one of the assistant examiners—he was hoping to get the next examiner's job that came around. He loved working there. Said it was always so interesting to see how peoples' minds worked, and the inventions they made. He would spend hours looking through all of the old patents and playing with the models, and he loved all of it."

"I can imagine that would be interesting. Were there any patents that Mr. Tufts worked on that weren't approved? And maybe the inventor was angry about it?"

"Oh, that happened all the time that a patent didn't get approved," she replied. "And of course the inventor would get their dander up and maybe write a letter or even come in and argue about it. But hardly ever did they get so mad. And Piney was only an assistant examiner, and so it wasn't him who made the final decision. So if someone was angry, they'd be angry with the top examiner, you know."

"And you don't know of any situation where a patent applicant was angry and holding a grudge?" She shook her head, her eyes clear and steady. Adam hesitated, then pressed on. "Mrs. Tufts, I imagine this is very difficult for you, but if you have any ideas or thoughts about this—or if you know of anything unusual that seemed to be affecting your husband or his mood recently, I need to know. He's dead, and very likely someone killed him. I need to find out why, so I can find out who."

A sigh burst from her and she wrapped her hands around the teacup. "I don't know if this matters, but all of a sudden, he had some extra money. It started about the end of May, a little bit of extra money. Then about two weeks ago, and then last week again. He said we'd be able to buy or rent a housekeeper again soon, and he was looking at a pair of horses so we could get a new carriage. He was going to take me up and down the Avenue whenever I wanted, he told me, and even said that I could have some new frocks."

"Do you have any idea where he got this extra money?"

She shook her head. "When I asked him, he just smiled and

said everything was going to be just fine, and that I shouldn't worry. He was being careful, he told me." She lifted her eyes to him at last. "'Being careful,' that's what he said. I didn't know what he meant by that."

Adam didn't either, but he reckoned it was a strange choice of words.

But apparently, Pinebar Tufts hadn't been careful enough.

CHAPTER 3

Sophie was a trifle irritated that Mr. Quinn hadn't taken up her offer to help him interview people who might know something about Piney Tufts, but that didn't mean she couldn't help on her own. After all, as a journalist, she was experienced at taking interviews and gathering information from people. However, the exasperation she felt about him declining her help was alleviated by the fact that he hadn't wanted Constance Lemagne and her sketchbook involved either.

Although she'd begun the day planning to listen to the Senate debate their absent members, the attraction of that now paled in comparison to working on the puzzle of Mr. Tufts's murder. Still, Sophie made a point of accompanying Constance to the gallery and getting settled there. Maybe she'd learn something else about Mr. Tufts—such as why and how he'd been inside the Capitol at night.

It had to have been at night, hadn't it? He'd obviously been dead for a while—and then there was the hat she'd found with his blood on it. What was a man like him—who worked in the Patent Office—doing in the Capitol so late at night?

"Mrs. Greenhow!" Constance had tucked away the satchel with her sketchbook and just finished arranging her skirts over the chair when she sprang back to her feet, waving at the woman dressed in mourning gray with black trim.

Sophie was interested in the newcomer in spite of herself, for she certainly had heard of the Washington socialite and her well-

attended salons. Rose Greenhow was older than she'd anticipated—in her late forties—and although she was fashionably at-
tired and carried herself with confidence, she wasn't the stunning
beauty Sophie had imagined when she thought of a popular society queen.

"Good morning, Constance. How kind of you to save me a
seat." The older woman looked at Sophie curiously. "Is this a
friend of yours?"

"Yes, indeed. May I present Miss Sophie Gates, Mrs. Rose
Greenhow." Constance's introduction was as proper and smooth
as could be, but the moment after Sophie and her friend ac-
knowledged each other, she launched into an excited description
of what had occurred that morning. "Did you hear about the
dead man in the Rotunda? Sophie and I were there when he was
discovered *hanging* from the machine in the middle of the room!
I declare, I can scarcely *imagine* how or why someone would do
such a thing!"

Mrs. Greenhow listened with rapt interest and proper horror,
then, dividing her attention between the two of them, asked, "Do
you know who it was?"

"His name was Pinebar Tufts," Sophie told her. "Apparently, he
worked at the Patent Office." That was convenient—she could ask
Miss Barton, who also worked there, if she knew anything about
the man. Mr. Quinn might not agree with Sophie's assessment
that Mr. Tufts was murdered, but she didn't doubt her own conclusion for a moment.

They weren't the only ones gossiping. News of the dead man
had spread, and Sophie caught many snatches of conversation
about it as they waited for the senators and their aides to enter
the chamber below. She sat quietly, listening for anything that
might be relevant, but was doomed to disappointment when the
conversations tended more toward the sensationalism of the
event than anything of substance, and then went on to frustration
and conjecture about *why hadn't McDowell done anything yet?* Everyone, it seemed, was expecting an announcement anyday that the
troops would be leaving for Richmond.

Drat. So much for wasting her time here.

Even Constance and Mrs. Greenhow had moved on from the topic of Pinebar Tufts and were talking about a big wedding that seemed to be imminent.

"Oh, look! And there's Mr. Monroe right there," Constance said, tugging at Sophie's sleeve as she looked down into the gallery. "He's the father. He knows everyone in Congress, doesn't he, Mrs. Greenhow?"

"He has quite a bit of influence," agreed Mrs. Greenhow in a throaty voice.

"And Miss Monroe—the one who's getting married—just returned from New York City with her dress," Constance continued to Sophie. "They had to have a special stand-up trunk made in order for it to fit inside without being crushed!" She turned to Sophie, her eyes dancing. "It's going to be the biggest wedding of the summer—surely you've heard about it. Felicity Monroe—she's Miss Corcoran's best friend and some distant cousin of the Monroes, you know—is marrying Carson Townsend, of the Richmond Townsends, the big milling family. They've got mills in Baltimore and Arlington. Her daddy knows absolutely *everyone*, and Mr. Townsend is filthy rich and horribly handsome. I'm simply *frothing* for an invitation, but I hardly know Miss Monroe."

Sophie, who'd had her fill of society gatherings, formal attire, and gossip when she lived in New York and was engaged to Peter Schuyler, could care less about such an event. Especially since there was a war upon them, and important work to be done for the troops.

Still, she couldn't subdue a small niggle of interest simply because descriptions of that sort of event were the type of journalism normally relegated to female writers—and since she'd thus far had no success getting stories about serious things like preparations for war or living in Washington during the early days of Mr. Lincoln's presidency published, she couldn't dismiss the possibility of such a story idea out of hand. If she could get even one story published in the *Times* or the *Post*, that could help with future, less-frivolous dispatches.

"I haven't been invited either," she replied, "but it's possible my aunt and uncle have been." Joseph Henry, her uncle, was the director of the Smithsonian Institute, and Sophie lived with him, his wife and their three daughters in apartments in the East Tower of the Castle. "I'll have to ask."

"Oh, do tell, Sophie, dear. The wedding is August first, so there's still time for me to finagle an invitation. I've invited Miss Monroe to meet me for coffee this afternoon and perhaps we will become friends. But if not, I'll want to know *every* detail if you attend," Constance gushed, then turned back to Mrs. Greenhow. Her voice dropped. "Wouldn't it be wonderful if Varina and Jefferson were back in time for the nuptials? I just know Miss Monroe must be *devastated* that they had to leave. The Townsend family knows them very well."

Back in March, Varina Davis, the wife of former senator Jefferson Davis—who was now president of the Confederacy—had sent out notes to all her society friends in Washington inviting them to a fete on May first in the President's House, anticipating a quick end to the war and her husband's triumph. That day had of course come and gone with Mr. Lincoln still ensconced in his rightful position and the Union intact, but the audacity of Mrs. Davis seemed to be echoed by Rose Greenhow and Constance Lemagne.

Thus far, the war had been limited to a few small skirmishes between the two sides, mostly in Virginia and Maryland, with hundreds of casualties—including one of Mr. Lincoln's particular friends, Captain Ellsworth. That was part of the reason everyone in Washington was on pins and needles, waiting for *something* to happen.

Sophie didn't know whether the conflict could be resolved within a few months; she certainly hoped it would be the case that one big battle would be decisive. The lack of accommodations and supplies for the wounded soldiers was appalling. She couldn't imagine what would happen if the conflict went on for much longer.

But Mr. Quinn wasn't the least bit confident. At the mention of that sort of quick resolution, his mouth would tighten and he would shake his head gravely. "I reckon that's a lot of optimistic thinking," he'd say.

Mrs. Greenhow smiled quietly. "I wouldn't be at all surprised if

that came to pass, Miss Lemagne. We must have faith in our boys."
Her expression was one that reminded Sophie of a cat that had
just finished off a dish of cream and was grooming the remnants
from its whiskers.

Sophie managed to hide her shock at such a boldly sympathetic statement—and in the Senate Chamber!—even when the
elder woman glanced at her as if to assess her reaction.

More of the senators had begun to filter their way into the
chamber, followed by their staff and other government bigwigs.

"I see Senator Wilson." Mrs. Greenhow straightened in her seat
and waved down at the portly gentleman who was the Chairman
on the Committee for Military Affairs. She looked at Sophie and
smiled. "We severely disagree on politics, but he is a generally
agreeable fellow, so I shan't hold it against him and will continue
to invite him to my home. And there is Senator Trumbull." Her
lips compressed with disgust. "He's threatening to bring a bill to
the floor to support that disgusting confiscation declaration by
General Butler. That would be an appalling overreach by Congress." She slapped her closed fan against the inside of her palm.

Sophie knew about the declaration to which Mrs. Greenhow
was referring—back in May, the Union's General Benjamin Butler had announced that any slaves captured by the Federal army
would be considered a contraband of war. His reasoning, which
made sense to Sophie, was that because the slaves were being
used by the Rebels to dig trenches or build blockades, they were
tools and supplies of warfare and therefore could legally be con-
fiscated as spoils of war by the Union and also put to use.

Since the Southerners *owned* the slaves, they were thus considered commodities—a concept which sat uncomfortably with Sophie, but nevertheless that was the way of things at the
moment—and therefore, by Butler's proclamation, meant that
any slaves could be taken and freed or otherwise put to use. Apparently, since Butler had made that announcement, word had
gotten around and slaves had been escaping to Monroe, the fort
held by Butler and his troops, and offering themselves up as contraband.

Despite her agreement with the concept, Sophie decided this was not the moment to debate with the outspoken Southern sympathizer who sat next to her. Still, the fact that Rose Greenhow was here, watching the senate meeting, was curious to Sophie. There were no senators from the seceding states, and in fact, that was one of the things the chamber meant to discuss today: whether the absent senators, like Jefferson Davis, should be expelled and taken off the official rolls of the senate.

Why would Rose Greenhow be so interested in the workings of the Congress for a country she obviously no longer supported? Perhaps she merely wanted to learn about the fate of Jefferson Davis in his former congressional role. Sophie gnawed on that thought as Solomon Foot, the Senate President *pro tem,* called the session to order. Or maybe Mrs. Greenhow was merely interested because the Congress could pass laws that would affect her friends in the South—such as with the confiscation predicament.

Possibly, it was just a matter of wanting to see and be seen, as a Washington socialite who invited both Unionists and Southern sympathizers to her salon.

Sophie mulled over Mrs. Greenhow's smile from a moment ago. *I wouldn't be at all surprised if that came to pass,* she'd said. As if she knew something . . .

For the first time, Sophie thought maybe she would like Constance to bring her to Mrs. Greenhow's salon.

Just so she could find out more.

When Adam left Mrs. Tufts with her daughter, both women were gripping each other's hands at the kitchen table, their faces flushed with tears of grief. Mr. Melvis, the son-in-law, was expected soon.

Adam had asked Priscilla Melvis the same sort of questions he'd done Mrs. Tufts, but the daughter had nothing of interest to add except to give him the names of some friends of her father.

Even so, it was nearly half ten when he closed the door of the small, neat house on M Street. Brian Mulcahey was sitting on the ground beneath a tree, his bony knees angled up and away from his body like that of a spindly grasshopper. At the sight of Adam, he launched to his feet like the energetic insect.

"Mr. Quinn, where are you about going now? Did you see that pair of bays? They were just prancing by, pulling a buggy, and I never seen two that matched so well." Even as he spoke, the boy was looking down the street after the horses in question. His eyes glowed with wonder. "Mr. Birch at the Willard said as how he'd be putting in a word with the groom there, that maybe he might be letting me help curry the horses for a few pennies. I told Mr. Birch, I'd be doing it for no pennies at all—just to be touching those beauties!"

"And what about going to school, young man?" Adam asked— then realized he sounded like Mr. Lincoln, who used to lecture him about the same topic back when Adam lived with Uncle Joshua in Springfield. "If you're running errands for me and helping Dr. Hilton and brushing horses at the Willard, there's little enough time for learning your letters and numbers."

"Oh, me mam's always going on about teaching me that. Every night she's about making me work on my letters," he said, brushing the idea away with a pale hand as he skipped along to keep up with Adam's long stride. "But a groom—well, he's not needing all that book learning if he's got a way with horses and knows how to care for 'em and talk to 'em. That's all the edu . . . *cation*"—he struggled a little with the word—"I'll be needing."

"Well, that's not what Mr. Lincoln would say," Adam replied. "And I reckon I'd agree with him. After all, if you own your own livery or stable someday, you'll need to add up all the money you're making and spending on oats and brushes, and you'll have to be able to read the papers for the horses you're buying so no one can cheat you."

Brian's feet slapped to a halt on the dirt. "Own my own livery? *Gor . . .*"

"I reckon anyone who loves horses as much as you do and who's as smart as you are should want to be in business someday." Adam mussed his hair.

"Mam said when school starts up in September, she'll be making me go. But I can still be helping you and Dr. Hilton, can't I? Before and after?"

"As long as you keep your studies up." They started walking again, and Adam felt as if he'd stepped into yet another occupation here in a city he didn't truly want to live in. It was as if Washington, D.C., was trying to put its hooks into him so that he would never leave. First he'd come as a jack-of-all-trades to the president. Then he'd been conscripted as a murder investigator. And now he found himself acting as parent to a young boy.

He didn't know where Brian's father was. The boy spoke of him only occasionally, and with neither malice nor grief. Just simple pragmatism.

"Where are we going, Mr. Quinn? Is it true there was a man hanging dead inside at the Capitol? I never been inside there, but my mam says all the men who run things work in that place. What's it like? It's awfully big. Why do they have to go on making a building so big anyway?"

"I'm going there now," Adam replied. He'd only had a brief look at the foot markings on the crane's beam. He wanted to examine them a little more with better light, as well as the hallway where Miss Gates had found the hat that belonged to Mr. Tufts. "Would you like to come with me?"

Brian slowed and trailed behind him a little. "I'm not allowed to go in there, Mr. Quinn. Not a place like that."

"Everyone's allowed in there. And I reckon if you live here in Washington, you ought to see inside the building."

The boy picked up speed to keep even with him, but Adam sensed his hesitation as they drew nearer. He reckoned he couldn't blame the kid—he was thirty years old, and the big, fancy, gleaming building made him feel like the dusty, ragged frontiersman he was. Or had been.

But when he climbed the broad steps of the grand building, Brian was on his heels. The boy nearly tripped on the top step, he was so intent on looking up at the dome. "*Gor . . .*" he whispered.

He stuck near Adam as they went inside, and Adam was pleased to see that Privates Strongley and Belcher had carried out his orders of not letting anyone onto the steps of the crane or down the hall where the hat had been found.

But that didn't mean there wasn't a ruckus about it.

"We've already had enough of a delay getting this work done," a man was saying to the two soldiers. "Do you see all those massive pieces of cast iron sitting out there on the lawn? The ones big as carriages? They've been on the grounds for months. We *paid* for them almost two years ago and I've been losing money on this sotted project now because of the damned war. I've got workers I'm paying, standing around waiting for this to be cleared out so they can get back to work, and a Congress who's scratching their arses waiting to give me the official go-ahead to start up again." The man wasn't dressed in the clothing of a construction worker but in a coat and fancy neckcloth, and Adam wondered who he was.

Private Strongley saw them approaching and said something to the man, who turned and started toward Adam.

"Are you the man in charge? What is going on here? How much longer until my men can get back to work in here?"

Adam removed his hat and shook the man's hand. "I'm Adam Quinn. I'm investigating the murder of—"

"Murder? A man hangs himself and it's murder now?" His frown deepened. "I just traveled all the way down from New York so we could get the construction going on the dome again. You see those big pieces of cast iron out there? The curved ones? All over the place, next to the big marble columns? They've been collecting dust and rain since May, and I'm losing money every day because I bought the material and cast it over a year ago and—"

"It's a murder investigation, Mr.—what did you say your name was?"

"Charles Fowler. I'm a partner with Janes, Fowler, Kirtland and Company—the ironworkers who are supposed to be finishing the damned dome on this building. A murder investigation? What are you—some sort of Pinkerton? Or are you a constable?"

"Neither. I work for the president, and the sooner I can take a look at the crane up there, the sooner you'll be able to get your men back to work." Adam offered him the card Mr. Lincoln had given him, then turned to Brian, who'd been alternately gawking at the interior of the Rotunda and watching the conversation. "I need two big lanterns. Ask Private Strongley over there to help you find them."

When Fowler returned the card, Adam asked, "Were any of your men working here yesterday or last night? What time did they arrive this morning?"

"On Independence Day? No, of course they weren't working. The crew started back last week, but no one was here yesterday—except maybe Walter—that's Thomas Walter—might have been here. He's the architect who designed the dome, and he's here most every day from what I hear. In fact, it's him who's been trying to get the project going again, while that bast—while Captain Meigs shut it all down."

Fowler didn't appear to be very fond of Montgomery Meigs, an engineer who'd just been named quartermaster general of the Union army. Meigs was the one who'd conceived of the idea of using a crane to install the dome instead of scaffolding, and he'd been in charge of the entire Capitol Expansion.

"Now that he's working for the army, Meigs says construction's suspended until the end of the war. We can't have that. We can't have that at all." Fowler looked around, his lips tightening again as his expression became thunderous. "Three hundred thousand dollars' worth of cast iron, just sitting—"

"What time did your men arrive this morning?"

Fowler collected himself. "They're to report by seven o'clock. Usually a few of them get here earlier than that."

"I'd like to speak to whoever arrived first." When Fowler opened his mouth to argue, Adam said, "You can give me their names when I get down from up there. Now, I reckon if you'll excuse me, I'll get my work done and then you can get back to yours."

Brian was trotting toward him, carrying two large lanterns. "We're going up *there?*" the boy said as Adam pointed to the steps that wound up through the gigantic crane's base.

The lanterns cast two expansive glows as they climbed. Adam

was satisfied that they'd illuminate the crossbeam in question well enough for him to see the fine details. "Now just keep that right there, Brian, so it shines on those footprints and doesn't cast my shadow over them."

"What are ye doing there, Mr. Quinn?" asked the boy as Adam crouched close to the markings in the dust, holding his own lantern right next to them.

"I'm looking at the footprints to see what happened here. It's like a story," he said even as he absorbed the meaning of the tell-tale disturbances. "One person, a man, stepped off the steps and walked onto the beam. He threw the rope over up above here, and then tied it tightly. And then . . ." His voice trailed off as he noted the smudge in the dust that ran along the edge of the beam where the rope had dangled.

Adam frowned. It didn't seem right. There was a long swath along the edge; if Piney Tufts had dropped the noose around his neck and jumped—even though there wasn't a set of footprints near the edge where he would have done so—his weight would have snapped the rope nearly straight down. It wouldn't have swayed or moved so much along the edge of the beam, he didn't think.

No, he was sure of it. And as he looked and read the signs, he became even more certain that Tufts hadn't launched himself off the beam.

"How can ye tell all that, Mr. Quinn?" Brian had edged as close as possible and the lantern shivered with his movements. "All's I'm seeing is dirt and lots o' boot marks."

"Well, I reckon I've been practicing for longer than you've been alive," he replied. "I learned it from an Indian friend of mine—his grandfather, really."

"*Gor.* You've met a *savage?* With red skin? I ain't never seen one of them. Did he try'n scalp ye?"

Adam couldn't let that comment go without a careful response. He turned where he squatted and looked squarely at Brian in the wavering light. Their eyes were level and he saw the flash of surprise in his young friend's as he began to speak. "My friend Ishkode isn't a savage, young man, and neither are any of his people." His voice was firmer and sharper than he'd ever used when he spoke to the boy. "He is part of the Ojibwe tribe, and they were always very kind to me"—especially Ishkode's sister—"when I knew them in Wisconsin. They understand nature far better than anyone I've ever met with white skin, and one of the things I learned from Ishkode and his grandfather Makwa is that all living things should be respected and honored—no matter whether they have red skin or black skin or white skin or fur or scales or feathers or whether they are trees or grasses or rocks."

Brian's eyes had gone so wide Adam could see the whites all around his irises, as well as a faint pink in his milky cheeks. "Yes, sir, Mr. Quinn," he said, obviously abashed—although Adam wasn't certain the boy fully understood what he was saying. Nevertheless, he'd planted the seed and would continue to nurture that thought because he himself had felt the same way Brian did before he got to know and understand his friends of the Ojibwe. Now he looked at things very differently than most people of his acquaintance.

"Now," he said, turning his attention back to the mussed-up dust and dirt, "if you look here, Brian, you'll see how this foot-print is wider at the back—the heel. What do you think the man was doing when he stood here, to make it wider at the back?"

Brian hesitated a moment, then eased forward to look. He was silent for more than a minute, then finally spoke. "Mr. Quinn, I don't know. I'm about trying, but I can't see much difference be-tween that mark and the one I'm seeing next to it."

"I reckon that the man was standing here and he turned slightly, on his toes, and that scraped his heel mark, making it just a little bit wider. Do you see how it's just a trifle wider?"

"*Gor.* I do now, but I wouldn't-a never seen that, Mr. Quinn. Never in my whole life."

"As I said, it takes a lot of practice." Adam realized he needed a piece of string or something with which to measure the size of the marks. "Brian, go down below and ask the privates for a measuring tape or a stick. Or Mr. Fowler—his crew might have something."

As the boy clambered down, the lantern's light swaying with his movements, Adam checked the front of the beam again where the rope and its burden had passed by on its way below. Tiny threads of rope had caught along its sharp, unfinished edge, confirming that the length had scraped back and forth along it for some distance.

While he waited for Brian to return, Adam manipulated himself along the beam to examine the rope itself without disturbing the footprints he wanted to measure. There was nothing notable about the line, but he did discover a small cluster of hair caught in a splinter of the rough wood. Whoever had tied up the rope—and since the hair was very pale blond, perhaps even white, it had not been Piney Tufts—had not been wearing a hat and scraped his head against the beam above.

Adam had taken to carrying a pencil, along with small envelopes and scraps of paper on his person—he'd have to add a small measuring tape to his pockets as well—so he used the tip of his penknife to remove the tuft of hair and drop it into the protective crease of a packet. By now, Brian was pounding back up the steps. The crane was so well-made that it didn't shiver in the least with this activity, but the noise of his feet rang out in the round, marble-walled chamber.

"Here you are, Mr. Quinn. What are you going to be doing with this measuring tape?"

Adam explained as he set about measuring the length and width of the footprints—more than one of them just to make certain he had the right measurements and that there really only had been one person up here—and then he noted the way the front of the boot narrowed, and the width of the toe. With a pencil, he drew it roughly on one of his papers and thought briefly of Miss Lemagne and her sketchbook and how handy it would be if *he* could draw.

"All right, Brian. I reckon we're done here." Once on the ground, Adam approached Mr. Fowler. "I'll need to speak with whichever of your men arrived first this morning, but in the meanwhile, you can get back to work with the crane."

The other man nodded. "It was Alexander Provest—he's the

marble finisher—who got here earliest today, and then my man Hamlin Jenkins right after him. I've told them to wait for you."

"Much obliged. I'll return in a short while. I've got one more thing to look at." Without waiting for a reply, Adam started off down the corridor toward the wing where Miss Gates had found the hat. He was fairly certain it was the hall that led to the House's new chamber, but wouldn't attest to it. Miss Gates had described the location she'd found the hat and Adam crouched with his lantern to see what tracks he could find.

As it had been dry for the last few days, only some faint smudges of dirt marred the marble floor. He was used to looking for the smallest of disturbances or marks, so he spotted a minuscule streak of blood. Then, in the corner behind one of the half-columns that lined the walls, he noticed a walking stick.

It was topped with a heavy brass knob, but there was no sign of blood or hair on the end which might have been used to strike the blow on the back of Tufts's head. Yet a walking stick simply lying against the wall of the corridor was strange.

Adam examined it closely, but there were no personal stamps on the stick nor any distinguishing marks that might help identify its owner. Still, he'd keep it.

With Brian dogging his footsteps, Adam went back to the Rotunda where the crew had wasted no time getting back to work under Charles Fowler's watchful eye. A man in scrubby work clothes approached him and introduced himself as Hamlin Jenkins.

"Fowler said you wanted to talk to me," he said, scratching a grizzled chin while holding a long metal tool. He was sucking on a plug of tobacco in his mouth.

"Yes, much obliged. You're aware that a man was found hanged here this morning. Did you see anyone or anything unusual when you arrived? Did you go inside?"

"No, sir. I can't get inside until someone lets us in—either Provest or Bassett or Cluskey. I sat there on the West Front steps and had my meat pie from Cory's while I was waiting, watching out over the Mall. It's quieter than the Avenue side, even with all the cows down there on the grass, mooing. It'd be a nice view if there wasn't so much marble and iron pieces all over. The grass is growing all around them, they've been sitting there so long. The smells from the chimneys though—from the bakeries down in the cellar—that's pretty nasty and kind of takes away from the scene." He gave that long speech while managing the chaw of tobacco in his mouth with nary a drip or splatter.

"Who let you in today? Was it Mr. Provest?"

"Yassir. He's usually here early—he does the marble finishing, he and his men, and anyway, it's nice of Mr. Fowler to put us back to work even while he's not getting paid. Mr. Walter, he's going in front of Congress tomorrow to ask them to give the money to keep the work going." Jenkins shrugged. "It's either we keep working, or we start up soldiering for the army. Me, I'd rather keep working." He scratched his chest and shifted the plug of tobacco in his mouth as if he were ready to expel it.

Adam automatically looked for a spittoon, didn't see one, then back at Jenkins, who'd tucked the chaw into his cheek. "All right, then, thank you." As the ironworker ambled off, Adam pulled out the envelope with the hair tuft in it. "Brian, I need you to take this to Dr. Hilton and tell him I found it near the scene. And bring back word from him when I should come—and on your way back here, stop at Cortland's Bakehouse on the Avenue and get us a pair of meat pies." He handed the boy a dime. "If I'm not here, I'll leave word with Mr. Bassett—that's the doorkeeper there— where I've gone."

"Yes, sir, Mr. Quinn. I'm glad I am that you wanted a meat pie too. Hearing that man talk about them made me hungry. But my mam says I'm always about being hungry—like my legs are hollowed out or something, and I have to keep eating to be filling them up." He started to go, then spun back and looked up at Adam. "Thank you for letting me come inside here, Mr. Quinn," he said in a whisper. "I never thought I'd see a place like this ever in my life. It's just like I thought America would be when we were coming over on that ship—big and grand and new. And important."

Adam nodded and felt his throat burn a little. "Go off with you now, Brian. I'm hungry for that meat pie too."

Big and grand and new. Important.

And still under construction.

Yes, the United States was all of that . . . or had been. Whether it would remain a big, grand, important Union—and whether it would be finished—was yet to be seen. Adam prayed that Mr. Lincoln would succeed in keeping it that way.

CHAPTER 4

*G*eorge Hilton was about as blessed as a black man in America could be, he thought—and reminded himself of it regularly.

He had an occupation that he had loved since he was thirteen, had money to live on—which was helpful, as most of his patients paid him in pennies or half loaves of bread or bartered labor in exchange for his services—and had recently embarked on a new and fascinating tangent to his medical career by helping Adam Quinn, a man he considered a friend, seek justice in the cases of murder.

And that was all due to the fact that he was a free man who'd been smart enough to cling to his mama's womb for a full nine and a half months.

His mama had always told him being slow and steady—and even stubbornly so—had thus served him well. Somehow he'd known to wait for the day she got her freedom papers and *then* to decide to be born—to a free woman. Either that, or God had just kept him there until it was safe.

And then, when he was twelve, Dr. Theodore Raitz had come along.

The Quaker man was a neighbor of the Methodist minister for whom George's mama worked, up in Philadelphia after she got her freedom. At first, George had simply assisted the physician with keeping his office clean, the stoop swept, and the woodstove going. But then Dr. Raitz began to ask him to help with other tasks, including medical work. Meanwhile, the minister taught George how to read and do his numbers. And before he knew it, George was apprenticing—as Dr. Raitz called it—with him in his office. The unmarried, lonely doctor said he was "gifted"—though George didn't understand what that meant until he was much older, and even now he was skeptical—and eagerly taught him what he could.

The kind, practical Quaker had had no family. When he died from cancer at forty-six, he left his house and money to George—along with something even more precious: a letter of recommendation to his own mentor, Dr. Caldwell, at the Toronto School of Medicine.

And that had sealed George's fate—in the best way possible.

Not that it had been easy, being the only black man studying medicine in Toronto. And not that he hadn't had more than a few beatings in his life because of the color of his skin and his "uppitiness" in wanting to be a doctor. But he was still alive, still healthy, and was doing what he believed God wanted him to do, right here in Washington City, seeing to his people in a number of ways.

Because who else was there to do it?

Today, he wasn't expecting any patients in his partly-subterranean office beneath Great Eternity Church—but that didn't mean none would show up. Therefore, he hung up the heavy blankets he used to separate what he thought of as his morgue with the rest of the office and examining area so that he could lay Pinebar Tufts out on the table.

He knew his work was dangerous—considering that it was illegal for even free blacks to have any sort of occupation as educated professionals—and particularly since he was cutting open a dead white man to discover what secrets his body held. Yet he'd found it fascinating and rewarding to be trusted with such a task the two previous times Adam Quinn had asked it of him. And for the President of the United States.

He rolled up his sleeves and slung on the butcher's apron he'd acquired to use during surgeries, and now postmortems, then lit the ten kerosene lanterns he'd strung up over the table. They were expensive but necessary, and though George hated feeling as though he was profiting for doing an unpleasant yet important job, he had no choice but to allow Adam or the president to pay for these supplies.

George pulled back the blanket that had been used to wrap the body and looked down once again at the unfortunate who'd been hanged in such a public place.

Pinebar Tufts was a forty-three-year-old man of approximately five feet seven and a half inches, and one hundred fifty pounds. He had brown hair, pale skin, a trimmed beard and mustache, and an old scar near his right eye. The noose was still around his neck, and George took care when he cut it free so that he didn't nick the flesh swelling around it. After that, he methodically removed Tufts's gloves, boots, and stockings, all the while carefully examining every bit of skin that was revealed. Trousers were next, then the man's coat, waistcoat, neckcloth, shirt. He'd let Adam dig through the pockets and examine the clothing when he arrived. All the while, George looked for signs of injury as well as watching for anything that might tumble or scatter from the clothing.

He'd learned that even a smattering of hair or a slightly different shade of black fabric could be an important clue to the investigation, and so, as always, he took his time: with painstaking care. Next were the undergarments, which George rolled up carefully and placed on the rest of the clothing he'd folded and put aside.

The body was rigid due to rigor mortis, and the muscles of Tufts's arms and legs were still very firm.

So that meant Tufts had been dead for approximately eight to eleven hours—which put his death after midnight and well before dawn.

Now, with his ear half-cocked toward the door of his office in case anyone came in, he looked over the entire naked body of the pasty white man. As he'd told Adam, the cause of death seemed obvious—the thick red mark from the rope around his neck was gruesome—but there could be other bits of information that might tell them where he'd been before going to the Capitol, or any other injuries—

Ah. *Here we are.*

George paused, for he'd tipped the body up onto its side and discovered a soft, sticky mass at the back of the head. He probed and examined the split scalp and chunk of damaged hair that nearly covered it. The contusion was from a single blow that had been enough to stun or knock out the man, but not enough to kill him. The strike would have happened before the hanging, but how long before he couldn't say for certain; the blood had congealed and there wasn't all that much of it. The man might have been wearing a hat, which helped to soften the assault.

George looked closely at the broken skin, bringing near the one lantern he kept handy for such close work. The contusion wasn't a narrow slit, as if from an edge or corner—like a marble wall, for example—but was smashed as if whatever had struck the blow had a curved or rounded shape.

He finished his thorough study of the exterior of the body but found no other recent injuries. George was just getting ready to make the incisions that would open the chest cavity when he noticed bruising on one side of the neck, just below where the noose had cut into the skin.

What's that?

He set down the scalpel he'd been about to use and brought his lantern closer once more, fumbling for the magnifying glass he'd recently acquired. *Well, that's odd.* He angled around to get a better look and reached for a small pair of forceps.

Just then, the door to his office slammed open.

"Doc! *Doctor!*"

George nearly dropped the lantern. He spun around as he heard feet thudding toward the dividing blanket. He whipped a covering onto Pinebar Tufts as he called back, "I'm coming. Wait there please!"

But it was too late—the dividing blanket was flung aside and a white man with blood streaming down his face stood there, gasping for breath, eyes wide, face flushed alarmingly. "Doctor! Can you come? There's been a . . ." His voice trailed off and he looked at the table.

Damn. George moved quickly to shift the sheet that hadn't quite covered up Pinebar Tufts from the prying eyes. The stark white of the corpse's naked skin seemed to shine like a beacon of guilt.

Still staring at the table, the new arrival found his voice. "What—"

"This way," George said firmly, trying to batter back the flicker of fear. "What's happened?" He began to blow out the lanterns, cursing silently over his clumsiness at not getting the sheet completely over Tufts. Next time, he'd have to lock the office door. He couldn't take the chance.

"It's Frederick Smuts," said the man, ignoring the dark smear of blood dripping from his face. "He was doing the brickwork over to the—"

George took him by the arm and directed him back to the main area of his office. The blanket swung back into place behind them, but not before the newcomer's eyes trailed toward the backroom once more. "Let me get you something for your face," he said, trying to keep focused on the moment instead of what damage might have been done by this unexpected interruption. "What's your name? And tell me what happened to Mr. Smuts."

"I'm—I'm Bartle. Fred—he *fell.* He fell down from up top the chimney we was building, and he landed on a pile of bricks. He wasn't breathing too well when I left," said the man, becoming frantic again. "He warn't moving either. I come to you—they said you can put people back together, Doc."

"All right, let's go," George said, gathering up his satchel. He slammed a hat on at the last minute and swung a coat around his shoulders—not that anyone here in Ballard's Alley cared whether he was in shirtsleeves or not, but it was habit. "What happened to you?"

"Fell down the brick wall myself. Just got my face, slid against it on the way. Hurry, Doc, hurry!"

George took the precious time to lock the door of his office, but even as he did so, he knew it didn't really matter.

Now that someone—a white man—had seen that he had the corpse of another white man back in there, a lock wouldn't make much of a difference.

Clearing his mind of the nauseating worry, George started off after Bartle. He had a man to put back together.

He hoped.

Adam found Alexander Provest, the marble finisher, with his crew working on setting the steps near the East Portico. The mason was an energetic man with a small, wiry figure that seemed at odds with an occupation dealing with massive blocks of stone. His clothes were covered with a fine glittery dust that clung to and scattered from every wrinkle or crease when he moved. Even his thick brown mustache and beard were sprinkled with the grit.

Three men were working with a block of stunning white marble that shone in the midmorning sun, carefully easing it into position as Provest supervised with a running commentary. "Ease her in, now—careful there! Yes, in like a dream . . . ahh, yes, there she goes . . . right into her spot . . . slick as a whore and twice as pretty . . . and . . . *there* she is. Snug and tight as a virgin."

Relieved that Brian wasn't around to hear and ask questions about such talk, Adam caught Provest's attention when he dragged off his cap to swipe a bead of sweat from his forehead. "Adam Quinn," he said, offering his hand to shake the other's gloved one. "I need a moment of your time."

"You're the one Fowler told me about," Provest grumbled, then turned to his crew. "Miller, finish cutting that piece there. Reston, you and Pultney polish up the next piece for the steps there. And find Garrick. Tell him to get his arse back to work—how long does it take a man to piss? There's a tree over there, for pity's sake."

"I only have a few questions," Adam said, looking around at the blocks of marble in various stages of cutting, polishing, and lining up to be set. The grounds of the Capitol looked like a disaster had struck.

"Well, what is it? Not that I'm in any hurry to get back to work seeing as we aren't getting paid," Provest said. "But can't just let the damned block sit there forever, and I figure the government's good for it, no matter who wins this damned war. You know Jeff Davis is the one who originally approved the contract for our marble?"

Adam chose to ignore Provest's implication that the Union might not remain intact and got to business instead. "You heard about the man found dead in the Rotunda this morning. Name of Pinebar Tufts. Did you know him?"

"Never heard of him before today. Guess the bastard hanged himself? Why the hell anyone would do a thing like that in the middle of the Capitol, I don't know. First we had to get the damned soldiers out of the building, now we gotta wait for a body to be cleared out. God rest his soul," he added mournfully.

Adam cleared his throat. "Mr. Provest, what time did you arrive this morning? Did you go inside the building, or see anyone leaving?"

Provest had replaced his cap and now he squinted up at Adam. "Got here at sunrise. Like to watch the way it pours over all the marble there—first it's nothing but gray and dark lumps, then it goes all soft and brown, then golden, and finally all stark white. Beautiful. You know we mined that up in Massachusetts. Italian marble's got some pretty colors—pink, veined red, black, and more—but that pure white from up north . . . ain't nothing like it." He brushed lightly at his clothing. "I always come home wearing some of it too—like the way she sparkles. Damned impossible to get out of the clothes, though, no matter how hard my missus washes 'em. Them little gritty sparkles make me trousers and coat look like the starry sky."

"Did you see anyone coming from the Capitol? Or anyone around?"

"Can't say that I did. No one else around but me. Even the Auxiliary Guards were off duty by then. That is, if Billy Morris even came on last night. Just as likely he was watching the fireworks with a bottle of whiskey in his hand and slept it off under the tree over there."

"Do you have any idea how Tufts might have gotten into the building overnight?"

"Well, like I said, Billy Morris ain't really worth the sole of the boots he walks on when it comes to patrolling the grounds and keeping the Capitol safe at night. Since the troops moved out and Morris got assigned here, I can't say I've seen him more than once or twice, though he's supposed to patrol at night. And I'm here every day, all day, just before sunrise up till after sunset."

Adam got the name and address of Billy Morris and thanked Provest for his time. As he walked away, he heard the marble worker referring to the next slab of stone as a "sleek and willing woman, sliding into her bridal bed" and was again thankful Brian wasn't around to hear.

But his stomach felt empty and he wondered how soon the boy was going to arrive with the meat pies, for Adam had left the President's House in a hurry this morning and with nothing in his belly. That had been nearly five hours ago, and truth to tell, he'd had several ales last night during the fireworks. That made a man's stomach grumbly, especially when it was half a day later and it was still empty.

As he stood on the portico facing east, overlooking Pennsylvania Avenue, Adam remembered the last time he'd been standing on this very spot: March 4, the day Mr. Lincoln had been inaugurated. That night, a man had been murdered at the celebration ball, and that event had sent Adam into the turmoil of having to find the killer. The president had asked him to help, and then again in April when a soldier was found with a slit throat in the White House, as Lincoln had begun to call the Executive Mansion.

Adam reckoned he should tell the president about this latest death, especially if the investigation was going to keep him busy and away from the president. He didn't have a particular job working for Mr. Lincoln—which Adam found both frustrating and liberating—but was usually set to doing special projects the president didn't trust anyone else to do in a town filled with Southern spies, political maneuverings, and countless people who only wanted Mr. Lincoln to give them a job or grant some other favor.

Just as Adam started down the steps of the portico, he heard a shout, followed by the shrill, horrified whinny of a horse. He spun in time to see it happen: a two-nag merchant's wagon overturned, crashing into a smart, sleek but flimsy landau pulled by a single black filly. The nags shrieked and reared, and the filly went down hard onto her tail in a tangle of legs, lines, and bridle. Her driver was thrown out of the open-sided landau, whose red-painted wheel splintered horribly as the small carriage crashed to the street with its driver's foot caught up in it. The contents of the merchant's wagon—mostly barrels of flour—tumbled to the ground, rolling into the road beneath the hooves of a pair of chestnuts that almost didn't stop in time.

Adam wasn't the only one running toward the disaster, but he was one of the first to arrive. Seeing that the injured landau driver was being attended to, Adam gave his attention to the filly. He came from behind the downed horse and snagged her reins in an effort to calm her so she wouldn't kick anyone or injure herself further—a difficult proposition in itself, but made moreso by his handicap. But the filly's eyes were wild and her elegant, spindly legs worked frantically. Adam was trying to settle her so he could unhitch her and determine how badly she was injured when a small body shoved up next to him.

"She's scared," said Brian Mulcahey, thrusting a warm, aromatic package at Adam as he crouched next to him at the filly's head, resting a small pale hand between her sleek black ears. He bent close enough to look her in the eye and began to speak in some lilting language Adam didn't understand—Irish.

It sounded soothing even to Adam's ears, and somehow, the words or their cadence penetrated the young horse's wall of terror as Brian patted her cheek, looking her in the eyes as he murmured on in a lyrical sort of fashion. After a moment, her heaving sides and terrified eyes settled, and she blew out a last agitated snort before she settled on her side, legs sagging to the ground.

Adam, still holding the packet of meat pies—and, oh, the smell was making his mouth water!—was dazed by his young friend's calm manner and skill. He patted Brian on the head. "Nicely done, young man. You certainly do have a way with horses. Will you stay with her while I see about her owner?"

"She's not hurt bad," Brian said in a low, confident voice as he continued to stroke the shiny black nose. "She'll be getting up in a minute. This little lass is a real beauty, she is." He paused as if to listen, leaning close to the filly. He murmured something else, all the while stroking her over the forelock and down her nose. "She's hurt, but she'll be all right. It's her tail."

Adam looked past the filly's withers, which were flecked with sweat, and saw the odd angle of her tail. It had obviously broken as she fell onto it. If that was the only injury, then he reckoned Brian was correct—the slender girl would be all right in a few months.

But her driver was likely a different matter. He'd been badly caught up in the accident, his foot wedged between a wheel and the carriage as he was tossed from the vehicle.

Adam had just pulled to his feet to see if he could be of help with the injured man when he heard a shriek. "Daddy! *Daddy!*"

He recognized that voice—Miss Lemagne—and turned in time to see her in a flurry of yellow skirts and trailing ribbons. She flung herself onto the street next to the landau driver, who'd just been extricated from the accident and was now lying in the street.

"Miss, please," said one of the men who'd been kneeling next to the man Adam realized was Hurst Lemagne. "I need some room to—"

"Daddy, are you all right? It's me, Constance." Miss Lemagne wasn't about to be budged from her father's side. "I'm here . . . I'm right here. *Please* open your eyes, Daddy."

Adam hurried toward her and navigated between the others trying to comfort Lemagne. He bent, offering her an arm. "Miss Lemagne, why don't we step back and give them some room to see if he can be moved? Look, he's opening his eyes—he's awake. Did someone call for a doctor yet?" he added, looking around at the crowd of people.

"Yes, they sent for him," replied a woman, who was helping to keep a small crowd of children from getting too close even while she eyed the goings-on herself.

"Daddy, it's *going* to be all right." Miss Lemagne had barely glanced at Adam before returning her attention to her parent, who was gray-faced with pain, and panting. "I'm here, and the doctor is coming. He'll fix y'all up, Ah *know* it." As usual, her southern drawl became more pronounced during a moment of high emotion.

Despite her optimistic words, the situation seemed grim. Hurst Lemagne's leg was bent at an odd, ninety-degree angle with his left knee toward the other knee, and he was clearly in intense agony. Three men were carefully moving his limbs, trying to find a comfortable position for him—but nothing seemed to ease his discomfort. His daughter took off her shawl and bunched it up, then placed her sketchbook satchel under his head and used the shawl for padding. After, she knelt next to him and refused to leave his side, holding his gloved hand in hers, murmuring to him.

As there was nothing he could do to assist Miss Lemagne and her father at the moment, Adam helped to roll the barrels back and load them onto the wagon, which had been righted while he and Brian were seeing to the filly. Two of the barrels had split, coating the street, horses, and bystanders with flour, and the owner of the wagon was shouting at someone—apparently who-ever had caused the whole accident. Due to their warmth and de-licious scent, Adam was acutely aware of the meat pies he'd shoved in his pocket, but now wasn't the time to pull them out. But his stomach was gnawing, urging him not to wait too long.

Two constables and one of the provost guards finally arrived and began to try and sort things out while Brian continued to sit with the pretty black horse. She was making signs that she might be ready to stand up.

"*Where* is the doctor?" Miss Lemagne cried, looking up with blue eyes filled with tears. "Isn't he coming? Mah daddy's in such *pain.* Can someone bring a drink? He's thirsty."

Adam thought privately that a big swig of whiskey might be more appropriate, but when a young woman offered a jug of water, he said nothing. Instead, he crouched on the other side and helped lift the man's head enough so his daughter could dribble some into his mouth.

Just then, a small carriage similar to the one Hurst Lemagne had been driving, arrived with a great clatter of hooves and jingles. A tall, portly man climbed out hurriedly, carrying a medical bag. "I'm Dr. Forthruth. Let me take a look. . . ."

Now Adam moved around to Miss Lemagne's side and this time, he took her arm and gently but firmly pulled her to her feet. "I reckon we'd best give the doctor some space to do his job."

"He's going to be all right, isn't he?" she asked, looking up at him. Her bonnet was askew and her eyes glistened with unshed tears. "He's awake, and he said my name—so he's *going* to be all right." The second time it wasn't a question but a statement, and Adam squeezed her arm gently.

"I'm certain the doctor will do whatever he can." Adam wasn't as optimistic. The odd angle of Lemagne's leg indicated a serious situation. In the best case, the man might be confined to a wheelchair for the rest of his life. And that was the most optimistic.

"Broken femur," said Forthruth grimly once he completed his examination. "Right there at the hip. Going to have to set it—"

"Miss Lemagne, I think it's best if you step over here with me for a moment," Adam said, keeping a firm hold of her arm when she would have turned back.

"No, Mr. Quinn, I-I just can't. I can't leave my daddy."

"I understand that, but I reckon you don't want to see what they have to do to put his leg back into position. Please, Miss Le-

magne. As soon as they've finished, you can go right to his side."
He hoped that while he kept her here—talking, distracted, turned
away—the doctor and a few strong men would get the job done.

He knew what they were going to have to do, and he glanced
over just in time to see the doctor at Lemagne's foot and two men
at the other end of the injured man's body, holding down his
shoulders. The physician would have to pull steadily on the shin
to get the bones to fit back into place. It was a shame it had to be
done on the street in front of everyone, but at least Miss Lemagne
wasn't looking in that direction—

The doctor moved sharply and Lemagne screamed, arching in
agony. Miss Lemagne tore from Adam, crying and running over
to her father as Adam spun to go after her.

Hurst Lemagne was panting and gasping. His face appeared
grayer than before and seemed to have shrunken into his skull.
His leg was still in the same awful, awkward position it had been,
flexing inward, toward the right knee. Miss Lemagne was crying
and holding her father's hand, batting at the three men who'd
gathered around to try and set the leg. They stared at her, panting from exertion, when she tried to push them away while hud-
dled next to her father.

Adam took matters into his own hands. There was no reason to
continue this on the street. "Forthruth, we're going to take him
home—or to your office. Your choice. But not here. You're not
doing this again here. We need a wagon," he added, calling into
the spectators, who'd crept in closer as the horrible medical work
had begun. "Constable! A wagon to transport this man. Some
whiskey too—quickly!"

Then he turned to Brian, who'd been standing there with the
filly—and miraculously back on her feet—holding the bridle and
watching with horrified eyes. "Follow us with the girl, all right,
Brian? She can walk all right? Here's your pie." He dug out the
packet and thrust one crumbly, glorious-scented beef pastry at
the boy. Then, reluctantly, he shoved the other back into his coat.

"Miss Lemagne, come now," he said, pulling her to her feet

once more. "Let's get your father somewhere more private, and something to help with the pain."

"They hurt him," she said furiously. "They just pulled on him—"

"Yes. They have to do that to get the broken ends of the bone to fit back together or it won't knit together and heal."

"I know that, but why do they have to be so *rough?*" She began to sob quietly, and Adam realized he didn't have a handkerchief to offer her as it was still in Mrs. Tufts's possession. "They were *hurting* him so badly!"

"I know," he said. "It's an awful thing to watch. We'll get something to help dull the pain, and I reckon they'll try again. Surely it'll work the next time." Adam held her arm firmly as one of the constables drew a wagon closer. "They're going to load him in there. Is there a place at Mrs. Billings's house for him? On the main floor?"

Miss Lemagne blinked back the tears and seemed to come back to herself. "Yes, yes, I should make a place for him. That's right, Mr. Quinn."

"Constance? Constance, is everything all right? Mr. Quinn, what's happened?"

Adam heaved a great sigh of relief when he recognized Miss Gates's voice. He turned to find her and Clara Barton, whom he'd met previously, standing there with two large satchels bulging with fabric. He remembered she and her friend had been intending to solicit supplies for the military hospital. It appeared they'd found some donations of bandages and blankets.

"My daddy," Miss Lemagne said, then burst into tears, her hand waving helplessly at the men loading him into the wagon.

"Miss Gates," Adam said, giving her a pleading look. "I reckon Miss Lemagne would appreciate some assistance, as they are bringing her father back to her house. He's injured quite badly, and she could—well, maybe you could help her."

"Of course." As he'd hoped, Miss Gates stepped up to the problem and took the other woman's arm. "I'll be happy to help her, Mr. Quinn." She gave him a look that indicated she knew exactly how relieved he was to see her—and why.

Having turned Miss Lemagne over to the capable Miss Gates, Adam went to assist the men settling Hurst into the wagon. The man had fainted again, which was just as well—maybe they'd be able to pull his leg into place before he came to. Adam shook his head as he looked at the patient again. He'd never seen a leg in that position before. Something was very wrong. His optimism, already low, dropped further.

He was just considering whether to go with the Lemagnes when someone shouted, "Mr. Quinn!"

Adam turned to see William Johnson, who worked for both the Treasury Department and the president as a messenger, hurrying toward him. The young man had come with the Lincolns and Adam from Springfield as Abe's valet, and despite his new job, he still went to the mansion every morning to groom and shave the president and lay out his clothing.

Reading the writing on the wall, Adam gestured to the doctor to take the wagon and his patient on without him, once more thankful that Miss Gates had appeared at a most opportune moment. He would have felt guilty about leaving Miss Lemagne to go on with only strangers to help her. "Hello, William." He called out and waved so the messenger knew he'd wait.

As the dark-skinned young man loped up to him, out of breath and hat in his hand, Adam plucked the meat pastry from his pocket and at long last broke his fast.

"Mr. Quinn, sir, the president is a-wanting you soonest. I been looking for you for more than an hour, sir, and so I think we'd best go back right away."

Adam licked his fingers to get the last of the pastry crumbs and nodded, starting off down the Avenue toward the President's House.

As he did so, he realized he hadn't had the chance to ask Brian about a message from George Hilton. He hoped if there was news that it could wait until the president was finished with him.

"Hanging in the Capitol Rotunda, you say?" Mr. Lincoln, whose gray eyes were filled with sober compassion, looked up at Adam from the large table he used as a desk.

"Yes, sir. He was found early this morning, when they opened up the doors." Adam glanced out the window of the president's office, which overlooked an elliptical expanse of grass to the south. The stinky, swampy Canal was beyond the long, broad lawn, down a little incline, and it ran all along the length of the National Mall. One of the troop regiments—he couldn't remember which one—was practicing a game called baseball there on the lawn.

He could make out the white, pencil-like stub of the unfinished Washington Monument out on the Mall. Next to it was the slaughterhouse that had been constructed in order to provide food for the troops. About a month ago, an entire herd of cows and steers—which had been left to graze on the Mall—had fallen into the Canal. It had taken a dozen men more than a day to herd the cattle out of the sludgy water, and even then, they lost six of them.

"A terrible thing, to be sure. And a shock to those who found him," the president said. "Poor man."

"Yes, sir. There was a small crowd of people just coming inside—apparently to hear the Senate this morning."

Lincoln nodded and reached for a bowl of peanuts among the papers on his desk. "They found him hanging, and someone called you in to investigate." A glint of satisfaction flared in the president's eyes. "Your reputation begins to precede you, Adam. Mr. Pinkerton might soon have a competitor to contend with." He chuckled and swiped up a scoop of peanuts in his knobby hand. Twisting, cracking, and then popping the shell apart, Lincoln tossed a few nuts into his mouth. Adam suspected that was the extent of the man's meal for the day thus far, as Mrs. Lincoln was out of town and not there to badger him into eating. "Who was it that thought to send for you?"

Adam gritted his teeth, though he wasn't certain why he was hesitant to answer. "It was Sophie Gates and Constance Lemagne, sir."

"Both of them?" The president's dark bushy brows rose into the shock of unkempt hair that flopped on his forehead. Adam was reminded that he himself wasn't the only scruffy, uncouth frontiersman attempting to live among the society of Washington, D.C. "How fortuitous that both young ladies were present." Lincoln chuckled as he twisted, cracked, then liberated several more nuts, popping them into his grinning mouth. "I reckon you've got some admirers, Adam. Not an untenable place to be for a handsome young man."

"They're both very nice young ladies," Adam said. As he did so, it came as a mild shock to him that one of them seemed to intrude on his thoughts more often than not—and at unexpected moments. It had been a long time since he'd even thought about wooing a woman, let alone met one that was appropriate to woo. Especially since he'd lost his arm.

"Not the least bit hard on the eyes, neither of them, if I recollect right—and I'm sure I do." Lincoln grinned, then picked up a pen and stabbed it into the ink bottle. "Well, I must say I fully support the idea of you sparking one—or both of them," he added with a sudden twinkle. "There's something to be said for a soft, warm, sweet-smelling woman in a man's life—and, one hopes, eventually in his bed. I highly recommend it, Adam."

Adam's face warmed, not because of the sentiment so much as the fact that it was the *President of the United States* who was making a lewd comment—*and* because Lincoln's very circumspect secretary John Nicolay was sitting at a nearby table, scritch-scratching at some document or other. Fortunately, he didn't seem to be paying any attention.

Or at least, Adam didn't think the sober, correct Nicolay was paying attention until he saw the man's mouth curve in suppressed laughter behind his mustache. "Mr. President, might I remind you that General Scott and General McDowell will be here at any moment."

"Damn. I suppose that means I'd best drag myself down the stairs. Scott can't make the trip up them anymore, the plagued old goat. Couldn't even stand at yesterday's parade. 'Course that made me easiest the tallest man on the stand, even without my hat, so I'm not complaining." Lincoln chuckled to himself and unfolded that long, angular body from its chair. "Especially since I was the recipient of a kiss from a handsome woman."

Adam frowned. Unlike his secretaries and bodyguards, Lincoln had found it amusing that yesterday, during the Independence Day parade of soldiers past the Executive Mansion, a woman had run from the crowd, somehow bounded up the steps of the stand in her skirts and crinolines, and given the president a large, smacking kiss on the cheek before turning and slipping back into the crowd. And no one had stopped her.

"Let's be thankful she wasn't carrying a knife or a pistol she meant to use," Adam said flatly. "She got close enough to do either—and easily enough. Abe—"

"And let's make certain Mrs. Lincoln don't hear about that," the president added hastily, looking at Adam with a jaundiced eye. He hated getting lectured about the lack of security around himself and refused to do a thing about it, and he knew the rare moments Adam called him by his familiar name meant he was about to call upon their friendship and history and pressure him. "Never can tell what will set that woman off."

As Mrs. Lincoln's fits and moods were a common topic among those who lived in the President's House, Adam was inclined to agree. Knowing it was a losing prospect to continue the conversation about the president's safety and that he would have to leave for his meeting, he said, "There's something I must tell you about Mr. Tufts—"

The door flew open and two bodies hurtled themselves into the room. With them came a flurry of white cards that fluttered into and around the chamber, landing on every surface as the boys shrieked and spun in circles.

"Look, Paw! We made a blizzard!" lisped Tad, Lincoln's eight-year-old son as he dumped over a pail with even more white papers in it. "It's *snowing!*"

Willie, who was ten and not quite as exuberant as his younger brother, nonetheless laughed and lunged to the ground, scooping up a handful of what Adam recognized were calling cards and tossing them back into the air with glee. "It's snowing in July!" he cried.

"And so it is," their father replied gravely, an affectionate twinkle in his eyes. "And now someone had best shovel all this snow from my office before it melts and gets my papers all wet." Seemingly nonplussed by this interruption and the ensuing mess, the president began to shuffle through one stack of papers among many on his desk. He used a long, bony hand to flick a pile of cards to the floor, then kept on digging.

Tad shrieked and swung his bucket around and the last few fluttered out. Then he reluctantly began picking up the mess, then tossing them into the air again, muttering, "Snow! Snow!" Willie bent and got a few handfuls, but they'd only retrieved a small portion of the calling cards when the office door opened again.

"General Scott's carriage is here," Hay, the other John who was a secretary to the president, said as he poked his head into the office. He was younger and not quite as staid as the German Nicolay, and he gave the boys a wink then backed out of the way as Tad and Willie charged out of the room—leaving the "snow" to "melt" all over their father's desk.

"Damn," said Lincoln again, seeming to sink down into himself despite his tall stature. "I reckon it's going to be another fight about whether the soldiers are ready to move out yet. Blast it all. We've got the press and the public who want this war over, *now*— and most of our mustered troops, well their subscription's over end of July. They're wanting to finish this up before then."

Adam had heard all of this before—multiple times; in fact, daily, over the last three months—but he only nodded. His friend and mentor had few people to whom he could rail about these things, and he felt honored to be one of them. He also considered it part of his patriotic duty to listen and to offer support and advice as appropriate.

"Scott and McDowell—they're saying the boys aren't ready. Though I think they're looking better, myself," the president said thoughtfully. "Washington—nor anyplace here in this country— never saw such a vast army together as we had marching down the street yesterday." He sighed and scratched his head as he continued to shuffle through his desk. "You ever hear of Manassas, Adam?"

"Yes, sir. Isn't in Virginia?" Adam had most definitely heard of the small town that had seemed to come up more and more as the place that would be a decisive battle against the Confederates. The "big" battle that so many people were hoping for.

Lincoln nodded as he stuffed a sheaf of papers under his arm, then surveyed his desk as if looking for another set. "Thirty miles from here. Near a creek called Bull Run. Now, what were you saying about Mr. Tufts? Nicolay, find that map for me, won't you?"

"Yes, sir."

Adam followed Lincoln, who now had a thick wad of paper under his arm, a bundle clutched to his chest, and another sheaf in his big hand. As he reached the door, which led into the hallway where several people waited to see the president—though not as many as there used to be only three months ago—he said, "Mr. President, I reckon there's one thing you should know about Mr. Tufts's death."

Lincoln stopped with his hand on the knob. He was only an inch taller than Adam, but his presence made it seem much more; particularly with the aura of responsibility around him. "Don't tell me—let me guess. He didn't do it to himself. It was murder."

Adam nodded grimly. "I believe it was."

"Well, then, I reckon you'd best see to it. Who else is there to do it?" Lincoln shook his head as he opened the door. "And that's yet another problem requiring my attention—Mayor Barret's still complaining about the clashes between our soldiers and his residents here in the city. Even the Provost Guard hasn't helped keep the military in line enough for him. I'm certain the city's going to need a new police force to help keep the peace. But that's for another day."

"Mr. President," Adam said quickly, following him out into the corridor. "You sent for me hours ago—what was it you needed?"

Lincoln paused. "Oh yes, I did, didn't I? Damned if I can remember what it was. Too many thoughts in this old head of mine, Adam." He smiled wryly. "It mustn't have been as important as the investigation of a murder—ah, yes. I remember now. It was regarding some missing rifles." He glanced at the cluster of people in the hallway, most of them visitors to the mansions and hoping for something from the president. "Best if you ask Stoddard about it—he was there when Stanton and I were discussing the problem."

Adam nodded, but Lincoln probably didn't notice. He was off on his long legs, striding down the corridor past the oval library and the bedrooms he and Mrs. Lincoln used, to the stairway which led to the main floor—all the while nodding and acknowledging, but not stopping for, the line of people waiting for him.

Watching him go, Adam, burdened by the responsibility of finding justice for Pinebar Tufts, knew that the president felt such a weight a hundredfold more than he.

Sophie felt for Constance Lemagne. She really did. Her father was gravely injured and in incredible pain. She was living in a home that wasn't hers—although, apparently, Mr. Lemagne was going to be marrying Mrs. Billings, assuming he recovered from the accident—and therefore she was attempting to settle her father into an unfamiliar place where she had no real authority over the servants. Mrs. Billings was mostly bedridden, so she was of little help.

But as sympathetic as she might be to the other young woman, Sophie did have her limits. And one of them was when Constance ordered her—she didn't *ask*, she *ordered*, as if Sophie was a servant, and that was the whole reason it got Sophie's back up—to run around to Mrs. Greenhow's house and tell her what happened, and to give her Constance's regrets for the salon that evening.

"Run off and tell her, Sophie" were the exact words Constance used, even as she sat in the wagon next to her unconscious father, holding his hand, tears glittering in her eyes, waiting for the house to be readied for him.

It was Sophie's opinion—which she kept to herself, of course, considering the situation—that sending regrets to a friend's weekly meeting was not a priority when there was a bed and linens to prepare for a first-floor sickbed, as well as an entire rearrangement of the parlor in order to make room for the patient and what would surely be a prolonged rehabilitation.

Not only that, there were servants to be managed—especially since Mrs. Billings was upstairs, and Mr. Lemagne would be downstairs, and ne'er the twain should meet, at least in the near future. And aside from all those perfectly reasonable considerations, there was Brian Mulcahey, who waited patiently for direction in the front of the Billings house with the elegant black filly that had somehow emerged relatively unscathed from the disaster but still needed medical care herself.

It was young Brian who helped Sophie make up her mind that it was more important for her to stay and assist Constance than to take a message about news that she suspected Mrs. Greenhow would hear all on her own, considering the size of the crowd around the accident and how quickly news did travel in Washington. She wrote a brief letter on the notepad she always carried and sent the boy off with the paper after he relinquished the horse—whose name predictably turned out to be Midnight—to James, one of the servants.

The housekeeper, Louise, was dispatched to the closest livery stable to obtain the name of a veterinarian to call for Midnight, and then Sophie turned her attention to Constance.

"What did Mrs. Greenhow say?" asked the distraught young woman, grief and shock glazing her eyes as she looked down from the wagon, which was parked in front of the house while they waited. Clearly, she had no concept of how little time had passed since she ordered Sophie on her errand.

The poor thing. Sophie's annoyance ebbed a trifle, and she fibbed. "She was horrified at the news and said that of course she expected you would stay with your father tonight. And she hoped for all to be well, soonest." She was confident that the actual response would be along the same vein when it arrived. "Now, it should only be another moment before the bed is ready for your father. How is he doing? Has he opened his eyes again? Do you think he could drink some whiskey? I'm certain the doctor will give him chloroform once they move him inside, but a little whiskey might help until then."

Dr. Forthruth and the man who owned the wagon they'd borrowed to move Mr. Lemagne had been conferring in a grave manner near the front of the cart. Everyone had agreed that they didn't want to move the injured man more than once, and that he should wait until the parlor was readied for him. Sophie had been the one to speak to the servants after an initial appearance by Constance before her father arrived in the slower wagon.

"He's in so much pain," the other woman replied. "Where is Mr. Quinn? I thought he would be here too." She looked around through tear-filled eyes.

"Mr. Quinn was called away. He said he'll call as soon as he's able." That also was a fabrication, but again, Sophie was all too certain such an event would come to pass. Surely nothing, save an invasion, would keep the affable, utterly responsible Mr. Quinn from checking on the southern belle and her father.

Constance appeared ready to speak again when her maid, a motherly black woman—and, Sophie assumed—a slave, appeared at the front door and waved them to come inside. Apparently all was in readiness for Mr. Lemagne.

It was a painful and difficult process to carry the injured man inside on a board. Sophie was glad she was there for Constance, as it was terrible to watch the trio attempt to maneuver him through the narrow front door without jarring the awkwardly bent leg. Whenever the doctor did his best to shift it to a different position, Lemagne arched and cried out, even screaming at times.

Constance burst into tears after the first outburst and cried, "Can't you be careful? You're *hurting* him!" She was squeezing Sophie's hand so tightly Sophie feared she might lose the use of her fingers for a while.

At last, Lemagne fainted again and the determined men thrust him as determinedly—but as carefully as possible—through the doorway.

Before Sophie could follow them and Constance inside, a small barouche pulled up in front of the house. She saw two women passengers: one about her age, and another who was probably a servant or other chaperone.

The younger woman rose impatiently, and the driver hurried to help her down as she managed her abundance of skirts and crinolines. Sophie recognized the expensive quality of her frock and, just as immediately, unashamedly coveted the fetching bonnet of sky blue trimmed with airy pheasant feathers and tiny forget-me-nots. The new arrival was a stunningly beautiful woman with a perfect nose, a full, bow-shaped mouth, and a dusky rose complexion. She had slashing dark brows that still managed to make her look elegant, and her coloring along with thick, inky hair suggested she was French or Italian.

"Hello," Sophie said, moving forward to greet the visitor as she started toward the house. She wasn't certain how to announce that this wasn't the most appropriate time for a social call, but the young woman spoke before she had the opportunity.

"Is Constance Lemagne home? I heard about her father, and I wanted to come and see if there was anything I could do to help." She spoke in a smooth, dulcet voice with a swath of the South.

"I'm afraid he's in a very bad way," Sophie replied. "And Constance is with him. They've just managed to bring Mr. Lemagne inside and I expect the doctor will be seeing to him for quite some time. My name is Sophie Gates. I'm—a friend of the family." She went on to explain what she knew of the injuries. "It will be a long recovery, I fear."

"I'm Felicity Monroe. Miss Lemagne and I were supposed to meet for coffee this afternoon, but when I heard about the accident—well, everyone heard about it; it was all anyone's been talking about besides the man they found in the Capitol this morning. I just wanted to find out if there was anything I could do to help."

This was the young society woman whose wedding Constance had been "frothing" to get an invitation to. Sophie supposed her chances had just increased, considering that Miss Monroe had made a specific trip to call on her and offer support and assistance. Unless she merely wanted to fill up her gossip bucket so she could be the one touting the latest news among her group of friends . . . but that wasn't the impression she got from the young lady. Miss Monroe seemed genuinely concerned by the situation.

"I'm not certain Miss Lemagne is prepared to have visitors right now, but suppose I go inside and see what the situation is." Sophie thought that either Constance would be unwilling to part from her father's side, or that she might *need* to step away as the doctor and his assistant tried once more to set the bones of his leg. She shuddered at the thought.

"Oh, thank you, Miss Gates," replied the young woman. The fact that she didn't attempt to wheedle her way inside made Sophie think she truly was concerned and not so much interested in gossip. "I'll wait right here."

When Sophie walked in, she heard a shriek and knew it was time for Constance to give the physician space to do his difficult job. She took her friend—she supposed Constance was now her friend, of sorts—by the arm and said, "Felicity Monroe is outside. She's very concerned about you. Perhaps you'd like to step out and speak with her for a moment while Dr. Forthruth is seeing to your father."

Constance didn't argue, but she did stumble as she looked back over her shoulder as the men gathered around her parent once more. "Daddy," she whispered, and clung tighter to Sophie.

Once out in the sunshine, Constance seemed to collect her bearings—and, unexpectedly, her southern manners. "Miss Monroe," Constance said with a nearly perfect hospitable inflection. "How kind of you to call."

And people said the British had stiff upper lips.

"Miss Lemagne, I'm so, so terribly sorry to hear about your father," said her visitor, clasping Constance's hand.

Sophie drifted toward the house as the two young women exchanged hand squeezes and leaned toward the other in intense conversation. She wondered if it would be possible for her to leave, now that Miss Monroe had arrived and Mr. Lemagne had been settled. There wasn't much else she could do, and she'd abandoned Clara Barton, leaving her to manage the two large sacks of bandage and blanket donations for the Union soldiers at the infirmary.

She'd not had the chance to ask her friend about Pinebar Tufts, her coworker at the Patent Office, and so she hoped to intercept Clara leaving the hospital before she went home for the afternoon. A quick check of the watch pinned to her shirtwaist told Sophie that it was nearly four o'clock, and she ventured toward the two other young women, who seemed to be chattering along with less emotion and angst.

"Constance, I hope you'll excuse me, but I must leave to meet up with Miss Barton," Sophie said. "Perhaps Miss Monroe will stay with you for a while until Dr. Forthruth is finished."

"I certainly will," replied the lovely and agreeable Miss Monroe, still clasping Constance's hand. "I can send Bitty home, and wait until Carson—er, Mr. Townsend I mean—can come to fetch me." Her cheeks turned slightly pink.

Sophie remembered that Mr. Townsend was the fiancé of Miss Monroe, for whose wedding she'd had a dress sewn in New York that required a specific trunk to be made to accommodate its size when sending it back (the actual size and design of such an extravagant dress Sophie found impossible to imagine). "That would be very kind of you, Miss Monroe."

"Oh, would you, Miss Monroe?" said Constance, glancing worriedly toward the house.

"Of course. Miss Gates, could I have Vancy drive you somewhere?" She indicated the barouche, with its waiting driver and the woman inside—presumably the aforementioned Bitty. "There's no sense in you walking about with all of those soldiers everywhere, crowding the streets and making all sorts of ruckus. Why, my papa won't even let me walk to the market anymore."

Surprised at her kindness, Sophie accepted with enthusiasm. "I very much appreciate it, Miss Monroe. Constance, I hope things will go well with the doctor, and your father won't be in too much pain. I'll call tomorrow to see how he—and you—are doing."

"Thank you for everything, Sophie." To her surprise, Constance enfolded her in a heartfelt embrace. "Such a terrible day it's been—what with finding Mr. Tufts hanging at the Capitol, and then poor Daddy . . . and poor, sweet Midnight . . . well, at least *she's* going to be all right." Her words choked off and she dabbed at her nose with the lace-edged handkerchief she clutched.

"Mr. Tufts?" said Miss Monroe. "Did you say *hanging*? At the Capitol? Was that who it was?" Her expression was stricken.

"Yes. His name was Pinebar Tufts. He worked at the Patent Office," Sophie said, watching her curiously. "Did you know him?"

"My papa does. If it's the same Mr. Tufts," she added, giving a short laugh. Then she sobered. "How absolutely horrible. Just horrible to do something like that."

Sophie opened her mouth, then closed it. Perhaps it wasn't the best time to mention her belief that Mr. Tufts had been murdered. But that didn't mean she couldn't do some subtle interrogating. "Was he a friend of your father's?"

Miss Monroe tilted her head. "I'm not quite certain. My papa is a lobbyist for the mining companies, and he knows so many people I can't keep count of all of them, or why, or how. I don't really pay much attention. We're always having important dinners at our house—the congressmen come, and some of the senators too—though there are fewer now with the secessionists having gone south. Other business people too—like the men who cast the iron for the new Capitol dome. I don't remember whether Mr. Tufts was at one of papa's dinners because of business, or if he knows him some other way. I just know Papa has spoken of him—his name is so unusual, I remembered it."

Sophie decided that was all she was going to learn from Miss Monroe, at least for now. But she'd mention it to Mr. Quinn the next time she saw him . . . which she would make certain was soon. She wanted to find out what he'd learned, if anything, so far.

Perhaps it wasn't exactly justifiable, but Sophie had already begun to think of the investigation as "hers"—this personal attachment due to her having determined almost immediately that Mr. Tufts had been murdered.

CHAPTER 5

Since Ballard's Alley was in the First Ward—the area of the city which butted up to the north side of Lafayette Square and the President's House—Adam decided a visit to George's office would be the next stop in his day. Surely the doctor would have some news for him by now, because it was almost four o'clock in the afternoon.

Adam had just finished a lengthy meeting with Stoddard about Mr. Lincoln's concerns regarding Union military guns being stolen and sold to Washington residents and possibly even being shipped south to the Rebels. The president wanted Adam to look into a particular regiment commander who could be spearheading some of the illegal sales. It wasn't urgent that he do so immediately, so Adam decided he could take the time to speak with George Hilton.

As always, when he walked along the neat street lined with comfortable houses, Adam found it unappetizing to know that behind the row of pretty, well-kept homes was a sort of inner mews, a hidden alley, where the poor and indigent scraped out a living. One could walk up Fifteenth Street, and then turn on L Street and then onto M Street and never realize that between the two strips of houses was an unseen neighborhood filled with rickety structures and muddy, refuse-strewn walkways with the occasional scrawny chicken or goat. Both enslaved and free blacks lived in the shacks clustered in these blind alleys, as well as immigrants—mostly from Ireland and Germany.

Tucked into one of these subset neighborhoods of the capital city was a tiny, whitewashed church called Great Eternity. The only thing that indicated its role as a place of worship was the small cross perched on the peak of its roof and another one hanging on the main entrance. Adam didn't climb the four steps to the front door, but instead walked around the sparse, muddy lawn to a set of stairs on the side, which descended to a subterranean entrance.

When he tried the door, Adam found it bolted tight from the inside. He frowned. That had never happened before.

Slightly unsettled, he looked around, then climbed back up the stairs. What if George hadn't made it back to his office with the body? What if he'd been intercepted on the way—while in possession of a white man's corpse? He set his jaw grimly.

There were two small windows on the back of the half-buried wall, only inches above the ground—which was a godsend, considering that the type of work George Hilton did required some ventilation. The subterranean room also helped to keep the space cool.

He was crouched on the ground trying to look through one of the skinny windows when he heard the metallic clunking sound of a bolt being thrown open.

"Adam," said the doctor, standing in the doorway to the cellar. He sounded strangely relieved. "I've been expecting you."

Adam lifted his brows. "Really? You're locked up tighter than a drum in here."

George shook his head and stepped back for Adam to enter. His mouth was in a flat line. "Didn't want anyone to walk in on me—again."

Adam didn't need the details; it wasn't difficult to realize what had happened. He made a quick decision. "I'm going to ask Mr. Lincoln for a letter for you to have—to show people in case someone asks." When George began to shake his head, he continued. "I reckon it'll be better than nothing."

The other man just turned and walked to the back of the space, flinging aside a heavy blanket that separated the room as he passed through. "I haven't done as much as I'd hoped—got called away to an injury on The Island. Man fell off a chimney, landed on his back on the pile of bricks below. Nothing I could do for him—by the time I got there, he was dead."

"Sorry to hear that, Doc. There was a big accident down in front of the Capitol too. Hurst Lemagne was injured pretty badly. I don't think he's going to walk again."

"Miss Lemagne's father? The southern woman who draws? She came here with her maid."

"Yes. The doctor who came to the scene says Hurst broke his leg—thigh bone."

"Femur."

Adam shrugged. "I reckon. Anyhow, they tried to reset the bone there on the street, and they couldn't do it. I don't know whether they got it in place once they got him home or not." He was going to have to call on Miss Lemagne to find out.

"A femur fracture is serious," George said soberly. "You're likely right—he won't walk again."

"Doesn't look that way. Never seen anything like that before—the leg's just kind of turning inward, but it looks strange and it won't straighten out at all. Doctor said the break is right at the hip, but every time we tried to pull it to realign the bone, it just shifted back the way it was. Poor sot."

George sucked in a breath between his teeth. "I hope they gave him chloroform or laudanum."

"After the first try, yes. The doctor was going to when they got him back to his house." Discouraged by that and so many other things, Adam shook his head, then looked at Pinebar Tufts's pale body. Although unclothed, it was covered from the waist down. George had sliced into the body's throat and abdomen, leaving dark red lines where the incisions had been made. Adam didn't look at that part too closely, for he still hadn't gotten used to the sight of a man's insides being exposed or extracted—even in the name of science and justice. The smell was bad enough—and as it was July, he expected it to get a lot worse pretty damned quickly.

"I left his clothing over there," the doctor said. "I didn't look at it closely—nor dug through his pockets. Thought I'd leave that to you. There was a note pinned to his coat?"

"Yes. I've got it here." Adam showed George, who looked at it closely, then turned back to his work. "I know you've just started, but have you found anything I should know?"

"Yes, I have." There was a hint of excitement in his voice—which was saying something, for George was usually very even-keeled in tone and action. Only rarely did he make a jest, and even then it was dry and subtle. "This man didn't hang himself. He was murdered."

"I thought so," Adam replied, and was amused to see the enthusiasm in the other man's eyes deflate.

"You already knew."

"I suspected as much—thanks in part to Miss Gates, who pointed out to me that a man doesn't generally hang himself while wearing gloves and a coat."

"I have proof, not merely conjecture," the doctor replied, a bit stiffly.

Adam smothered a grin. "And I reckon that *proof* is exactly why I pay for your kerosene lanterns."

George shot him a dark look, but his lips twitched from behind the cropped beard and mustache. "I've been going through lots of oil lately, here, Adam. You keep anticipating me, and I might be buying more lanterns need to be filled."

Adam chuckled. He not only admired the doctor's skills, but he liked him as a man as well. And it was a testament to George's trust in him that he would make such a jest—him being a black man and Adam being a white one. Even free blacks generally showed extraordinary deference to whites, rarely letting down their guard, for there was always the chance that the wrong word to the wrong person could send them off for a whipping by one of the constables, to jail, or, worse, sold illegally into slavery.

"So, what sort of proof do you have? A blow to the back of the head maybe? Something that might have left blood on a hat like this?" Adam gestured with the bowler Miss Gates had found and showed the doctor the bloodstain.

"That, and more." George carefully lifted Tufts's head and shoulder, rolling the body onto its side. "As you seem to already know, here's where he was struck. Notice the shape and type of contusion—it looks like he used something rounded or blunt. Not very large, though. Even with the hat on, a sharp edge would have split the skin in a line. Here you can see it crushed it open more than sliced it."

Adam nodded. "Like the head of a walking stick."

"Coulda been."

"But that alone doesn't prove Piney Tufts was murdered," Adam mused. "You said there was more."

"Oh yes. Look at this." George let the body roll onto its back once again. "You've got the thick, rounded mark of the rope dug into his throat from where he hung. It goes around the neck at an angle, along under the chin and then up in the back, as one would expect from a hanging rope and the body's weight pulling down. It's cylindrical-shaped contusion. But do you see that dark mark on the side of the neck?"

"It's not angled. As if the rope went straight back instead of up, at least part of the way on the side of his neck." Adam looked at him. "As if the rope moved?" He didn't understand.

"That's what I wondered. So I took a closer look, and I found this." To Adam's horror, George used two large fingers from each hand to pull apart the skin at the incision that ran down the front of the throat. Adam automatically reached up to touch his own neck. He couldn't—nor did he care to try—identify any part of the red, pink, and white insides exposed by the doctor's hands.

"The larynx is crushed," said George. Though his stomach was turning a little at the grisly sight of mincemeat where the throat was, Adam watched as George used the tip of a pair of pincers—forceps, he thought they were called—to probe into the open skin.

"Wouldn't that happen from the rope?"

"No. The larynx might be bruised or even damaged, but not in this manner, and not in this location. The neck would break, the and windpipe squeezed off, but the larynx wouldn't be demolished like this, not here. It's as if a great weight pressed into it, or onto it. That's not from a hanging rope."

Adam raised his eyes to find George watching, as if waiting for him to catch up. It didn't take him long—he was so used to reading markings and interpreting them. "So you reckon he was killed first, then? With something . . ." His voice trailed off as he tried to picture how it had happened. "Something pressed across his windpipe."

"That's the only explanation I have for that sort of damage," George replied. "The shape of the breakage and the marks on the skin indicate something long and hard, pressed against his throat, like you said. Asphyxiated him. Tufts was dead before that noose went around his neck—do you notice how pale his face is? Not purple or red like it usually is when a man dies at the noose. Whoever did it killed him first, then strung him up to make it look like he hanged himself."

"Something across his throat." Adam tried to imagine it, how it would have to happen. It came to him. "Like a stick—a walking stick or a cane. The same thing they hit him with, maybe. Whoever it was pushed the stick against Tufts's throat—held him on the ground, or up against a wall—until he suffocated. The force was so hard it made a straight mark across his throat instead of a rounded one like a rope. But the position of the rope hid most of the evidence."

"Except for the smashed larynx," George said quietly.

There was no doubt that Pinebar Tufts hadn't crushed his own windpipe, then climbed up the derrick and thrown himself over with a noose around his neck. If the body had simply been taken away without such a close examination, no one would have been the wiser and Piney Tufts would have wrongly been accused of suicide.

"And so murder it is," Adam said, drawing in a deep breath. That meant he'd be continuing this investigation for certain. And Miss Gates would be more than gratified to know that her suspicions were correct.

"Now to determine who—and why." He looked at the doctor. "Can you narrow down the time of death any further?"

"After midnight, likely in the early hours of the morning. He was completely stiff when I first saw him—that was at half eight—so time of death would have been not long after midnight."

"Whoever wrote the note killed him. That's almost certain. Did you find anything on Tufts that might help identify the murderer? Hair? Threads?" Adam went on, musing more to himself than aloud, "Since Tufts was unconscious, whoever suffocated him probably did it when he was lying on the ground, instead of while he was standing, so we can't reckon how tall the killer was by the position of the stick across his throat. But he bumped his head on the beam above him on the crane, so he must have been at least tall enough to do that. Which would put him at . . . at least five feet and nine inches. And he had very light hair. Blond or white. Straight."

"I didn't find any hairs on the body that didn't match the color of Tufts's own hair," George replied. "But I didn't examine his clothing carefully."

Adam wandered over to the neat stack of clothes and shoes. A brief study of Tufts's boots told him that he hadn't made the footprints on the crane—his feet were smaller than the longer, narrow marks. Another confirmation of their conclusion.

One by one, he picked up each article of clothing and examined it with the same care and lantern illumination George used for the corpse.

The pockets of his coat were empty but for a few coins, a key, a handkerchief, and a small pocketknife—the sort of things most men carried. Adam also found a tattered receipt from the Willard, along with an order from a tailor. Nothing unusual—except the note that someone had pinned to his coat.

When he was finished, he refolded the clothing. The strong, distinct smell of blood and internal organs indicated that the doctor had continued his own work. Adam glanced at the corpse just long enough to see that flaps of skin had been pulled away, exposing the glistening, smelly insides of a man.

"What are you looking for in there?" he asked.

"Nothing in particular," said the doctor cheerfully. "But as much information as I can find. I may be able to tell you what he ate for his last meal, and possibly when. By examining the organs like the heart and liver and lungs, I may also be able to see if he had any medical conditions."

Adam nodded. Though it might not be important, he reckoned an investigator could never have too much information in the case of a crime. It was his task to pare through the details and determine what was helpful and what wasn't.

He should take his leave, but for some reason, Adam wasn't ready to go. Instead, he stood back, not exactly watching but not really ignoring him as George continued about his business. Adam didn't need to see the details as the doctor carefully removed the stomach and set it on a wooden countertop. All the while, the smell of death filled his nostrils and Adam mulled over what he knew about Pinebar Tufts and his murderer.

"He had to have planned it," Adam said after he'd let his thoughts stew for a while. He'd become mostly used to the raw, ironlike scent of the corpse. "The murderer. He brought the rope with him. And the note."

George looked up at him with hands still plunged inside the abdomen of the corpse. Adam tried to ignore the squishing sounds the doctor's fingers were making. He wondered if his friend ever got the smell and blood completely washed away.

"Not necessarily," said George. "He could have found the rope at the Capitol. It's a construction site. All sorts of tools and supplies lying around. And there's paper in offices too."

Adam scratched his bare chin. "On the grounds, yes, there are a lot of tools and supplies. I didn't see anything like that inside. I reckon if he found the rope on the grounds, he took them inside for that purpose, and then bashed Tufts on the head."

"Or he bashed him then decided he needed to finish the job and kill him. So he went back outside to get the rope."

Adam shook his head. "No, I don't think so. I think he planned it from the beginning. Tufts was hit from behind. That means the killer sneaked up on him with the intention of doing harm. Killing him or at least wounding him. It wasn't a fight gone bad."

"I'd agree with you there," George said, nodding. "No other

marks on the body that might have been from a fight. And it means the killer knew Tufts was going to be there. Either he followed him, or he somehow knew."

"Right. They could have had an appointment to meet there, or he knew for some other reason that Tufts was expected to be there. But inside the Capitol Building? After midnight? Why?" Adam shook his head and George grunted his implicit agreement that it was a strange prospect.

"I reckon if we find out what Tufts was doing inside the Capitol after midnight, we'll have a good idea why someone did this—and who it was."

"And how he got inside," George put in. "Isn't it guarded?"

Adam curled his lip. "The Auxiliary Guard is supposed to be responsible for patrolling to keep the government buildings safe at night, but since the war started, more than half of the Night Watch ran off to the South. Not that they did much good before. I've got to talk to Billy Morris—the one assigned to the Capitol—and find out whether he saw anyone. Either way, Tufts *and* the killer got inside. The killer sneaked up behind him and smashed him on the head. And there was a walking stick left behind in the corridor where Tufts's hat was found. It could have been his walking stick, or it could have been the murderer's.

"And think about this—if you're clear-headed enough to strangle a man and then go to such lengths to make it look like a suicide, you're not acting in a fit of rage or in a moment of high emotion," Adam went on, musing aloud. "You've planned it out for some reason. Otherwise, why not just hit him on the head a few more times and leave him there to be found? Why go through all the trouble to make it look like suicide anyway? Why not just kill him then leave?"

George lifted out a shiny, floppy organ Adam thought might have been the liver, but he averted his eyes before he could be certain. The smell of blood and raw flesh was thick in the close air. "You're making a good point. People—they kill in anger, and they're not thinking clearly. That's us'ally why they kill in the first place." He set the liver down carefully and picked up a scalpel. Adam looked away again before the blade sliced into the organ.

"Whoever did it meant for people to think Tufts had hanged himself—but why would he do that? In the middle of the Rotunda? Such a public place." Adam couldn't understand it.

"Sounds like a lynching."

The words hit Adam like a blow and it was a moment before he could speak. "A lynching. By God, that's what it was, wasn't it? A type of lynching."

Adam tasted bile at the back of his throat. He'd seen such things—the violent results when a man—most often a black man—was hanged from a tree as the pro-slavers in Kansas gathered around with their rifles and jeering voices and blazing torches.

Eerie and ugly and dark. Those were memories he didn't care to revisit.

"Seems to me if you hang a man in a public place like that—even if it's meant to look like he done it himself—you've got a reason. A real hatred for him." George's voice was steady and low, but Adam sensed the undercurrent of emotion there.

"And the note could have been meant to be written by Tufts, or it could have been a judgment on him by his killer. '*For my sins,*'" Adam said slowly.

Yes. Whoever hanged Pinebar Tufts had loathed the man, and, he thought, either wanted to make a point by making it appear as if the man had done it to himself, or was hanging him in judgment. Or hatred.

A lynching. A public statement of hatred and judgment.

Right in the center of the Capitol.

In the most important building in a country torn in half by war.

Adam felt the hair on the back of his neck prickle.

Yes, there had to be a message there. Some sort of ugly, dark message in the murder of Pinebar Tufts.

Constance didn't know what to do.

The doctor and Miss Monroe were long gone. Evening was approaching, and now there was only herself, her daddy, and Mrs. Billings—besides the servants, of course—left in the house, and *she didn't know what to do.*

Dr. Forthruth had tried to fix her daddy's leg, but to no avail.

Her father was still in incredible pain, and every time the doctor tried to pull it straight to set the bones, the limb refused to cooperate and it sprang back into the awkward, angled position with one knee curving toward the other. It made Constance queasy every time she looked at it.

At last the doctor had left in a swirl of frustration and defeat, but not before mentioning the dreaded word: *amputation*. Constance hoped her father hadn't heard him say that, for despite the chloroform the doctor had given him, poor Daddy had been in and out of consciousness during the ordeal of trying to straighten his leg. In fact, Constance had been the one to call off the physician after his fourth attempt; she couldn't bear it anymore.

But Dr. Forthruth's pronouncement sent shivers down her spine and made her skin clammy. Amputation.

"There's nothing more I can do but that," the physician said. "He'll not walk again without a crutch, because the break is so close to the hip and we'll have to take the whole leg. And even that's only if he survives the amputation. But something's got to be done soon, Miss Lemagne."

She didn't disagree. The shocking change in her father's face— not only the color of his complexion, going from a healthy pink to a pasty white to a dull gray, and now there was an ugly blueish tinge to the gray—but also the way his skin sagged in places, as if the skull and bones beneath it were shrinking from the pain, retreating from life. And the manner, in other places, in which the flesh tightened to a shiny, unhealthy pallor, molding so tightly at his cheekbones and eyes.

The smell of chloroform hung in the air, as well as heavy perspiration rolling off her father's inert body. His breathing was unsteady and rasped at times, while other times, it seemed to stop completely, bringing Constance to his side at a dash. Her maid, Jelly, had sponged him off as much as possible, but the barest touch near his torso or legs had him moaning and shuddering.

Constance was cold with fear.

Back in March, she'd worried that her father would be put in prison for the murder of Custer Billings—and if he did, what would happen to her, in this Southern town that was now becoming a Union stronghold, where she knew very few people—and even fewer with her political inclinations—in the middle of a war.

But if Daddy died, that would be far, far worse. How would she get back to Alabama? Would she even be able to go? Mrs. Billings was kind enough, but she was quite sickly and rarely rose from her bed. Constance didn't know anything about how her father accessed money here in Washington when everything they had was back in Alabama, let alone how to *get* back to Alabama. She didn't think one could take a carriage or a train when there was a war going on.

But she wasn't going to dwell on that right now. Daddy wasn't going to die. She just couldn't let that happen.

But how could she let them cut off his leg?

She paced the small dining room, grateful that the cook, who was also the housekeeper, had left her a supper, then gone back to her own little house for the night. The two black women who worked here—one was Lacey, the upstairs maid who saw to Mrs. Billings as her nurse, and the other was Louise, the cook and housekeeper—and the one black man, James, who acted as groom and a sort of butler now that Mr. Billings was dead—were all hired help. They weren't slaves—unlike her own dear Jelly, who was more of a mother to her than a maid since her mama had died when Constance was young.

It had come as a shock to Constance when she learned that the servants in the Billings house had some nights off and returned to their little houses in the back alley for the evening well before everyone went to bed. Back home, the slaves were up before she was, and there to make certain she had everything she needed as she went to bed. It was strange. The whole arrangement was different than what she was used to, but Mr. and Mrs. Billings had been abolitionists and they refused to have slaves.

Constance could hardly believe that her father—a staunch Southerner—was planning to marry a woman who thought all blacks should be freed. What on earth was he thinking?

From where she paced in the dining room, Constance could
see the little fenced-in yard behind the house—just like there was
behind every other house on Mrs. Billings's street. Beyond those
little courtyards were rows of shacks and lean-tos where the servants lived. The space between the house and the alleys was called
"the area" and that was how the servants and slaves traversed to
their place of work—from the back, through the rear entrance.

It reminded her of the alley where that Negro doctor had his
office. Dreary, crowded, dirty, ramshackle.

But George Hilton's office—if you could call it that—she remembered, had been neat and clean and surprisingly well-lit. She
still couldn't think of him as a doctor, although she'd seen plenty
of evidence that *he* thought himself one. And Mr. Quinn apparently did as well.

The thought crossed her mind—then was immediately dismissed, of course—that perhaps George Hilton could set her
daddy's leg. He looked strong enough. He was far more muscular
than Dr. Forthruth; she'd seen his bare arms once when his shirtsleeves were rolled up. That was why darkies were such good
workers. They were strong and could work long hours like horses
or mules.

She sighed and tried not to think about how ragged her daddy's
breathing sounded. And how weak it was. How he hadn't even
opened his eyes the last time she went to sit next to him and hold
his hand. Instead, she allowed herself to reflect on her surprise
visit from Miss Monroe. Or, Felicity, as she'd asked Constance to
call her.

That was the only—the *only*—good thing that had happened
today. And even the chance to get to know the sweet, beautiful,
and socially connected Felicity Monroe better didn't come close
to making up for the horror of what happened to her daddy.

And Felicity had been so kind and sympathetic, even going so
far as to asking Constance if she wanted her to stay and sit with
her all evening. "I can send word for Carson—Mr. Townsend—to
pick me up at eight o'clock," she said.

Constance found it quite adorable the way Felicity blushed
every time she stumbled over saying her fiancé's familiar name

and then corrected it to his formal title. It was as if she herself couldn't believe she was about to wed such a catch. "Oh no, thank you, Felicity, that's not necessary. But it's so kind of you to ask." She was hoping that Mr. Quinn might call later, and she confessed that to her new friend. "And then we might be able to . . . well, to talk privately for a while."

Felicity's dimples—they were just as adorable as the rest of her—danced as her eyes lit. "I understand completely, Constance." Then she frowned, a charming little line appearing between her delicate brows. (Was everything about the woman so simply perfect?) "Mr. Adam Quinn? Isn't that the man who helped find the killer at the President's House in April? He's like a detective—like a Pinkerton, but he's not a Pinkerton, is he?"

"Why, yes, that's who I mean." Constance didn't realize people knew about Mr. Quinn and his investigative abilities. "And no, he's not a Pinkerton. He works for Mr. Lincoln." She managed to say the name without too much of a sneer.

"Do you know him well? Mr. Quinn, I mean." Felicity appeared to want to say more, but then paused and looked down.

"What is it? Why do you ask about Mr. Quinn?" She had no need to worry that the other woman's interest might be romantic; clearly she was madly in love with her Mr. Townsend.

Her new friend shook her head, her head still bowed. "It's just . . . someone like him might be able to help me. I was going to see about hiring Mr. Pinkerton himself, but he's so busy, and he travels back and forth to Chicago so much. And . . ."

"Felicity, is something wrong?"

She nodded her head mutely, and when she at last looked up, her eyes glimmered with tears. "I just don't know what to do, Constance! I'm just so afraid that something will happen and—" Her voice broke and she dabbed at her eyes with the handkerchief.

"What is it?" Constance said again. "You can tell me. And I'd be happy to introduce you to Mr. Quinn. I'm certain he could help you—with whatever it is." She wasn't exactly certain, because she didn't quite know what was bothering her friend, but she did have confidence in Adam Quinn.

"It's just so horrible." Felicity's voice was so choked with tears that Constance could barely understand her.

And then, before she could press her further, a knock at the front door announced the arrival of none other than Mr. Carson Townsend, come to fetch his fiancée.

Felicity quickly dried her eyes and held her breath to help the flush fade from her cheeks. But there was nothing she could do about the pink tinge to her nose—again, charming and adorable— so when Mr. Townsend saw her, he immediately asked what was wrong.

"It's just so terrible for Miss Lemagne," Felicity said, tucking her hand through his arm. "Her father is in such pain, and there's not much that can be done for him."

Constance accepted Mr. Townsend's sympathies as well, along with his offer of assistance if there was anything she should need. The handsome young couple took their leave, with Felicity giving her friend a last pleading look over her shoulder as they went out the front door.

If nothing else, Constance thought, Felicity's problem would give her a chance to contact Mr. Quinn—if he didn't call on her himself.

A knock on the front door startled her from her reverie, and Constance drew up her sagging shawl. It wasn't chilly, but she was so very cold.

She opened the door to find Bettie Duval standing there, and although Constance had to submerge a twinge of disappointment that it wasn't Mr. Quinn, she was glad to see her. She smiled and invited her in. She'd met Bettie, who was about her age, several times at Mrs. Greenhow's house and they were becoming friends.

"Oh, Constance, I'm so terribly sorry to hear about your daddy. And Rose is too," said the pretty young woman, who was holding a small basket. "She sent me on over to bring you this bread and to give you her love. We both feel terrible. Is there anything I can do?"

"That is very kind of her," said Constance, taking the basket. "Let's sit in the kitchen, shall we?" She didn't want to take the chance any of their conversation might be overheard by Mrs.

Billings, whose bedroom was at the top of the stairs. "I was just about to make a cup of coffee. Would you like some?"

Bettie accepted her offer, and Constance—who'd only recently learned how to actually brew coffee, now that she was staying at Mrs. Billings's house and had to do for herself sometimes—turned up the flame on the stove. As she poured water from the pitcher Louise had left into the kettle, she said in a low voice, "I'm terribly disappointed I won't be able to attend Rose's meeting tonight."

"Of course she understands," Bettie said. She leaned forward, her eyes sparkling. "She's going to send me instead."

Constance suppressed a bump of disappointment, along with a trickle of relief, and replied, "Thank goodness. I was so terribly afraid Daddy's accident would ruin it all. But I simply can't leave him now, or anytime soon."

"Rose completely understands. After all, she is still mourning Gertie—she knows how difficult it is when someone is ill, or worse. She wanted you to know that she would have come here herself, Constance, but Senator Wilson had sent a message that he was coming to call."

Constance nodded and sat at the table. "Oh, that's splendid. I'm certain she'll be able to get any information she needs from him. He's completely besotted."

The two laughed softly, clasping hands on the table. "Unionist fool," said Bettie. "Speaking of Unionists . . . Rose was wondering if you had gleaned anything from that handsome Mr. Quinn."

Constance shook her head. "I hadn't seen the man for weeks until today—we were there at the Capitol when that man was found, *hanging* there. And then Daddy's accident . . . no, I've hardly had the chance to talk to him. But he doesn't talk much anyhow."

Bettie nodded. "I'll tell Rose you don't have anything to add." She squeezed Constance's hand. "I'm both terrified and *terribly* excited she's trusting me to do this! I do hope they'll let me cross over the river."

"Of course they will," Constance replied, once again quelling a pang of disappointment. She'd wanted to go, *wanted* to somehow do something exciting and dangerous to help her Southern boys—but of course she simply couldn't leave Daddy, even to deliver such important information. "You're young and pretty, and you look very innocent. All you have to do is bat your eyelashes and look confused and worried about getting to see your old granddaddy down in Alexandria, and those soldiers will let you pass right on by."

"I know. Rose and I have been talking about it all day. She wanted to wait until you could do it yourself, Constance, but the information has to get to General Beauregard right away."

"Shhhh," Constance hissed, rolling her eyes toward the ceiling. "Don't say the name."

"Right." Bettie winced. She dropped her voice to a bare whisper. "If there really is going to be a battle at Manassas, this could make a big difference."

Constance nodded, smiling. "If he gets the information in time, he'll be ready for those dratted Yankees. And then the war will be over." *And Daddy and I can go home.*

Then everything will be the way it was.

It was well into the afternoon before Billy Morris peeled open his bleary eyes and crawled out of bed. His head was pounding, as it often did when he woke to bright sunshine—or really, when he woke most every day—and he was already anticipating getting his hands on a big mug of frothy ale.

But first he would have something to eat, and maybe some coffee, because his belly was empty and gnawing and tasted a little sour. He and the rest of the Auxiliary Guard didn't have to report for the Night Watch until the bottom of the sun was at the top of the Treasury Building, so he had a few hours to see about getting some food and maybe even have time to play a little poker with some of the other men who were part of the Guard. He was particularly good at poker, because he knew how to bluff and how to lie and how to keep a blank face when necessary.

When Billy stepped out in to the bright, warm sunshine, he almost turned around to go back inside and catch a few more winks. But that gnawing in his belly was insistent, and he smelled sausage cooking in Mrs. Melody's kitchen. His dry mouth somehow managed to water at the delicious scent.

He considered the possibility of going around to the kitchen door and trying to sweet-talk her into a link, but Mrs. Melody was strict when it came to her boarders following the rules. And one of her rules was: no breakfast after eight o'clock.

Another of her rules was that her boarders needed to shave before sitting at her table—something he hadn't managed to do today either—and comb their hair and wash their hands. He supposed he could manage that last one, but Mrs. Melody was pretty damned frightening when people didn't obey her rules. Hell, she was pretty damned frightening all the time. There was no Mr. Melody that he'd ever heard of, and he suspected he knew why. The only reason Billy rented from the giant, red-headed harridan was because she did his laundry once a month and would sew on a button if he needed it (for an extra fee, of course).

Still, since it was nearly three in the afternoon, Billy wondered if he might be able to convince her that he *was* following the rule, because it *was* before eight o'clock . . . in the evening . . . but he didn't think she'd find that amusing. She'd probably go after him with a frying pan, like she did to Jim Westley the time he asked her for a piece of bread and cheese to take with him on his walk to work—at quarter past eight one morning.

Billy was just about to walk on by when Mrs. Melody herself came rushing out of the front door he'd just exited. Her fiery red hair was bundled into a tight bun at the back of her head, and her dark brown eyes snapped with excitement. Her tall, large-boned body was dressed in a dark blue dress with a pinstripe apron over it. The apron was covered with flour all down the front. She had the largest feet he'd ever seen on a woman, and therefore he could hear her whenever she moved about the house.

"Mr. Morris! I was hoping to see you this morn—erm—today," she said, wiping her floury hands on a towel. "Why don't you-all come into the kitchen and set yourself down and have a piece of breakfast? I've got some sausage cooking, and I can fry up an egg with some toast. And how about a big cup of coffee?"

Billy blinked and resisted the urge to rub his eyes. Was he still sleeping? Was this a dream?

Was she actually smiling at him?

"Well, all right then," he said warily, following her back into the house. "That sausage smells good," he ventured as she squeezed through the doorway into the kitchen.

She was all business as she plunked a metal platter down in front of him with a glistening piece of sausage and a lightly browned piece of toast. He nearly fell off his chair when she stuck a small ceramic pot of apple butter—something she'd never offered anyone in the four years he'd lived there—on the table in front of him, then turned to the stove to fry him that egg.

"Ma'am, could I please have some of that coffee?" he asked, then hunched his shoulders nervously as she spun around.

"Oh, lands, of course! Silly me, to forget all about that. A man's gotta have something to wash it all down with, now, doesn't he?" She poured the drink into a speckled blue metal mug and set it next to his plate.

"Thank you, ma'am," Billy said, still unable to believe his good fortune. The sausage tasted like heaven, and he nearly moaned as he bit into it and the juices exploded in his mouth. The toast was crunchy and warm, and the apple butter a delicious addition. He was just gathering up his nerve to ask for another piece of toast when Mrs. Melody slid two fried eggs and that second piece of toast onto his plate.

And then she sat down across from him with such a great thunk that the table moved half an inch toward him. For some reason, the expression in her dark eyes made Billy's hair stand on end and the rest of him want to make a quick escape.

"Now, Mr. Morris," she said in a brook-no-nonsense tone, "Tell me everything you know about it."

He looked at her blankly, and her eyes widened, then narrowed. "You ain't heard yet about what-all happened up to the Capitol this morning?"

He swallowed the last bite of sausage and shook his head. "No, ma'am."

"But you were there last night, then, weren't you?" she said, leaning closer across the table. "Patrolling the grounds. So surely you seen something."

"Yes, ma'am. I mean, no, ma'am. I mean . . . yes, I was there all night"—it wasn't a lie, because even when he was sleeping under the portico roof, he was still *there*—"but no, ma'am, I don't know if I saw anything because I don't know what you're talking about happening up there." In self-defense—for surely she was about to swipe that plate away from him at any moment—he forked up one of the eggs and stuffed it plus an entire piece of toast in his mouth.

Mrs. Melody's expression flickered with irritation, but she smoothed it out immediately and said, "There's a man was found hanging by his *neck* up inside that big room under the Dome this morning."

Billy just managed not to choke on the ungainly mouthful he was chewing. His eyes bulged as much as his cheeks did, and his mind began to race. What did this mean? Why was she telling him this?

"At first they said he done it to himself, but now they're saying someone else hung him up there to die," Mrs. Melody went on. "That means *murder*."

The large swallow of food nearly stuck in his throat, but he gulped a big draught of coffee to help it go down. "Murder?" he managed to say.

"That's right. If they're right about it anyway," she said. "I don't know how they can tell if a man killed himself or if someone else strung him up—there was even a note on himself, pinned to his coat!—telling why he did it—but if someone *did* kill him, then there's a murderer loose around the Capitol. And I'm thinking to myself this morning, 'Why, Janie, you know someone who might just have seen that murderer last night,'—that being you, Mr. Morris, and the fact that you're responsible for patrolling around the Capitol Building and all every night, I just knew I had to talk to you about it."

Billy nodded, and all at once his comfortably full belly felt queasy and unsteady.

"Now, Mr. Morris, tell me what you saw." That avidity in her eyes dared him to disobey, and her large, strong hands rested on the table as if ready to reach out and grab him by the coat if he didn't answer the way she expected.

His thoughts wheeled in all directions and Billy tried to corral them so he could say something she'd want to hear. But the truth was, he didn't remember much of last night. He'd drunk a whole bottle of whiskey—it was Independence Day, after all—and he only vaguely remembered making his rounds about the building once or twice.

Then he realized how he could salvage his breakfast and his relationship with Mrs. Melody. He manufactured a great sigh. "Ma'am, can I be frank with you?"

Her eyes widened with surprise and she leaned even closer. "Yes. Yes, of course you can, Mr. Morris."

He hemmed and hawed for a long moment, drawing out the suspense and making it seem like he wasn't sure he could trust her. It was like when he held a full house in poker and he was pretending to be nervous over his bet. "I ain't supposed to say nothing to you or nobody because it's a big investigation. I could lose my job if they found out."

"That's why you didn't let on you knew about it!"

"That's right," Billy replied immediately. He took another gulp of coffee while he pretended to consider her.

"I won't tell a soul," Mrs. Melody said with nearly believable sincerity. "I swear it, on Mr. Melody's grave."

"Well," he said, leaning toward her and still pretending to be reluctant. "There was a man. I saw him, and he was sneaking around the building. I thought he looked suspicious at the time."

She leapt on it. "You did? Where was he? What did he look like?"

"He—now, Mrs. Melody, I'm not supposed to be saying all this.

Are you sure I can trust you?" He lifted the coffee mug again to hide his smile as she stammered out her assurances. "All right, then. The truth is, I been wantin' to tell someone about it . . . and seeing as I can trust you . . ."

"You can. You truly can."

"All right, then. Well, he wasn't too tall, and he wasn't too short. And he wore a hat—a top hat it was," he said, still making things up. "And a long, flowing cloak."

"Was he carrying anything with him? The rope he used to hang him up with?"

"Mrs. Melody, how could you know about that?" He acted impressed. "That's exactly what I saw—the man was carrying a bundle of rope over his shoulder, tucked under his arm. The moonlight shone over him, and I started to follow him when he went into— well, now I really can't say anything more. Right now I mean," he added hastily when she drew herself up. "But," he continued as a brilliant idea struck him, "I wager I'll be able to talk some more about it—to someone I can trust, I mean, like you—tomorrow. After my shift tonight, of course." Then he realized the last thing he wanted was to be met at the front door by his landlady when he came stumbling home at dawn. "When I wake up, after my shift tomorrow, I mean."

"Lands," Mrs. Melody said, appeased. "Imagine that! My own boarder being the one to see the murderer—and being involved in the investigation too! Why, that old crone Mrs. Craskey is going to be swamp-green with jealousy when I—when she hears." She smiled innocently at Billy.

He decided now was the best time to make his escape, and rose. "The truth is, Mrs. Melody, I've got to be on my way now. I've got people to talk to—"

"Like those Pinkertons?"

"That's right. They're waiting for me. I'm going to see if I can find out what they know about the situation." He slapped his bowler hat onto his head. "After all, it can't be just me telling them what-all I know—it's only fair they give me information too."

"That's only fair," she agreed, standing to tower over him. "After all, if there's a murderer lurking around the Capitol Building, you need to know all there is to know in case you might run into him. He might even come back tonight, you know." Her eyes gleamed with delight.

"Right," Billy said, and thought about the fact that he would be by himself, patrolling around the Capitol all night tonight. Where a murderer might be lurking.

All at once, his breakfast didn't feel quite so satisfying.

CHAPTER 6

After Bettie left, Constance felt even more alone. She'd wanted to be Rose Greenhow's messenger—it had given her something to *do* while trapped in this horrible city where most of the interesting people had left, and chickens and goats wandered the streets. And the mud caked her shoes and hems and splattered up every time a wagon or carriage went by.

She *loathed* Washington.

And there were soldiers *everywhere*. Yankee soldiers, who foolishly talked about how easy it would be to put down the rebellion. Constance knew better: the men and women of the South wouldn't lay down easily. No, indeed. They had grit and determination, and the Yankees were in for an unpleasant surprise if they thought they'd whip the Confederates so easily. Their entire way of life was at stake, and if the states wanted to leave the Union, she didn't understand why it was worth going to war over. Just let them *leave!*

Thus, meeting Rose Greenhow had been a turning point in Constance's life, and had made the necessity of staying here almost pleasant—and it had given her purpose.

She was looking forward to the triumphant return of President Jefferson Davis and his lovely wife, Varina, when they took over the President's House.

But now . . . *Daddy.* Tears welled in her eyes and she blinked them back. Sitting in the chair next to his bed, she looked down at him and felt such a range of emotions—fear, affection, worry—and, suddenly, *resolve.*

Something had to be done. She was a woman of the South. Though she dressed in frills and carried on superficial, giddy conversations, and allowed men to assist her (so they felt capable), she was far stronger and more intrepid than she let on. Mrs. Greenhow and even Sophie Gates had taught her that a woman could be feminine and charming, but also have steely conviction to make things happen.

Someone had to help her daddy. Someone had to set that bone.

Constance stood, all at once resolved and hopeful.

She was going to send for that George Hilton. Surely he had enough brute strength to do it, and she could tell him where the bone was broken and how to pull it into place. It just needed more strength than the portly Dr. Forthruth could muster.

Almost giddy with relief, she rang the bell for the servants, then paced rapidly from the kitchen to the front door and back while she waited. Her skirts swirled and her shoes clicked as she imagined what George Hilton would say when he was summoned to her house. She'd pay him of course—which was probably more than he ever got from the other patients he treated.

And then Constance stopped abruptly. Would he even come?

That man was uppity enough to ignore such a message, wasn't he?

She gritted her teeth. It would be mortifying if she sent for him and he didn't come, the dratted man.

And *where* were the servants? She reached for the bell again just as Jelly appeared at the top of the stairs. She'd been in Constance's bedroom, doing her mending.

"Yes, Miss Constance?"

"I need James," she said. "I can't imagine why he hasn't responded yet. It's only eight o'clock."

"He went on home, Miss Constance."

Constance ground her teeth. Drat. She'd forgotten about that. "Well, I need him to go somewhere to get help for Daddy. To that doctor—that Negro doctor, the one who was looking at your foot?—we went to before. Go and fetch James for me, and I'll send—I'll ask him if he'll go."

Jelly lumbered down the stairs. "I'll go'n ask him, Miss Constance."

It took more than ten minutes before Jelly returned—without James.

"He not there in his house. Nor Louise nor Lacey neither. Ain't no one there."

No, Constance shrieked inside her head. She wasn't going to be thwarted. She knew if something wasn't done soon for her daddy, he was going to die. And she was *determined*.

She slammed her hands on the kitchen table, making hers and Bettie's coffee cups jump. "Fetch your cloak. I'm going and you're going with me."

"Oh, Miss Constance . . ." Jelly began, then snapped her mouth shut when her mistress gave her a look. Nonetheless, Constance heard her grumbling and sniping under her breath as she went off to do as told.

But Constance was stubborn. She'd be perfectly safe. It wouldn't be dark for another two hours. Plenty of time to get to Ballard's Alley and back, especially if they hired a hack. And then she could *make* George Hilton come with her. If Midnight hadn't been injured, Constance could have driven her with the landau, but then she would have had to leave her tied up when they ventured down Ballard's Alley—for the carriage wouldn't fit and it was too dangerous to try and drive a horse through the narrow ways.

Fortunately, earlier Constance had changed into a simple around-the-house-dress that only had one crinoline and no hoops, which would make their journey easier. She found her daddy's Colt revolver and loaded its six chambers, then carefully tucked it into the deep pocket of her dark cloak. She wasn't a fool. Not only was Ballard's Alley not the safest place, but all those wild soldiers could be unpredictable.

Regardless, neither were a match for a determined Alabama woman. She tucked her hair into a simple bonnet and pulled on her gloves.

"Miss Constance," Jelly said one more time in a pleading voice, but Constance just marched out the door.

She knew the older woman would follow her, and she did.

It was simple to find a hackney on Seventh Street, and moments later she and her maid were being helped into the carriage by the driver. It was none too clean, but beggars couldn't be choosers—though Jelly lifted her nose and sniffed with disdain when she was required to whisk Constance's skirts off the floor and tuck them into the seat.

"Ain't gon' make any difference anyways," Jelly mumbled. "Streets so filthy here in this town. Miss Constance, are we really goin' to that alley again?"

"Mr. Hurst needs help, Jelly, and I *have* to do this or he's going to *die*." Her voice broke a little, and her maid reached over and patted her hand.

"It gon' be all right, little lady," she said as Constance fought back tears in the dim interior of the carriage. "That Dr. Hilton, he a good man. If we git there safe—and praise be to God if'n we do—then he'll fix Mr. Hurst up right."

All the way to the First Ward, Constance prayed that Jelly was right. If she found it astonishing that she was putting all of her hopes in a Negro doctor, she didn't examine that fact too much. Instead, she focused on asking the Almighty to look down favorably on her and her family and this mission.

"Are you sure you wanna get out here, miss?" asked the hackney driver when she and Jelly climbed out of the carriage. He was a black man and scratched his forehead beneath the lip of his cap, but he was looking at Jelly and not Constance when he spoke. He had a large wad of tobacco in his mouth.

The narrow, refuse-strewn alley angled off into a cluster of shacks and lean-tos. A single scrawny dog prowled around a pile of waste. In the distance, a baby screamed bloody murder and someone shouted from a different direction.

"Yes," she replied briskly, and carefully counted out the money for him. The sun was still above the horizon, but it had fallen quite a bit during their ride—faster than she'd anticipated. For the first time, Constance wondered what she would do if George Hilton wasn't at his office.

"If you wait here for us for fifteen minutes, I'll pay you double to take us back," she said.

"Yes, miss. But it goin' on nine o'clock, miss, and I done got the curfew at ten."

"We'll be back in fifteen minutes," she said firmly, even as Jelly muttered under her breath.

"Yes, miss. I'll wait right here for you."

As they started into the alley, Constance realized she hadn't thought to bring a lantern. She hadn't expected it would be this dark, but with the close buildings crammed in behind the stately homes of the more wealthy white people, there was hardly any way for the lowering sun's light to filter into the area.

But Jelly had thought ahead, and she produced a lantern from beneath her cloak. "You gonna light this up for us, man?"

The driver, who had a lantern hanging from his carriage, complied and moments later, Jelly and Constance started into Ballard's Alley.

"This ain't gon' end well, Miss Constance," grumbled her maid. "It's jus' askin' for troubles."

Constance started to reply, but at the last minute was required to dodge a very large, shiny, pungent pile of something she didn't care to identify. After that, she paid attention to where her feet were going instead of what her maid was going on about.

"It's not much farther," she said as they turned onto an off-shoot of the main alley. She remembered it from her last visit, for there had been a group of women sitting right on that old up-ended cart there, doing laundry. This evening, there were people—black and white, but all dressed in worn clothing—going about their business—cooking mostly, or taking down laundry and emptying washbasins—and they gave her and Jelly curious looks. But no one spoke to or stopped them, and for that she was grateful—although she kept her hand around the butt of the revolver in her cloak pocket. She noticed that, along with the lantern, Jelly had produced a large wooden stick the size of a baseball bat.

"There it is," she said when the gleam of a whitewashed building became discernible in the lowering shadows.

My goodness, it was getting dark quickly now. Thank Providence they'd made it to Hilton's place without incident.

Constance walked more rapidly, and Jelly puffed along behind her, still grumbling—or maybe she was praying—with the lantern swaying in her grip and the club mingling with her skirts. Her heart sank when she saw that the building seemed dark, but then remembered to walk around to the side door and the half-buried windows. A dim light shone through them, but she would have to crouch—a difficult prospect in her corset—to see into them. One of the windows was propped open with a stick, and from inside she heard a loud crash, followed by a tumbling, falling noise.

Frowning, Constance turned and hurried down the four steps to the door that led into the cellar. She was startled to find it ajar.

More alarming noises were coming from inside. It sounded like some sort of altercation. Instinct told her to pull out the Colt, and Constance gripped its thick handle in her hands. She stepped through the door, Jelly hot on her heels with the lantern.

She took in the scene in an instant: three white men were grappling with George Hilton, who was sagging between them as they took turns pummeling him. There was blood everywhere.

"What is going on here?" she demanded in the imperious voice she used when the slaves needed to be reprimanded. She aimed the revolver in the general vicinity of the combative men and was gratified (and slightly terrified) when they all turned to look at her.

"Leave that man alone," she ordered as Jelly moved in close behind her. She had no idea why those men were beating on George Hilton, but she *did* know that she needed him to help her daddy, and he wouldn't be able to do that if he was beaten to an insensate pulp. "Step away or I'll shoot you. And my daddy taught me not to miss," she added.

"This nigger," panted one of the men in a thick German accent, "he's been cutting up *white men*. Probably been *eating* them."

"Nonsense," Constance snapped. She gripped the Colt tighter, hoping her trembling wasn't visible to the men. She hadn't lied—

she knew how to shoot, and well, but there were three of them and only six shots. "He does work for Mr. Lincoln."

"Mr. Lincoln?" sneered the tallest of the three intruders. "A nigger working for the president, cutting up white men? Who are you? His pretty white nigger-loving bitch? Maybe you could find a better man than this ape to do your—"

Constance's vision went red and her finger curled on the trigger before she could stop it. The revolver's ball blasted into the room in a puff of dust. The sneering man dropped to the ground with a cry, holding his leg at the knee, and the other two men stumbled away from him.

One of them called her a filthy word and lunged toward her. Jelly bellowed a terrible, blood-curdling yell Constance had never heard as she launched herself between the attacker and her charge, swinging her club. The awful sound of wood cracking against bone reverberated in the small room, but Constance hardly heard it as she pulled the trigger again.

Boom! Another explosion of powder, and now her wrists were hurting from the double kicks of the firearm, and from a death grip on a handle that was too big and heavy for her hands.

All at once, there was silence. Her breath heaving, Constance looked around to see one man on the floor, gripping his leg as blood streamed from it. Another man was cursing, curling his arm against his body where, she thought, Jelly had hit him and— from the looks of it—broken his forearm. And the third man was edging toward the door, as if trying to escape.

Constance whirled on him, her emotions high with fear and anger and determination. She'd never felt so unsettled, so terrified, so furious and vengeful—yet so in *control.*

"I'll have you thrown in jail if y'all ever come back here again," she cried, unabashedly exaggerating her influence. She could tell from the looks of this man that he was a poor and mean immigrant, and would believe this threat. At least, she hoped he would. "Get your friends and get out of he-ah." Her accent had gone thick and Southern. "And don't y'all come crawlin' back t'ask the doctor he-ah to fix you up after what y'all did to him. You find someone else to do it."

She trained the Colt on the trio of attackers as they helped each other out of the cellar, not even attempting to suppress groans of pain. "Cowards, all of y'all," she panted after them.

It was only then that she turned her attention to George Hilton, who was standing of his own volition—albeit unsteadily. Jelly was fussing over him like a mother, cleaning off the blood from his nose and cuts on his face with a rag dipped in water. One of his eyes was going to be swollen shut by tomorrow. He was breathing heavily and holding an arm at his ribs—drat, she hoped he wasn't too injured to fix Daddy after all she'd gone through to get to him—and he was looking at her with baleful dark eyes.

"I cannot even imagine what brought you here, Miss Lemagne," he said in a stiff, careful voice. "What a foolish, *damned* foolish thing to do."

Her breathing was finally settling, and the red haze that had colored her vision eased. Her fingers loosened and the revolver threatened to slip from her grip. "I need you to see to my daddy." Her voice broke.

He lifted an eyebrow, then winced as if suppressing a gasp or even a hard bark of laughter. "I see." But he didn't seem to see; he seemed utterly confused and bothered.

"I need you to come with me. Are you—are you injured?"

George looked down at himself as if to check to see whether he was, then looked back up at her with an arrogant expression that, if he'd been her slave, would have prompted her to give him a good tongue-lashing. "Not much—just a fractured rib, I think, and maybe a sprained ankle. A loose tooth here in the side of my jaw, and—"

"Are you going to come with me or not?" she demanded. She was almost ready to cry, now that the danger and anger were over, and she was only contending with an uppity black man who was her last hope to save her father's life. Constance's knees were shaking and her vision was watering up with angry, frustrated tears. She shoved the revolver into her pocket lest she drop it from nerveless fingers.

"Jes' hush a minute there, Miss Constance," Jelly said in an uncharacteristically snappish voice. "This man is hurt and he ain't gon' be no good to you if'n he faints dead away."

"I'm not going to faint," replied George flatly. But his voice was more thready than usual, and Constance's concern grew.

"Fine. Fix him up then, Jelly. I'll wait over here." Constance stalked to the blanket that sagged from where it had been hung to separate the two areas. It appeared to have been halfway torn from its moorings.

"Don't go back—"

But it was too late, of course. And it wasn't as if Constance hadn't seen the results of George's work in the past—so she wasn't completely horrified by the sight of the body on the table. Fortunately, Mr. Tufts—she did recognize him because his face was the only place she dared look—was mostly covered up from his chest on down. Still, the sheet revealed some red cuts that had obviously been made by the so-called doctor and she had to swallow hard when the smell of dead flesh and organs fully assaulted her.

Or maybe she just hadn't noticed the stench in all the excitement earlier.

By now, her knees were shaking ominously and Constance barely made it to a chair in time before they gave out. She tried to take deep breaths—already restricted by her corset—but every time she did, she inhaled the horrible smell and felt sick again. She needed air.

She flung the blanket aside and stumbled across the room to the outside entrance. Before she went through the door, she caught a glimpse of Jelly helping the doctor—who'd removed his shirt—to wrap his torso in a tight bandage and then, finally, blessedly, she was outside, gulping in fresh, summer night air. She managed to keep the contents of her stomach inside, but then the tears came.

She fought them back when she heard voices from inside coming closer, but the moment of indulgence had helped. She waited for Jelly and the doctor to come out of his office. At least, she hoped he was going to come. He hadn't looked all that healthy. Nor all that willing.

But when the door opened and her maid stepped out, she was followed by George Hilton. He was carrying a large black bag and though he moved slowly, he was moving.

And he was coming to help her daddy. Constance nearly wept again with relief and hoped, once more, that all of this had not been in vain.

George was not at all happy about the turn of events. Here it was, after nine o'clock—only an hour until curfew, which, though he'd broken it many times in the past still was a risk—and he was sitting in a hackney with a beautiful, stubborn, arrogant white woman and her *slave* maid. His head throbbed from the beating he'd taken, and his ribs ached like a son of a bitch, and he wasn't going to be able to open his left eye come morning.

He knew it could have been worse, much worse, and so he leaned back in the carriage and closed his eyes in an attempt to stave off the pounding in his head.

What in the hell was she thinking, coming to his office?

George stifled a moan. Considering the entirety of the situation, it would be a miracle if he woke up tomorrow still a free man without any more bruises or aches. And another miracle still if his office was still intact and his work untouched.

After a ride that was both interminably long and far too brief, the hackney carriage pulled up in front of a pleasant-looking house at G Street, near Twelfth. George managed not to groan as he bestirred his aching body to climb down first, then to offer a hand to each of the women in turn. Miss Lemagne was wearing gloves, of course, and once on the ground, she moved briskly past him toward the house without saying a word.

He and the maid walked more slowly, which gave him the opportunity to ask, "How is that aching middle toe of yours, Miss Jelly?" He'd been too stunned and confused to mention it when she was tending to him back at the office.

"Why, it's still givin' me a world of pain, Dr. Hilton. Isn't there anything you can do about it?"

"I'm fixing to have a new remedy that might work. You'll have to come visit me at my office"—if he still had an office—"next week, then, all right? Tuesday?" When there was a new moon and it was as dark as it got in the summer.

"I'll do that, Dr. Hilton," she said, opening the door to the house. "I'll shore do that."

Miss Lemagne was already inside waiting for them, and to George's surprise, she was holding one of the largest slabs of meat he'd ever seen. "You'd best put this on that eye, uh," she said, clearly not sure how to address him and obviously unwilling to use his title. "Or y'all won't be able to see what you're doing. Daddy's this way. Dr. Forthruth"—no hesitation on the title that time—"says his thigh bone's broken, but he wasn't able to pull it back, to put it into place so the bones could heal. He said he's going to have to amputate or Daddy's going to die."

The cold meat felt like Heaven on his angry, hot, swelling eye. "Thank you," he said.

"Would you—would you like some coffee? Or some whiskey?" Miss Lemagne asked, surprising him again.

"No, thank you, miss," he replied. "I'd like to see your daddy. That's why you brought me here, isn't it?"

"Yes." She spun abruptly in a rustle of skirts and he followed her into a small parlor. "Jelly, bring some more lamps so—uh—so he can see what he's doing."

Hurst Lemagne lay on a narrow bed in the parlor. He was dressed only in a nightshirt and stockings. His pallor was sickly, and when George touched his forehead, he felt the burn of fever and the clamminess of pain. He had to relinquish the comfort of the slab of meat in order to do a thorough examination, and he gave it to Jelly after she'd brought in a sufficient number of lamps.

Even with them, the parlor wasn't as well-illuminated as his morgue, but he could see well enough to note that Hurst Lemagne was dehydrated, in extreme pain, and his life was fading. Dr. Forthruth's assessment in that, at least, was correct.

He pulled back the blankets to reveal two pale legs, uncovered from above the knee to the top of the stockings. The left femur was adducted and the entire leg appeared to be shortened, with the knee rotated and turned into the other thigh. George frowned as he dunked his meat-scented hands into a basin, then wiped them on a towel Miss Lemagne had provided. Something wasn't right.

"What is it?" she demanded breathlessly.

He merely shook his head as he carefully palpated along the upper part of the femur, feeling for the fracture that Dr. Forthruth had diagnosed and had been unable to set. When he reached the top near the hip joint, he felt an unfamiliar sensation of looseness that didn't match what he'd anticipated, what he expected, for a fracture. And when he attempted to adjust the leg, just the slightest bit in that vicinity, Hurst Lemagne shrieked and his eyes flew open.

To George's surprise, Miss Lemagne didn't fly into a rage or shout at him to stop. She was watching him through eyes glistening with tears and her hands clasped into tight fists, pressing into her mouth. Her breathing was rough and loud, competing with that of her father's for volume in the small room.

Taking her silence as implicit permission to continue, George finished his examination and confirmed his suspicions. The femur wasn't fractured at all, and all of the attempts to set the bone had been unnecessary and incomprehensibly painful, possibly even doing more damage. No, the femur wasn't broken, but it had become dislocated from the hip. And if it wasn't moved back into place very soon, the hip would die. It was a good thing Miss Lemagne had come for him tonight. If she'd waited until tomorrow for Dr. Forthruth—who might have eventually made the correct diagnosis—it would have been too late.

"Is there someone else here who can help? Someone strong?" he asked. The pelvis would need to be held completely immobile while George attempted to fit the femur back into the hip socket. At least one man, maybe two, would need all of their weight and strength to hold Lemagne's hips down.

"Jelly, go see if James is returned," Miss Lemagne said, then said to him, "There's no one else besides me."

George shook his head. "You're nowhere near strong enough,

miss." He wasn't confident a single man would be able to do the job, either.

"Can you fix it? Can you set his bone? Will he be able to walk again?"

George shrugged, unwilling to say much else unless he was successful. It was a leap of something—he didn't think it was faith so much as desperation—that had caused Constance Lemagne to ask a black doctor for help, and her lack of trust was already so apparent that he knew he must tread carefully.

"I need bindings. Rope or strips of cloth to tie him to the bed."

Miss Lemagne gasped and her eyes widened with horror, but instead of arguing, she left the room, presumably in search of the items. While she was gone, George checked the right hip and femur, and confirmed that everything was still in position there. The familiar movement of the joint working properly on the right side was an even stronger confirmation of his diagnosis, but he took the time to palpate the left hip area once again. Yes, the femur was definitely dislocated—there was swelling behind the pelvis much further back than the hip. And all of the nerves, muscles and tendons, and blood vessels were dangerously compressed.

Miss Lemagne rushed back in with a bundle of rope and an armful of cloth. "Will this do?"

George took the rope, and was reminded briefly of Mr. Tufts, lying on the table in his morgue, and how this time last night he'd still been alive. And how later someone had used a coil of rope just like this one to make it look like he took his own life. And now George was about to use a stretch of rope to save one—at least figuratively speaking.

He hoped.

Miss Lemagne was surprisingly helpful and calm as she stood on the right side of her father and helped George to wrap the binding across the hips and under the bed, then around and around. He tied it as tight as he could, despite Hurst Lemagne's weak protests.

"Daddy, be still. This—this man is going to help you. Oh, if only we had some more chloroform for him."

When George produced a small bottle of the pungent medicine, drawing it from his medical kit, she seemed surprised and relieved. He pressed some over Hurst Lemagne's nostrils and mouth and watched as the man eased into unconsciousness. He didn't know how long it would last, considering what was coming, but it would help.

George was really feeling the lack of cold meat on his painful, swelling eye by now, and he was just about to ask if he could have it back when a door at the rear of the house opened and closed. Heavy, rushed footsteps told him that Jelly had returned—presumably with James.

The newcomer wasn't as tall or muscular as George, but he would be some assistance. He gave the trussed-up Hurst Lemagne a long look, then turned a grave expression toward George. "I'm here to help, sir. Doctor."

"All right. Stand on his left side, right there by the hip. You'll have to lay your whole weight across him, James, because the pelvis *has* to stay as still as possible." George hesitated, then climbed onto the bed, facing the head, and stood over the patient. Ignoring the shocked gasp from Miss Lemagne, he lifted her father's right calf, lifting it so the knee bent at a ninety-degree angle. The patient stirred and moaned, but his eyes didn't open. "Are you ready? Don't let him move."

Aware that Miss Lemagne and Jelly were watching with wide, horrified eyes, George forced himself to concentrate on the task at hand.

Still standing over the injured man, he carefully, firmly, lifted the foot and calf—keeping it at a ninety-degree angle—and began to try and slide the femur back down into position. He lifted, twisted, manipulated, feeling his way—because that was the only way to do it—trying to work the ball of the femur down into the hip socket. The deadweight leg was heavy and it was difficult to lift and lower—lift and twist and sidle and lower—the largest bone in the body back into a place it wasn't certain it wanted to go.

Lemagne struggled, crying out, trying to tear free of his bonds, but James—God bless him—held him and his arms down as George sweated and worked, fighting the agony in his own battered body. His vision flashed light, then dark, for it was impossible, strenuous work. He lifted, lowered, then lifted, twisted, lowered some more, pulled, pushed, twisted, trying to feel his way into the slot—all the while blocking out the cries of his patient and the horrified, muffled shrieks from Miss Lemagne and trying to keep himself from fainting on top of his patient.

"Stop, stop, *stop!*" Miss Lemagne screamed at last. "Stop it, I said, *stop it!* I knew I shouldn't have called for you!" She was beating on him, her small fists raining down on his legs and torso as he strained, ignoring her, focused on the movement of the leg because he was almost there . . . *it was almost . . .*

There.

George heaved a sigh of relief as he felt the top of the femur slip down into place with a satisfying sort of *thunk.* The room was spinning when he dropped Hurst Lemagne's leg, and all at once, there was silence except for Constance Lemagne's furious sobs.

"Get out! Get out of here!" she cried, tears streaming down her face as she continued to flail at him. "You—you—horrible, awful ni—"

"*Miss Constance!*" Jelly took her mistress by the arm, pulling her away just as she landed a solid fist on George's broken rib. "Look! Look at your daddy, Miss Constance. He did it."

George barely held back his own cry of pain from the blow and stepped back to get away from her, away from the situation. He wanted to leave, to curl up somewhere and nurse his own hurts.

The room was silent now, except for Miss Lemagne's heaving breaths and her father's much more regular ones.

"His leg," she said. "You fixed it. It looks—it looks *right.*"

Jelly and James were unraveling the rope around Lemagne's body, and the patient hardly moved. Now that the leg was back into position, the nerves and vessels weren't compressed and although he'd be sore, he wasn't in pain.

"It wasn't fractured," George said, really wishing for the cold meat slab. The exertion had caused his own blood vessels to swell and heat and throb, making him even more fully aware that he'd nearly been beaten to death.

He would have been if this little missy hadn't come demanding his help, and for that he had to be grateful.

But he didn't have to like it.

"But Dr. Forthruth said it was," she argued, taking up her father's hand in hers. "He already looks better," she murmured. "His color is coming back already. And his breathing . . ."

"It wasn't fractured," George said again, as calmly as he could muster. "The doctor was wrong. The left hip was dislocated from the femur. Now that it's back into place, he should have much less—if any—pain."

She was watching him with round blue eyes. The skepticism was fading. "It wasn't broken after all?"

"No, miss."

"Will he . . . will he walk again?"

"There's no reason he shouldn't regain full use of his leg," George said, now more confident giving his prognosis. "If you'd waited until tomorrow—or even much later tonight—that might not have been the case. The blood vessels and nerves that run through the pelvis to the leg were being compressed, and if we hadn't fixed it and relieved that pressure, they would have died. And then his leg would have been useless for certain. And half of his body as well. At least."

Miss Lemagne was staring at him silently. "Jelly, James. Go and get . . . Dr. Hilton . . . some coffee and another slab of meat. And something to eat. And pour a good shot of whiskey in that coffee, do you hear me?"

By the time Billy Morris played a few hands of poker and got several ales into his belly, he was feeling pretty damned pleased with how things were working out.

Not only had he definitely finagled another breakfast—whenever he happened to roll out of bed tomorrow morning—from the terrifying Mrs. Melody, but he was the center of attention at the Screeching Cow. Of course everyone had heard about Pinebar Tufts being found in the Rotunda, and word was getting around that no, he hadn't actually hanged himself, but it appeared someone had done it *to* him.

Which meant, that, like Mrs. Melody, everyone wanted to hear what Billy had to say instead of talking about the damned troops and when they were going to actually *fight*. And Billy Morris had plenty to tell them.

And with mugs of ale being purchased for him as quickly as he finished each one, Billy's tongue loosened up more and more, and he dredged up (and fabricated) more details from his foggy memory.

The more he thought about it, the more he was certain he *had* seen someone lurking about the Capitol after the fireworks were done. And, yes, the man had been wearing a top hat, which meant he was one of the rich people in town. Most working men wore bowler hats or caps, and they didn't carry walking sticks. Not usually.

There'd been a carriage parked nearby—Billy remembered that, because he'd seen the fancy markings on it when he took his first (of many) breaks and drank from his bottle of gin last night.

"Slick and black it was," he said to the small crowd at the Cow. The Screeching Cow was a small pub not far from the Division— the area where a man could pay for any pleasure he wanted from the ladies who walked the streets and beckoned to a man as he strolled on by. There were the fancy houses with fine ladies and red plush sofas, like Mrs. Hall's, but that was where all the senators and congressmen went. Billy couldn't afford the likes of those establishments, but it was just fine with him if he slipped into a small, simple room instead of one with lace curtains and a fancy brocade bedcovering. Or even an alley, if he was in a hurry.

"Do you think it belonged to the killer?" asked Totty, who was another of the Auxiliary Guard. He patrolled the Patent Office and was one of Billy's good friends because he wasn't all that great at bluffing in poker. Billy tended to like playing cards with him because Totty usually lost all his money.

"It had to," Billy said with a vehemence he had no right to feel. "All them gold markings on it. Or were they silver . . . ?" He scratched his head, trying to make sense of the muddled memories. He *had* seen a carriage, hadn't he?

"Time to report," said a loud voice. "Let's go. Don't want-ta be late, do we, boys?"

Billy sneered into his beer. That damned Wendell Popper could never stand it when anyone else was getting attention. And he always tried to boss everyone around, even though he wasn't a supervisor or nothing. Just another Night Watch guard who thought he was as good as God or something.

Nonetheless, Billy stood. He'd considered taking the night off—why not, after what he'd been through last night?—but decided it would be more to his benefit to go on as usual. Then he'd have more information and more stories to tell. Hell, he might be able to draw this out for a few more days, get sausage and ham and eggs for breakfast and ales bought for him every night.

The crew of Auxiliary Guards shuffled out of the Cow, and Billy cast a glance down the street. He might just make his way over to the Division to find a pretty lady some night soon. He deserved it after what he'd been through, after all. A man was due a little pleasure and relaxation every so often.

It was a short walk from the Cow to the Capitol, and the sun was nearly to the horizon by now. So Billy was going to be a few minutes late starting his patrol. That was all right. There wasn't no one to care except that Wendell Popper. The streets were surprisingly empty tonight. Maybe it was because of the thunder rumbling in the distance. Everyone was going home before the rain started.

Though he'd lost count of how many ales he'd had, Billy was hardly drunk at all. Sure, he stumbled a coupla times, and his head was a little muzzy, but he was perfectly capable of walking around the long white building, keeping an eye out for mischief-makers—and now, for killers—all the while avoiding the blocks of marble and the huge pieces of cast iron. It wasn't a bad job, but with his newfound fame, Billy thought he might be able to get something better.

Besides, there was talk about Congress getting rid of the Auxiliary Watch. They didn't think the patrol was effective.

Effective. He'd show them effective. Hadn't he seen the killer?

Wasn't he the one the detective—what were they saying his name was? Adam something? That detective was going to need to talk to him, to Billy, to get the information. Maybe Billy should be a detective himself. Ole Pinkerton could use someone like him on his staff. Someone who knew how to get around in the dark and make friends and get people to talking. Someone who was quick on his feet, like Billy was.

Yessir, that was exactly what he was going to do. Once this murder investigation was over, Billy was going to quit his job and join up with the Pinkertons. That would be far safer than joining up for the army—where he'd probably get himself killed.

Billy had hardly finished that thought when a shadow fell across him from behind. Next thing he knew, something crashed into the back of his head.

Ten minutes later, Billy Morris had gotten himself killed.

CHAPTER 7

Saturday, July 6

*T*he day was beautiful. Bright and clear, with the sky as blue as blue could be. The tall silvery, silken grasses of the Kansas prairie undulated in regular waves beneath a gentle breeze. The sun blazed above, and as he rode, Adam removed his wide-brimmed hat to wipe a trickle of sweat from his brow. The scent of sweetgrass and wildflowers mingled with the familiar tang of his horse. Adam drew in a breath of fresh, warm air as he noticed a group of hawks circling in the distance. They were above a lone tree that sprang from the ground, probably at the side of a small river or creek.

But Adam knew what circling hawks or turkey vultures meant and a pang of concern had him urging Patience, his brown, into a canter. He gripped his rifle in one hand and managed the reins with the other, feeling the comfortable weight of his pistol tucked into his coat pocket.

No one rode without a firearm in Bloody Kansas, especially if you were a Free-Stater like Adam.

His pleasure in the day evaporated as he and Patience flew through the waving grasses, drawing closer to the tree where he could see that something—someone—was hanging from the longest, lowest branch.

He flung himself off his mount as soon as he was close enough, and a cry of rage and grief choked up inside him as he recognized Johnny Brown, a free black man who'd been homesteading on the other side of Green Creek. Adam and Johnny had shared a campfire and fellowship one night when they both rode back from Leavenworth after a trip to the general store there.

Adam was too late for Johnny. Too damned late. Whoever had done this, *strung him up, lynched him in broad daylight, was long gone—and so was Johnny's soul.*

Still in the saddle, Adam had to maneuver a reluctant but obedient Patience close enough to the hanging body so he could reach high enough to cut down Johnny. The thick flies and dried, congealed blood from the beating Johnny had gotten before he was hanged upset Adam's brown, but she was a good girl and she held steady while he sawed away at the rope. Adam blinked back tears of rage and grief as he worked.

Just before Johnny fell to the ground, Adam saw his face. He reared back in horror. Not Johnny. It wasn't Johnny. It was George Hilton.

Oh God, not George too.

So much waste. So much violence. So much hatred.

Johnny. George. How many others?

Adam was just climbing off Patience so he could see to burying his friend when a shout in the distance caught his ears.

He spun, diving from his horse toward the rifle he'd propped against the tree while he was cutting, but he was too late. All at once the men were there—five of them, on furious horses with foaming mouths and red, rolling eyes—bearing down on him.

They wore the wide brimmed hats and rough clothing of the prairie and carried rifles and revolvers. One of them brandished a coil of rope.

Shots rang out in a sudden maelstrom of noise and violence. Patience screamed and reared, rolling back onto her tail and then to the ground with an ugly thud that twisted her body. Adam kept running toward his rifle, but he wasn't getting any closer . . . he couldn't reach it, and his revolver was no longer in his coat pocket.

The group descended upon him, shooting and shouting, whooping and cursing, flailing out with whips and rocks. Adam felt the slice of a streak of leather across his face, his arm, the backs of his legs and he stumbled, falling as he tried yet again to get to his rifle. He had to get his rifle, he had to save Tom and Mary, and sweet little Carl before the mob stormed the house, set it on fire . . .

The searing pain in his left arm made him scream and fall to his knees, the rifle still somehow—always—out of his reach, the mob surrounding him with their leering faces. One of them produced a noose, and as Adam fought the pain in his arm, they descended upon him with the rope, fitting it around his neck, tightening it as he struggled and kicked and—

"Quinn! Wake up, man. Quinn!"

Someone was pulling at him, yanking, dragging him . . . and he opened his eyes to discover that he was no longer in Kansas, no longer at the mercy of the Pro-Slaver mob, no longer at the lynching site of poor Johnny Brown and George Hilton.

But his arm . . . it screamed and burned with remembered pain, and when he went to cradle it with his right hand, his fingers closed over emptiness. There was nothing there.

Adam blinked, shook his head, tried to bring himself back to wherever he was. It was mostly dark, and he was in bed. His missing limb throbbed with pain and he gritted his teeth against it as someone brought a lantern near his face.

"Adam. Are you all right?" It was Thomas Burns, the White House doorkeeper's assistant.

"Yes. What is it?" It was all Adam could do to keep his tone civil when he was still shuddering inside from the memory-dream, and combating the agony in his phantom arm. "What time is it?"

It was dark enough to need a lantern, which meant it was too early to get up—at least in his estimation.

"It's almost five o'clock. Dawn's coming now. Sorry to wake you," Thomas said, his voice doubtful. "There's been another body found, up to the Capitol. They thought you'd want to know."

Adam stifled a groan but pushed himself up in bed with his remaining arm. His torso ached with pain from yesterday's activity when he'd been hanging from his prosthetic arm on the crane. He had scrapes and bruises all around his ribs and shoulders from the mistreatment. "All right. I'll be down as soon as I can."

It was never a simple or fast process for him to dress with only one good hand, let alone accounting for the reattaching of his prosthetic, which required buckles and straps that wound around his shoulders, torso, and under his arms.

His head still partially in the dream, which was only slightly accurate as far as what had actually happened—he hadn't been alone when Johnny Brown had been found, nor was that the incident when he'd taken the bullet that shattered his forearm bones—Adam splashed water on his face. Worst of all, the image of George Hilton hanging there would not leave his mind—settling there like a vulture, ready to swoop in and become reality. He tried to shake it off and rubbed his hand over his chin and eyes. The stubble needed to be shaved today as he'd not had the time yesterday morning. Then, when his eyes still felt bleary and his mind groggy, he simply dunked his entire face in the basin.

That was more efficient that trying to scoop up water with only one hand. He only wished it were colder instead of tepid from the warm summer night.

Then he set about the task of reattaching his Palmer arm over abused skin and overtaxed muscle with fingers that didn't want to cooperate this morning. As he did so, it occurred to him to wonder why *he'd* been called to look at a dead body.

Was he now the only person in Washington City who could assess a murder scene? Or investigate a crime? Or was it because the body had been found near the Capitol, and they—whoever had found it—thought there might be a connection to Pinebar Tufts's murder? He fervently, grouchily hoped it was the latter and that he wouldn't have yet another insurmountable task to see to.

And then Adam stopped suddenly, sharply, and was angry with himself. He sighed and passed his hand over his face. Good God. A man was *dead*. Adam had no business grumbling about being awakened at dawn when a man was dead and he was still alive and well, dammit.

At that moment, realization struck him—hard and fast, like the flat of his mama's hand on his behind when he was young, or the sudden shock of a dunking in the ice-cold creek.

You have the gift of knowing—something that is rare. This gift will be instrumental on this path of your life and its work. Use it wisely and well. Use it for good, not for harm. Do not doubt it. Trust in it. Allow it.

The words had been spoken to him by Makwa, Ishkode's grandfather, who'd taught him how to track and to read all of the most subtle signs in nature, and to understand how all living things connected and communicated.

To *know*, as he described it—to sense and inherently understand the story of what had gone there as he interpreted what the tracks and signs meant. At the time the old man had told him this, Adam had been barely twenty years old, still young enough to believe he was in control of his life. Too young and inexperienced to understand what he meant.

But now, here he was: thirty-three, living in a city he disliked, missing half of an arm, and unable to farm, homestead, or cowherd; not able to enlist in the army to defend his country; no longer able to play his grandfather's fiddle . . . filled with grief and loss and witness to far too much violence and hatred—with more to come as the war marched on.

Adam was . . . lost. He felt lost.

Until now—for it was *now*, at this moment, like a lightning strike—that he realized how the path of his life had led him here. That everything he'd done until now—meeting Abe Lincoln as a boy, going to Wisconsin to trap with the Ojibwe, moving to Kansas and experiencing firsthand the determination of the Pro-Slavers . . . even losing his arm.

He realized that he was no longer useless and floating willy-nilly down a river that he hadn't remembered jumping into.

It came to him with a sudden bolt of clarity that the gift he'd discovered through Makwa was now serving him even as he used it to serve others: as a way to seek justice for those who could no longer seek it for themselves. As a way to do right by them. As a way to do right, period. As a way to contribute to the nation, to the city, to his president, to those around him.

He had a gift, a talent, an inherent ability that had been unearthed, honed, and polished by his Ojibwe friend and mentor. Now he had the responsibility to use it.

And he would. Willingly. Readily. Honorably.

And never again would he call into doubt his ability to do so.

With this startling revelation, Adam felt enlightened and energized in a way he hadn't been for years. He finished dressing quickly and left the bedroom he slept in just down the hallway from Mr. and Mrs. Lincoln.

As he stepped into the corridor of the second floor, which was dimly lit by a single lamp, he nearly bumped into the president himself. The other man was still wearing his nightshirt and looked just as startled to see him.

"Good morning, Mr. President," Adam said.

The president laughed ruefully, gesturing to his bare legs and slippers. "I don't reckon too many people could say that with a straight face when confronted by this sight, Adam. No need for such formality when you've seen me in my altogether, anyhow, now is there? Where are you off to so early?"

Adam submerged the distant memory of the time he had, in fact, glimpsed the gleaming white arse of the man standing before him after one of them stumbled from the outhouse while the other stumbled in, decades ago. "Someone sent for me to see a body that's been found by the Capitol. I reckon they think it might be connected to Pinebar Tufts's death."

Lincoln nodded, grave and thoughtful despite his knobby knees and darkly-haired legs. He cocked his head at a loud thump followed by an alarming rattle from his sons' bedchamber, then shook his head affectionately and said, "I'm thankful for you taking on these tasks, Adam. I hope you know that. I appreciate that I can trust you."

Now Adam felt even more confident about his previous realization and newfound confidence, and he nodded as one of the boys screamed and there was a loud thud from down the hall. "Thank you for your trust in me. I'll do my best, sir." He began to go, then thought of something else. "Mr. President—er, Abe," he said when the other man lifted a brow and gestured pointedly to his nightshirt, "I'm worried about George Hilton. His safety, I mean. He was able to confirm that Tufts was murdered and that he didn't hang himself, but by doing the postmortems on—that is, cutting up—white folk, he puts himself in danger."

Lincoln nodded. "Yes, I can see that being a concern. What can I do?"

"I reckon if you give him a card like the one you gave me, that might help—even in this city," Adam said dryly.

"I'll see to it today. Thank you for bringing that to my attention," the president replied, making Adam feel a little guilty for adding yet another thing to the man's interminable list of problems, tasks, worries, and conflicts. "And perhaps you might want to have William see to that beard you refuse to grow when he's here today. You're looking altogether too scruffy, and Mrs. Lincoln is due back today." He winked and mussed Adam's hair like he used to do when he was much younger. "You might as well avail yourself of his services while you're still living in this big white house."

"Thank you, sir, I'll do that," Adam replied.

Lincoln was whistling to himself as he opened the door to his bedchamber, and Adam thought it might have to do with Mrs. Lincoln's imminent return. The president was always happier when his wife was around.

Just then, the door of Tad and Willie's room opened and the two boys burst into the hall. "Papa! Papa!" Willie shouted, and they barged into the bedchamber of the President of the United States without hesitation.

Adam shook his head at the hooligans' raucousness—he wasn't certain which was worse, the Lincoln boys or the twenty thousand undisciplined troops that filled the city—and continued on his way down the stairs. By the time he walked out the front door of the "big white house," the sun had begun to spill her golden glow over the city. Unlike yesterday, however, he was walking out with a hunk of bread and an apple to munch on as he hurried along with the soldier who'd been dispatched to send for him.

"Man named Wendell Popper found him," said the young man from Ohio, whose name Adam had heard and then promptly forgotten. He had cornsilk hair and a nose much too large for his face, and he looked like he was no older than sixteen—a fact which saddened Adam, for the boy was much too young to be fighting in a war. "He's another of the Night Watch guards."

"Who is it that's dead?" asked Adam as he waved to the Willard's ever-present Birch, whose pristine glove and smile both flashed white when he waved back.

"Name's Billy Morris," replied the soldier, and Adam nearly stopped right there. *Damn.*

He'd needed to talk to Billy Morris about whether he'd seen anything happen on the night of the fourth while he was on his patrol, and now he'd never be able to do so. And with the man turning up dead? He reckoned that was not a coincidence.

Despite the early hour, there was a small crowd gathered near Billy Morris's body. Two more soldiers—at least the abundance of troops in the city were a benefit by helping with some keeping of the peace—were stalling the gawkers at a distance.

The dead man had been found slumped against a large oak tree just beyond the construction area, in the shadow of the Capitol, on the west side. The National Mall stretched out beyond with its stub of the unfinished Washington Monument in the midst of muddy grass, and Adam understood why the killer would have left Billy here, on the less-traversed side of the building.

The Smithsonian Castle sat on the left side of the Mall, its gothic shape and seven red-orange brick towers a striking contrast to all of the other national buildings, which had been designed in the style of classical architecture. Or so Adam had been told by none other than Miss Sophie Gates, who tended to impart random facts during casual conversation.

He reckoned she'd be mightily disappointed not to have been here on the scene of another dead body.

With that thought causing his lips to curve in a slight smile, Adam turned his attention to the more difficult problem at hand and took a look at the scene.

It had rained a little last night, and so the ground was soft beneath the muddy grass. Most footmarks had probably been washed away by the showers, depending when the killer had attacked Billy. But Adam was adept at reading even the slightest impressions in grass, and the thickly leaved tree provided some cover from the rain, so he was able to discern markings that told a tale.

Two parallel marks, so faint that they were only noticeable to someone who knew how and where to look, indicated that Billy Morris had been dragged to his current position leaning against the tree. A single footmark in the soil near the trunk had Adam crouching closer to examine it. He hummed with satisfaction—

he'd have to measure it, but it looked like the same size and shape as the one in the dust on the crane. And now that the mark was in the soft ground, and not on the wood of the crane, he could see more details. It appeared the back heel on the right foot had a chip out of one of its inside corners. He'd like to see another clear print of the right boot just to be certain, but if so, it would be helpful in identifying the murderer.

Now that he'd looked for tracks, he was able to get closer without fearing he'd obliterate any signs. He crouched next to Billy Morris.

The first thing he noticed was the strong scent of spirits wafting from the man, who appeared to be in his forties. He wasn't wearing a hat or cap, and his clothing was worn but clean. His head was slumped down, chin to chest, and his ungloved hands curled in his lap. There were no obvious signs of violence—no blood on his face, clothing, or hands.

As was his custom, Adam paused for a moment and said a prayer for the dead man. And this time, he added a silent promise: *I'll do my best to find your killer.*

"I couldn't wake him," said a man standing close to the tree. He'd been introduced as Wendell Popper. "Not unusual for Morris—he'd as soon have a swig from a gin bottle as take a breath—but when I shook him, I realized there was something wrong."

"You didn't move him?" Adam asked.

"No, sir, just to shake him. His head kinda rolled around like that, and he started to tip over. And he was stiff. So I—well, I pushed him back up like that. And then I called for help."

"Were you looking for him?" Adam asked, craning his head to peer up at Popper. "How did you find him here, so far out of the way?"

"I'm on the Night Watch with him, and those of us who are usually see everyone walking back after the shifts. He—well, he had a lot to drink last night—more than usual, because everyone was buying him ales after what happened yesterday, him being here and seeing things and all, and when I din't see him come back, I thought I should check and make sure he wasn't passed out somewheres. And when I found him, I thought, that was exactly what he did—passed out here. But he didn't move or respond, and he was so stiff and *cold* when I touched him. That's when I realized he was dead."

"What did he say about what happened yesterday?"

"He was jawing on about seeing the killer, and how he was wearing a top hat and had a fancy carriage—but I didn't believe none of it, being truthful, there, sir. He was saying one thing, then when someone said something or asked a question, he changed his story to match what they said. I think he was just talking so's he could get the attention. And refills on his mug."

"All right." Adam grimaced and returned his attention to the body. So Billy Morris had been talking about what he'd seen yesterday—or not actually seen. And the killer had probably gotten wind of it and decided he didn't want Billy Morris spreading any information that could identify him—whether it was accurate or not. So even if Adam could get people to repeat what Billy had said, he'd have no way of determining which parts were correct. He looked at the soldier who'd walked him from the President's House. "Go and fetch George Hilton, in Ballard's Alley in the First Ward. Cellar of Great Eternity Church. Tell him I asked for him."

Now, at last, Adam began a closer examination of the body, which was quite stiff and difficult to move. The first thing he noticed was a bloody mass on the back of the head—just like that on Piney Tufts. He was certain that blow wouldn't have killed Billy Morris, however. With a sense of inevitability, he lifted the dead man's head as much as he could with the rigor of the body.

He didn't have to lift it far to see the dark red mark indenting across the front of Billy Morris's throat, extending onto the sides of his neck. With a little more work, he lifted the chin even more and could see that the man's voice box was crushed from something long and hard pressed across it—just like Piney Tufts's had been. Only this time, the killer didn't even try to hide his work.

Adam reckoned the murderer had taken the same walking stick he'd probably used to hit his victim on the back of the head, stunning him enough to be able to use the walking stick to choke

Billy Morris to death. He looked at the ground near the body again to see if there were any marks that supported this theory.

Nothing except the dragging marks in the grass.

Dragging marks. Had he been dead when the killer brought him here, or had the killer finished the job in the shadow of this leafy oak?

Adam looked at Billy's shoes, lifting each foot one by one to examine them. The backs of the heels had collected small bits of grass and scrapes of dirt from when he was dragged from wherever he'd been hit. Not only grass and dirt, but a fine white grit with a subtle, silvery glitter.

Marble dust.

Adam straightened. "Wait here for George Hilton to arrive," he said to one of the soldiers who'd been keeping the crowd back. "Don't let anyone touch the body or get close to him, understand? If Dr. Hilton asks for anything, you see that he gets it. This is an order from the president himself."

"Yes, sir." The soldier gave a salute, which Adam—though he wasn't enlisted—returned.

Then he went off to follow the trail made by the dragged heels.

If he hadn't had the instinct and the experience, Adam would have lost the trail many times due to the rain and many footprints that marred the area. The marble dust was a clue that indicated from which direction the body had been dragged, and Adam doggedly examined the area until he found part of the trail, then another part, then another until he was approaching the clutter of marble blocks in the shadow of the building.

The sun was fully up and Provest's crew was at work again. As he drew closer, he smelled the smoke churning from the basement bakery and saw the soot flushing into the sky from the chimneys. A large wagon laden with barrels of flour had pulled up to the first floor of the building.

"Mr. Provest," Adam said, approaching the marble finisher. "I reckon it's not going to make you happy, but I need you to keep your men out of this area for a short while."

The other man removed his hat and scratched his head, squinting into the bright sun as he looked up at Adam. "I heard there was another body found. Poor Billy Morris. Not much of a watch-man, but he never did nobody no harm." He leaned closer. "Was he murdered too?"

Adam nodded.

Provest frowned, then shouted at his men to take a break. "What're you looking for? Isn't any dead body hereabouts," he said, following Adam as he did a slow, careful survey of the place where the dragged heel trail temporarily ended.

"But there was," Adam replied. "There." He crouched next to a pile of large, uncut blocks of marble.

The story was as clear as in the page of a book: the marks where Billy Morris had dug in his heels as he struggled, kicking in vain to free himself from the stick crushing his throat; the imprints from two knees on the ground that had straddled his body as the killer did his work; the marks from the frantic scraping of shoulders, elbows, and arms as the victim tried to fight off the attack. Even a smear of blood mixed in with dirt and marble dust from the broken skin at the back of Billy Morris's head. Adam reckoned the blow must have been just enough to stun Morris and knock him to the ground, then the murderer did the rest.

Adam found more footprints from the killer and was even more certain they would match the ones found on the wooden beam of the derrick. He followed them back to the north side of the Capitol, noting where the killer stopped behind a bush next to one of the lampposts, waiting for Billy to walk by. The slightly deeper impressions of the fronts of his shoes when the killer swung his walking stick to smash into the back of Billy's head— and there, beneath a bush, was a cap that Adam reckoned belonged to the dead man.

The trail ended there, for too many people had passed by on the walkway where the killer approached from Penn Ave.

That made Adam wonder whether the killer had driven his own carriage, or if he'd walked here, or if he'd taken a hackney cab and been dropped off—nothing more unusual than a gentleman taking a bit of air. There wasn't any way to tell unless someone had seen something.

He hoped if someone *had* seen something, they wouldn't be as loud about it as Billy Morris had been. Since someone had already killed two people in less than twenty-four hours, there was no doubt he'd kill again.

He looked back at the footprints where the murderer had waited for his prey, and was delighted to see an excellent impression in the soft dirt—the deepest, clearest one he'd seen yet and he was able to confirm that there was definitely a chunk broken off the corner of the inside of the right heel. It wouldn't impede a man's stride, because it was on the inside, in the middle of the sole, but it made the footprint—and therefore the boot—distinctive.

At the sound of his name, Adam turned to see the young soldier he'd dispatched to fetch George Hilton. He was running at top speed up the hill toward him.

"What is it?" he asked as soon as he was close enough to hear the boy.

"I went to find that George Hilton, sir, and he wasn't where you said he was. No one was there—exceptin' a dead man, and he was all cut up something fierce! His guts were—everywhere." The boy gagged and swallowed hard, his face colored with a definite green cast. "And it looked like there was a big fight went on in there—furniture was all smashed and there was blood everywhere. I don't think it was from the dead man, though."

George. No.

The image from his dream lodged back into his mind as Adam's stomach plummeted to his feet. For a moment, he didn't know what to do—where to go, whom to contact, where to look for his friend. For all he knew, George could be in manacles on his way to Mississippi or Georgia by now. Then just as quickly, his mind cleared: he could start with the scene, see what he could learn from the tracks and then decide what to do.

He left short, sharp directions for the soldiers and the constables—who'd finally arrived—to wrap up Billy Morris's body and put it in a wagon until he returned or sent word, and then hailed a hackney driver to take him up to Ballard's Alley. He had no time to waste and climbed up to sit next to him so he could give easier directions.

When he told the driver, a friendly black man with a huge wad of tobacco in his jaw, where he meant to go, the man scratched his head. "Why, that's funny. I done took a coupla women up there last night. They was gwan to see a doctor or somepin, which I thought was a strange thing, that time-a night. White woman, she was, with her nanny. And she had a southern accent thicker than my mama's waist. She's rich too; paid me double t'wait for her—and though she took longer than she said—and it was gettin' on to curfew, y'know, and I din't wanna get no fines—she come back, she and her nanny, and wit'em a Negro man was beat up real bad. That was after I heard some gunshots over from there too."

Adam was only half listening until the driver went on and said, "Sounded like her daddy was hurt real bad too, and that Negro was gonna help her—though he could hardly stand up, so I dunno how he was gwan do nothing anyways."

"This woman, was she very pretty, with blond hair?" When the driver nodded, Adam continued. "Do you remember where you took them? With the man who was beat up?"

"I shore do. Was over to G Street."

"Never mind going to the First Ward. Can you take me there?" Adam's apprehension eased a little, and he sat quietly as the driver navigated the way to what he believed was going to be Althea Billings's house.

When the hack stopped in front of the familiar house, Adam saw another carriage parked there and recognized it as Dr. Forthruth's. He quickly paid his driver, then hurried to the front door.

It was Jelly, Miss Lemagne's maid, who answered the door to him, and although she seemed surprised to see him, she didn't have the opportunity to say so, for there were raised voices in the other room.

"Oh, Mr. Quinn, you'd best go in there and see what they'se doin," she said. "That black doctor o' yours come and fixed up Mr. Hurst, but that other doctor ain't likin' it."

Adam went into the parlor to find Dr. Forthruth whipped up into quite a state, as his mother used to say. His face was red and his eyes bulged. Miss Lemagne was standing on the other side of her father's sickbed, hands on her hips, chin jutting out in a stubborn position Adam had seen before. Hurst Lemagne was lying there, his eyes open and himself propped up in the bed—clearly in a much better condition than yesterday.

And George Hilton, whose one eye was swollen closed and his face bruised and scraped, stood a little behind Miss Lemagne, hands raised as if in an effort to settle the furious doctor.

"Good morning, Miss Lemagne," Adam said cheerily—and he was indeed more cheery than he had been, now that he was assured of his friend's continued freedom and good health. "Good morning, Dr. Hilton," he said, deliberately using George's title. "And Dr. Forthruth. And Hurst. You're looking surprisingly recovered this morning."

"I certainly am," replied the Southern gentleman in a much more civil voice than he'd ever used with Adam. Hurst Lemagne was not a supporter of Mr. Lincoln—in fact, quite the opposite—and transferred his antipathy for the president and the Union toward anyone connected to him. "I'm sore, but the pain is gone and I can move my leg—carefully though. That man there"—he jerked his head toward George—"says I'll be walking in a fortnight." His tone was colored with disbelief as well as hope.

Before Adam could respond, Dr. Forthruth exploded. "That confounded darky had no business touching one of my patients. You're damned lucky he didn't kill you! And don't be calling me back when your leg starts to shrivel up and you get a fever, Mr. Lemagne." He yanked up a medical bag, but not before Adam saw a sharp, lethal blade sticking out of it.

The same type of blade they'd used to cut off his own arm.

He'd been partially conscious during the surgery, for they'd not dosed him with enough chloroform, and he well remembered the flash of the blade as it came close to his burning, bleeding, macerated skin.

He shuddered and stuffed the thought away before the memory came flooding back, but a streak of pain shot through his short arm and into the limb that was no longer present. "Good day, Dr. Forthruth," he said as the doctor brushed past him.

"Mr. Quinn!" Miss Lemagne gave her father's hand one last pat then, in a rustle of petticoats, flowed over to greet Adam. Her hair was smoothed back in a simple knot and she wasn't enclosed by the usual amount of fabric in her skirts. "How kind of you to call." She took his real hand with her ungloved ones and looked up at him.

"Of course. I wanted to see how your father was doing. It appears he's taken a turn for the better." Adam found it strange to be holding a woman's bare hands, especially in front of her father and his own friend. He gently extricated his fingers.

"Dr. Hilton fixed him up," she replied. "His leg wasn't broken after all. That Dr. Forthruth had got it all wrong, and then he came here this morning to cut off Daddy's leg!" Her eyes were narrow with disgust as she slammed her hands on her hips.

"I reckon you won't have to worry about Dr. Forthruth bothering you again," Adam replied. Then he said to George, "Have you seen yourself in a mirror?"

"Can't get too good a view with only one eyeball working," replied the doctor dryly.

"Heard you had a little bit of trouble," Adam said. "I sent for you this morning, and word got back to me about the condition of your place."

"He was in a bad way until Jelly and I rescued him," Miss Lemagne said, slipping her hand through the crook of Adam's false arm as she directed him out of the parlor. "Daddy needs some sleep."

Adam cast a look over his shoulder at George, who appeared as mortified as a man whose face looked like it had been through a meat grinder could look. "You and Miss Jelly went to Ballard's Alley at night?"

"Of course we did." Miss Lemagne looked up at him with soulful blue eyes. "My daddy was in a bad way, Mr. Quinn. I wasn't going to let him die. Or worse—have his leg cut off. And so I thought maybe Dr. Hilton could help set my daddy's broken leg. It needed someone horribly strong, I thought. But when we came upon Dr. Hilton here—why, he was being pummeled to death by those three terrible men. So I shot one of them."

Adam barely managed to control his shock at her blithe state-

ment. "Is that so?" Did that mean he had another dead body to
see to?

"Yes. Right in the leg. And Jelly swatted another one of them with
her club. And then I chased them off. They were good-for-nothings,"
she added flatly. "And I needed Dr. Hilton."

Adam glanced at George, who still looked pained. But there
was a bit of worry limning his gaze, and Adam doubted the fact
that a young woman had "chased them off" would be an end to
his problems. "And as it turns out, I'm in need of Dr. Hilton's particular skills right now as well, Miss Lemagne."

"Why is that? *Oh*. There's another murder?" Her eyes sparkled
with interest. "I'll fetch my sketchbook so I can get a good drawing of the scene. Daddy will be just fine resting with Louise and
James to look after him." She hurried from the room before
Adam could attempt to dissuade her.

"Who died?" George asked—likely before Adam could do the
same and question him. Adam understood that his friend didn't
want to discuss the events of last night.

"Billy Morris—the Night Watch at the Capitol—was murdered.
His throat was crushed—looks like someone took a long stick and
choked him with it. I'll feel better if you take a look at him—
somewhere else than your office," he added. "We need to move
you somewhere safer."

George shook his head. "I can't do that, Adam. I got patients.
I'm not leaving my place."

Adam pursed his lips. "I reckon I might need to find someone
else to do the work, then, George, if it's going to cause you a black
eye and a busted-up face."

"Coupla broken ribs too," the other man replied. "And if that's
what you want to do, I'll not stop you."

"It's not what I *want* to do. Next time it could be worse," Adam
said.

"I'll be more careful. Lock the doors. Have a rifle handy. Maybe
I'll get a dog."

Adam nodded, then allowed a glint to creep into his eyes. "Or
you could just set Miss Lemagne up with a revolver at the door."

George said something under his breath that sounded like, "Lord save me from interfering women," and shook his head.

Miss Lemagne bustled back into the front room, satchel in hand with her sketchbook in it. A simple bonnet with ribbons trailed from her other hand. "Jelly, I declare, I can't seem to pin this on straight."

"Miss Constance, you can't go out looking like *that!*" her maid said in horror. "Why, that's only an at-home dress, and your hair ain't even done! Lookit the edges of your petticoats—they're plain and not even hemmed! No, Miss Constance, I can't let you go out like that. Your daddy would whip my backside if'n I did."

Adam seized the opportunity. "Miss Lemagne, I appreciate your willingness to help, but Mr. Morris's body has already been removed and so there's nothing at the scene to be sketched. And I reckon I've got to excuse myself, as Dr. Hilton and I must attend to the problem right away. I hope your father continues his recovery."

She looked as if she wanted to say something, but George spoke up quickly. "If you like, I'll come back and check up on your father later today, Miss Lemagne. Thank you for letting me stay here last night."

"Well, I couldn't let you go home after curfew," she said sharply. "And after everything else. Yes, I'm sure Daddy will want to see you later today. Good-bye, Mr. Quinn." Her tone was *frosty*, without a hint of southern in it.

Adam grimaced but managed a smile before he fled with George close on his heels.

CHAPTER 8

Sophie hurried up the walk to the front door of the Executive Mansion—or, as President Lincoln had begun to call it, the White House.

"Good morning, Mr. McManus," she said to the wizened old man who opened the door for her.

Despite the number of times she'd been to the great mansion—and in fact, she'd even lived at the President's House for several nights in April when everyone was certain the Rebels were going to come across the Potomac and invade Washington—Sophie was always mildly surprised that anyone could gain admittance to the house for any reason. There was no security to speak of, despite the war going on, and people came and went as they liked. There were always job-seekers and other favor-mongerers loitering about, waiting for the opportunity to press Mr. Lincoln for their requests.

"Top o' the morning to you, Miss Gates," Old Ed McManus replied. "If it's that handsome Adam Quinn you're after seeing, lass, well, he's not here."

At this news, Sophie screeched to a halt just inside the door. "He's not? Why, it's only half nine! I thought for certain he'd still be here." *Drat.* Now she'd never be able to track him down—that man moved around faster than a raindrop fell.

She'd wanted to find out whether he'd learned anything else since yesterday about Pinebar Tufts. And she was going to advise him of her intention to meet Miss Barton at the Patent Office today and use the opportunity to do some snooping around at his place of work.

"No, lass, he was called out just before dawn this morn'. There's another body was discovered up on the hill at the Capitol."

Double drat. Another body meant another crime scene that she wasn't able to see with her own eyes. "All right, then. Thank you, Mr. McManus." Sophie adjusted her bonnet and was just about to leave when Old Ed opened the door once more.

To her surprise, she recognized the young woman who hesitantly stepped inside.

"Miss Monroe!" Sophie exclaimed. "What are you doing here?" she added before she realized how peremptory that sounded. "I mean, what a surprise to see you again."

"Hello—Miss Gates, isn't it? How wonderful to see you here." The pretty young woman rushed over to her and took Sophie's hands as if they were old friends. "It's a bit intimidating, coming in here like this, isn't it?" She looked around with wide eyes, and then Sophie recognized the moment Miss Monroe saw the shabbiness of the entryway of the house and surprise flickered in her gaze.

Unfortunately, the president's house was in dire need of renovation and sprucing up. To be sure, Mrs. Lincoln was hard at work spending far too much money (if one believed the rumors) to get new furnishings and decorations, as well as painting, repairs, and other updates. But especially the entranceway, which was separated from the main corridor and stairs to the rest of the house by a pebbled-glass wall, was as sterile and unexceptional as the entrance to a bank.

"The Blue Room is absolutely beautiful," Sophie replied with sincerity. "Mrs. Lincoln always makes certain to have fresh flowers on every table too. I hope you'll be able to see it someday. What brings you here, Miss Monroe, if you don't mind my asking?"

The other young woman hesitated, then plunged on. Later, Sophie was to wonder why she was so immediately open and trusting of someone she'd just met, but realized it was likely because she had no other options and that a young woman her age would presumably be a sympathetic listener. And it became obvious Miss Monroe desperately needed someone to talk to.

"I wanted to speak to that Mr. Adam Quinn," she said, startling Sophie.

"Mr. Quinn? Why, whatever for? And he's not here at the moment anyhow. I came to see him as well." Sophie realized how that might sound, and the last thing she wanted was anyone—including Old Ed, who apparently already had the idea—to think she was chasing after Adam Quinn. Good grief. That was the *last* thing she would do.

"He's not here?" Miss Monroe's face fell. "Oh dear. I was hoping he could help me. He's the one who does all the investigating—like a Pinkerton?"

Sophie, spurred on by curiosity and her intrinsic need to advise others, said, "He is. But perhaps I can help in his stead."

Miss Monroe looked at her, and Sophie was shocked to see tears glistening in her eyes. Whatever was bothering the young woman was clearly weighing heavily on her. "Let's walk together," she said, slipping her hand inside the crook of the other lady's arm. "We can talk and you can tell me about it. I work with Mr. Quinn on his investigations, you know."

"You do? *You?* A woman?" Miss Monroe seemed both shocked and delighted by this fact. "Why, that's wonderful!"

Sophie thought so too, but she suspected it was for a different reason. "Do you want to send your carriage on home? Or have them follow us? I prefer to walk whenever possible, because it helps keep one in good health." She remembered how Miss Lemagne was out of breath after climbing up the steps of the Capitol yesterday and was glad she kept her own corset as loose as possible.

Miss Monroe seemed intrigued by the idea of walking as well, and did as Sophie suggested. "Besides," she said as they walked away from the White House, past the statue of Andrew Jackson in Lafayette Square, "this way, no one will hear what I have to say. Even Vancy and Bitty shouldn't hear this."

My goodness. Now her curiosity was truly piqued. "What is it?" Sophie asked, her interest and impatience warring with the need to treat her companion with kid gloves. "What's bothering you, Miss Monroe?"

The other woman stopped and looked at Sophie. "Please call me Felicity. It's—it's only right, for what I'm going to tell you is—is—" Her dark eyes filled with tears and she shook her head so suddenly and violently that her bonnet bounced. "No. I can't. I shouldn't. Yet it's a secret I can't bear to keep, because I don't know what to do! It's just . . . *awful.*" Her whisper broke with emotion. "I have no one to talk to about it. I *can't* talk to anyone about it."

The tears were coming faster now, and Sophie dragged a handkerchief out of the small drawstring purse that hung from her wrist. "Well, dear Felicity, perhaps you don't need to actually tell me what the secret is, but *why* you're so upset about it. And how I or Mr. Quinn could help."

Felicity took the handkerchief and looked at Sophie with stunned eyes. "Why, that's . . . that's such an unexpected thing to say. Most people are so salacious, they would only want to hear the gossip, and they would try and convince me to tell them."

Privately impressed by her use of the word *salacious,* Sophie shrugged. "I know what it's like to have a secret—and how difficult it is to trust anyone. Or even whether you should. A secret is meant to be kept. Why don't you just tell me what you can without actually telling me what it is?" She automatically swished her hems out of the way of a muddy, smelly dog trotting past.

They'd left the President's House and Lafayette Square behind and were walking along the Avenue, just approaching the Willard. Although they passed people, the walkway was fairly clear. There was no one close behind them, so it was unlikely they would be overheard.

"My nanny died," Felicity said, sniffling a little. "Just in May. I loved her so much. She took care of me from the time I was a baby until April, when she got very sick. We did everything we could do for her; even Mr. Townsend sent Deucy—his manservant, that is—over with a home remedy," she said with a bashful smile. "She was like a member of the family . . . but she died anyway. And she—she told me something on her deathbed. A very big, terrible, *shameful* secret. Something I can never tell anyone. It's a matter of life and death." Felicity's eyes were downcast and she was fairly trembling as she bumped against Sophie while they walked.

Sophie's heart squeezed, for it was clear that whatever burden her companion was carrying, it was horrendous. Or at least, *she* thought it was horrendous. Sophie had enough experience to know that perception was not always reality. "Did you tell anyone?" she asked.

"No. But I think someone else knows. Or—or knew."

"Why do you think that?"

But here Felicity stopped talking and shook her head. They walked past the hotel and continued on down the Avenue with Sophie's hand tucked through the crook of Felicity's arm as if they were old friends. It hadn't escaped her thoughts—for Sophie's mind was always whirring—that she'd resisted the idea of doing so with Constance at the Capitol yesterday morning, but now, here she was with a woman she hardly knew but felt comfortable enough to do so.

Or perhaps it was simply that she knew Felicity was in desperate need of support, and Sophie was willing to give it, just as she had ended up doing for Constance yesterday after her father's accident.

"I'm getting married on August the first," Felicity said. "Carson Townsend is the most wonderful man I've ever met—after my father, that is." She managed a smile through her tears. "He even looks a little like him—I've always thought of my papa as a this big, friendly, golden giant, and my mama is this sweet angel hovering over me, a little dark-haired girl. And Carson is handsome and kind and I'm so very lucky to be marrying him."

"But this secret . . . you're afraid if it comes out, it'll make him call off the wedding?"

"Yes. How did you know that?"

Sophie forbore to explain how obvious her conclusion was, and instead replied, "Does Mr. Townsend love you? Or is this more of a family arrangement?"

"Oh yes, yes, he loves me. I know he does. We met at a fete last summer, and it was—it was love at first sight. That's what he said." Her dusky cheeks had grown more pink and some of the grief had faded from her eyes. "He knew my daddy from some business arrangement; I don't really know what it was. His family owns a big flour milling company, and—oh, I'm not certain. I think they were talking about investments and such. Incidentally, my mama is beside herself with happiness."

"But you're afraid if Mr. Townsend learns about this secret, he'll decide not to marry you. He'll cancel the wedding." Sophie was beginning to have an ugly suspicion about what Felicity's nanny had told her on her deathbed.

"Oh yes. He definitely will. He—he couldn't marry me, if he knew. He just couldn't." The tears were back in eyes that were dull with grief. "No one could," she added in a whisper.

And that was when Sophie figured it out—what Felicity Monroe's secret was.

Her insides clutched, because the young woman was exactly right. It was a matter of life and death, and her entire world would change if the information became known—the information Felicity's black nanny had told her when she was dying.

All of this conversation in conjunction with Felicity Monroe's dark hair, dark eyes, and dusky skin suggested for Sophie that the woman standing next to her must be part Negro. And, likely, that the dying nanny, who'd raised her from a child, was in reality her mother. Not just her nanny.

That information would indeed be enough to not only destroy Felicity's social standing—as well as that of her family—but could make her eligible for being sold into slavery. Surely her father would never do that, but if someday he weren't there to protect her . . .

Sophie shivered at the thought, and said, "Felicity." Her voice was sharp and urgent. "You can *never* tell anyone the truth. About what your nanny told you. *Never.* You understand that, right?"

"You . . . you know?" Her companion seemed shocked, stumbling to a halt. "But—how did you know?"

"I figured it out from what you were saying. And if I could, someone else could as well. And that would be so very dangerous to you." She squeezed her new friend's hand and thought about how awful it must be to discover that you weren't who you thought you were—who you'd been told you were—all your life.

"That's the problem," Felicity cried softly. "I think someone has found out. I believe someone has been threatening my father with it. Threatening to tell the truth."

Sophie's mind whirled with this new information. "What makes you think so?"

"Papa has been so different lately. Over the last few months. He used to be so jovial and happy, and so pleased about the wedding and proud of me, but not as of late. It was a sudden change too. And it's the way he looks at me—like he's afraid. For me. It's—it's in his eyes. He's afraid of something. He's afraid someone knows."

"What about your mother?"

"She's the same as she always has been. She doesn't seem any different. I don't think she knows . . . I mean to say, I don't think she's worried that someone else knows the truth. Of course she must know about—about me. My nanny—Dodie, was her name— she said no one in the world knew except herself and my parents. None of the other s-slaves knew because I was born when we all three were away somewhere, and when my papa came back, he sold all of the house slaves and bought new ones. And then six years ago, Papa moved us here so he could work as a lobbyist. And we got all new servants then too—free ones. So no one else could know. But now I think someone does."

She dashed away a new spate of tears. "I wanted Mr. Quinn to help me find out who it was—who is threatening my papa—so we could just pay the money and he'd leave us alone. That's what they call blackmail, isn't it? When you pay someone to keep from telling a secret about you?"

Sophie's heart broke a little more for Felicity Monroe. Not only was the young woman in a tenuous position—and would be for the rest of her life—but she was also determined and intuitive, while at the same time being terribly naive about certain things.

Sophie didn't know herself exactly how blackmail worked, but she suspected if someone demanded money from a person in order to keep their secret, that once they received the money, there would at some point be the desire to demand more. If it worked once, it would work again.

And if the person paid, they would pay again. And again.

Until they ran out of money or patience. And when the victim ran out of patience, what would he do?

"Do you have any proof that your father is being blackmailed? Any specific reason to think so?"

"There was a letter." Felicity started walking again, this time a trifle faster, as if she needed to put the situation behind her. "I didn't think anything about it at the time except that it upset my papa. But the last week, when another one came, I remembered before. Both times, my papa took the letter and—and his face. When he read it. Do you know how people say that someone's face turned white? Like they'd seen a ghost? That was exactly what happened to Papa the first time.

"I was standing there in the foyer with him when he was flipping through the mail our butler put on the front table. He was teasing me about all the bills for my trousseau—there were some in the pile—and how I was going to put him in the poorhouse." From the side, Sophie could see Felicity's lips curve softly at the memory. "And then when he opened this particular letter, he got very still and I actually heard him gasp. His face drained of all color, and all of a sudden he looked as if he'd been hit by an anvil. I thought he was going to drop dead right there, Sophie. It was so awful. It was like his whole self had gone away, but left his body."

"I suppose you didn't get to see the letter."

"No, he just turned around and walked away without saying anything to me. He went into his study and shut the door and he didn't come out for a long time. He wouldn't even open the door to Mama when she knocked. He didn't eat dinner with us that night either." Felicity's voice was so lost and woebegone, but she went on speaking as if she could no longer keep it pent up.

"I didn't really think much about it after that," she confessed. "Mama and I were going to New York for my dress and to buy more clothes for my trousseau, and I was missing Dodie so much that I allowed myself to get distracted. And then another letter came. I remember, because it was on July the first and that was the day some of the congressmen were expected back in town. Papa was entertaining some of the senators at the Willard that night, and he was in a fine mood.

"And the mail came. I brought it to him in his study where he was reviewing some papers. When I handed it over and he saw the letter on top, he did the same thing as before—he seemed to freeze, and his face turned gray. He took the mail and told me to leave. But it was his voice. It was so dead and—and quiet . . . Papa is never quiet. He has a big personality and a powerful voice, and this was just so . . . different. It was awful. He was so defeated."

Somehow, they'd reached the foot of Capitol Hill, and now stood beneath a large oak tree at the foot of the broad steps. It was almost the same location of the accident that had injured Hurst Lemagne yesterday. There were people and carriages milling about. Sophie glanced around quickly in case Mr. Quinn was in the vicinity—hadn't he been called to investigate another death at the Capitol?—then returned her attention to her companion.

"All right, Felicity, let's think about this. Your father could have received bad news about any number of things. What makes you think those letters were someone blackmailing him about—about you?"

The other woman paused, stopping right there on the sidewalk so quickly that Sophie kept going and jerked her arm. "Well," Felicity said, "I hadn't really thought about why. I just . . . knew. But *how* did I know?" She was quiet for a moment, then nodded. "I remember now. I could tell it had to do with me, because he sort of looked at me with those haunted eyes and said my name. Felicity. As if he were about to deliver to me the worst news ever. Then he shook his head and said *no* in this sort of agonized whisper."

"That was the first letter."

"Yes."

"And that was after Dodie told you about . . . everything."

"Y-yes. It was just before we were leaving to go to New York. So it would have been May twenty-fifth."

Sophie mulled on this. "And the second letter that came—that made him react that way—was only on Monday. When you gave your father the mail, you must have seen the letter on top—the one that caused him to react so strongly. Do you remember anything about it?" she asked, pulling Felicity gently away from the middle of the sidewalk to make room as a group of three men strode toward the Capitol steps.

To her credit, Felicity didn't respond immediately. After a moment of quiet, she said, "It was smaller than the other letters. That's why I put it on top. And the color of the paper was a little darker than some of the other envelopes." She closed her eyes as if to picture it. "Black ink, not pencil. The writing was a little smudged on the left. I noticed that because Papa's name—Henry—looked like 'Benry' and I thought it was amusing."

Sophie nodded. "Do you think there's any chance your father kept the letter? Or the envelope? If we could look at it, maybe we could learn something more."

"It was almost a week ago," Felicity said slowly. "I don't know. Papa's study is usually very cluttered, and he doesn't like the servants to move things around in there. But they do clean, and we do reuse old paper, of course. It might still be there."

"Do you think we could look around his study and see if we can find the envelope—or even whatever was in it?" Sophie tried to tamp down her enthusiasm for such an exciting prospect. "Would you recognize it if you saw the letter again?"

Felicity gaped at her. "Search my papa's study? Oh my goodness, I don't think so. He wouldn't like that."

Sophie privately thought Mr. Monroe probably liked being blackmailed even less, but she didn't say so. Instead, she was trying not to think about the logical conclusion of her previous thoughts: what happened when a blackmail victim no longer wanted to—or could afford to—pay?

Was it only a coincidence that Mr. Monroe had received a pre-

sumed blackmail demand on July first, then four days later, someone he knew named Pinebar Tufts was found murdered?

Yes, there were many people who died every day in Washington
City. Even more than one who might be killed on a given day. Sophie knew that. But there was something about this coincidence
that made her feel prickly all over.

Mr. Monroe must know the inside of the Capitol well, for he
conducted his business there, meeting with members of Congress
as he lobbied on behalf of the mining industry. He'd know how to
get inside the huge building undetected, and where to go to remain unseen. How to stalk someone . . .

Sophie did *not* like where her thoughts were going. At all.

"Did you and your family watch the fireworks on Independence Day?" she asked. If Mr. Monroe was otherwise accounted
for that night, he couldn't have been killing Pinebar Tufts.

"Oh yes!" Felicity seemed relieved at this change of subject.
"We were spread out on a blanket on the National Mall under a
tree—just over there, beyond those marble blocks on the other
side. It was a wonderful display."

"And your parents were with you?"

"Yes, and Carso—I mean, Mr. Townsend. And my mama's brother,
too, my uncle Stuart. He lives here in Washington as well. He's an ac-
countant and Mama teases him about being so boring he can't find
a wife. So instead he makes things—all sorts of contraptions. When
I was little, he made me a little dolly that had arms that waved
when I pulled a string. He doesn't live with us but Papa lets him
use part of the stable for his workshop." She smiled. "And there
were some of Mama's friends as well sitting with us because Ur-
sula—our cook—makes the best fried chicken and cornbread,
and no one ever wants to miss that. Even Miss Corcoran and her
beau stopped by to say hello when they were out driving before
the display. They just wanted some of Ursy's cornbread."

"It must have been dark by the time you went home after the
fireworks," Sophie said.

"Mr. Townsend drove me home. Papa allowed it this time, because he and Mama and Uncle Stuart were in the carriage behind

us. But it was just Mr. Townsend and me in his landau because his manservant died over a month ago and he hasn't b-bought . . ." Her voice trailed off, but she went on. "He hasn't bought a new one." She looked down and Sophie suspected she knew what was going on in Felicity's mind. When she looked up and added flatly, "Mr. Townsend believes strongly in the peculiar institution."

Sophie nodded, and didn't speak for a moment. Her heart squeezed. Imagine loving a man who didn't—wouldn't—love who you really were? She'd always thought her situation with Peter and his family had been untenable because they wouldn't allow her to be who she was—but that was nothing compared to Felicity Monroe's awful plight.

"Did you all go right to bed when you got home after the fireworks?" she asked after they'd gone another half block. "Or did you sit around and talk for a while?"

"Why, we sat in the parlor and—why?" Felicity's frown was delicate, creating a charming little line between her brows.

"Oh, I was just curious." Sophie decided it was best to change the subject, though she was disappointed not to have learned more. "Shall we walk around and see if we can find Mr. Quinn? He was called to come here to the Capitol. Maybe he's still close by. Then I can introduce you."

But to her surprise, Felicity balked. "I'm—I'm not sure, Sophie. You're right—someone *might* figure out what Dodie told me, and if I talk to Mr. Quinn about it, he'll know and that's just one more person who could tell."

"Mr. Quinn would never tell anyone," Sophie told her firmly. "He's one of the best men I know. But if you don't want to talk to him about it, I can take your case. And do the investigation, if you want."

Felicity's eyes widened. "Would you? Oh, thank you, Sophie. I trust you. I'll pay you, of course. I have money of my own."

The idea of getting *paid* notwithstanding, Sophie felt more than a little pleased with herself. Yet she was a trifle nervous at taking on such a task. Dismissing her worries, she took her new friend's hand. "Thank you. But I must warn you—there might be

a time"—very soon, in fact—"when I have to share *some* information with Mr. Quinn." She was thinking that if her investigation
coincided with his inquiry about Mr. Tufts, that it would be un-
avoidable.

"All right," she said again. "You can tell him whatever you need
to. I just—I don't want to be there."

"He won't tell anyone. And—and your secret wouldn't matter
to him anyway," she added, thinking of how Mr. Quinn had always
acted around Dr. Hilton. And the way he talked about his Ojibwe
friends, who'd taught him how to track and read signs in nature.

"Just like you," Felicity said, blinking back a glimmer of tears.
"Even after you divined my secret, you—you haven't changed.
You haven't looked at me differently. Or treated me differently.
That's not going to be true for many other people."

Sophie's heart squeezed. "Felicity, you're the same person you
were before I knew. Nothing has changed."

And with that, her friend burst into tears. "If only I thought my
fiancé would feel the same way."

"It seems pretty obvious that the same man killed Billy Morris
as did Pinebar Tufts," Adam said as he helped George lift the
night watchman's body onto a table in the workshop under Great
Eternity Church.

"I'll take a close look over him and see if there's anything else
to find," replied the doctor, stooping to pick up a lantern that
Adam reckoned had been broken in the fight.

"I'm going to have a couple of soldiers posted outside your
door," Adam said, worry gnawing at him as he looked around the
mess of his friend's workshop. Drops of blood, broken furniture,
and the condition of George's face along with the way he was
moving funny at the torso were enough to have him taking extra
measures. "There are plenty of them around, and God knows
they could use something productive to do."

"No," George replied flatly.

"But—"

"You think my patients will walk up to the door if they see soldiers standing there? White soldiers?"

Adam went silent. The man had a point. "At least, let's get the door fixed and some better locks."

"I let them in. It was my own damned fault. Next time, I'm not letting anyone in unless I know them or they've got a real medical problem. And definitely not three at a time. Two I can handle, but those three took me by surprise. Now, get off with you and let me do my work."

Seeing that he didn't have any choice in the matter, Adam did so. Besides, he thought he should pay another visit to Mrs. Tufts to find out whether she knew what her husband was doing at the Capitol after midnight on Independence Day.

Since he'd dismissed the hackney, Adam walked back to Pennsylvania Avenue. He was just passing City Hall when he heard a female voice calling his name with great urgency.

Ah. He reckoned Miss Gates had heard about Billy Morris's murder. Adam couldn't control a smile, and he turned, walking toward her so she didn't have to get out of breath running up to him.

Today, Miss Gates was wearing a light blue dress, but the same straw bonnet with pink ribbons she'd had on yesterday. She was also moving toward him at a speed his mother would have called unladylike but wasn't actually running.

"Mr. Quinn, I've been looking all over for you," she said, wheeling to a halt in front of him.

"Well, I reckon if I'd known that, I'd've stood still all day long until you found me," he replied with a grin.

Her eyes widened a little. "That was a joke," she said, looking up at him as if unsure to believe her assessment. A little smile played about her lips.

"Indeed it was," he replied, then surprised himself by saying, "I'm on my way to speak to Mrs. Tufts again. Would you care to walk with me? Or we could take the omnibus a few blocks if you don't care to walk."

"Walking is fine. And my accompanying you would be an excellent use of time," she replied, and started off in the opposite direction he needed to go. "I have several things—oh," she said, turning back when she realized he wasn't following her. "Where does she live?"

Adam pointed and she fell into step with him. He reminded himself that her legs weren't nearly as long as his, so he kept himself to what felt like a snail's pace, but had Miss Gates trotting along quickly. He slowed a little more.

"I have a number of things to tell you," she said. "The first thing is, there's a young woman named Miss Felicity Monroe who was looking for you this morning."

Another one? Adam resisted the urge to rub the dent in his chin. What on earth was it about women coming out of the woodwork, wanting to talk to him? It made him feel a bit scritchy, having to deal with a lot of females. Just one—the right one—would be fine with him.

"She's a particular friend of Miss Lemagne's, and she stopped by to see how Mr. Lemagne was doing yesterday. When she found out you and Miss Lemagne were friends, she wanted to meet you, and I encountered her at the White House this morning, as I had gone up there to speak with you about Pinebar Tufts. But you had already left. I understand there's another body, then. Is it related to the Tufts case?"

"It was the same man who killed them both," Adam replied.

"So you're certain it was murder." She gave him a satisfied smile. "I told you it was."

"You were correct, Miss Gates," he replied gravely, though he found her grin contagious and had to fight one back of his own. He didn't think it was seemly to smile when one was talking about murder. "Dr. Hilton was able to confirm your suspicions."

"Confirmation is always helpful. How was Billy Morris killed?"

"It was the same way, except it wasn't made to look like suicide." He explained the conclusions George had drawn about Pinebar Tufts's death and how Billy Morris was killed.

"How awful," she said, rubbing her slender white throat as if in sympathy with the night watchman. There was no hint of a smile left.

They walked another half block before she spoke again. "Miss Monroe wanted to speak with you about hiring you for an investigation, but she's decided to retain me instead—since you weren't available. That is," she added, giving him a quick upward glance from beneath her bonnet, "I offered and she accepted with alacrity. In fact, she seemed quite relieved and even pleased to hire a female investigator instead. It's a . . . delicate situation."

Adam wasn't certain whether to be relieved not to be involved himself, or concerned about Miss Gates putting herself in such a situation. "I see."

"But as it turns out, I think it's very possible that Miss Monroe's situation is connected to Pinebar Tufts's death."

"I suppose you'd better tell me about it then, Miss Gates," he said dryly. "Although I reckon you were going to anyway, whether or not I needed to know."

"I assured Miss Monroe you would be discreet," she said primly, then launched into her explanation. "Miss Monroe's family is quite well-off and has impressive social standing, and she's about to get married to a man named Carson Townsend, who's the son of a big milling company in Richmond or perhaps it's Baltimore. Apparently, he's been living here in Washington for several years— managing this arm of the business, I suppose; maybe they supply to the government—but nonetheless, he and Miss Felicity Monroe met last year and fell in love. Their wedding is going to be a big society event on August the first.

"But Miss Monroe's family has a very big secret, which she just learned about only in May. The secret is scandalous enough that it would give Mr. Townsend ample excuse to call off the wedding. And Miss Monroe is convinced that her father, Henry Monroe— who is a well-connected lobbyist for the mining industry and knows everyone in Congress—is being blackmailed over this secret."

Adam appreciated her concise explanation, and they walked in silence for a few moments as she allowed him to absorb the information. He wondered what the secret was, but didn't ask.

"All right, go on and tell me why you think this is connected to the Tufts and Morris murders," he said instead.

"Not only did Miss Monroe mention that her father knew Pinebar Tufts," Miss Gates said, "but I find the timing very suspicious." She went on to explain about two letters Henry Monroe had received and how his daughter had come to the conclusion that they were blackmail demands. "The most recent one arrived on July the first, and Felicity—Miss Monroe—gave it to her father herself. And then four days later, Mr. Tufts is murdered. Mr. Monroe would have great familiarity with the Capitol building, of course," she added unnecessarily.

Adam nodded. "So your theory is that Mr. Monroe paid the blackmailer the first time, but when the second letter came, he reckoned the process could go on forever, and decided to put an end to it by killing Tufts."

"Yes. And for all we know, he might have received more letters in between the two Miss Monroe knows about, and he might have made other payments. I'm certain that the first letter she saw him open was the first one he ever received, based on her description of his reaction. According to her, he was shocked beyond words and his face drained of color. Surely the message had been the first of its kind."

"All right." Mrs. Tufts had mentioned her husband beginning to get more money around the end of May. The timing was definitely right. Before Adam could say more, Miss Gates continued.

"I suggested to Miss Monroe that we search her father's office and attempt to find the letters—or at least the envelopes—so we could try and identify the blackmailer, but she was too faint-hearted to do something like that." Her tone was disgusted, and Adam hid another smile. He reckoned that secretly digging around in someone's office was high on the list of things Sophie Gates yearned to do. "The only thing she could tell me about the envelope that contained the letter was that it was smaller than usual, and the paper was slightly darker than the other letters she had. And there was a little bit of an ink smudge on it. Not much that is helpful," she said, still obviously put out by the lack of information.

"Here we are," Adam said as they arrived at the Tufts home.

"This is your second visit to Mrs. Tufts?" she asked as they approached the door. "Is there anything I can do to help?"

"My second visit, yes. The first one was difficult, so I reckon having another female here might help Mrs. Tufts. She took the news badly and was doing very poorly when I left."

"The poor woman," Miss Gates murmured as he rapped on the door. "Have you told her that it was definitely murder?"

"She suspects, but I will confirm it today," he replied, just as the door opened a crack. "Mrs. Tufts? This is Miss Sophie Gates with me. She and I would like to speak with you for a moment. It's about your husband." Adam was more relieved than he wanted to admit, having Miss Gates present. And this relief became even more pronounced when he saw the red eyes and sallow, sagging expression on the widow's face.

Unlike the previous time when he called, Mrs. Tufts opened the door immediately, wordlessly.

"Mrs. Tufts, I'm Sophie Gates. I'm so very sorry for your loss. Thank you for letting us speak to you. I know this is a very difficult time. Would you like to sit down? I can make some coffee. Or tea?"

Adam fell back and let his companion take the lead with the grieving woman. It appeared that she was home alone at the moment. As Miss Gates maneuvered the other woman toward the kitchen, he took a moment to look around the main floor of the house. He'd only been in the front sitting room and the kitchen, and he was curious as to whether Piney Tufts had had a study at home, and what sort of paper he might have had to use.

Miss Gates's conjecture made sense, although he agreed with her sentiment that simply because Monroe knew Tufts, and Tufts had been murdered within four days of the most recent blackmail demand, might only be coincidental. Still, he'd take the opportunity to look around because so far it was the only lead he had. With a glance toward the kitchen—he noticed Miss Gates had maneuvered the seated Mrs. Tufts so that her back was to the front of the house, and he didn't have to wonder whether she'd done so purposely—he slipped across the short hall into the only other chamber on this floor.

It was, as he'd hoped, a parlor that seemed to double as a study or office. A bookshelf leaned against one wall, and there was a small desk crammed in the corner. A brocade sofa and one stuffed armchair were arranged in the center of the room with a tiny table in front of them. A small lacy thing was draped over the top of the table and a woven rug was centered beneath it.

With one ear cocked toward the kitchen, from which the sounds of conversation and the clanging of dishes—he couldn't imagine what Miss Gates was doing in there so loudly—came, Adam began to search the area. It was immediately apparent that the desk and its paperwork belonged to Pinebar Tufts, and if one hadn't already known he worked for the Patent Office, that fact would have become obvious as well.

There were all sorts of scraps of paper with notes about patents, designs, measurements, and even drawings. Tufts might have been an inventor himself, or at least a dreamer. There was a stack of Patent Office stationery where he'd made notes to himself— things like *review Patent no. 0004556* and *need an extra copy of no. 0003897,* and *check P. Martin's work on no. 0002321 & etc.* It seemed that Pinebar Tufts had taken his work home with him.

Nothing seemed unusual or suspicious, but Adam did remove one of the Patent Office stationery papers that had Tufts's writing on it. He wanted to compare it to the note that had been pinned to the dead man's coat. He was just about to leave the parlor when he noticed a sheaf of papers tucked on top of the row of books on the highest shelf.

Being so tall, Adam found it easy to reach the papers, and the fact that they were stored high enough that Tufts himself would have needed a stool to retrieve them suggested they were either intended to be kept from his much shorter wife's notice, or that they were so unimportant that they were put away in an inconvenient location.

Just as he pulled down the papers, he heard the sound of Miss Gates's voice carrying clearly through the house. "I can't imagine where he got to, Mrs. Tufts. Maybe Mr. Quinn stepped outside to—to see about paying the hack."

Adam swiftly moved across the room as he tucked the papers into his coat pocket. He was on his way to the kitchen just as he heard the sound of a chair being pushed back from the table, and saw Mrs. Tufts rise.

"I beg your pardon," he said as he walked into the kitchen. "I had to—er—see to the hack." He never lied, but in this case, Miss Gates had already set up the story and he couldn't think of another excuse quickly enough. It wasn't as if the house was large enough to become lost in. "Mrs. Tufts, thank you for agreeing to speak to me again."

The widow sat back down gratefully. Her eyes, though still tinged red, were clear. "Miss Gates has just told me that you're certain my Piney was *murdered*. Is that true?"

Adam glanced at Miss Gates, then returned his attention to Mrs. Tufts. "Yes, ma'am. There's no doubt that he was murdered, and then it was made to look as if he'd hanged himself."

To his surprise and relief, the older woman merely took in a shaky breath and nodded. "I knew he would never do such a thing to himself, my Piney. In a way, it's a bit of a relief to know."

"Yes, ma'am." Adam couldn't help but agree. "Now I'm trying to find the man who did this to your husband, and so I've got to ask you some more questions."

Mrs. Tufts nodded, curving both hands around the teacup in front of her. Adam smelled the strong coffee that wafted from it and before he could think to ask for some, Miss Gates set a full mug in front of him. He gave her a grateful smile as she took the third seat at the small table.

"Someone wanted your husband dead, Mrs. Tufts," he said quietly. "Do you have any idea who might have wanted to kill him?"

"You asked me this before, but I-I was in such a state that I just couldn't think at the time. But I've done been thinking about it, Mr. Quinn, ever since you left, and I still can't think of anyone who'd want to harm my Piney. He was a good man. Lived in his head a lot sometimes—always wanted to hit a gold streak like those miners did, or make it rich somehow. Why, if it wasn't for me and Priscilla, I know Piney would have gone to California back in the 'Fifties. But he stayed here with us—Pris was just a baby, and I was expecting another . . ." Her voice trailed off and

Adam knew better than to ask what had happened with her second pregnancy.

"Piney loved working at the Patent Office because he got to see all of the different ideas people had—all the strange and wonderful inventions people come up with. If he'd had the money, he'd have invested in some of the ones he thought were good ideas. He told me all the time, 'Marybelle, I wish't I had some money to put down on number' . . . whatever it was. He'd rattle off the patent number like it was his own birthdate." She laughed affectionately, looking down into her mug. "My Piney wasn't any sort of inventor himself, but he had a good mind and he fancied he knew what was going to make it and what wasn't. He even made suggestions to some of the people who applied for patents—sending them off his thoughts on improving their inventions. He received many thank you letters from the inventors over the years."

Adam was quiet for a moment, then said, "Did Mr. Tufts know a man named Henry Monroe?"

"Henry Monroe . . . that name does sound familiar." Mrs. Tufts said thoughtfully, then suddenly she looked at him. "That's the daddy of that Miss Monroe, who's getting married to that handsome young man from Richmond, isn't he? I read about it in the society pages." She blushed a little. "I do enjoy reading about all the fancy dresses, and who is sparking who, and all of the other gossip."

"And why not?" Miss Gates said. "It's a fascinating study of human character. I always read the society pages when I lived in New York. Do you know how your husband knew Mr. Monroe?"

"Now let me think. I certainly recognize his name—oh, yes. I remember now." Her face lit up with pleasure. "It was through the Patent Office. Mr. Monroe was interested in putting money toward a particular invention, and Piney was meeting with him and the inventor to talk about it. Not that Piney was an expert, you see, but as I said, my Piney had good ideas. Some of the local inventors always wanted him to be the one to file their patents when they came in so that he could tell them what he thought."

"Did Mr. Monroe invest in the patent?" Adam asked.

"Oh. Oh, good heavens, well, I don't know."

"Do you remember when your husband met with Mr. Monroe?" Miss Gates asked as she gestured with the kettle, silently offering Adam a refill on his coffee. He shook his head.

"Oh. Well. It must have been in the spring I think. I don't remember exactly when."

"What about when he died? Do you know why Mr. Tufts was at the Capitol Building that late at night? We reckon he got there after the fireworks were over and was killed shortly after." Adam finished the last swallow of his drink while waiting for her reply.

Mrs. Tufts drew in a deep breath. "He didn't tell me where he was going that night. All I know is that Piney said he had an appointment. An important appointment that, if it worked out, everything was going to change for us. That's when he was talking all about the carriages and new dresses and all of that." She flapped her hand vaguely.

"Did he give you any idea who the appointment was with?"

She looked at him. "No. And it seemed . . . well, I'm not even sure he had an appointment with anyone at all. He mentioned something about the time, and how he wanted to be there early before something was dropped off."

Adam exchanged glances with Miss Gates, then, when she shook her head to indicate she had no other questions, he pushed back his chair. "Thank you very much for your time, Mrs. Tufts. If you can think of anything else that might help us, I hope you'll send for me at the—"

"Or you can contact me," Miss Gates interrupted, giving him a quick, quelling look. "I live at the Smithsonian Institute with my uncle, the director, Dr. Henry. You can get word to me by sending over to the Castle." She rose and began to stack the mugs and kettle on the counter next to the water pump and sink. "Did you say your daughter would be here soon? Would you like me to stay until she arrives?"

"Yes, Pris will be here at three o'clock. Oh, thank you, Miss Gates, but there's no need for you to stay. I'll be fine alone."

Moments later, Adam and Miss Gates were back on the street.

Before he could speak, she said, "The Tufts are Secessionists, and so I didn't think it would be prudent for you to mention you were living at the President's House."

"And since your uncle is rumored to be a Southern sympathizer, it was safe for you to mention him," he replied.

"Precisely. And it's only a rumor. Well," she said briskly, "that was a very helpful and enlightening conversation, don't you agree?"

"It certainly sounds as if Tufts was going to pick up something at the Capitol."

"A blackmail payment, surely. But the blackmailer decided to lie in wait for him and kill him instead," Miss Gates replied with such relish in her tone that he looked at her quizzically.

"You sound so delighted about Mr. Tufts's demise," he said.

"Not at all. It's just that things are falling into place rather neatly, don't you think?" She smiled up at him and suddenly Adam felt particularly good-humored. It must have shown on his face, for she said, "What's so amusing, Mr. Quinn?"

"I reckon I never thought of you as the type of woman to pore over the society pages. Did you call them an example of the human character?"

"A fascinating study of the human character," she replied primly. "And I was simply trying to create empathy with Mrs. Tufts so she would open up to us—me—more readily. I had very little interest in the society pages even when I lived in New York and was required to read them. I could care even less about them now. Incidentally, I find it quite surprising that you even know what the society pages are, Mr. Quinn." There was that smile again.

"I reckon I ought to confess right here that I haven't the least bit idea what society pages are," he replied truthfully. "Or why anyone would be required to read them, living in New York or not."

Miss Gates laughed. "Indeed."

Without thinking too hard about it, Adam offered her his arm as they crossed the street. To his mild surprise, she had no comment and slipped her gloved fingers around his forearm—his real one—as they stepped into the road.

"I suppose we should speak to Mr. Monroe," she said after a few moments of them walking along.

"We?" he asked, glancing down. He could only see the top of her bonnet and a hint of chin and nose now that she was walking so close to him. But at the same time, he felt the brush of her skirt against the leg of his trousers, and the warmth of her fingers. He decided that was a fair trade.

"I think it's only right, as I was the one who made the connection between him and Mr. Tufts," she replied tartly.

"I reckon I can't argue with that, Miss Gates."

"How is Mr. Lemagne doing? He was in a bad way yesterday when I left," she said suddenly. "I'm certain you've been by to call on the family."

"Yes, in fact I was there just before noon. As it turns out, Dr. Hilton was able to fix up Mr. Lemagne's leg last night. He says he'll be able to walk again within a month—perhaps sooner."

"That's wonderful news," she replied enthusiastically. "I'm certain Miss Lemagne was relieved."

"She was."

"She must have been happy to see you when you called," Miss Gates said.

"Yes, she was." For some reason, Adam felt strange about this turn of their conversation. "She was—uh—very grateful to Dr. Hilton for his help. I arrived just as she was telling Dr. Forthruth to see himself out."

"Was she?" Her question was posed in a way that he knew didn't require clarification.

Suddenly feeling awkward, Adam fell silent as they walked along, navigating between other passersby on the sidewalk.

"Have you ever met Miss Lemagne's friend Mrs. Rose Greenhow?" his companion asked after an unusually long silence.

"Yes, I have. Briefly." He wished he could see her face, but that damned bonnet blocked the view unless she was looking up at him. Which she wasn't at the moment.

But then she stopped. They had just reached the bottom of Capitol Hill on the Pennsylvania Avenue side, not far from where he knew Billy Morris had been killed. She pointed to a bench. "Would you mind sitting for a moment? I find it annoying to have to crane my head to look up at you, Mr. Quinn, and I have something important to tell you."

"Of course."

Miss Gates plopped down onto the bench with little fanfare, ignoring the way her skirts settled, bunching around her.

Adam took a seat next to her, but far enough away that he could see her beneath the bonnet. "What is it, Miss Gates?"

She huffed out a breath and looked up at him. "First, I believe it would be permissible for you to call me Sophie—if you like. Now that we're working together on these investigations, we needn't be so formal, need we?"

"I'd like that, Sophie," he said, and liked the way her name felt when he said it. "And you must feel free to call me Adam."

"Excellent. Thank you. Now, for the other thing I wanted to tell you . . ." She hesitated, then plunged on. "It's about Mrs. Greenhow. I don't trust her. In fact, I think . . . well, I think she might be a spy for the Confederacy."

CHAPTER 9

Monday, July 8

*I*t was late in the afternoon on Monday by the time Sophie was able to visit the Patent Office, even though it was just a stone's throw from the Capitol and the White House. But she'd been required to spend time with her aunt, uncle, and cousins Saturday afternoon and all day Sunday—including attending church services and having dinner with some of Uncle Joseph's colleagues.

During the last few days, however, Sophie mulled over whether she'd been right to tell Adam Quinn her suspicions—slim as they were—about Rose Greenhow. The last thing she wanted was for him to think she was trying to tarnish Constance with the same brush as Mrs. Greenhow—which she absolutely wasn't. Just because Mrs. Greenhow was acting suspiciously, that didn't mean Constance was involved.

But that didn't mean she wasn't.

Adam had listened to her reasoning with that sober, thoughtful expression with which she was familiar, but in the end gave her no indication whether he believed her, agreed with her, or would even do anything to investigate.

So, she decided, if he wouldn't, she would. But first, Sophie was going to follow up on the Pinebar Tufts case by poking around the Patent Office. She hadn't been inside the grand building before, although her friend Clara Barton had talked about it often. Built in the same neoclassical style as the Treasury and War Buildings, the Patent Office took up the entire block between F and G Streets, and Seventh and Ninth Street. A massive, three-story structure with elegant columns and a jutting pediment above its portico, it housed the entire Department of the Interior. The place was one of the busiest government buildings in the city.

A regiment from Rhode Island had been barracked there back in May, when the sudden influx of troops had overwhelmed Washington, but according to Clara, they were gone and the office had been put back to rights. Sophie walked up the steps, noting the scores of other visitors coming or going, most of them well-dressed men. Some of them were carrying large boxes with complicated machinery jutting out of the top or satchels.

Inside, she made her way to the receptionist and asked for her friend.

"Miss Barton is a copyist in the north wing," the man behind the counter told her. Sophie felt the disdain rolling off him, likely over the fact that a woman was working in the office. Clara was the only female who currently did so, although Sophie wondered if that might begin to change. "Through that door, to the right."

She found her friend without incident, following the hallway lined with offices. Clara's work area was in a large, low-ceilinged space clustered with desks. Half of the desks were empty of workers, but laden with piles of paper, bottles of ink, and pens.

She found Clara carefully writing out the description of a patent from an original document on her desk.

"Sophie! How nice to see you." She rose and stretched her arms and shoulders, slightly twisting her back. "I was just going to finish this page, and then go home for the day." Clara was older than Sophie, in her thirties, and had never married. She was a petite, shy woman who'd nonetheless managed to get a job in the male-dominated office—a feat in and of itself.

It was Clara who'd started the movement to collect donations of supplies for the Union soldiers after a trainload of injured troops had arrived from Baltimore in April. Sophie had met her then, and they'd been friends ever since.

"I was hoping you could show me around your workplace a little," she said to Clara.

"Are you thinking about trying to get a job here?" her friend asked in a low voice. "It's not as busy as it was, so I don't know if they are hiring."

"Oh, probably not," Sophie replied vaguely. "Goodness. How many copies of each patent do you have to write?" she asked when she saw the stacks of paper.

"Ten. At least. Sometimes more, if the inventor wants to pay extra." Clara flexed her fingers, which were gloveless and stained with ink. "It can be tedious work, but it pays well enough."

Sophie followed her around as she showed her the copyist's room. "There are twenty of us right now, and we write copies of patents as well as any correspondence that go out between the examiners and the inventors."

"Wasn't Mr. Tufts one of the examiners?"

Clara's eyebrows shot up. "Oh, I see why you've come to visit," she said, smirking a little. "Yes, Piney Tufts was one of the assistant examiners in the Civil Engineering Division. With the war, submissions have slowed down quite a lot and Commissioner Holloway just released five assistant examiners and five second assistant examiners—some of them were because of their sympathies, you know. But with Mr. Tufts gone, they may need to hire another one. Did you see all the models when you came in?"

"Models?"

"Oh, you must have come in from the south if you missed the display. Come with me."

Sophie followed as Clara explained. "Every patent that is submitted must come with a working model of the invention, no larger than twelve inches by twelve inches. And since we receive over three thousand patents a year, that means there are a lot of little machines and gadgets that need to be stored."

"Oh, that's why there were so many model shops on F Street," Sophie said with a laugh. "They must do a lot of business."

"It seems like every week a new one opens, usually right in this area," Clara replied.

"So *all* of them are on display?" Sophie said, just as they walked into the great hall in the west wing. She gasped at the sight.

The gallery was three stories high, with a vaulted ceiling and a curved glass roof to let in the light. Three levels of walkways passed along its great length, with an open center from the ground floor to the ceiling. Glass cases lined the walls everywhere from the white tiled floor to the roof. People—mostly men—crowded the area, peering into the cases one by one.

Miniature machines and gadgets crowded each case. Sophie identified several of them—a sewing machine, a strange-looking frying pan, a unique water pump handle—but there were many other models whose purpose was lost on her.

Nonetheless, she couldn't pull her eyes away. "It's amazing. It's like an inventor's dream. Or a toy shop."

"Or nightmare," Clara said. "Anyone who wants to have a patent approved needs to look through all of the other patents that have been previously approved—and the models—to determine whether their invention is, in fact, new and unique. That's why there are so many people here," she added in a low voice. "Lawyers and inventors and examiners are always milling about, digging through the cases, looking for information about previous patents. And that's why we copyists have to make so many copies—so they can be sent out to the libraries in other big cities. Not everyone can travel to Washington every time they want to file a patent."

Sophie was standing in front of a case, staring at a miniature piece of machinery crammed in amid several other models. It was a container that had clawlike hands and snakelike pipes writhing from it. "What on earth is this?"

Clara laughed. "I have no idea. It looks like some sort of fancy water bucket—with a drain, perhaps?" She sighed. "Unfortunately, when the Rhode Island troops were here, they broke a lot of the cases—Mr. Bronwick, the clerk for the Agriculture Division, told me that four hundred panes of glass have to be replaced because of the destruction. And some of the models were stolen too." Her face was set grimly. "Heaven knows we need our troops, but they should show respect to our national buildings and property."

Sophie knew Clara was likely referring not only to the destruction here at the Patent Office, but also what had been done when soldiers were barracked in the Capitol. They'd both been inside visiting soldiers during that time and had seen the mess firsthand.

"The troops need something to do," Sophie said. "Soon. All the ones that came from the north, right after the firing on Fort Sumter—their ninety days are almost over. Then they can go home."

"Everyone here keeps talking about a battle in Manassas," Clara replied as they strolled along the hall. "If old Fuss and Feathers is going to send them off to fight, he'll have to do it soon or he'll lose all of his men."

"Mr. Quinn says there is a lot of argument over whether the men are ready to go," Sophie told her. "And the president is torn between what General Scott and General McDowell are telling him—that they aren't ready—and the pressure Congress is putting on him to do something. They want him to act decisively before the men all go home."

"Oh, Mr. Taft," said Clara suddenly, pitching her voice toward a man on the other side of one of the cases. "Do you have a moment?" She dropped her voice and murmured to Sophie, "Mr. Taft is an examiner in the Civil Engineering and Firearms Division. Mr. Tufts was one of his assistant examiners."

"Yes, Miss Barton? Why, Miss Gates, is it?" Mr. Horatio Nelson Taft gave a brief bow of recognition. He was in his late fifties, with thinning white hair combed straight across his head and a clean-shaven, pleasant face. "How are you doing today, ladies?"

If Clara was surprised that her coworker knew her companion, she didn't comment. Sophie responded, "What a pleasure to see you again, Mr. Taft. I'm enjoying the beautiful weather—and am simply fascinated by all of these inventions. What an interesting place to work. Tell me, how are your boys doing?"

She'd met Horatio Taft during the week in April while she stayed at the White House when everyone expected the city to be invaded by the Southern forces. Adam had insisted on her living there temporarily, for Sophie's aunt, uncle, and cousins had evacuated the city and he didn't feel it was safe for a young woman to be staying alone in the Smithsonian. Sophie hadn't disagreed too vehemently—after all, the man had a point, *and* living in the Executive Mansion would give her a unique perspective for the news stories she wanted to write.

"Bud and Holly are just the same as always—filled with energy and always getting into trouble. Of course," he added with a smile, "they're usually not alone in their predicaments, are they?"

Sophie laughed heartily. "Not at all. In fact, I think everyone agrees it's more Tad than anyone else when it comes to those four boys stirring up trouble." Tad and Willie Lincoln were inseparable friends of the Taft boys, and anyone who spent any time around the President's House knew what havoc the quartet could wreak. The Tafts' oldest child, fifteen-year-old Julia, was often sent to accompany the boys to and from their playmates' house. She was at the White House nearly as often as her brothers, and Sophie had also met the pleasant young woman several times while she sat in one of the parlors reading books that her father wouldn't approve of.

"That wouldn't surprise me," Mr. Taft replied. "Why, last week Julia came home and told me that Tad and Willie had arranged it so all of the servants' bells in the whole house rang at one time, summoning the entire staff to Mr. Lincoln's office at once. He was in the middle of a Cabinet meeting." He appeared both pained and amused by the situation. "Fortunately, the president only laughed and sent the servants on their way. I spoke severely to Holly and Bud, but of course, Tad and Willie do have the run of the mansion."

"Indeed they do," Sophie replied, having seen herself the way the two Lincoln boys charged down the corridors and in and out and through whatever rooms they wished, at any time, at any volume. It was difficult to fault them though, for they were darling, funny, intelligent boys—especially the older one, Willie, who was adored by everyone. "Is it true that Tad was riding in his wagon pulled by goats, and he drove it into the house one day?"

Mr. Taft's lips twitched, but he kept the smile in check. "Yes— right down the hall past the Red and Green Rooms and into the

Blue Room. Several congressmen and a senator nearly got their heels taken off and their legs bruised when he raced through the house. One of the ones whose feet were run over told me that Tad is 'more numerous than popular.'"

"Dear Heaven," Sophie said, grateful that she wasn't in charge of the little boys. She changed her expression from amusement to soberness. "It was just awful about Pinebar Tufts, wasn't it? I happened to be at the Capitol last Friday when it—when he was found."

"Just terrible. Tufts was a pleasant man, easy to work with. Had a good eye for patent work too, and mechanics," Mr. Taft said. "He was brought on not long after I was, about four years ago." He tilted his head to look at her. "Julia says that Adam Quinn is investigating the case, as he did with the killing at the White House back in April."

Sophie hid a smile. Apparently, Adam's—it was still strange to think of him by his familiar name—reputation was growing, whether he wanted it to or not. "Yes, and I've been assisting him, as I did before."

Mr. Taft's brows rose up his tall forehead. "I see."

Sophie could tell that he didn't really "see," but she plunged into her interrogation. She saw no reason to beat around the bush. "Did Mr. Tufts ever mention Mr. Henry Monroe or an invention Mr. Monroe was thinking of investing in?"

"Henry Monroe? Well, yes, I do think Piney was working with him on something. It wasn't a patent that came through my division, though. Something in agriculture, I believe. But it was his brother-in-law—Henry's wife's brother—who'd filed for the patent. It was approved, if I recall correctly."

Sophie remembered Felicity mentioning her uncle Stuart who was an inventor. "So Mr. Monroe was considering investing in the production of this patent? And Mr. Tufts was advising him?"

"Piney had a way of seeing things about gadgets and machinery where he could pinpoint the shortcomings. He couldn't make up his own inventions, but he could see the faults in others. I think he was helping Monroe and his brother-in-law—blast if I can remember his name—to smooth out any wrinkles in the idea before they went to find investors. But who knows—now that the war is here, they might have a more difficult time."

Sophie nodded. "That's very interesting. Do you know of anyone who might not have gotten along with Mr. Tufts, or who might have wanted to harm him?"

Mr. Taft drew back a little and his expression settled into something grave. "So the rumors are true, then? Piney was murdered?"

"Yes. It's been proven without a doubt by Mr. Quinn and Dr. Hilton. Do you have any idea who might have done such a thing?"

He shook his head. "No, I can't think of anyone who had a problem with Piney. He was just the sort of man who mostly got along with everyone. He did his work and lived for inventions and gadgets." He smiled softly. "I'll miss him around here. He was a good assistant examiner—and I was going to suggest he be promoted, but then everything slowed down here, with the war." He rubbed his clean-shaven chin. "I'll have to get the wife over to call on Marybelle Tufts again, poor woman. Mrs. Taft heard about Piney and went over on Saturday, but she wasn't home. I'll go with her next time. Piney was a good man. And I'm—well, while it's terrible that someone did such a thing to him, I admit I'm relieved he didn't do it to himself."

"Whoever killed him also killed Billy Morris," Sophie said. "The Auxiliary Guard who patrolled the Capitol."

Mr. Taft's eyes widened with shock. "Why, that's terrible. I hadn't heard about that. I—"

"Mr. Taft!" A young man came rushing up to their little group. "I've been looking for you. Your daughter, Julia, is downstairs. She says your sons are missing—along with the Lincoln boys!"

Adam had been unusually busy since Saturday afternoon, when he and Miss Gates—or, rather, Sophie, as she was now known to him—had called on Mrs. Tufts. Unfortunately, the tasks and problems with which he'd been occupied were unrelated to the murders of Pinebar Tufts and Billy Morris.

Pressure to end the war was growing from Congress, now that

they'd reconvened, and President Lincoln was wavering between the two factions pushing and pulling at him: that of the generals, who wanted more time to drill their troops, and the inflamed members of Congress, who wanted action—quickly and decisively. And with the majority of the thirty thousand troops of the Army of the Potomac nearing the end of their commission, something had to be done or most of the Union Army would disintegrate as the men returned to their homes up North.

Over the last two days, Adam had been sent off to meet with seven different regimental leaders as an unofficial representative of their commander in chief, as well as being involved in security arrangements for Mrs. Lincoln and the two boys. He was also starting to look seriously again for a private room at one of the boardinghouses near Penn Ave. He'd moved out of the President's House in late March, taking rooms in a small boardinghouse run by a Mrs. Hunter. But then the war started and Mrs. Hunter had evacuated the city, evicting her tenants in favor of the safety of Philadelphia, where her family lived. But it was time for him to find his own quarters again, now that it was clear he'd be staying in Washington for the foreseeable future. Adam had come to the conclusion that since he couldn't enlist with only one arm, his contribution to the nation and the war would be by serving Mr. Lincoln.

And, apparently, by solving crimes such as murder.

Despite all of these matters, Adam had also taken it upon himself to discreetly ask around about Mrs. Rose Greenhow. He knew the city was rife with Southern spies, and since Allan Pinkerton had returned from Chicago, he and his team had been spending a good portion of their time rooting out the informers, while doing some spying of their own.

But Adam didn't want to mention anything to Pinkerton about the widow—who, he'd learned, had recently lost her daughter Gertrude—or do anything to besmirch Mrs. Greenhow's reputation unless he had evidence. Or at least something more tangible than Sophie's hunch.

Along with all of these matters, the deaths of Pinebar Tufts and

Billy Morris continued to nag at him. He was determined that justice would be served to whomever had done the deeds; but he felt as if the investigation had come to a bit of a standstill. The only suspect he had so far was a man he'd been unable to speak to—Henry Monroe—simply due to the fact that he kept missing him at home or his office or at the Capitol.

Finally, late Monday afternoon, Adam had the opportunity to make his way to Monroe's office, which was just a few blocks from the Capitol. It was a rainy day and surprisingly chilly, and so Adam wore the coat he'd left home yesterday in the blistering heat.

As he walked, he felt a crinkle in his pocket. All at once he remembered the packet of papers he'd thrust in there as he exited Pinebar Tufts's office and was immediately annoyed. How could he have forgotten about them?

He found a bench in front of City Hall and sat down to look over the papers. Each was a folded note inscribed with a brief message. *In the Small House Rotunda beneath the North-side bench. July 4. No earlier than midnight,* read the top one.

The second one read: *Inside the Rotunda Crypt between the two outer columns at the South-most side. June 14. Between midnight and two o'clock. Deliver before noon June 15.*

A third one was similar, listing what Adam reckoned was a pickup location and then a drop-off date and time. That date was May 31.

Approximately every two weeks since the end of May. Who was picking up what? Were these directions for Tufts's blackmail victim? It appeared that when he'd arrived to collect his money on July 4, the victim had lain in wait to put an end to the harassment.

It made sense. But why did *Tufts* have the notes, if they were directions to his victim? Copies, perhaps. But why would he keep copies of such incriminating documents? Adam mulled this over, looking at the letters.

All were written in the same hand, and as he examined them, he realized the author must be left-handed because of a few light ink smudges from the writing hand as it passed over the fresh ink. Other than that, the notes provided no other clue to the identity of the writer. The paper wasn't any sort of stationery and was of common weight and color. None of the notes had envelopes, although they appeared to have been folded and sealed at one point, for Adam found a trace of blue wax on the edge of one, which strengthened his belief that these letters weren't copies Tufts had kept for himself, but messages that had been sent to him.

Adam frowned. Maybe Tufts hadn't been blackmailing anyone after all. Maybe someone had been blackmailing *him.*

But then why would someone have killed him? It didn't make any sense.

Adam folded the papers and stuffed them back into his pocket. As soon as possible, he'd compare the writing to the note that had been pinned to Tufts's coat. But since there were only three words on that note, it would be difficult to determine if the same person had written it.

He rose from the bench and continued on his way to Henry Monroe's office. Adam had just turned onto Seventh Street when he heard a male voice shouting his name.

It wasn't an uncommon occurrence to be hailed that way—how else was one to get his attention when he was two blocks ahead of them on the street?—but Adam was acutely aware of how often that had been happening lately. He turned and started toward William Johnson, Mr. Lincoln's valet and messenger, who was running toward him at top speed.

That told him something urgent was happening, and Adam picked up his own pace to meet William. The young man was out of breath. "Mr. Quinn, sir . . . the Lincoln boys . . . are missing! No one can find them . . . and they ain't been seen . . . since dinner . . . at noon . . ." He was huffing and puffing, and the expression on his face was one of fright and concern. "Taft boys are . . . with them."

"Does the president want me to come back to the White House to search there, or has the search gone beyond the grounds?" Adam asked.

"Tracks," gasped William. "Can you follow . . . tracks?"

"Yes." It was just as fast to walk as it was to find and hire a hack down the busy Avenue, so the two men started off back to the President's House on foot as Adam tried to quell his fear. The last thing his friend Abe needed on top of all of these war worries was for something to happen to the children.

Could they have been abducted? Intended to be used as hostages in the war?

Adam's chest felt tight as he began to run, leaving the already out-of-breath William far behind.

CHAPTER 10

"*I* just can't thank you enough for sending over Bettie to visit, and for all of the food as well," Constance said, reaching over to pat Mrs. Greenhow's hand. Indeed, her family had dined on several loaves of bread and a roasted chicken her friend had had one of her servants deliver. "My daddy is doing so much better, and the—uh—doctor says he should be able to begin walking within a fortnight."

It was late in the day Monday, and they were sitting in the elder woman's parlor in her well-appointed home at 398 Sixteenth Street. No one was present except the two of them and Mrs. Greenhow's eight-year-old daughter, Little Rose, who sat in a corner working on her embroidery.

"I expect Bettie is across the river and well on her way to the general by now," replied Mrs. Greenhow with a smile taut with nerves. "Please God, she'll get to Beauregard safely."

The two women clasped hands tightly for a moment, then Mrs. Greenhow released Constance's fingers and settled back in her chair with a sigh. "I declare, the waiting is so very difficult. I can't hardly sit without worrying about a knock at the door, coming with bad news—or good news." She sighed again. "Would you like some more coffee?"

"I'll pour it, thank you," Constance said. "Mrs. Greenhow—"

"Oh, you must call me Rose, Constance," she replied firmly. "We've become so close and have done so much together that it

strains the bonds of friendship for us to have such formality between us."

"Thank you. I feel the same way. As if you're the mother I never
had," Constance replied truthfully, for her mother had died when
she was ten. "It's so refreshing to be able to speak openly to you
about my hopes for the South. My daddy is so besotted with Mrs.
Billings—and she's *such* an abolitionist—that even he doesn't
speak as strongly about our boys anymore. I begin to wonder if
he's giving up on our way of life."

"And what about that handsome Mr. Quinn? Have you been
able to spend any more time with him?" Rose asked.

Constance sighed and settled back in her own chair. "He's
been so busy, and I've hardly seen him at all." It still bothered her
that he seemed to have forgotten she'd moved from the St.
Charles Hotel to Mrs. Billings's house. "And even then, usually
there are other things happening and I have no chance to speak
to him privately." But even as she spoke, Constance sensed a little
niggle of guilt. She liked Adam Quinn very much, and although
she liked—*loved*—her Confederate brothers more, she still felt a
trifle unsettled over trying to pry information from him.

There was something about Mr. Quinn—his loyalty, his integrity, his calm and intelligent demeanor—that made Constance
uncomfortable about using him for information. She was reluctant to tarnish those qualities that she so admired.

Which was silly. Because this was *war*. And if the Federals won,
if they somehow managed to quash her Southern boys, then their
entire way of life would be destroyed. Her daddy's plantation
would be in ruins because there'd be no one to work the fields.

And besides, if all the slaves were freed, what would they do?
They'd be completely lost without their masters. How would they
make a living? What would they even *do?* The image of Dr. Hilton
popped into her head and was immediately and vehemently dismissed as she went on to think about her dear Jelly. Why, if she
were freed and turned out of their house, the poor woman would
be inconsolate. She loved Constance like a daughter.

"Perhaps it's just as well," Rose said, "that you've been unable to acquire any information from Adam Quinn. Because then you'd be under suspicion if you were caught." Her eyes glinted with something that had Constance sitting upright once more.

"What do you mean?" Her heart galloped with excitement.

"I've come into possession of a very interesting map. Courtesy of a certain member of the Military Affairs Committee," Rose said with a sly smile. "Unfortunately, Bettie left on her errand before I obtained it, but the information would be of great interest to a certain Creole general in the vicinity of Manassas."

All at once, Constance's palms went damp beneath their gloves and her insides were fluttering. "I'll go. Rose, you know I'll go. I can, now that Daddy is recovering so well."

"I was so hoping you'd say that." Her friend smiled warmly. "How soon can you be ready?"

"Is tomorrow soon enough?"

"July ninth . . . the day General McDowell is supposed to leave with his troops? Yes, I think that will do just fine. One woman alone will travel much faster than that motley crew."

It was after five o'clock when Adam arrived at the White House to find it in disarray. Troops were searching the grounds while Mrs. Lincoln, her female relatives who were visiting, and the staff were still going through every nook and cranny in the house. He didn't waste time going inside to speak to the president—Mr. Lincoln had plenty to do besides talk to him—nor did he stop to interview anyone in the house about what they knew or where the search had gone.

Adam was looking for tracks.

His goal was to determine whether the boys had left on their own, or whether an adult—a potential abductor—had been with them, and of course, what direction they'd gone. He paused only to ask whether the guards stationed on the flat roof of the White House had seen the four boys on the grounds. They had, but it was much earlier in the day from when they'd gone missing, which was sometime after one o'clock.

No one had seen them in the stable, where their little wagon and pet goats were kept—along with ponies, horses, and a turkey that had been pardoned at Thanksgiving and saved from the oven. Tad's most recent critter acquisition—a scrawny, stinky hound—wasn't with him either, and was found sleeping under a tree by the stable.

None of the servants' children—with whom the Lincoln boys often played on the lawn—had seen them for hours, nor had any idea where they might have gone. The rooftop, where Tad and Willie often patrolled with empty rifles or turned into a pirate ship, was empty of shrieking, running boys. And most tellingly, no one had heard Tad's shrill bugle for hours.

Adam began by examining the grounds closest to the house. It took him nearly an hour as he made a circle from the east side of the mansion around the portico to the south, carefully trying to make out the trail he needed among all the other prints from patrolling officers and the search team. Along the way, he learned that a crew of men had gone from the mansion across the Ellipse down to the Canal. They were looking for signs the boys had gone in that direction, hoping none of them had fallen in. Another group of searchers walked around Lafayette Square and to and from the War and Treasury Departments, asking everyone if they'd seen the boys. They knocked on doors and stopped workers and hackney drivers.

Adam knew Tad and Willie particularly favored exiting the mansion from the ground floor, going out through the conservatory so they could play on the grassy lawn after pretending the huge greenhouse was a forest or adventure world. Because of all the searching that had already taken place, it was difficult to isolate any footprints, but Adam was finally able to find some of their much smaller foot markings that had been brought through the dirt on the floor of the greenhouse.

The greenhouse, which was connected to the White House by an enclosed glass walkway, was a magical place, and it was no wonder Tad and Willie liked to play there. The high, peaked ceiling was decorated with twelve colored transparent images, one for each month of the year. Now, in July, some of the doors and windows were open for a fresh breeze to today's unusually cooler weather, but in the winter, the place was closed up tightly and heated water created the humidity that allowed plants to grow all year around.

There were lemon and orange trees, large terracotta pots arranged on green tables like blankets and hillocks of colorful flowers. The rich fragrance of herbs, roses, lilies, and more filled the warm, heavy air. Baskets hung with spills of colorful blooms, and there were spirea, poinsettia, camellias, jasmines, ferns, and many other plants Adam couldn't identify. In the middle of the greenhouse was a large water tank that boasted goldfish the boys liked to try and catch with a net, the murky water topped by silky white and pink water lilies. And in the center of the conservatory was a large Sago palm that had once belonged to George Washington.

The only sign of the boys was a recent set of footprints exiting at the far, west end of the greenhouse, and it was that trail Adam began to follow. The process was tedious because of the thick grass outside and the many feet that had trampled the area since the boys had gone missing. The sun was still high in the sky, but it was beginning to touch the tops of the trees along the west stretch of the Potomac, which meant Adam had about four hours of full daylight left.

He was able to discern that the boys had left on their own— that is, without an adult or potential abductor—and based on the length and pattern of the strides, it seemed they had a destination in mind instead of playing and losing track of time and place. Adam followed and lost the trail several times over the south lawn of the Executive Mansion's grounds, but it appeared the quartet of Lincoln and Taft boys were walking without hesitation down to the Tiber River—which was an offshoot of the Potomac, directly south of the White House's huge south lawn. It was slow work, for several times the trail was obliterated by a cross path or other

footsteps, and Adam would have to start making concentric circles around the marks he'd followed to determine which direction to pick up the trail.

However, he saw no indication that anyone had joined the children, which relieved some of his worry over them being taken as
military pawns instead of merely going off on their own and for-
getting to come home. But there was also the fear they'd taken a
tumble into the Tiber, which flowed from the Potomac into the
Canal, or even, knowing Tad and Willie, gone as far as the big,
broad stretch of the Potomac and fallen in there.

Adam hurried as quickly as he could, for it was cloudy and now
the sun was dipping below the trees. The light was getting chancier
and the details of the sway or clipping or bending of the grass he
relied on to see direction and speed would soon be lost in the
dimming light. He reached the spot where the Tiber fed into the
Canal, which flowed the length of the north side of the National
Mall. Across the water, the Washington Monument, only half-
constructed, cast a stubby shadow over the slaughterhouse next
to it. Even from here, he could smell the stench of raw meat and
rotting entrails.

Cattle mooed and roamed as Adam followed the boys' trail and
was relieved to see it led to the bridge from Fourteenth Street
that crossed the Canal. As he loped over the murky, smelly water,
he heard the nearby, regular reports and answering echoes of
rifle shots. A portion of the Mall was also an area that had been
designated as a shooting range for some of the troops. Once on
the other side of the water, he lost the trail for a moment, and
Adam had a bad moment worrying that Tad—because it would
be Tad, the hooligan—had coerced his friends and brother into
joining the soldiers for shooting practice—or simply had gotten
too close to the targets.

Although he was certain someone from the search party would
have already checked that area, Adam shielded his eyes against
the lowering sun and peered toward the rows of soldiers as he
hurried toward them. No short, slight bodies in sight.

Instead of walking over there, he pivoted and went back to where he'd lost the trail. The Capitol Building was directly ahead at the east end of the Mall, frosted with pale yellow in the setting sun. The Smithsonian Castle and its seven towers spiked into the heavens just ahead of him to the right, and the waning sunlight made its red-orange brick glow like a blazing fire against the dark blue sky. He wondered if Sophie was there, and considered whether to ask at the Castle whether anyone had seen the boys. Surely someone else had already done so . . . if they could conceive that four young children would have gone that far on their own.

Anyone who knew Tad Lincoln wouldn't doubt that they would cross the Long Bridge into Virginia if they had a mind to do so, and that thought spurred Adam on. The boys could be anywhere, and conjecture wouldn't help. He'd keep his attention on marks and prints, relying on fact instead of supposition.

He crouched once more, trying to find the trail the foursome had left behind just over the Canal. At last he was able to pick it up two yards farther east—the boys had splashed around at the edge of the water for a while. Adam grimaced, thinking of the sludgy, sewagelike water in which they'd been mucking around. They'd be filthy and stinky—and probably cold, for it wasn't a warm day.

The trail he picked up had the quartet heading directly down the Mall toward the Capitol. He could see that they were in a hurry, and once more with a destination in mind—all because of the even lengths of the strides, the way their feet landed in the soft, muddy grass, and the lack of hesitation in any step.

Moving more quickly now, for this area wasn't as trampled or overwalked and the trail was easy to follow, Adam picked up his speed. By the height of the sun, he guessed it was after half-seven. The shadows were growing longer faster and soon he wouldn't be able to see much at all.

Then the tracks took a sudden sharp turn left, north, toward Centre Market on Seventh Street at Pennsylvania Avenue. Adam cursed under his breath, for he'd have no chance of following the path in or around the largest and busiest market in the city.

Sure enough, the boys had made their way to the large shopping area. A large, somewhat rickety building that had been constructed back when Jefferson was president housed booths for farmers and other merchants to offer their wares. Half the city visited there every day.

Adam stewed for a minute, standing there, wondering how he would ever be able to discern the boys' footprints from here.

"Mr. Quinn!"

At any other time, the sound of Sophie's voice would have been most welcome, but at the moment, Adam was frustrated and concerned. Nevertheless, he started over to meet her as she rushed toward him.

"Have they been found? The boys?" she asked. Her eyes were wide with worry, and that was when Adam noticed Mr. Taft and his daughter, Julia, hurrying along behind her.

"Not yet," he said, pitching his voice enough for the other man to hear. "I was tracking them from the President's House—"

"I *knew* it," Sophie exclaimed.

"But I've lost them here," he continued, trying and failing to keep the disgust from his tone. "There are just too many marks here, in and around the market. Mr. Taft, I'm sorry about this."

"I was at the Patent Office when Julia came with the news," Sophie said by way of explanation as she edged aside for a family making their way through the crowd. "We've been walking up and down the Avenue from the White House to the Capitol, asking everyone if they'd seen them. Even Mr. Birch at the Willard didn't notice the boys."

"I reckon I'm going to keep trying," Adam told her, scanning the area of vendor stalls, parked carts and wagons, and the milling crowd in the slim hope his great height would help him locate one of the youngsters. "And if no one has seen them on the Avenue, maybe they went back down to the Mall."

She spun in a slow circle as if looking as well. "So many people are helping to search. I'm sure they'll be found soon." He reckoned Sophie was about as optimistic as they came. "All sorts of people have joined in to help."

"I'm glad to hear about that." Adam couldn't push away a new, niggling worry that maybe someone had heard about the lost boys and had lured them away from the market. But surely they wouldn't take all *four* of them . . . even if it was for a military or hostage situation.

He hoped.

"Mr. Quinn! Mr. *Quinn!*"

With a sense of inevitability, Adam turned to see Brian Mulcahey flying toward him. "Mr. Quinn! I know where they are!" he shouted as he threaded none-too-gently through the crowd of people. He nearly knocked a loaf of bread from one woman's hand in his haste, and tripped with his too-big feet over the peg leg of a fish cart. He barely caught himself before he went sprawling, stumbling up to Adam in a mess of gangly limbs.

Adam looked down at him and swore the boy had grown two inches since he'd seen him Friday. "You know where the boys are?"

Brian nodded, gasping for breath. He pointed urgently and Adam followed his finger.

"The Capitol?"

"Yes," the boy managed to squeeze out. "I saw'em. I . . . talked . . . to 'em." He was clutching his middle as if it pained him. "Mr. Birch . . . told me you . . . was about lookin' for . . . them. I was on . . . to . . . getting home to Mam when I saw . . . him."

"All right. When you catch your breath, you can tell me more." Adam was already starting toward the Capitol, and as expected, Sophie, Brian, and the Tafts fell in with him.

It took a block before Brian could give a coherent explanation. "They're fun boys," he said right off, "even though they're younger. They were looking around back there, all around the Market, seeing if there were any live lobsters they could poke at, and that's when I met them. I was about showing them where the men were cutting off the frogs' legs, and then they were on about how hungry they were and how the bread smelled so good, and so I was telling them about the big bread ovens in the Capitol—remember, Mr. Quinn, you told me about them? They're baking them for all the soldiers?"

"Yes, Brian. Go on."

"And so they wanted to see the ovens. They were all about pretending they were soldiers, and so they were thinking they could be getting some of that bread for themselves, and so we all went up there to look. I didn't want to go inside," he said, glancing bashfully at Adam, "but they said as I could, because they were the President's sons—*gor*, I didn't even know that till then!—and I had their permission. And that they'd be getting a loaf of bread for us, pretty as you please, because they were fighting their Paw's war. And so that's what we did."

"And they were still there when you left?" Adam said.

"My mam would tan me if I wasn't home in time, so I had to leave before those boys. But when I left, they were on about having a pirate's treasure hideaway in the cellar there." Brian seemed disappointed that he'd been required to leave the fun.

"Thank you for finding me and telling me this. How long ago did you leave them?"

"Only just as long as it was taking me to walk from the Capitol to Willard's and say hi to Mr. Birch."

Adam felt relieved. Far less than a half hour, he reckoned. At the very least, there'd be fresh tracks to follow if the boys had left the Capitol—which was as good a possibility as any, knowing Tad and Willie.

"Good. Now, I suppose you'd best be on your way home so your mama doesn't tan you," Adam told him. "I reckon you ought to take her a peach pie for being late—tell her it's from Mr. and Mrs. Lincoln in thanks for helping to find their boys." He gave Brian fifty cents and gestured to one of the stalls that was just closing up.

Brian took the money and turned away, albeit reluctantly. Adam could see the regret in every step he took—he wanted to go back with them to find the boys, and, probably more likely, to continue the fun. "Off with you now, before your mama gets more worried."

Now slightly less anxious than he'd been, Adam automatically offered his arm to Sophie, who was doggedly trying to keep up with his longer strides. He slowed once again.

By the time they reached the Capitol building, she was a little out of breath, but still able to speak. "Where do we go inside? The main entrance leads to the second floor, and I think beneath the Rotunda is the Crypt. The"—she had to catch her breath—"basement must have its own entrance."

Adam, who'd circled and examined the grounds of more than half the building during his investigation, knew the answer to that. "The bakery is in the galleries under the Senate Chamber," he explained, reminding himself again to slow down.

With a glance behind, he saw that Mr. Taft and Julia were still making their way up the hill, but he saw no reason to wait for them. He directed his companion to the Senate Wing on the south—and farthest—side of the building.

The exterior ground floor entrance, built into the side of the partially subterranean wall, was cluttered with covered wagons, horses, and soldiers unloading supplies and loading up finished loaves of bread to be delivered to regiments all over the city. Adam and Sophie went inside to find even more activity within: large canvas bags of bread, ready to be loaded, sacks and barrels of flour stamped with the name of their mill, crates of eggs, buckets of water, tubs of yeast, and more.

The workers rolled barrels down the center of the broad, two-sided marble stairway that led from the ground floor into the basement. Shouts rang out and echoed in the cellar, which had high, vaulted ceilings. The place smelled like yeast and heat and fresh bread, and Adam felt the twinge of a hunger pang.

He counted fifteen ovens and thought there were even more beyond the columns holding up the high ceilings. The massive chimneys and an array of coal stoves shot up along the walls, and he wondered where they led or opened into the floors above. Surely not into the Senate Chamber itself . . . ?

Adam approached one of the bakers who was manning four of the ovens. He assumed he was one of the few who'd been in the same location for a while and so he asked, "Have you seen four boys, about ages eight and ten?"

The man shoved a long-armed wooden paddle into the deep brick oven, using it to move a tray of bread around inside. Adam felt the waft of heat from within and appreciated why the man was wearing only shirtsleeves and a pair of trousers. "Saw 'em and chased 'em on out of the way," he said. "Were about to get theirselves burnt, poking around in my ovens."

"Do you know which way they went?" Sophie asked.

"Don't know. Told 'em the bread was for the soldiers, and they tried to tell me they were ones." He laughed and swiped an arm over his damp forehead, pushing a swath of hair out of the way. "Maybe down yonder." He gestured to the right with his paddle, then moved on to another oven.

Adam and Sophie went off in that direction. He hoped to try and track the boys, so he kept his eyes open for smaller footprints made in the dirt and flour that covered the floor. They spoke to another baker, and one of the workers who was tossing cooled loaves into a large canvas sack to be delivered. Each time, they pointed them in a different direction, and after a while, they found themselves in another part of the basement, some distance from the bakery.

The noise of activity could still be heard, along with shouted directions and even some singing plus the sounds of dull thuds rang in the distance. But this was an almost deserted part of the cellar, and the floor was dirty and the damp foundation walls were covered with cobwebs and patches of moss and algae. Only some of the gas lanterns hanging from the walls worked, and the ones that did gave off a small, sickly glow.

"They must have been underfoot everywhere," Sophie said with a pained laugh as Adam paused to check the floor at the junction of three corridors that led even deeper into the basement. "Tad! Willie!" she called, cupping her hands around her mouth and aiming down a narrow, dark hall. "Bud! Your fathers are looking for you!" Her voice echoed into the cavernous space.

"This way," Adam said when he at last found their prints—the smallest sets of the myriad of marks throughout the area. He gave a mental sigh of relief when he recognized all four of the boys were still together. "No surprise—they're going down this empty hall here." Watching the floor, he took two steps, then jolted to a halt when he saw the footprint next to the trail he was following.

Like those of the boys', the mark was outlined clearly in flour—so clear, in fact, that he could tell the back heel of the right boot had a chunk missing from its corner.

CHAPTER 11

"Adam? What is it?" Sophie asked when she realized he'd stopped dead.

"Go on back and tell Mr. Taft that I'm on the boys' trail," he replied, but there was a tension in his voice that alarmed her. "Get him and some of the others to come and help."

"What is it?" She carefully crouched to look at the footprints he'd been examining, using the wall to balance herself since her dratted corset would hardly allow her to bend at the waist. "Are one of the boys injured? Did you see some blood?" She knew what an exceptional tracker he was and didn't doubt he could tell that or more.

"Sophie, please go back and do as I ask," he replied, looking into the darkness ahead of them. His false arm had come out in front of her, as if to keep her back—or to offer protection.

She looked up at him and pulled to her feet. "Adam, what's wrong?"

"Please go back and get Taft and some others," he said once more, this time from between clenched teeth. He reached for one of the lanterns that hung at the junction of the hallways and looped it over his prosthetic hand. "It might be dangerous."

She sighed, warring between exasperation that he wouldn't tell her, and embarrassment. The latter finally won out. "I would, but . . . I don't think I can find my way back." At his muttered exclamation, she defended herself. "We took so many twists and turns, I lost track. I was so busy looking for them and calling for them that I didn't pay attention." She looked up at him in the dim light and forced a smile. "I'd probably get lost myself."

"All right." She could feel *him* battling with himself now—she sensed he couldn't decide whether to lead her back or to allow her to come along. There was no doubt that *he* hadn't lost track of where they were. "I don't want to take the time to go back."

He shifted and dug through the pocket of his coat, and Sophie was shocked when he pulled out a revolver. "Please tell me what's going on," she said.

He pointed down. "That footprint belongs to the man who murdered Pinebar Tufts and Billy Morris."

She managed not to gasp, but didn't quite keep herself from taking an involuntary step backward. Even she could tell that the footprint was very fresh.

Suddenly, she wasn't enamored with the idea of going into a dim, narrow tunnel where a murderer might be lurking. But then—

"The boys!" Her eyes flew wide. "You don't think he's after *them*, do you?" She would have started off down the passage if he hadn't grabbed her by the arm and pulled her back.

"Quiet. And slow," was all he said, and started into the tunnel. "Don't step on the tracks—stay to the right side, please, Sophie, so I can see what they're doing."

Well, if she had to go into a dim, dark tunnel where a murderer might be lurking, the one person she'd want to go with—if it was only one, and not an entire troop of armed men—was Adam Quinn.

The vaulted ceiling had given way to a narrow, low, flat-topped covering that was only inches above Adam's head. The walls were still constructed from stone, but huge masonlike blocks instead of the costly marble that made up the more showy part of the building. Although they had their own light, its illumination was bolstered by occasional kerosene lanterns that somehow remained lit. Sophie hadn't been exaggerating—she had no idea what direction they were walking, or which way to go to retrace their steps.

She stayed close to Adam, holding the lantern for him as she listened carefully for the sounds of voices or footsteps. But even though she listened for them, she didn't call out for Tad and Willie as she'd done before. It seemed safer not to draw attention to any of them.

A sleek shadow moved at the periphery of the small circle of lantern light, streaking across the floor in front of them, and she didn't so much as snatch in her breath when she saw the long tail of the rat. Nor did she make a sound when a heavy swath of cobwebs caught on her bonnet and trailed across her face, clinging like a sticky veil. But inside she was shuddering and, if she were honest, even shrieking a little in her head.

It was dark, dank, dirty, and creepy down here, and knowing there was a murderer lurking about made it even more dark, dank, dirty and creepy. But Sophie was not about to leave those four little boys to the mercy of a killer even if she had to dodge rats, mice, spiders, and whatever soft, smelly things oozed in piles on the floor. She thought maybe she should consider starting to carry her own little derringer—especially since this was the third murder investigation she'd been working on, and she'd nearly gotten herself killed during the last one.

With that unpleasant memory now accompanying her, Sophie continued on, hoping this time she wouldn't actually come face-to-face with *this* murderer.

The going was slow, for Adam was now tracking two trails of prints. He didn't tell her that, but Sophie could see the way his attention scanned over the breadth of the narrow hallway, jumping from one area to the other. The fact that he kept the revolver in his hand and his other arm slightly back, nearly across her midriff, made her feel more comfortable.

Just so long as the killer didn't sneak up behind them.

She glanced back to make sure, and nearly bumped into Adam when he stopped.

They were at the junction of another corridor. She heard him mutter under his breath and without being asked, she brought the lantern closer to the ground where he was studying traces in the dirt.

"The boys went that way," he said, pointing to the left. "The killer went that way." To the right.

"At least they're not together," she said.

"Yes." Adam looked down at her, and she saw the consternation in his face as his jaw moved slightly.

She understood immediately. "I can go after the boys," she said. "You should try and find the—him." It was silly, but she couldn't get herself to say "killer" as they stood there in the empty, distant, foreboding tunnel. "Even I can follow their tracks from here."

She felt confident of that, at least, for the tunnel was so lightly traveled it was easy to see the marks of the smaller footprints.

But Adam shook his head. "No. You might get lost, or something else might happen." Like the killer somehow showing up. Sophie grimaced at the thought. "The most important thing is to find the boys. I can come back and tr—"

A shriek reverberated through the hall, coming from some distant location ahead of them. It was followed by another horrible screaming sound.

"Tad! Willie!" Adam bolted down the corridor, leaving Sophie to follow as well as she could. She gathered up her skirts in one hand and ran behind him, the lantern swaying wildly from her other hand. More shouts and bloodcurdling shrieks echoed through the dim warren of tunnels. Even when her foot landed in something soft and squishy, she kept going—although her insides twisted and heaved at the raw, putrid scent that now clung to her shoe.

Soon, Adam was so far ahead of her she couldn't see him or even hear his footsteps, and the calls and shrieks had stopped.

Sophie slowed to a fast walk, panting. She held the lantern high and clutched her skirts as she hurried along, ignoring the stitch in her side. She sincerely hoped there wouldn't be a turnoff in the corridor where she'd have to make a decision about which way to go.

Then she heard voices—exuberant, boy voices—and the sounds

of enthusiastic movement in the distance. No one sounded distressed, and they seemed to be coming closer.

"Adam?" she called as loud as she could, though she was still panting a little. Her voice echoed down the expanse of tunnel. "Willie! Tad, are you there?"

When Adam's response echoed back—"Coming! They're here!"—Sophie felt such a wave of relief that she stopped in the hallway to catch her breath.

They were near, and she could actually hear the boys bouncing and running as they made their way toward her.

"Miss Gates!" cried Willie, who was the first one to come into view. "We had so much fun!" He threw himself into her arms for a hug, which she happily gave back. He really was the sweetest little boy.

"It was like a pirate's treasure cave," Tad shrieked, barreling down the hall toward her. He was carrying a long stick and narrowly missed jabbing it in the ground—and his brother and Sophie—as he came dashing up. "Me and Bud was torturing them—Willie and Holly—for them's treasure!"

Sophie met Adam's eyes as he came into view behind the quartet of loud, bouncy boys. There was a mixture of relief, exasperation, and levity in his face and Sophie concurred with each one of those emotions.

"Come on, you ruffians," he said firmly, gesturing to the hall in front of them. "It's long past time for your dinner. March."

"But we had some bread!" Holly spun as he shouted at the top of his lungs, surely just so he could hear the words reverberate down the tunnel.

"Let's go," Adam said, a trifle less patiently. "Straight ahead, right at the next tunnel. March, young men."

"But we didn't get to explore—"

Tad's complaint was cut off when Sophie took him by the ear. It was the only way to get his attention. "Young man, do you know how worried your mother has been all these hours you've been gone?" she said, giving him a stern look. "Not to mention your papa? You don't want to keep them worrying anymore, do you?"

To his credit, Tad—who adored his father—sobered. "We was gone a long time, wasn't we?"

"You certainly were," she said, still stern. But she released his ear and took his small hand, ignoring whatever grimy, sticky, gritty mess was on it. "Everyone in the whole house, and lots of other people in the city were looking for you, and now they all want to go home and have their dinners. And besides, your dog—what's his name?"

"Splot," said Tad, trotting along with her. "Like a *splot* of something falling on the ground."

Sophie thought she knew exactly what he meant by a splot on the ground because she'd stepped in one. "Splot, then, is waiting for you to feed him. He's awfully hungry too."

This appeared to make sense to him and his friends, and although they seemed to be nowhere near running out of energy, the four moved along without distraction now.

Sophie and Adam walked behind them, and although they didn't converse, he seemed far more relaxed than before.

But Adam still had his revolver in hand, and Sophie noticed he didn't put it away until they reached the bakery.

Mr. Taft was relieved to see his sons, and he immediately took them off, Sophie presumed, to give them a bit of a tongue-lashing at home. Although she suspected he'd be somewhat lenient, as it was always Tad and Willie who were the instigators in their adventures and they merely dragged the Taft boys along like flotsam on the river of their activity.

"I can take the boys back to the President's House," she told Adam as they walked out of the Capitol. "If you want to . . . go back in there and see what you can find with those tracks."

"No," he replied. "It's after dark, and it's most certainly not safe for you to be walking down Penn Ave, even with those hooligans. Too many soldiers with nothing better to do than cause trouble."

Sophie opened her mouth to argue—for heaven's sake, there were plenty of people about and the Avenue was the most well-lit street in the city—but the expression on his face stopped her short.

"Very well, then, I suppose I can have no argument, Mr. Quinn," she replied, giving him a prim look from beneath her bonnet— then realized there were cobwebs dangling from it. With a sound of disgust, she untied the ribbon and temporarily removed the hat so she could pull off the remnants of the sticky veil as they began to walk back to the White House.

Adam had already sent a messenger off at a run to deliver the news to the Lincolns posthaste, and at last they set off down the Hill to the Avenue. As the two of them went, along with the boys— who finally were showing signs of exhaustion, setting a surprisingly slow pace, Sophie finally had the chance to speak to Adam.

"So the killer was in the tunnels," she said, pitching her voice just loud enough for him to hear, but not the two Lincoln boys. "What do you think he was doing there?"

Adam shook his head. "I reckon there's lots of reasons he might have been down there. Could be he works in the Capitol and was just going from one place to another. Could be he was looking for something—or someone."

"Do you think he was after the boys?" she asked, tilting her head so she could see him beyond her bonnet brim. "Everyone in the city knew they were missing."

By the way his jaw set, Sophie knew Adam had wondered the same thing. "I don't know."

"Tad. Willie," she said, and stepped forward to catch each of them by the hand. "When you were playing pirate in the tunnels, did you see anyone down there with you?"

"There was lots of people," Tad said. "They kept chasing us away, and all we wanted—"

"She means when we got aways from those baking people," Willie told him loftily.

"Yes. When you were way deep inside the tunnels, did you see anyone?"

"A man? With light-colored hair?" Adam said, giving Sophie a bit of information she hadn't known. So the murderer was fair, was he? "Not so tall as your pa, though." Hmm. Another crumb of information.

"Oh yes, we seen a man in there," Tad replied.

"Did you talk to him? Where was he?" Adam asked.

"He was in the tunnels, walking along like he was going some-wheres—he told us to quiet down and stop disturbing people. So we went a different way to get away from him," Willie said. "He was mean."

Sophie's heart lurched. "Was he mean to you?"

"Not to *us*, but he talked mean. And he had a mean face," Tad said.

"Was he wearing a hat? Could you tell whether he had light-colored hair? White, like Mr. Taft, or maybe just yellow, like corn-silk or butter?"

"He had on a hat but I could see his hair and sideburns. Yes, it was like that hairy stuff on the corn we have to pull off, I guess," Willie replied.

"Yeah," Tad said, not to be outdone. "It was white like Mr. Taft."

"Was there anything else about him you noticed that was inter-esting? Or different?" Sophie asked, still holding on to their hands.

"Naw, he was just a man, is what I said," Tad replied.

"Was he older than your pa? Or younger?" she pressed.

"I dunno. There's home!" Tad pulled his hand from hers and with a sudden burst of energy took off running the last half a block along Lafayette Square to the mansion's east portico.

"It was hard to tell, Miss Gates, in the light, whether he was real old. But he wasn't bent over like Fuss and Feathers is or Old Ed, if'n that's what you's asking. He did have a walking stick, though—there's Ma! *Ma!*" He yanked free and bolted off, leaving Sophie with no choice but to chuckle and look after them.

"Good heavens. If I ever had that much energy . . ." she said, shaking her head.

"I reckon it's safe for me to see you back to the Castle, now that those ruffians are safely in their mother's care," Adam said, offer-ing his arm.

"Thank you," she replied. The knowledge that a murderer was still out in the night made her acutely aware of how dark it was. The midnight blue sky was cloudless with only the barest sliver of moon showing and a faint scattering of stars very high in the heavens.

"I wasn't able to tell you what I found in Mr. Tufts's study last Saturday," he said as they walked down Fourteenth Street toward the canal.

"You found something in Mr. Tufts's study?" she exclaimed. "And you're just now mentioning it? After the way I brilliantly worked things out so you could snoop around in there while I talked to Mrs. Tufts?"

"I apologize, Miss Gates. Sophie, I mean." His voice shook a little as if he were suppressing a laugh. "I would have told you before, but I'd actually forgotten about it until earlier today. The President has had me running in all directions what with McDowell getting the troops ready to go off and other concerns." He went on to describe a packet of papers he'd discovered, and the three messages on them. "The timing is right for them to be blackmail letters, but I don't reckon why Pinebar Tufts would have had them if *he* was the blackmailer."

"That is an excellent point," she replied thoughtfully as they approached the narrow pedestrian bridge that crossed the Canal. "And there's something else that's bothering me. This secret of Felicity Monroe's—I suppose I should tell you: it has to do with her parentage," she added, because now that they were neck-deep in this investigation, Adam needed to know all of the details. And she knew Felicity's scandalous secret wouldn't make any difference to him. "With who her real mother is. It would be very disruptive if the information came out."

"I see," he replied, and she suspected his quick mind definitely did.

"The secret has been kept for over seventeen years . . . and now, all of a sudden . . . someone finds out about it and black-mails her father. But *how* did the blackmailer find out about this very carefully-kept secret?"

He made a quiet sound of agreement. "Yes, that is curious and an excellent question. When did Miss Monroe learn about the—uh—truth of her parentage? How long has she known?"

"She only learned from her nanny when she was on her deathbed—back in May."

"May. The end of May. That's about the time the first blackmail letter came."

Sophie nodded. "Yes, it is. She said her nanny died in the middle of May. And she saw her father with the letter shortly after. A week or two later."

"So I reckon that Miss Monroe's learning about her parentage just before the blackmailing began isn't just coincidence." He looked down at Sophie. "Would she have told anyone about this secret?"

"No. She didn't even tell *me,* but I was able to figure it out."

"I reckon someone else must have figured it out."

She shook her head. "I don't know. Felicity knows how devastating this secret would be to her and her family. I'm certain she wouldn't have told anyone."

"Except for you," he said mildly.

"Yes, but not really. She didn't actually *tell* me. And the only reason she even told me there *was* a secret was because she wanted to hire you to help her because she knew her father was being blackmailed. So until that happened, she had no reason to tell anyone."

They walked a few more paces on the narrow wooden bridge, then he said, "Could she have told her fiancé?"

"*No.* Definitely, certainly not. In fact, she's terrified he'll find out. He'd call off the wedding, she said."

"He would?" Adam said, and Sophie thought he sounded personally affronted.

"He would," she replied definitively.

It was a few moments before he spoke again. "I reckon if we find out how the blackmailer learned the secret, we'll be much closer to learning who the blackmailer is."

"You don't think it was Pinebar Tufts?"

He shook his head as they stepped off the little bridge onto soft grass. "It doesn't make any sense for him to have the blackmail letters if he was sending them. The wax traces on the messages indicate they were sent *to* him. Unless someone was blackmailing him as well. . . ."

Sophie stopped sharply. "What if . . . what if Mr. Tufts was only the messenger? The delivery person? What if *he* wasn't the blackmailer, but that he was picking up the—the money or whatever it was that Mr. Monroe was leaving for the blackmailer."

Adam nodded, rubbing his chin thoughtfully. "That would explain a lot. Because Tufts wasn't *acting* as if *he* were being blackmailed, was he?"

"No, he wasn't. He was acting optimistic and good-humored."

They fell silent as they started across the soft grass to the Smithsonian. Lights winked in the East Tower, directly across the Mall from them. Sophie was fortunate that Uncle Joseph and Aunt Harriet weren't as concerned about her daily whereabouts as her own parents—or her fiancé—had been. In fact, moving to Washington after the horrible scandal of her broken engagement had been the best thing that ever happened to her, even if she was in the middle of a war.

A few cattle lowed in the distance, but most of them had settled for the night in the stables built next to the Washington Monument. The smells of butchery and swamp sewage mingled with that of summer flowers, apple blossoms, and coal smoke. The evening was quiet but for distant shouts and a few gunshots . . . and one lone bugle, playing from somewhere across the Long Bridge. It was sad and slow, as if to portend what might soon come.

Sophie sighed and without thinking about it, curled the fingers of both hands around Adam's arm. Beneath his coat, she felt warm flesh and muscle as well as the unyielding surface of his false limb. "What's going to happen?" she asked quietly.

Somehow, he understood that she was talking about the war and not the murder investigation, and he sighed, long and quiet, and covered her gloved hands with his large one.

Carefully, as was his way, he replied, "I reckon it's going to be even more ugly than it was in Kansas. There'll be more bloodshed and deaths than we can even imagine. More than half the city—and Congress—reckon there'll be one big battle, and the Rebels will go running. It won't happen that way, Sophie. I saw the way it was out west. Just like Kansas, the country is torn in two, and it won't be repaired that easily."

She looked at the forlorn stub of the Washington Monument and saw the glitter of troop campfires across the Potomac, and sighed. "I wish you were wrong, Adam, but deep in my heart, I sense you're right. I pray we come through this."

His fingers tightened over hers again, and then they were at the ground floor door of the East Tower. "Good night, Sophie."

He looked down at her from his great height, and she tilted her head back so she could meet his eyes beyond her bonnet brim. Her heart gave a funny little trip. "Good night, Adam."

Tuesday, July 9

Five days after Pinebar Tufts's body was found, Adam finally got to speak with Henry Monroe at his office.

"Well, come in," the man said reluctantly when his secretary opened the door.

The tone suggested that Monroe had been getting the messages that Adam had been trying to reach him, and realized he could no longer avoid a meeting.

Adam had never been in the office of a congressional lobbyist before. His first thought was that it was far more comfortably furnished—and less busy—than the president's work space was. There were two dark upholstered chairs made from shiny walnut with a round table between them—something that seemed more appropriate for a study or parlor. On one wall was a built-in cabinet with bottles of whisky and Kentucky bourbon, along with empty glasses. Other walls were lined with shelves holding books, mementos, and even a display case that contained two very old revolvers.

Monroe's desk was massive and placed in front of a trio of tall, narrow windows. The surface had only two neat—small—stacks of paper on it, an ink bottle, a pen holder, and a wax seal. The windows looked out onto the street below, which was, of course Pennsylvania Avenue. And if he craned his head enough, Adam reckoned he'd be able to see the Capitol Building itself.

Henry Monroe was set up in a position that demonstrated his influence with Congress, as well as his own personal wealth. The loss of such prestige due to a family scandal would be significant.

The man himself was about sixty, with light hair going white and beginning to thin on top. He sported a neatly trimmed beard and sideburns that met at the edges of his squared jaw, and wore a pair of wire-rimmed glasses that sat high on the bridge of his nose. His clothing was well-made and Adam noted a tall hat hanging on a rack, with a walking stick and coat next to it.

Monroe was behind his desk as he entered, so Adam couldn't see his shoes—although he didn't think he'd be able to tell whether there was a chunk of heel missing from the right side just by sight. He'd need to see a print or the sole of the shoe.

"I'm here about the murder of Pinebar Tufts," Adam said, offering him the card from President Lincoln. "And Billy Morris."

Henry Monroe took the card silently and perused it, then offered it back to Adam. "Did you say *murder* of Pinebar Tufts? I thought the poor man hanged himself. And I'm afraid I don't know who Billy Morris is, in any event."

"Pinebar Tufts's murder was made to look as if he'd taken his own life, but he didn't." Either the man didn't listen to gossip, or he was pretending to be ignorant. Adam wasn't certain, yet, which was true.

"How do you know that?" Monroe's expression was sharp behind his glasses.

"Upon close examination of the body, as well as the scene of the crime, it became obvious. Billy Morris was the Auxiliary Guard who patrolled the Capitol grounds at night."

"Interesting. I'd like to know how one would go about proving that a suicide is actually murder. In any event, what can I do for you, Mr. Quinn?"

"I understand that you and Mr. Tufts were acquainted. I'm speaking to everyone who knew Tufts."

"Everyone? In the entire city? Well, no wonder it's taken you so long to get to me." Henry Monroe laughed, but it sounded forced.

"I reckon it wasn't for a lack of trying on my part, Mr. Monroe. How did you know Tufts?"

"He worked at the Patent Office, which surely you already know. And I assume you already know that he'd been advising me and my brother-in-law Stuart Howard on a patent he—Stuart— had filed—and, shockingly, had approved. I still can't quite cotton how that happened.

"My brother-in-law is quite a dreamer, Mr. Quinn. Like Tufts. They both live—or should I say, lived, at least the case of Piney— in their heads: dreaming, planning, inventing, wishing. Just from our brief acquaintance—as well as what I've heard about you, because of course I asked around after I learned a Mr. Adam Quinn was trying to see me—I can see that you're not that type of man yourself. You deal with reality, with what's in front of you, with specifics and facts and tangibles. Not in fluffy dreams.

"I'm the same way, Mr. Quinn. However, in the case of my brother-in-law, my wife's sibling, I was—erm—it was *prudent* for me to at least entertain the idea that Stuart's invention could be something quite lucrative. It wasn't enough that Beverly insisted we allow him the use of the old stable—which I'd intended to get fixed up, as I wanted to keep my own pair on the property instead of having to send off to the livery every day—for his workshop—and what a mess he's made of the place! Coils and wires and metal pieces everywhere. Noises and stink at all hours of the day and night. And then the wife wanted me to invest in his invention." His large hand slapped onto the desk as he shook his head in exasperation. "What one does for the woman he loves."

Adam had managed to follow this long and winding speech. "And how did Mr. Tufts help you with this potential investment?"

"Well, I had hired him to *advise* us, if you follow me. I knew there was no possibility anyone would invest in Stuart's confounded invention—especially with a war starting up. The only business that's going to be lucrative now is anything related to weapons and supplies for the troops. *That's* obvious to anyone with a head on their shoulders."

"And Stuart's invention wasn't anything that would be useful in wartime, then."

"I should say not! It was a new way to clarify sugar cane juice. He thought the machine was going to make him rich. But Beverly—my wife—insisted I hear him out, so there I was."

"And you hired Mr. Tufts to advise you?" Adam tried to steer the man back to the relevant detail. "How, exactly?"

"Well, Tufts was known to be a sort of adviser to people with inventions. He offered—usually unsolicited and unwelcomed—suggestions for improvement to a variety of inventions. Knowing this, I hired Tufts to meet with us, and to give Stuart all the reasons *his* invention wasn't going to be attractive to any investor. Unfortunately, Tufts got far too involved and he actually made several relevant suggestions to Stuart, which of course got my brother even more het up about the clarifier."

"Are you saying Mr. Tufts didn't do what you hired him to do?"

Monroe wagged his finger at Adam. "Now, don't try and trap me, there, young man. Just because the man didn't do what I asked him to do doesn't mean that I *killed* him. He made things more difficult for me, that's sure as hell true, but I wasn't going to kill the man."

"Where were you on the night of July Fourth?"

The other man reared back into his chair. "Is this an inquisition?"

Adam merely looked at him.

"Well, I'll be damned." He frowned, tapping his fingers on the desk. "Well, confound it, I've got nothing to hide. I saw the fireworks on the Mall with my wife and daughter and her fiancé, and of course Stuart. And then we went back to our house and had a glass of whisky—well, sherry for the ladies—and sat and talked until almost half eleven. And then Townsend and Stuart went on their way, and my wife and daughter and I went to bed."

"And you didn't leave the house again," Adam said.

"Of course not," Monroe snapped.

"You must spend a lot of time at the Capitol, Mr. Monroe."

"Of course. I'm there most every day Congress is in session." He smiled complacently. "I'm quite busy, you know, representing all of the mining companies' interest to the senators and representatives. Part of my efforts got the Morrill Tariff passed, you know."

Adam didn't know all the finer details of what the Morrill Tariff had to do with mining iron and coal, but he refused to allow himself to be distracted from his series of questions. "Do you ever go down into the bakery they've put in the basement of the Capitol?"

"No. Why on earth would I go down there? It's dirty and hot, and I have no reason to be there." He frowned with irritation.

"Mr. Monroe, was Pinebar Tufts blackmailing you?"

Adam couldn't have imagined a more intense reaction. Monroe froze, his face and even his hands draining of all color. Every bit of bluster and bravado and command evaporated from his person. He seemed to shrivel inside his clothing, shrinking into a small, beaten man.

"How do you know about that?" Monroe's lips were colorless. "The blackmail?"

"The same way I know that Pinebar Tufts and Billy Morris were murdered." Adam waited again patiently.

"I don't know *who* is blackmailing me," Monroe said after a long moment. "By God, I wish I did. Because if I did . . ." Then he sighed, the fury and desperation shriveling into defeat. His hand shook as he waved it weakly. "No. No, I wouldn't. Confound it, I'd just keep paying him. I have to. *Felicity.* And, oh God, Beverly . . ." His eyes shone as he blinked rapidly, looking at Adam. "She'd be devastated. She's been through so much already."

"Mr. Monroe, where were you on Friday night?"

The other man seemed to try and drum up his previous outrage and bravado, but in the end his response was subdued. "I was—we had dinner. At the Corcorans'. My wife and I and Felicity. We were home by half ten. I went to bed after that."

"And you didn't leave the house that night?"

"No."

"May I see the bottom of your right shoe, please, Mr. Monroe?"

"What?" The outrage had returned.

Once again, Adam merely waited. He knew the man could easily have him thrown out, and could deny his request. Not for the first time, he wished he actually had the authority—beyond the placard from the president—to impel people to comply with his requests.

The older man shoved his chair back and lifted his right foot, thumping onto the top of the desk. The ink bottle clinked. The boot's back heel was intact, but Adam could see that it was a new heel block that had hardly any wear.

"Thank you. It looks as if you had some repair work done on your shoe," he said, rising. "Recently."

"Is that a crime now, Quinn?" Monroe slid his foot angrily from the desk.

"I reckon it's not, but I'm curious anyway. When did you get the work done?"

"Damned heel had to be replaced. Got it fixed yesterday, if you must know. Sterling's shop, over on Fifteenth." He spoke through gritted teeth.

"Thank you, Mr. Monroe." Adam offered his hand, and to his surprise, the other man shook it. But that was the extent of any further courtesy. The lobbyist sat back down at his desk without another glance.

When Adam left, Henry Monroe seemed to be aimlessly shuffling through a stack of papers, unseeing and shaky. Pointedly ignoring his visitor.

Adam left the office, feeling more than a little unsettled by the devastation Henry Monroe was obviously feeling—the horror he,

Adam, had stirred up by asking about the blackmail and shocking him so badly. The man was clearly terrorized by the thought of the scandal coming out.

But Adam was investigating two murders and he couldn't afford to dance around the subject. He had to ask the questions that needed to be asked. Two people were dead, and Henry Monroe had confirmed that he was being blackmailed—which meant that he was still a suspect.

Fear and defeat didn't absolve the possibility that he'd killed in order to keep his family's secret.

No, Monroe could easily have rid the world of his blackmailer—and still be terrified that someone else would take his place. Monroe's reaction when Adam had brought it up indicated how shocked—and devastated—he was that someone else knew.

That could make a man even more desperate.

Constance's hands were damp with nerves, but she was *determined*.

Everyone in Washington was talking about how General Mc-Dowell was readying the troops to march to Richmond. A few of the regiments had actually begun to start on their way, to the great fanfare of the town, but there were many more who were still gathering themselves together and preparing to leave.

The talk was that the Federal troops, led by the Army of the Potomac, would rout the Rebels in Manassas, Virginia—a mere thirty miles away!—and then march on to take the Confederate capital in Richmond. And that, they claimed, would be the end of the war, the finish of the conflict, the put-down of the upstart Rebels.

That couldn't happen. It *wouldn't* happen, and Constance was one reason that was so.

It was in mid-afternoon, and she'd just left Rose Greenhow's house. In her possession was a map that her friend had somehow acquired—although Rose wouldn't tell Constance *how* precisely she'd come to have it. The map had red dotted lines that indicated the route McDowell's army was going to take to Manassas, and Constance was going to deliver it to General Bonham in the small village of Fairfax Court House. He would ensure it got to General Beauregard.

Constance was wearing a very simple dress with only one spare crinoline that she'd borrowed from Lacey, the maid who took care of Mrs. Billings. Rose had helped her to comb out her long honey-blond hair and then showed her a small packet, only the size of a large coin, wrapped in gold satin—to match her hair. The packet was rolled up in the long length of her hair and secured in place with three tucking combs that held the thick cylinder at the nape of her neck.

Constance's coiffure had never felt so heavy, so important, so *complicated* as it did right now—though it was the most simple of styles she'd ever worn. In fact, Jelly would be astonished to see her mistress in such a plain fashion. She looked like a young housemaid or laborer's daughter, with her hair parted in the front and merely a simple straw bonnet with a narrow ribbon to tie under her chin, and no other ornamentation. Only she and Rose knew how very unsimplistic she really was, with Union Army secrets bound up in her hair.

Rose had arranged for Constance to ride in a tanner's cart across the Chain Bridge to Virginia, and it was with no great trepidation that she climbed into the cart at two o'clock on July 9. The two mules hitched to the wagon stood placidly as a cloud of flies and gnats buzzed around them in the sticky, hot afternoon.

"Be still, miss," said the driver—whose name was given to her as Buck—when she fussed nervously with her skirts, although there was far less fabric, lace, and layers than she was used to. In fact, she felt almost indecent with only a simple, plain calico skirt and one thin layer of cotton beneath it, instead of the eight layers she was used to wearing. "Now, don't say nothing if anyone stops us, or when we cross the bridge. Let me do all'a the talking." He took a big pinch of tobacco and shoved it in his mouth, then "hawed" at the mules.

The Chain Bridge was on the northwest side of Washington, even beyond Georgetown, so it took nearly an hour to navigate through the clogged streets. Constance tried to keep her nerves steady by making conversation with Buck, and asked him about his occupation as a leather tanner.

It didn't take long, however, for her to wish she hadn't, for he rambled on and on about tree bark, of all things—all the while rolling, sucking, and chewing on his tobacco cud.

"Now, you take a hide and you soak it in the grit from ground up hemlock—the tree bark's got all those tannins in it—and it only takes maybe three, four months for it to tan," he said wetly. "So it's fast to make leather with hemlock bark. But chestnut—well, she takes longer—five months or more. But it don't crack when you use chestnut bark, and it holds the color of the dye longer." He shook his head, tsking. "That's why I do all my hides with chestnut oak because you buy black boots, you want'em to stay black—not get all cracked and lose the color and turn brown." He shot a stream of tobacco juice from between his teeth and she shuddered, focusing on the two mules plodding along in front of the wagon.

"But if you use hemlock, it makes the leather go heavier and thicker, annat means you can charge more for it at the saddler or the cobbler," he went on. "Make more money on the same piece o' hide because it's heavier. But like I says"—another stream of light brown juice squirted in a long arc—"it don't hold the black dye, and the good leatherworkers don't want bad quality like that with cracks and the dye fadin'."

Thus, Constance was almost relieved when they approached the Chain Bridge, even though this would be the first test—whether the Federal troops guarding it would allow them—*her*—to cross into Virginia.

She clenched her hands in her lap and attempted to appear bored as the driver drove the two mules up to the long wooden bridge that crossed the Potomac into Fairfax County. It was made from wooden trusses that crisscrossed thickly over the flat top and all along the sides. It reminded her of a long and deep garden archway where climbing roses might grow, except that this was *not* in a garden, was much longer, and—worst of all—it was populated by Union soldiers standing guard.

She swallowed hard and buried her twisting fingers beneath the light cloak she wore as the wagon rolled to a stop when two men blocked their way with rifles.

"Name, occupation, place of residence, and purpose for asking to cross," said one of the men. He sounded bored, and after one quick glance, Constance averted her eyes in an effort to escape notice.

"Buck Riffler," the driver said, rolling the wad of tobacco to the other side of his mouth. "I'm a tanner, and I live in Washington City. I'm goin' out to pick up some chesnut bark for the shop my supplier's got waitin' for me over by Pimmit Road."

"And who is this with you?" The soldier on Constance's side of the wagon tipped his rifle slightly in her direction.

"Oh, that's my sister. She's goin' to visit our cousins, live right there on Pimmit Road." Buck rolled the chaw into the opposite cheek.

"What's your name, ma'am?"

"W-Wisteria," she said softly.

The other soldier took up the interrogation again. "When are you going to return? And will she be with you or is she stayin' at the cousin's house?"

"Yeah, she's comin' back with me. Her husband don't like her gone more'n part of a day. He's like that." Buck scratched his forehead. "How long? Four hours maybe—gotta load up all that dried-up bark. It's in crates, but still takes some long time, specially if you drop one and the damned thing splits. Gets all over the damned place, and then—"

"All right, then. Go on." The soldier was apparently no more interested in tanning details than Constance was.

She exhaled softly as the wagon started up again. It seemed to take forever for them to cross, clattering over the bridge in what felt like an eternity, with the mules taking their sweet time. Every moment she expected to hear someone shout after them to stop.

But they made it to the other side without incident and passed by the soldiers patrolling the other end without slowing. Although they weren't in the clear yet, the worst was over. Now that they were in Virginia, there were many places to go and hide. And just as many sympathizers to their position as not.

"It's almost two hours to Fairfax Court House," Buck said. "If we don't get stopped again. You did good back there, just looking quiet and docile like my Berry there," he added, gesturing to the mule on the right.

In her entire life, Constance had never been called docile, and had never been likened to a mule—except the one time she remembered Jelly calling her stubborn as one. But she tucked away the sharp words she wanted to say and sat there silently as Buck jabbered on about tanning (what else was there to know? Good heavens, apparently a lot), as well as the weather, his mules, and a variety of other topics she lost track of and could care less about.

The whole time, her insides were tight and twisted, and her palms were damp inside their gloves. At every moment, she thought she might vomit or faint. Would they *ever* get there?

But at last they did. It was only just five o'clock when the wagon reached the outskirts of the small town.

Only a month ago, there'd been a small skirmish here between some Union and Rebel troops. Constance had heard about it— about how the Union troops tried three times to ride through the town, and how three times they'd been forced back by her boys. Eventually, they gave up and retreated back to their camp, and since then, the small town had remained in Confederate hands with General Bonham responsible for the area.

It was to him she must deliver the map—and only to him.

To her surprise and relief, the process was shockingly simple. With the town being in control of the Confederates, it was no difficulty asking for the general. Perhaps Bettie Duval's visit—if indeed she had made it yesterday as planned—had smoothed the way for Rose's other spy.

Spy.

Constance hadn't really thought of herself in that way until she was helped down from the wagon and escorted into the court-house, which General Bonham had taken as his headquarters.

She was officially a Confederate spy as of the moment she pulled the tucking combs from her hair and it all fell down past her shoulders, dropping the silk-wrapped packet to the floor.

CHAPTER 12

*I*t was going to be as dark as George had hoped it would be tonight. Clouds had rolled in, obstructing the sun before it even set. That boded well for him and Brownie and the task set before them.

Brownie Bixley was another free black man, and he and George often worked together. They'd outfitted George's wagon with a secret hiding place beneath the driver's bench. Taking one-third of the fronts of three barrels, they'd attached them together to create a sort of door that set just beneath and behind the driver's bench. On the back side of the barrel fronts, which were deep enough to appear real unless a man actually tried to move them, was the empty space under the driver's seat. A space large enough to hold more than a dozen rifles and their ammunition, an array of cannon balls, two or three small powder kegs—or a living person or two.

George unlocked the door to his office when he heard Brownie give his particular whistle outside. It was only getting on to seven o'clock, so they had three hours before curfew set in—but that would only be barely enough time for what they needed to do. It was a two-hour drive over to where they were going in Maryland.

"We taking cargo?" asked Brownie, and then his eyes widened. "What the hell happened to you?"

George grimaced. He was still bruised from the beating last Friday, and his broken rib had a long way to go before it healed so he didn't wince every time he moved. "Nothing."

"Nothing for cargo, or nothing happened?" Brownie asked. He was a strong, wiry man with a quick wit and a sassy, pretty wife who was home with their three kids tonight. Every time he and Brownie did a trip, George had to struggle with his guilt that if things went wrong, a woman and her babies were going to be without a husband.

But Brownie was just as stubborn as a certain white woman George couldn't seem to put from his mind, and the man insisted on helping his people just like George did. And so they were as careful as possible every time.

"Cargo should be here soon" was all George said on the topic.

"What the blazes is that awful smell?" Brownie said with a grimace. "You been cutting up dead bodies again?"

"Hush," he snapped, glancing warily toward the door, which was ajar. "I was, but I sent 'em away because they were too far gone to keep on ice anymore." He hadn't found anything interesting on Billy Morris's body, either, other than the obvious: he'd been strangled the same way Pinebar Tufts had been. And he'd had *a lot* of ale to drink beforehand.

"Still stinks in here. Can't you get some of them mothballs?"

George merely shook his head as they went outside to outfit the wagon for the journey. "Hope the cargo gets here in time."

Brownie didn't respond right away. He was probably remembering, like George was, that the last time their cargo didn't arrive on time was back in May. Deucy Short was supposed to be coming with his sister, and he never showed up that night.

Two days after, George heard what happened: Deucy had been beaten to death by his master the day before. That was a rare occasion for a master to whip his slave so hard he died—since the death of a slave meant the total loss of a worker, a financial waste. Sure, they often got beat to within an inch of dying, but not too often did the master go so far as to actually murder them.

But Deucy's master was one of the frighteningly mean and violent ones. No one knew whether he'd *meant* to kill his slave, or whether his temper had just gone too far.

Deucy's sister, Brilla, was still in the city somewhere, working in the same household. George had tried several times over the last two months to contact her secretly so he could help her, at least, but he hadn't been able to get word to her.

Just then a shadow fell across the small arc of light from their lanterns. George's head whipped up—yes, he was still far too het up about being taken by surprise—and he was relieved to see Jelly standing there. Her eyes were wide and her dark brown face seemed to have a touch of gray to its color, but determination rolled off her solid figure. She carried a small bundle clutched to her middle.

"How's that middle toe of yours, Miss Jelly?" he asked, to make certain she truly wanted to go through with this.

"It's still painin' me something bad," she replied, glancing at Brownie warily. "You hear anything 'bout my son, Dr. Hilton?"

"Jeremy's in Pennsylvania," he replied, then explained to Brownie, "Mistress Jelly here asked me to find her son who run off when he was sold away from her clear down in Mobile. That was, what, four years ago, ma'am?"

"That's right," she said. "He was only fourteen at the time."

"I got word of a Jeremy Poole in Chester, Pennsylvania. It's just over the river from Maryland, Miss Jelly. It's a three-day trip the way you'd have to do it. This here's Brownie Bixley, ma'am. He's really good at helping me fix sore middle toes." George smiled at her.

Having a sore middle toe was how Jelly had asked him for help to escape back in April. It was one of the ways in which his people communicated with each other. It was a sort of code—using certain phrases or singing songs with words that whites wouldn't notice or understand.

"All right, then," Jelly said. But her smile was still tense and nervous.

"How did you get away from home?" George asked curiously as he and Brownie prepared the wagon for their journey.

"The Good Lord was looking out for me, He was," she said, still clutching the small bundle—which was surely everything she owned. "Miss Constance left at two o'clock and said as how she wouldn't be home until late, and to just have her bed ready when she got back. And James and Louise and Lacey—they free, and they go home at night. Mr. Lemagne be sleeping, and Mrs. Billings was upstairs sleeping too. I jes' walked out that door, Dr. Hilton. I jes' walked out and I ain't never gonna look back." Her voice was strong and her eyes glinted with determination.

"All right, then, Miss Jelly," George said. "We're going to get you all settled here under the seat. It's gonna be a little uncomfortable—"

"Ain't no more uncomfortable than when my son was sold away from me," she snapped.

"You're right about that, ma'am," said Brownie with a sad smile. "Now let me help you up in there, all right?"

They got her all settled, lying down on a thin blanket beneath the driver's bench and with a hammer, in the unhappy event she needed to let herself out. Jelly tucked her bundle under her head and the last thing George saw before he replaced the trio of false barrelheads were her dark eyes glinting at him in the dark.

He said a quick, heartfelt prayer as he always did as he and Brownie nailed the barrel fronts in place. *Please protect us and all who help us in our mission, and deliver her safely to freedom and her son.*

And then, as Brownie hitched up the pair of horses, he climbed into his place on the wagon.

Moments later, they were off.

It was just growing dark when Constance and her driver reached the Virginia side of the Chain Bridge.

As before, she curled her fingers deep into her cloak—which was now a welcome covering in the cooling evening—as they approached. This time, however, she wasn't nervous or unsettled. She'd done what she came to do, and having dispatched the secret bundle, she was free from any indication of wrongdoing. Even if the Unionist soldiers stopped them, they couldn't prove she'd done anything wrong.

Nonetheless, as Buck drove the mules up to the bridge, Constance had to remind herself to relax.

As before, there were two soldiers, each with rifles, that blocked their way from entering the wood-covered bridge. Another four men stood just beyond them, on the bridge itself, talking among themselves.

"State your name, residency, occupation, and purpose for crossing," said the soldier.

Buck responded the same way he had on their way across, but this time explained, "I got me some bark for my tanning shop in the back there. Had to pick it up out to Pimmit Road. Took a coupla hours to load it up—but I told them on the other side when we cross—"

"And who are you, ma'am?" The soldier on Constance's side lifted his lantern to illuminate her face.

"That's my—"

"Let the lady answer for herself."

"My name is Wisteria Jones," she said smoothly, remembering that she was supposed to be married to a husband who didn't like her to be gone very long. "Buck—he's my brother—why, he dropped me off at our cousins' house for a visit while he was loading up the supplies for his shop."

As she spoke those words, Constance glanced over at the group of men, which was just starting to break up. In that moment, while she was brightly illuminated by the soldier's lantern, she saw the face of one of the men.

Adam Quinn.

Her entire body froze. Her insides dumped to her feet in a rush of nausea as their eyes met and she saw the flash of surprise and recognition in his face.

"Miss Lemagne?" he said, striding over to the wagon. He was dressed in a sort of army uniform: a dark gray coat instead of his long, flapping frontier coat, gloves, and a hat she'd seen some of the troops wearing in their parades.

Constance couldn't breathe, and her whole world seemed to darken and close in. *What were the chances? Dear God, what were the chances?*

"Miss Lemagne, what are you doing here?" said Mr. Quinn as he came to stand next to the wagon.

She couldn't speak; had no idea what to say.

"Lemagne? She said her name was Wisteria Jones," said the soldier. All at once his rifle was pointing at her. "What's your name, ma'am?"

Her mouth was dry and her heart was pounding. *What am I going to do?*

Next to her, Buck was tense and had even stopped chewing on his tobacco. At least he had the sense not to say anything.

"Miss Lemagne, why don't you let me help you down from there," said Mr. Quinn.

It was not a request.

She had no choice.

She offered him her hand, relieved that it was gloved so he wouldn't feel how icy it was, and was shortly on the ground. Her knees were weak and trembly and it was all she could do to keep them from buckling.

Why had she given the wrong name? If she'd only given her real name, she could easily have made up an innocent excuse for crossing the bridge. But to give a false name in the presence of someone who knew better was a very big mistake—an indicator of something to hide.

Oh God, she was going to vomit. Right here.

"I need to be getting on now," said Buck, picking up his reins.

"I don't think so, mister," said one of the soldiers. "We're going to need to search your cart. Step down and step away."

Constance didn't look at her driver, nor could she bring herself to look at Mr. Quinn, who'd taken her arm and was firmly escorting her off the bridge. She wasn't fearful for the tanner, for he was truly who he said he was and while she'd been with General Bonham, he'd loaded up his wagon with supplies, just as he'd said. There was nothing suspicious about him.

Unless they forced him to tell the truth about her.

A hot wave of nausea rushed over her, and she stumbled. Mr. Quinn's strong arm was the only thing that kept her from spilling to the ground. Buck Riffler knew exactly who she was and what she'd done. *Dear God, I'm a spy.*

"Miss Lemagne, what were you doing crossing the river?" Mr. Quinn had taken her off to the side and now he loomed over her, hat in hand. It was a testament to his standing and trustworthiness with the soldiers that he'd been left to deal with her privately—whatever that "dealing" might end up being.

"I . . ." Her mouth was so dry she could hardly form words. "I was just visiting a—a friend. On Pimmit Road."

He looked down at her, and for the first time, she was afraid of Adam Quinn.

Not because she felt violence or even anger emanating from him, but because she knew he had power and influence, and that he was filled with integrity and an unwavering black and white honesty. And that, above all, he was loyal to Mr. Lincoln and to the Union.

"Why did you give a false name?"

The question hung between them for a moment. Constance battled with herself—she must not appear guilty or nervous, even though she was. Oh God, she *was*.

She thought quickly, so quickly. And at last the words fell from her tongue. "I was visiting . . . someone . . . and I didn't want anyone to know, Mr. Quinn." Though splitting hairs, it was actually the truth.

"And the man you're with?" The raw suspicion made his voice sound cold.

"Just—just a ride across the river. I couldn't ask anyone I knew to take me," she added quickly. Again, truth. "I was . . . Mr. Quinn, you must understand how shameful it is to be—that is, that you . . . *know*," she swallowed hard, trying to make herself sound frightened and mortified—which wasn't the least bit difficult. Better to ruin her reputation than to be arrested for spying. "Or might guess. I was meeting *someone*," she said again, hoping he'd get the wrong idea—in fact, the very idea that she *wanted* him to get. "In secret. Please. I wanted to keep my reputation . . . intact." She looked up at him with eyes as guileless and pleading as possible.

Mr. Quinn looked down at her for a long moment, and it was all Constance could do to try and appear innocent and yet guilty at the same time.

"I'll escort you back" was all he said, and that left her with an ugly pit of uncertainty in her stomach.

He didn't say "home"; he said "back." Did he mean to take her to jail? To wherever they took spies? Where *did* they take spies?

Constance's stomach hurt so badly she could hardly move as he spoke to the other soldiers while he kept a firm grip on her arm.

A short time later, she was back in Buck Riffler's cart, and Mr. Quinn was riding along with them, across the Chain Bridge and into Washington City.

What would happen once they got to the Avenue, she didn't know.

CHAPTER 13

*A*dam might have believed Constance Lemagne's story if Sophie hadn't put the idea of Rose Greenhow being a spy into his head.

But he couldn't dismiss the things Sophie had told him about Mrs. Greenhow's comments in the Senate Gallery, and the fact that it was common knowledge the elegant widow entertained both Unionists and Southern sympathizers. He also remembered the last time he and Sophie had talked about the Union forces in Miss Lemagne's presence—back in April, when they were expecting an invasion at any day—and how there'd been that glint of interest in the southern belle's eyes.

Fortunately, Sophie had pretended to give out confidential information, inflating the number of troops purposely. He didn't know whether that information had ever gotten to the Confederates or whether it had been believed, but now he was even more suspicious that it had since they'd never invaded.

But would Constance Lemagne actually risk her pretty head to deliver military secrets across the river and into Virginia? Was she really that devoted to the cause? Someone like Sophie Gates, who'd been dressed as a man the first time he met her, and who'd infiltrated an all-men's club meeting, would certainly do such a thing if she believed in something strongly enough.

But Constance Lemagne, with all of her lace and flounces and yards and yards of skirts? He just didn't know.

Thus he struggled with his conscience as he rode alongside the tanner's cart, wondering how to proceed when they arrived at Miss Lemagne's house.

It was only dumb luck that he'd been there on the Chain Bridge tonight anyway. There'd been ongoing problems with rifles for the troops being stolen from certain regiments—or possibly even being sold by some of the enlisted men—and then either resold to civilians or, worse, shipped down to the Confederates. Mr. Lincoln had asked him to investigate, and he'd been talking to the guards at the bridge when he saw Miss Lemagne.

He hadn't decided what to do by the time they reached the Billings house on G Street. There was only a small, low light shining in the front window, which Adam found mildly surprising, as it was after nine o'clock. Had no one realized the young woman was gone?

He dismounted and tied up his horse, then helped her from the cart. Then he walked to the other side and, taking the bridle of one of the mules, gave Buck Riffler, the tanner—who'd proven to be a real tanner, with a solid business in the city—a measured look. "I don't think you'll be needing to drive Miss Lemagne to visit her friend again."

The tanner didn't say a word, but as soon as Adam released the bridle, he whipped his mules up as fast as they would go—which was to say, not very fast at all—and his cart rattled off.

Miss Lemagne was just as silent until they reached the door. "I'm much obliged to you, Mr. Quinn, for seeing me home," she said, not sounding obliged at all.

She reached for the handle and he put out a hand to stop her—one of the very few times he'd ever acted so discourteously to a woman. He thought his mama would understand in this case, yet nonetheless, he felt a trifle guilty. But not so much that he removed his hand.

"Miss Lemagne, I'd like to remind you that we are a country at war. It's your right to have sympathies that lie with your seceded statesmen, and even to help with any of the wounded who are here in the city. But if your actions include the sharing of confidential information with the Confederates, you can and will be arrested as a spy."

She pressed a hand to her throat and gave him a wide-eyed guileless look from beneath her bonnet. "I'm certain you don't need to tell me that, Mr. Quinn. And I don't know why you even should think to do so." Her southern accent had become more pronounced, and that told him he'd upset her.

Good.

The last thing Adam reckoned he ever wanted to do was arrest a woman—especially Constance Lemagne—as a spy.

But he wouldn't hesitate to do so if necessary.

He'd made certain she understood.

Constance darted into the house and locked the door behind her, panting with relief. She listened to make sure Mr. Quinn actually left, and then once he was gone, called for Jelly.

She needed her motherly Jelly. She needed someone who loved her, who would understand how frightened she'd been, who'd hold her and stroke her. She was safe, she was home, but her knees felt like custard: wobbly, weak, and a little wet.

"Jelly!" she called again, then went in to see her daddy. If only she could tell *him* what she'd done today—but he was so besotted with Mrs. Billings that even he might not understand.

She was relieved to find that Daddy was sleeping peacefully, but with the lantern still turned up. The tray with the remains of his dinner on it was on the table next to the bed. That was strange. Why hadn't Jelly taken care of it? James and Louisa would have gone home for the night some time ago, but Jelly was still here, of course.

Alarmed now, she hurried up the stairs and swished past Mrs. Billings's room where a low lamp burned and there was nothing to see but the lump of the woman sleeping in her bed.

"Jelly!" she called, bursting into the bedchamber that had been given to her—of course much smaller than the one she was used to down in Mobile, but certainly larger and more comfortable than at the St. Charles. "Where have you be—"

The room was empty. A lamp was on next to the bed, but her night rail wasn't even laid out. And the shawl she'd discarded before leaving for Rose's was still in a puddle on the chair.

Now she was frightened, and worried. What had happened to Jelly? Where was she?

She went to her maid's pallet on the floor in the corner of the room—there were no servants' quarters in this house—and flipped through the bedding there.

Jelly's things were gone.

She was gone.

Constance sank onto her own bed, numb with shock.

Jelly had run away.

Wednesday, July 10

Sophie had intended to visit Constance and Mr. Lemagne before now, but time had simply gotten away from her. Not only had she wanted to find out how the injured man was recovering, but she also wanted to try and find out more about Rose Greenhow—and hopefully get invited by Constance to one of her salons. Sophie hadn't been able to forget that snide, knowing smile Rose Greenhow had given that morning in the Senate Chamber.

Since Sophie felt so badly that it was nearly a week since Mr. Lemagne's accident, she came laden with gifts for the household: a chicken pot pie she'd made with the help of her aunt, a knitted lap blanket she'd worked on over the winter and meant to send to her father but decided to bring to Mr. Lemagne instead (not being an invalid, her father had no real need for a lap blanket), a container of strawberries from the market, and a tiny box containing two chocolates for Constance.

Because she'd waited for the pie to come out of the oven and cool enough to pack into a flat-bottomed wicker basket, Sophie wasn't on her way from the Centre Market until after three o'clock. That was just as well, for afternoon was a much more appropriate time for social calls than the morning.

Since she'd moved from New York to Washington and left high society behind her, Sophie had come to love the mornings. When she'd been engaged to Peter and interacting with the *crème de la crème* of the city, the mornings were for sleeping in after very long, late nights at balls, dinner parties, the theater, or other engagements. She'd seen more sunrises since moving to Washington six months ago than she'd ever seen in her life.

Because of her burdens, Sophie rode on the omnibus as far as she could to the Billings house. She generally preferred not to sit in the very crowded, unpleasantly close and aromatic bus—especially since it didn't run on any time schedule to speak of—but today she managed to squeeze into a seat on the edge of a row. The basket rode on her lap, the tantalizing scent of the pot pie helping to mask the malodorous smells on the vehicle.

It was with relief that she climbed down several blocks later and walked the rest of the way to Constance's house. She was surprised and pleased to see that Felicity Monroe's carriage was parked out front of the house as well, and hoped that she'd have the opportunity to speak with her privately about the case before they parted ways.

James, the butler and manservant of the household, greeted Sophie at the door and brought her in to the parlor where Constance and Felicity were having tea.

"Sophie, how nice to see you," said Constance, rising to greet her.

"I wanted to stop by and see how your father was doing," Sophie said, setting down her basket as she moved to embrace the other woman. "I should have come before now, and I apologize for not calling sooner. Hello, Felicity. What a lovely frock you're wearing! Pink looks wonderful on you." She hugged both of them, then took a seat on the divan next to Felicity. "How is your daddy doing, Constance?"

As soon as she got a good look at her friend, Sophie realized something was wrong. She hoped Mr. Lemagne hadn't taken a turn for the worse.

"Daddy's doing much better, Sophie, thank you. He should be able to walk in another week or two. That Dr. Hilton was able to put his leg back in place. In fact, he was only just here an hour ago, checking up on him."

Constance's response was perfectly polite and correct, but

there was something about her that was different. She seemed . . . hard. Brittle, even. There was an underlying sharpness to her, something very at odds with the normal personality of the gracious and sweet southern belle. It was as if something bad had happened, and the other woman was trying to hide it. Nevertheless, it showed in the tension at the corners of her mouth and a hard glint in her eyes.

Sophie wondered what was wrong, but she wasn't certain whether to ask. After all, she and Constance weren't terribly intimate friends.

Fortunately, Felicity spoke up, "Poor Constance has had another problem to deal with today. I'm so glad I was able to help, but it'll take some time for things to settle back into place."

Sophie, who'd been pouring herself a cup of coffee, raised her eyebrows in question at both ladies.

"My maid, Jelly, has run off," said Constance, fury underlying her words. "That ungrateful, conniving, lazy darky has run away!"

Sophie was shocked at the venom in her friend's voice. For once in her life, she didn't know what to say, and focused on adding lumps of sugar to her coffee. "That must have been quite a shock to you," she said after a moment.

"It's been quite a shock," Felicity said soothingly. "However, I was able to help Constance get a new maid right away. She's in the kitchen right now with Louisa," she added. "She'll be out in a few moments. So far, she seems to be settling in quite well."

"Felicity has been wonderful," Constance said. Her voice was still hard, but not nearly as venomous as before. "I've never had to get a maid before—Jelly has been taking care of me since I was a baby. And after my mother died . . ." Her voice shook a little, and this time Sophie recognized hurt and betrayal instead of anger. Constance picked up her coffee and brought it quickly to her mouth as if to hide the fact that she was nearly in tears.

Felicity seemed to realize that their friend needed a moment to collect herself. "I knew what it was like to lose a nanny I'd had from childhood, and so when I heard about Jelly, I had a brilliant idea. Mr. Townsend"—she blushed, of course—"had a housemaid that was going to be my ladies' maid when we got married. To replace my Dodie, who . . . passed away back in May." Her voice trembled a little, but she pressed on. "But he's not been very happy with her lately—she's been moping around because her brother died in an accident a while back. Mr. Townsend was going to sell her and let me find my own maid after we got married—I've been sharing with my mama since Dodie passed on, which has been quite a trial, as you can imagine—and when I heard about Constance needing a new maid, why I thought Brilla would be just perfect for her. Getting her away from the house where her brother died might help her get over the mopes, and she could start immediately for Constance." Felicity gave her a quiet smile.

Sophie, who'd only ever had her mother and their housekeeper to help with her hair and dress—even when Peter was courting her, and they went to very elite parties and other fancy engagements—and who'd certainly never had servants that were bought or sold could hardly relate to this speech. Nonetheless, she merely nodded, and picked up a cookie to shove in her mouth before she said something regrettable—which was something she often did.

Which was how she'd ensured she'd never marry Peter Schuyler, and never need a ladies' maid herself.

"She's quite timid," Constance said, in that same brittle tone. "But she'll do for now, I suppose."

Sophie supposed she could understand the hurt—and perhaps even a sense of betrayal—Constance was feeling, over losing the woman who'd been like a mother to her. But . . . the fact that Jelly had run away spoke volumes about *her* perspective.

"Oh goodness, I almost forgot," Sophie said, rising to retrieve her basket. "I brought some things for you."

"I wondered what that delicious smell was," said Felicity with a smile.

"Chicken pot pie. I brought some strawberries too—and this for you, Constance." Sophie offered her friend the box of chocolates. "And this lap blanket for your father."

Constance seemed pleased and appreciative of the chocolate. "That's so kind of you, Sophie," she said. But that cruel edge was still in her voice. "Brilla! Come and get this pie—"

"Oh, that's fine. I'm already up—I'll take it to the kitchen. I wanted to tell Louisa about how to heat it up anyway," Sophie said swiftly.

She hadn't even seen the new maid, but her heart went out for her. The poor young thing had just lost her brother, and now was in a new household with a mistress who was not at her best.

She swept out of the parlor before Constance could stop her, picnic basket over her arm. Something compelled her to go to the kitchen, to speak to the maid that had been shuffled to a new household without having a bit of say in the matter. At least Sophie had *wanted* to come to Washington. At least she'd had the *choice* to change households.

At least she was free to go and do what she wanted, even though at times she'd felt trapped in her life. But she hadn't been. Not really.

"Are you Brilla?" she asked once inside the kitchen. Since the young woman was the only person in there—Louisa must be in the yard attending to something—she supposed it was fair to guess.

The girl startled and looked at Sophie as if her question was an accusation. "Yes, ma'am," she said softly. "I'm sorry, I didn't hear no bell ring, and I—"

"It's no mind. I just brought this pie in here and wanted to tell Louisa to put it in the oven thirty minutes before supper. It's chicken pot pie." She smiled, trying to ease the girl's nerves. The poor thing looked as if she were about to cower in the corner if someone looked at her crossly. "I'm very sorry to hear about your brother," she added.

To her surprise, Brilla burst into tears, and then immediately and desperately tried to stop them. "Oh miss, I'm sorry, please don't tell no one, please." She yanked a rag from where it was tucked into her apron and wiped roughly at her face. "*Please.*"

"No, no, not at all," Sophie said, horrified by the unchecked display of emotion. How long had that been bottled up inside her? "Sit down, Brilla, please. I'm so sorry. I didn't mean to upset you. It must be awful, missing your brother and then suddenly being so-sent to a new place today. . . ." She found she couldn't even say the word "sold"—though that was exactly what had happened.

She eased the girl into a chair, hoping Constance and Felicity were deep in conversation in the parlor. She had a feeling Constance, in her present mood, with that layer of cruelty in her tone and expression, would not take kindly to her new maid sitting down in the kitchen—especially with a guest present.

"No, no, I can't—"

"It's all right." And that was when Sophie saw the bruises on her shoulder, slightly bared by the collar of her dress. *Dear God.* Her stomach flipped. They weren't the kind of bruise you got from bumping into something. They looked like purplish-black handprints on her smooth brown throat and neck. Sophie's heart squeezed, and she skimmed the other woman closely. There were more marks on her arm, and more on her thin, bare legs. One of them looked like a burn. *God in heaven.*

She wanted to tell Brilla that she didn't need to be so fearful here in the Billings house, but the truth was, she didn't actually know. She knew the Billings hired free blacks for servants, but the Lemagnes obviously had slaves.

And then it struck her. Brilla had been at Carson Townsend's house. She'd been his slave. The man her friend Felicity loved— the man she was going to marry—*beat his slaves.*

Sophie felt ill, and she sank into the chair across from the other woman. Her mind was so full, and yet so frighteningly empty, she didn't know what to do.

Brilla had mastered her sobs and now simply dabbed at her eyes as she watched Sophie warily.

"Mr. Townsend was your master?" she asked at last.

Brilla nodded, those dark eyes fixed on her. Terror lurked in them. "Yes, ma'am." Barely audible.

"Did he do that to you?" she asked.

Brilla's neck convulsed as she swallowed, but she didn't speak. Her fingers trembled against the rag she held.

"Brilla, you can tell me. I won't hurt you. Did Mr. Townsend do that to you?"

"Yes, ma'am," she whispered at last.

"Does that happen . . . often?" Sophie felt like she was going to vomit. What was she going to tell Felicity?

He couldn't *marry me, if he knew.*

Maybe Felicity already knew what her future husband was like. *Dear God.*

"Yes, ma'am," Brilla whispered. "To all of us."

Sophie didn't know what compelled her to ask, but suddenly she knew. But she had to make certain. "Your brother who died— was Mr. Townsend his master too?"

Brilla's eyes flew so wide the whites showed all around her dark brown irises. They filled with tears that suddenly spilled from them, running down her cheeks in misery. She nodded and wiped roughly at her face again as if desperate to scrub away any emotion.

"He didn't die in an accident, did he? Your brother?"

"No," Brilla said, for the first time above a whisper. "Master kilt him. He so angry, he beat Deucy so bad he kilt him."

Sophie pressed a hand to her middle, trying to ease her twisting belly. But she knew whatever she was feeling couldn't come close to the horror and pain Brilla experienced. "I'm so sorry," she said, overwhelmed by a sense of helplessness.

There was nothing she could do. *Nothing.* For Brilla, for any of the other slaves in Townsend's household—for any slave anywhere who was beaten by his or her master.

Or who wasn't beaten but didn't want to be there—who had no choice in their life or choice of work.

Sophie had always known the so-called "peculiar institution" was wrong; it never set well with her that one man should own another, no matter his skin color or makeup. But she'd lived in the North—she didn't see it, she didn't *experience* it. Sure, she'd heard the likes of the Grimke sisters and Frederick Douglass preaching about the evils of slavery, but it had been easy for her to hear those words, agree with them—and then go on with her life.

She could set it aside, ignore it, forget about it. Because she *could.* It wasn't there; she didn't live with it.

But that was no longer the case.

Her heart lodged in her throat, and Sophie was utterly paralyzed by this awful realization. Just then, Louisa slammed in from outside. Sophie started a little, but Brilla bolted from her chair as if it was burning, and she looked terrified.

"Lands, child, I ain't gon' swat you or nothing," Louisa said, giving her a pitying look. She glanced at Sophie, who was still so frozen in her own moment of horror that she couldn't react. "Hello, Miss Gates."

"I brought a chicken pot pie," she said, popping up out of her seat.

"I smell it, I sure do," said Louisa.

Sophie was so mortified by her own ignorance, she could think of nothing more to say. She gave one last look at Brilla, then fled the kitchen, confident that the pragmatic housekeeper could calm the younger maid better than she, a white woman, could.

"Why, Sophie, what on earth took you so long?" asked Felicity, which reminded Sophie yet again that the lovely woman in front of her was going to be marrying a brute.

"I . . ."

But before she could make up something, Constance stepped in. "As I was saying, Felicity, dear—I didn't find out until late last night when I got home. After Mr. Quinn left, I looked all over for Jelly, and she wasn't anywhere to be found."

Sophie slowed her reach for the cup of coffee she'd left on the table, then snatched it up quickly.

Adam had been here last night? With Constance? She felt even sicker.

"It was long after ten o'clock, and she was nowhere to be found," Constance went on in that strange, cruel voice. "I didn't notice until after Mr. Quinn had gone," she added.

And Sophie felt the other woman glance at her, as if to make certain she'd heard—and understood—the comment. She gulped the coffee, glad that it had gone cold or it would have scalded her mouth, and tried to appear nonchalant. But inside, she was reeling.

Only two nights ago, Monday, she and Adam had had that wonderful walk home after finding the boys. They'd talked about the case, and about other things, and she'd felt so comfortable with him. As if he respected her thoughts and ideas. Almost as if he thought she was as important in the investigation as he and Dr. Hilton were.

And there'd been that moment outside the East Tower when . . . well, there'd been that moment when she thought she felt something. And that he had too—with the way their eyes met. The way he'd looked down at her, with those eyes that crinkled at the corners and his fine mouth curving a little.

But he'd been out with Constance last night? Until long after ten o'clock?

For the second time in minutes, Sophie felt as if the rug had been yanked out from beneath her. As if she'd just been jolted from a comfortable, dreamy sleep.

Now she felt like she was tumbling down inside some great, deep well that never ended—out of sorts, confused, and completely off-balance.

And then she shook herself and came out of it. Whatever interest she'd had in being courted by a man had evaporated after the disaster with Peter. She sternly reminded herself of that, and of how content Clara was, being unmarried and living a life independent of a husband.

That was what Sophie had intended when she moved here to Washington. That was why she'd left New York behind. And it was just as well that Constance had reminded her of it.

CHAPTER 14

Saturday, July 13

Adam looked down at the note and rubbed his chin as he reread it for the third time, trying to see if he'd missed something. The penmanship was far neater than anything he'd ever manage, but almost masculine in its simplicity.

> *Mr. Quinn:*
> *I've been invited to a small garden fête on Saturday to celebrate the upcoming wedding of Miss Felicity Monroe and Mr. Carson Townsend. In the interest of continuing our investigation, perhaps you should attend as well.*
>
> *Both Miss Lemagne and I will be there at four o'clock tomorrow afternoon, Saturday, and Miss Monroe would be delighted to have you at her home for the festivities.*
> *—Sophie Gates*

There was something about the message that bothered him. Of course, he'd never received a note from Sophie before, but somehow he'd expected something she'd write to be more . . . well, interesting.

He'd read it twice yesterday when it first arrived, and each time, he felt as if he were missing some vital piece of information.

In the end, Adam reckoned he was just a little unsettled about going to a garden fête. Whatever that was. He'd been too bashful to ask Mrs. Lincoln, and had barely gotten a straight answer from John Hay, the only other person he'd had the opportunity to talk to.

"It's pronounced 'fate' not 'feet.' A party," he'd said, looking at Adam's battered frontier coat. "Outside. There'll be some food. Wear a neckcloth and don't forget your gloves, man."

Along with a neckcloth and gloves meant the new shoes Adam had worn to Mr. Lincoln's inauguration, and a crisp, white shirt that had been starched thanks to the White House staff. He was going to miss that sort of service when he left, but he'd found a small set of rooms in a boardinghouse just two blocks behind the Willard and would soon be moving to his own space.

Adam tugged at the coat he'd struggled into; it was a tighter cut and of finer material than the frontier duster at which Hay had curled his lip. It buttoned up the front over a waistcoat he'd had to borrow from Abe—though the man wouldn't miss it; he was even less interested in how he clothed his body than Adam was. When he looked in the mirror, Adam almost didn't recognize himself.

He didn't like it. He felt out of sorts and uncomfortable and stiff. Even his hair didn't look like his own—the barber who shaved him had combed it back from his face and temples so it rose like a low wave over his forehead. And he'd put pomade in it to keep it there, which made his hair stiff and smell like lemons.

But he had a job to do. And Sophie would be there. She'd probably look pretty fancy herself, and she might even laugh if he managed to make a joke. That would make it worth getting trussed up like a roast hen, he supposed.

And then he realized what niggled at him.

Sophie's message had implied they would meet at the fête. There was no suggestion that he should pick her up and escort her, and he wondered if she'd been expecting him to offer. After all, she'd sent the message early yesterday morning—with plenty of time for him to reply.

He grimaced. Damn it. This was the sort of thing he didn't really think about, and now he wondered if it was too late—if she'd already left for the Monroe house on her own—or, worse, if she was

waiting in vain for him to arrive at the Castle to take her. He
glanced at the clock—it was nearly four already because he'd daw-
dled as much as possible.

No, Sophie wouldn't wait. His lips twitched. No, if she hadn't
heard from him, she would take matters into her own hands and
go on by herself. And she'd probably flay him with her tart
tongue about the whole situation when he arrived. He grinned
again and rubbed his freshly-shaven chin. That could be enjoy-
able.

And then all at once he realized what *other* matters she might
take into her hands at the Monroe house—where Henry Monroe's office would be ripe for the snooping.

Damn. She was probably already there, and here he was, wool-
gathering and dragging his feet because his shoes were too tight.
He snatched up his gloves and a hat he'd also borrowed, but
sneered at the thought of a walking stick. Instead, he stuffed a
clean handkerchief into his pocket and was just about to the door
of his bedchamber when he stopped.

Turning back, he reached into the dresser drawer and withdrew his revolver.

He was going to a fête—whatever that was—and it was very possible a murderer was going to be there. He was going to be prepared.

"Why, Sophie, I'm so glad you could make it. And your frock is
so lovely!" Felicity embraced her in a cloud of scented rosewater.
"You look as fresh as a summer morning. Those tiny roses along
the velvet ribbon are just darling."

"Thank you! I brought it from New York when I came," Sophie
replied, smoothing her lemonade-colored skirt. "It was from Mrs.
Fancy's shop on Fifth Avenue—do you know it?"

She did have a particular fondness for the dress made from
Swiss-dotted yellow lawn with pale green trim and tiny gold rose-
buds along the bodice and the edges of her short, lace-dripped
sleeves. Two crinolines shaped her skirt in a small but elegant
hoop shape—wide enough to be fashionable but narrow enough

that she could fit through a doorway without crushing it. She'd worn a bonnet made from dark brown straw, but it had a tall, open brim that framed her face. She'd added a wide spring green ribbon that tied beneath her chin, and gold and yellow flowers with forest leaves for decoration.

For once, she felt just as well-dressed as Constance Lemagne, who'd arrived in a frock with broader hoops and more crinolines, but of a less flattering color (pale pink) and far too many layers of lace for an afternoon gathering—in Sophie's opinion.

But her reason for accepting Felicity's invitation was not about whose dress was the prettiest—her hostess's blue watered silk would obviously win that competition—but to do some investigating for the blackmail problem. This was her chance to try and poke around Mr. Monroe's office to see if she could find the letters from the blackmailer.

Whether Adam Quinn made an appearance was an entire other issue, and one that she didn't care to dwell on. It might be helpful if he were there to assist while she snooped, but it certainly wasn't necessary.

"Oh, of course I know the place! Mrs. Fancy's is one of my favorite shops to visit when I'm in New York." Felicity was still holding Sophie's hand. "Now, do let me introduce you to my parents."

Of course Sophie was eager to meet Henry Monroe, her chief—really, only—suspect in the Pinebar Tufts's murder, and she gave a brief curtsy as Felicity introduced them. "What a lovely home you have," she told the Monroes as she shook their hands. "And an even lovelier daughter."

Mrs. Monroe was tiny and birdlike with brown hair that wasn't nearly as dark as her daughter's black tresses, and a warm smile. "How kind of you to say," she replied with a sweet smile as she glanced down at the drawstring bag that dangled from Sophie's wrist. It was a little heavier than usual and had swayed, bumping her hostess's arm as they squeezed hands in greeting. Sophie quickly withdrew her hands and tamed the little bag as Mrs. Monroe continued. "I'm so pleased to meet you, Miss Gates."

"A lovely daughter indeed, but have you seen her trousseau

bills?" Mr. Monroe joked, and laughed heartily. He was as distinguished looking as Sophie had expected him to be—and she noted with satisfaction that his hair was fading from light brown to white. "I'll be more than happy when Townsend has to take them over." He chuckled, but Sophie sensed an underlying tension in his demeanor.

Mr. Monroe took his daughter's hand and patted it gently. "You know I'm only jesting, darling," he said, looking down at her with a fond smile. "I'll happily pay your bills as long as you need me to. Just don't forget about your old papa once you're married and moved off to Richmond."

"Oh, Daddy," Felicity said, blushing. "You're the sweetest man ever, and how could I ever forget you?"

One thing about Mr. Monroe: he seemed to truly love his daughter. He wanted the best for her, and he clearly adored her. Which explained the secret he'd so carefully kept for nearly eighteen years. But that sort of devotion could make a man desperate enough to do whatever it took to keep his beloved daughter safe and scandal free.

"Oh, and here's my brother—Mr. Stuart Howard," Mrs. Monroe said.

"Very nice to meet you, Mr. Howard," Sophie said, looking up at the tall, gangly newcomer. He, like the other men in this casual garden party, was wearing an informal, low hat, and his curling moonbeam-colored hair also caught Sophie's attention. Felicity's uncle was in his forties and was clean-shaven but for thick sideburns. He had solid shoulders and slender hands with a strong grip. "You're an inventor, Felicity tells me?"

"Why, yes, yes, I am," he said a little nervously. His Adam's apple bobbed above the collar of his shirt. "My workshop is over there if you'd like—"

"Behind those potted trees," Mr. Monroe added quickly. "We moved them there to—erm—try and camouflage the mess. Miss Gates isn't interested in seeing that messy place, are you, Miss Gates?"

Actually, Sophie would have been quite interested in seeing an inventor's workshop—for more than one reason. It hadn't occurred to her until this very moment that perhaps Mr. Monroe wasn't the only person being blackmailed about Felicity. Mr. Stuart Howard would possibly have just as much to lose as his niece and brother-in-law if the truth came out, or—

Sophie's thoughts stopped suddenly as she looked up at Mr. Howard. He had light-colored hair as well. And the Lincoln boys had mentioned sideburns when they described the "mean man." But why would Stuart Howard be blackmailing his own brother-in-law—over his own niece's secret?

Still, one of the niggling questions Sophie had was how the blackmailer had learned about the family scandal. Stuart Howard, an actual member of the family, could easily have discovered the information over the years, considering his proximity to the household and his relationship to Mrs. Monroe.

"Oh, Sophie, there you are again." Felicity was suddenly back at her side, despite the fact that Sophie hadn't taken two steps from where she'd been moments ago. "I'd like you to meet my fiancé, Mr. Carson Townsend." Felicity beamed up at the tall, fair man whose arm she gripped as if afraid he'd flit away.

"A pleasure to meet you, Mr. Townsend," Sophie said, forcing herself to sound normal—and to offer her hand to the man who had a princelike bearing.

But when he took her hand and bowed briefly over it, it was all she could do not to snatch it away. The idea that the very hand that took hers so gracefully, that was gloved in such a gentlemanly manner, should have *beaten* a man to death—and bruised a woman—made her ill.

But there was no trace of such ugliness in his eyes when he winked at her and released her hand. "Felicity has been telling me about you for days. She's fascinated that you live in the Castle. I'd always hoped to see the inside of it someday—beyond what's open to the public—and now that I know you, Miss Gates, perhaps that will actually come to pass."

"Oh, certainly," she replied in a breezy manner she didn't feel. "Do stop by whenever you like." Sophie simply wanted to get away from him—and she wished with all her heart she could take Felicity with her.

"There's Miss Lemagne," said Felicity. "Carson, let's go say hello. Sophie?"

"I believe I'm going to fetch a glass of lemonade," she replied. "I did hear someone mention lemonade, didn't I?"

"Of course—it's in the shade beneath that spreading oak. There's a shrub—lavender and thyme—to drink in the punch bowl as well."

Sophie thanked her, and when the engaged couple walked off, she strolled aimlessly across the yard.

The Monroe home was one of the mansions only a few blocks off Penn Ave and Seventh Street. Its yard was bordered by a tall black fence, and pink, red, and yellow flowers spilled in clumps through the spires of the fence.

The gathering was in the shady backyard of the mansion. The house itself was four stories tall and made of pressed red brick. Small tables had been set up just beyond the entrance to the house, where guests could rest their punch glasses while they nibbled on small squares of cornbread, fresh strawberries, tiny peach tarts, and shelled peanuts tossed with spices. On each table was a small vase with colorful flowers wrapped in a colorful ribbon.

Sophie estimated about forty people were in the yard, talking and chatting. She wondered how easy it would be to slip into the house and find Mr. Monroe's office. With it being such a large house, it might take her a while to determine which room was his study.

There was no time like now, she told herself, and began to make her way around the periphery of the yard toward the house. There were two large French doors that opened from a sitting room onto a small brick patio that gave way to the lush lawn on which the guests were milling about.

She gave a quick glance to make sure no one was watching and slipped inside.

A tray of cookies and muffins was set out on a table in the sitting room, leading Sophie to believe that the house was open to the guests as well, although they were clearly encouraged to be out in the summer air. She hurried out of the sitting room and found herself in the main hallway that stretched from the main entrance of the house to the back. There were several closed doors, and at the front of the hall, a stairway led to the upstairs. Sophie decided it was more likely Mr. Monroe's study was on this floor, and she cracked open the closest closed door.

It led into a small, elegant parlor with dainty furnishings and a lot of flowers. Definitely not the man of the house's office.

She tried another door and found herself peeking into a music room with a piano and plenty of seating.

The third door, nearest the front entrance, was her last option before climbing to the second floor, and Sophie was relieved when she peeked inside. It smelled of tobacco and was furnished with a large, heavy desk and many bookshelves.

Heart pounding, she slipped inside, grateful that the sun shone brightly through the windows—which faced the side of the house, not the back where all of the guests were—and gave her excellent illumination for her search.

Sophie had never actually snooped before, so at first, all she did was stand over Mr. Monroe's desk and look at everything without touching it. It was fairly neat, and the few stacks of paper were letters and envelopes that, at first glance, appeared to be messages about the position Monroe's clients wanted him to take with the congressmen with whom he met. An inkstand, pens, wax seal, and paperweight were on the right side, and on the left was a photograph of Mrs. Monroe and Felicity.

She saw no personal correspondence, and realized that of course Mr. Monroe wouldn't leave blackmail letters just sitting out on the desk for anyone to see. So she was going to have to dig a little deeper. Her heart pounding and her hands damp beneath her lacy gloves, she carefully pulled one of the desk drawers open. She started when she saw a revolver sitting in there, pretty as you please, along with some ammunition. She closed the drawer quickly, a little harder than necessary, and grimaced when it made a sharp thunk.

Slow down, she told herself, and took her time opening the next drawer. Ink bottles and pens, blotting cloths, and a small wax stick for sealing, along with a small penknife and some coins. In another drawer she found personal correspondence—letters from friends and family. She quickly flipped through them to make certain that was all there was, keeping a look for a darker colored envelope with a slight smudge that made "Henry Monroe" look like "Benry Monroe."

Nothing caught her attention in that drawer, and she was just pulling open the fourth drawer when she heard footsteps outside the door. She froze, staring at the knob, and when it began to turn, she looked around in panic before diving under the desk.

Oh God, oh drat, oh no, oh God . . .

She curled herself into the smallest ball possible, thankful that the cubby under the desk was only open on one side. The only way someone would see her would be if he or she came around to the sitting side. Maybe it was a servant, coming in to fetch something for Mr. Monroe. *Please.*

She held her breath, trying not to pant—but her corset made it nearly impossible to take a good breath while crunched up like this. And she'd laced it tighter than usual today, blast her vanity. It was a miracle she'd actually been able to fold herself down and under the desk, to be honest. Just then Sophie realized she'd left the chair away from the desk, not pushed in, and hoped that Mr. Monroe—or whoever it was—didn't notice.

When the footsteps came over to the sitting side of the desk, Sophie began to feel very sick. And it wasn't just because she couldn't breathe in her stays. She carefully pulled the edges of her hem as close to her as possible, tucking them under her knees where she cowered.

Just don't sit down. Please don't sit down.

She held her breath, trying to make herself as tiny and as far away as possible as two trousered legs—a man, as she'd suspected—came to stand in front of the desk. They were dark blue or black; it was difficult to tell, but because she was terribly focused on watching them, prepared to react the moment they bent to sit, she noticed that the fronts of the trouser legs glinted a little in the sunshine as the man stood at the desk, moving papers around. It looked as if there were minuscule sparkles in the fabric, and she was fascinated and curious at the same time.

His black shoes were polished but were broken in and worn. She observed them carefully, as she imagined Adam would, in case she needed to identify the man. The stitching on the boots was neat, but there was a tiny thread loose on the left foot. Also a little crack near the toe of the same shoe.

That was all she could see as the man rummaged around on the desk, muttering to himself. When the chair moved, as if he were pulling it back to sit in, Sophie nearly gasped aloud—then suddenly she heard voices too, and the sounds of people coming closer.

The man cursed and grabbed something hard from off the desk, then hurried away. A moment later, Sophie heard the door open and close, and she *thought* she heard him go out.

But she waited quite a few minutes just to make sure she was alone—and that the voices in the distance went away—before climbing out from beneath the desk. She crawled on her hands and knees and poked out from the side first and assured herself she was alone.

At last able to take a full breath, and feeling faint with relief, she stood there at the desk, looking down. She was certain it hadn't been Mr. Monroe who'd come into his own office and hurried out as soon as he heard people approaching.

So it had been someone else. Another man, but she hadn't been able to see anything but his trouser legs and shoes.

And someone in the office didn't mean anything in and of itself—but whoever it was had clearly not wanted to be caught. So what would a guest of the party be doing here, snooping around in the office of the host anyway?

Sophie felt herself flush, for of course, she was a guest and was snooping around in the office. But she had a good reason to be doing so . . .

It couldn't have been Adam—Mr. Quinn—could it? She snick-

ered quietly. That would have been very amusing if they'd encountered each other in here, searching the office for clues.

The house sounded silent, and Sophie thought she'd best take
the opportunity to leave in case whoever had been looking around
decided to come back. She moved swiftly to the door and listened
before opening it to peer down the hall.

No one was there.

Giving a relieved heave of breath, she slipped out and into the
corridor, closing the door behind her.

Just as she stepped into the hall, she felt rather than heard
someone behind—no, above her.

She spun to see a shadowy figure standing on the stairs that led
to the second floor. He was looking down at her.

CHAPTER 15

"Mr. Quinn," she said, stumbling back in surprise as he came down the stairs. "What are you doing up there?"

"I reckon the same thing you were doing in there," he said, glancing toward Mr. Monroe's office. "Looking around."

"Was that you who came in there a few minutes ago?" She was certain she would have recognized him by those long legs if he had, but . . .

"No. Someone came in there while you were—?"

Footsteps and laughter cut him off, and a pair of young women appeared from around the corner of the sitting room that opened to the party. Neither of them seemed to find it odd that Sophie and Adam were standing in the corridor; they merely nodded to them as they passed by to climb the stairs.

"Gertrude will have it fixed up in no time," said one of the girls to the other. "She's an absolute wizard with a needle."

"They must be going there to freshen up," Sophie said. Then she looked at Adam. "I'm glad you were able to attend today," she said formally.

He looked so different. He was holding a hat, and his hair was combed back in a high, smooth pouf instead of sort of falling in waves around his face like it usually did, and he was wearing a tight collar with a dark blue neckcloth and a striped navy waist-coat. His coat was tailored and showed off his broad shoulders, unlike the loose, flapping thing he usually wore. And he had on gloves. She didn't think she'd ever seen him dressed so formally before—except maybe at the Lincolns' first levee, when she hardly knew the man, and even then, his hair hadn't looked like that.

"I didn't see you when I first arrived, so I reckoned you'd gone inside to riffle through Mr. Monroe's study," he said, looking down at her with a sort of twitch to his lips.

"Well, I—well, yes, of course. That was exactly why I decided to attend. When would I get another opportunity?" Her cheeks were warm.

"My thoughts as well." He offered his arm and she took it, noting it was his real limb and not the false one. "Now that you've done so, you can tell me all about it outside. I understand there's lemonade."

"That does sound good." She was parched—mainly from being dry-mouthed with fear while hiding under the desk.

They walked down the hall to the sitting room, then out to join the party. The first person Sophie saw was Constance, standing in the middle of the party in her yards of pink and lace. Her mood soured like the lemonade and she smoothly pulled from his grip. "Oh, there's Miss Lemagne. I'm certain she'd like a glass of lemonade."

He flickered a glance in the direction she was looking but made no move toward Constance. "I spoke with Henry Monroe on Monday," he said instead, and thus captured her full attention.

"Did you learn anything?" Sophie glanced around to make certain no one could overhear them.

"I'll be happy to tell you about that while you tell me what you found in his office just now. I reckon we could sit over here out of the way, Ss—er, Miss Gates." He was looking at her strangely.

She batted at her bonnet and touched her face. "Is my bonnet crooked? Do I have a smudge?" Drat! She'd probably completely disheveled herself when she dove under the desk. Perhaps she should go upstairs and check in the mirror.

"No, of course not. You look very pretty," he said.

"Well then, why are you looking at me like that?" she replied, sinking onto the bench he'd motioned to.

"I reckon because I can't seem to look anywhere else."

"Oh." Sophie's face went hot and she nervously fussed with her skirts to spread them out—something she never did. "How kind of you."

He sat next to her and she smelled a waft of fresh, crisp lemon. "Is something wrong?"

"Of course not. What would be wrong—except the fact that there's a murderer loose in the city and he might very well be *here,* right now." She kept her voice low as she looked out over the party, her nerves growing tighter. "I'm certain it's either Henry Monroe or Felicity's uncle, Stuart Howard. They both fit the description Tad and Willie gave us—light colored hair with sideburns—and neither of them are stooped or old. Either or both could have been being blackmailed by Piney Tufts. Tell me what you learned when you spoke with Mr. Monroe, please, Mr. Quinn."

He shifted on the bench, then gave a quiet sigh of acquiescence. "Henry Monroe is definitely being blackmailed. He's distraught about it, and I reckon he'd do whatever he needed to do to keep his family safe. Although he claims to have no idea who's blackmailing him. I tend to believe him about that. He also says he was in bed on the nights Tufts and Morris were murdered. What did you learn?"

"I didn't find anything of note in his office," she confessed. "Not that I expected to see blackmail letters sitting out anywhere, but even when I looked through the desk drawers, there wasn't anything interesting."

"But someone came in while you were in there." His expression was grave. "Did he see you?"

"No. I hid under the desk."

He smiled and his eyes crinkled at the corners. "You did? I reckon that wasn't very comfortable."

She chuckled. "Not at all. It was a miracle he didn't discover me—if he had sat down and pulled the chair in . . . well . . ." She swallowed hard. "It wasn't Mr. Monroe, because as soon as he heard people coming, he got out of there. That's why I asked if it had been you." He shook his head, still smiling. "I wondered why anyone else would be digging around in his study. It sounded like he took something off the desk. Do you think it could have been the blackmailer?"

Adam's grin faded and he nodded. "That is a question. If it was the blackmailer, I reckon he was looking for something or was going to leave something for Monroe."

"Maybe. But I'm certain he took something with him. There was a dull clunk and a quick little scrape like he was picking up something hard. Maybe he put his hat down or his walking stick while he was poking around. He didn't open the drawers, which was good, because one of them had a revolver in it."

"What side of the desk was the ink pen and bottle?" he asked.

"The . . . um . . . right side," she replied after a moment of trying to picture the desk. "Why?"

"Henry Monroe didn't write the letters to Pinebar Tufts about where to deliver and pick up whatever it was he was picking up—I reckon it was the blackmail money, but we don't know for certain."

"How do you know he didn't write the letters?"

"Because they were written by a left-handed person, and if Monroe's inkpen and bottle are on the right side of the desk, he's not left-handed."

Sophie's eyes widened. "That's brilliant. Of course. So obvious, but I didn't even think of that. I probably *would* have, given time, but—well." She smiled up at him. "We didn't really think Mr. Monroe wrote the letters Mr. Tufts had, but it's good to know that he didn't. So what *do* we know?" She mulled for a minute, then began to list the items she knew.

"We know that Mr. Monroe is being blackmailed. We know that Pinebar Tufts received letters written by a left-handed man telling him certain dates and times to pick up something and where to deliver it. The pickup times seem to coordinate with the times Mr. Monroe received blackmail letters, so I really do think it's possible Mr. Tufts was involved somehow. Maybe just as a messenger."

"It's the only thing that makes sense. Whoever was—or is—blackmailing Henry Monroe was having someone else do the dirty work by picking up the money. Could be so that if Monroe decided to watch the pickup location—where he was directed to leave the money—Tufts would be identified as the blackmailer instead of whoever is really doing it."

"Which means he would be killed by the person being blackmailed, instead of the blackmailer being killed."

"Yes. And Tufts told his wife that he was 'being careful.' And that things were going to change—to get even better. As if he expected to be getting even more money later. Could be . . . could be he discovered what the blackmailer was doing and wanted more money from him."

"Blackmailing the blackmailer? Why, that's so smart!" Sophie slapped her hands together, the sound dulled by her gloves. "That's got to be it. Tufts figured out what was going on, and tried to extort more money from the blackmailer, and the blackmailer killed him. But who is the blackmailer?"

"Whoever he is, I reckon he's also our killer. He was protecting himself by murdering Tufts, and then Billy Morris."

Sophie shuddered. "If whoever came into the study was him, I was right there. I *saw* him—or part of him anyway."

"All right. What do you remember about him?"

"I only saw his legs from just above the knee to his shoes. The boots were polished, but they weren't new. The stitching was very tight all around the edge of the sole, but on the left shoe, there was one loose thread. I couldn't tell if he left a funny footprint with a piece missing out of the heel—but we're outside, Adam, maybe he left a mark here."

"It's mostly grass, and he might not be wearing the same boots, but there's a chance to find a good print." He nodded. "I'll look around. Did you notice anything else about him? What color were his trousers?"

"Dark. Either black or dark blue. The fabric has a little bit of a shimmer to it—something I hadn't seen before."

"A shimmer?"

"Like tiny, tiny sparkles on it."

"Sounds pretty fancy for a man to be wearing trousers with tiny sparkles. How high were his knees, could you tell?"

Sophie showed him by measuring off the ground, and he nodded again. "That would make him tall enough to be the killer."

"So what we know about the killer is that he's left-handed, light-haired, not old, and has a funny shoe print. The man in the study today could have been him, or not. Oh, did Dr. Hilton find anything enlightening about Billy Morris's body?" Sophie asked.

"Nothing that gives us any more information about the killing. Morris had a lot of ale and gin in his belly, which was no surprise. But there was nothing else to lead us to the killer."

She mulled quietly for a moment, then said, "I was thinking about the fact that he hung up Piney Tufts. Why would a man do that? Why not just leave him on the ground like he did Billy Morris, if he was already dead?"

"That's a good question, Sophie. I reckon when we figure that out, we'll have a better idea who it is."

"And if we can figure out how he learned there was a family secret to use as blackmail, that will also be a big clue. That's why I'm suspicious about Stuart Howard. He's Mrs. Monroe's brother and he's here all the time in his workshop. Maybe . . . well, maybe he overheard Dodie, Felicity's nanny, when she made her confession when she was dying."

Adam nodded, and was just about to say something when a very familiar voice scorched over Sophie from behind. "Why, Mr. Quinn, I didn't see you until just now. And Sophie, dear, we've hardly had a chance to talk since you called the other day, but I do believe Felicity was looking for you. She wanted to show you something . . ." Her voice trailed off uncertainly as she looked over the party. "My stars, she was just right there."

Adam sprang to his feet for Constance to sit and dutifully said, "I was about to fetch Miss Gates a lemonade. Would you like one as well?"

"Oh, Mr. Quinn, that would be marvelous. Thank you so very much." No sooner had he started off than Constance continued. "Felicity was standing there just a moment ago, with her Mr. Townsend, Sophie." She gestured vaguely toward the crowd of people.

Sophie, who had no desire to remain with Mr. Quinn and Constance, gladly took the excuse offered to her and walked away.

Now that she and Adam—Mr. Quinn—had compared notes, she could get on with the investigation and leave him to Constance.

When Adam returned with two glasses of lemonade, Sophie was nowhere to be found. Instead, her seat on the bench had been taken by another young woman whom Miss Lemagne introduced as Miss Turner.

He offered one glass to Miss Lemagne and stood uncertainly for a moment until she said, a trifle impatiently, "If you're looking for Sophie, she's gone off somewhere."

"Miss Turner, would you like a glass of lemonade?" he asked belatedly, offering her the drink. She accepted, smiling up at him with a warm look. When two more young ladies approached— each attractively dressed and perfectly coiffed—Adam found himself reluctantly drawn into conversation with them before he could determine how to make a polite exit.

While they prattled on about the sunshine, the flowers, and the war—talking about the latter as if it were a theatrical performance they were watching—Adam dutifully listened and responded as required. At the same time, he was watching the rest of the party and trying to formulate an excuse to leave.

This was precisely why he disliked formal gatherings like this: he had to make conversation about things he knew nothing of and cared about even less, he was wearing uncomfortable clothing, and he always had to be on his guard in order to make certain he didn't step in any unpleasant societal puddles.

He was just about to excuse himself when one of the ladies shrieked and launched herself directly off the bench. She slammed into him, and he barely managed to catch her using his false arm.

"Oh my goodness!" The young woman in question—he'd forgotten her name—spun away and was dancing around, swishing her skirts and gasping, "It was a bee! A bee landed on me! Is it still there? Is it?"

The other ladies bolted from their seats as well, backing away carefully as Adam gingerly looked over the distraught woman from bonnet to hems. He thought her name was Miss Upton, but wasn't certain.

"I don't see any bees on you, miss," he said. "But there's a— er—a bug on your bonnet."

"Oh! Please take it off," she squealed. "I do abhor outdoor parties for this very reason. My auntie was stung by a bee and she up and *died* from it, and ever since then I can't *bear* to sit outside."

Adam gingerly removed the spider that had landed on the top of her bonnet. He considered it a good decision on his part that he hadn't mentioned it was a spider. Having three sisters, he had an idea of what sort of reaction that would have caused.

The spider safely removed from the brim of Miss Upton's bonnet, Adam seized the opportunity to make his escape. He wondered if Sophie was afraid of bees, and decided that even if she was, she'd be more likely to merely shoo one away than to shriek and dance around like a mad person.

And then he remembered their excursion in the tunnels beneath the Capitol—the cobwebs, the spiders, the rats and mice and other unpleasant items—and decided that Sophie Gates was definitely made of sterner stuff than Miss Upton and her friends.

As if he'd conjured her up, suddenly there she was, walking across the lawn in that pretty lemon yellow dress. She'd done something different to her dark hair today, and it made fetching little curls around her face beneath the bonnet. Her small hands were enclosed in delicate white lace gloves, and a little drawstring bag dangled from one of her wrists.

He wondered what was in the bag, for by the way it swung to and fro, he could tell whatever it contained was heavier than a handkerchief and a comb. What else would a woman put in a bag like that anyhow?

"Mr. Quinn, I don't believe you've had an opportunity to meet the future bride and groom," Sophie said as she approached.

Adam dragged his eyes away, noticing for the first time that she wasn't alone and had brought the party's two honored guests with her. Close on the heels of that, he realized that he'd been there for over an hour and hadn't greeted his hosts. He grimaced inwardly. Another reason he should never attend formal gatherings.

"Mr. Quinn only arrived a short time ago and was kind enough to wait for me while I went upstairs to fix one of my rosettes," Sophie said, neatly excusing him for his unintentional rudeness. "It was dangling by a thread, and I didn't want to lose it, for then my sleeves would be asymmetrical." She went on to introduce him to Felicity Monroe and Carson Townsend, the soon-to-be-married couple.

They were a handsome pair—quite attractive together, Adam thought, even though that was hardly the type of thing he normally noticed. Miss Monroe's secret heritage was quite obvious once one knew it existed, with her dusky complexion and thick, coarse black hair. She was a stunningly beautiful woman, and he understood why a man could easily fall in love with her—at least as far as looks went. Townsend was the opposite in coloring—tall, fair, and solid.

As she introduced them, Adam sensed a reserve beneath Sophie's normally easygoing personality. He wondered what was bothering her, but there was no opportunity to ask as they conversed in the center of the yard.

"Have you met Miss Monroe's uncle?" Sophie interjected at one point, looking over his shoulder. "He's an inventor."

Following Sophie's hint, Miss Monroe hailed her uncle and Adam was again subjected to introductions and even more pointless conversation. But he paid closer attention to Mr. Stuart Howard in consideration of Sophie's suspicions of him. The man was tall enough to be the killer, and although he was slender, Adam thought he could easily have carried and strung up the more slight Pinebar Tufts.

Howard didn't say much until Adam asked him about his invention, and then the man had plenty to say. Too much, in fact. He had a moment of sympathy for Henry Monroe, who likely had to listen to the finer details of clarifying sugar cane far more often.

"Townsend, so sorry to have disappeared for a bit. Did you find my pipe?"

Adam turned as Henry Monroe himself ambled up to their little group. The older man didn't notice him at first, as he was speaking to his future son-in-law.

"Yes, sir," replied Townsend, pulling a tobacco pipe from his pocket. "It was right on your desk, as you said."

Sophie's eyes widened and she met Adam's gaze. He saw her look down—probably at Townsend's boots—then back up. She nodded and he understood: yes, Townsend had been the one in the office while she was hiding under the desk, apparently at Mr. Monroe's request to retrieve his pipe.

Well, that explained that.

Monroe took the pipe, tapping it against his palm as if to loosen any tobacco inside. "Didn't know if you were looking for me—Mrs. Monroe had me seeing to something in the dam—er, the confounded—kitchen to see about making the cherry-bourbon punch, and I had to go down and unlock the cellar for the servants to get the bourbon. Apologize for my absence." Turning, he noticed Adam for the first time, and his demeanor cooled sharply. "Mr. Quinn. I didn't expect to see you here."

"Daddy, I invited Mr. Quinn. He's a friend of Sophie Gates and Constance Lemagne," Miss Monroe said, quickly covering up the awkward moment. "I thought it would be nice to have a few more gentlemen to round out the numbers, especially if we play croquet—it's a game Daddy heard about when he was in England last summer," she added, looking around at the group. "You play it on the grass outside and it sounds quite fun. Anyhow, Daddy, Mr. Quinn works with Mr. Lincoln up at the White House, you know."

"So I've heard," Monroe replied, his voice still cool.

"It's a very nice party," Adam said. "Thank you for inviting me, Miss Monroe. And thank you for the hospitality, Mr. Monroe."

"Of course," she replied, giving him a dazzling smile as her father excused himself. "Don't mind Daddy," she said after he walked away. "He's always annoyed when he doesn't know about something."

"No mind at all," Adam said, resisting the urge to shift from foot to foot.

Sophie must have noticed, for she said, "Mr. Quinn promised me a glass of lemonade *ages* ago, Felicity. Do you mind if I take him up on it?"

Her friend laughed and waved her off, slipping her hand around her fiancé's elbow. "Have fun, darlings. Do try the bourbon punch when it comes out—it's not too strong and Daddy puts dried oranges and bourbon-soaked cherries in it."

"Thank you," Adam murmured at the top of Sophie's bonnet as they walked away, arm in arm. He wished women didn't have to wear those things—the brims were so high they made it difficult to lean close enough to speak and be heard. He felt foolish talking into a curve of straw and fabric flowers. And it was irritating that he couldn't see her face unless she was looking up.

"Well, that was informative," she said as they made their way toward the beverage table. "Mr. Townsend was in the office with a perfectly reasonable excuse. Although it certainly sounded as if he were snooping around, looking at the papers on Mr. Monroe's desk. I suppose he left in a hurry because he didn't want anyone to see him being nosy."

"You don't like him, do you?" Adam said, suddenly realizing that was what had bothered him when Sophie introduced them. There'd been a subtle, cold reserve when she looked at Carson Townsend. "I didn't realize you'd met him before."

She was silent for a moment as they approached the table and he selected two cups of lemonade. Each had paper-thin slices of lemon and strawberry floating in it. It wasn't until they strolled away that she said, "No. I don't like him. I wish Felicity wasn't going to marry him."

Adam knew he didn't have to prompt her to explain, so remained silent, waiting for her to go on. Of course she did.

"He beats his slaves," she said quietly, fortunately tipping up her face so he could hear. "He beat one of them to death."

Adam couldn't help but recoil. A sour feeling settled in his stomach and he glanced over at the handsome man, who was talking and gesturing gregariously with several other partygoers. One would never guess that about him.

"I can't decide whether I should tell Felicity or not. She might already know. How could she marry someone who's so horribly violent?"

Sophie didn't say it, but Adam silently filled in the rest of her thoughts: If he beat his slaves, what would he do if he learned his wife was part black?

"I suspect she might already know because she's so terrified that he'll find out about . . . you know."

He nodded, glancing over yet again. "I—"

"Oh there you are, Mr. Quinn." Miss Lemagne was suddenly there in a flurry of pink skirts and her own high-brimmed bonnet. "Is that lemonade for me?" She fluttered her lashes prettily and he obliged by handing her the glass he hadn't yet touched.

"Of course," he said gallantly.

"I need to speak with Felicity," Sophie said. "Excuse me, Constance. Mr. Quinn." She was gone before he could say a thing.

"I understand that Mr. Monroe is about to bring out his famous cherry-bourbon punch," Miss Lemagne said. "It's *legendary* here in Washington."

Adam murmured something noncommittal, still trying to understand why Miss Lemagne kept seeking him out—considering the last time he'd seen her, he'd threatened to report her if she was a spy. He thought she'd been subdued and even afraid of him that night, having been caught red-handed.

But perhaps his instincts were wrong, for once, and she *wasn't* a spy after all. If she had nothing to hide but the secret visit she was making to a friend—who clearly was a gentleman friend—perhaps it was her way of making sure he knew that she had no reason to avoid him.

In that case, he reckoned he should be apologetic for accusing her of being a spy. But at the moment, he really just wanted to be somewhere alone, where he could think about this murder investigation.

"Miss Lemagne, it's been a pleasure to see you again. I hope you'll excuse me, for I'm just about to take my leave from the Monroes."

"Why, Mr. Quinn, how very convenient, as I was just about to do the same thing myself." She beamed up at him and had his elbow in her gloved hands before he could react. "I told my daddy I'd be home before dark to see to him, now that Jelly's gone. This way I don't have to try and find a hackney all by myself. Surely you could help?"

Adam had no choice—he couldn't refuse, and he certainly wasn't going to suggest using the Monroes' footman—or whatever the position was of the servant who'd greeted people at the door and taken their horses or carriages around. Even though helping to hail a hackney was part of the young man's duties. "Of course I'll help you find a hack."

Of all the luck: Sophie was standing there, talking to Miss Monroe and Miss Upton when Adam was directed up to the group by Miss Lemagne. He felt as if he were being dragged to his execution as they approached the group.

"Felicity, it's been such a lovely party, but I've got to get home to Daddy," she said. "I promised I'd be home before dark, you know, because Brilla is still new and all. Thank you so much for having me, and for such a lovely party. I'm so very excited for the wedding!" Her voice rose in a little squeal.

Adam just stood there for a moment. He wasn't truly ready to leave; he'd hoped to speak to Sophie one more time, and maybe even walk her back to the Castle if she was ready to go. But Miss Lemagne was holding on to his arm and everyone seemed to be looking at him expectantly.

"Mr. Quinn is leaving too," Miss Lemagne said after a pregnant pause. "He's offered to help me with a hack. You *know* how difficult it is to find them sometimes."

He glanced at Sophie, who was intent in conversation with one of the other ladies and who was absolutely not looking in his direction. Damn. He couldn't even catch her eye. "Thank you for a very nice afternoon, Miss Monroe," he said, having no polite choice. Someday, he'd have to talk with his mother about how to extricate himself from an untenable situation like this without embarrassing anyone—including himself. "I wish you all the best with your upcoming wedding."

Sophie still wasn't acknowledging him or the fact that he was leaving, even as he looked back over his shoulder when he and Miss Lemagne walked away.

Well, he could get her into her hackney cab and then go back into the party and talk to Sophie. Maybe she'd be ready to leave too.

Sophie was irritated enough by Miss Lemagne and Mr. Quinn's sudden departure that she decided it was time for action. She needed to do something instead of standing around feeling helpless about everything.

"Felicity, do you think I could have a word with you, inside, for a moment?" she said, giving her friend a warm but meaningful smile.

"Of course, Sophie." They linked arms and walked into the sitting room, and when Felicity would have taken a seat on the sofa, Sophie balked.

"Is there somewhere more private we can talk?"

"Oh. Is this about . . . the investigation?" she whispered, looking about. "Yes, of course. We can go into the parlor."

"How about your father's study?" Sophie asked. She wanted an excuse to be in there one more time, just in case she had the chance to look through that last drawer.

"Well, I suppose. Daddy doesn't really like me to go in there, but . . . all right. It is more private."

As Sophie had hoped, Felicity acquiesced and led the way to the study.

"What is it? Did you find out who the blackmailer is?" Felicity asked right away.

Sophie took her friend's hands and led her away from the door. Standing in front of the large desk, she drew in a deep breath. "No, but there's something else I feel I need to tell you."

"All . . . all right. You look so serious, Sophie. What's wrong?"

She drew in another breath. "I learned something about Mr.

Townsend that I thought you should be aware of. Something that might change your decision to marry him."

Felicity blanched. "What do you mean? Of course I'm going to marry him!" She withdrew her hands from Sophie's and seemed a little angry. "What is it that you think would make me change my mind?"

Sophie decided it was just easier to say it out right, fast and smooth. "Mr. Townsend beats his slaves. He hurts them. He beat one of them so badly he died."

Felicity stared at her, eyes wide, face draining of color. Her mouth moved, but she didn't seem to be able to form words.

"I thought you should know, Felicity, because . . . well, *because* . . ." Sophie spread her hands around to encompass the entire situation. "If he ever found out about . . ." she added barely above a whisper.

"I . . ." Felicity was still staring at her. "No, no, it's . . . it's all right. Of course I'm going to marry him. He'd never hurt anyone—he'd never hurt *me*."

"But, Felicity—"

"No, Sophie. There's—just stop talking. Carson loves me. He's so kind and gentle—he'd *never* do what you're saying. I don't believe it. It's a lie. Whoever told you that is *lying*." Now her lovely face was flushed red and she was so agitated her hands were flying around. "It's a *lie*."

"Felicity, it's true. I saw it. I saw evidence of it—didn't you notice the bruises on Brilla? He gave them to her. He beat her brother to death. He's a brutal, violent—"

The door to the study slammed open and both women spun around as Henry Monroe stalked in, followed by Carson Townsend.

"What is this all about, Townsend?" Mr. Monroe was saying. He appeared agitated and upset. The younger man had a more calculating, set look on his face that instantly made Sophie nervous.

When Mr. Monroe saw the two women standing by the desk, he halted. "What are you doing in here? Felicity! What is the meaning of this?"

"Is it true, Carson?" Felicity said, spinning to him, her eyes wild and glittering with tears. "Did you beat a man to *death*? One of your slaves? Did you?"

Townsend's expression changed from calculating and determined to one filled with loathing. "Get away from me, you damned darky bitch." He shoved her hard, and she stumbled backward, nearly falling to the ground.

Sophie gasped and stepped back, bumping into the desk as Henry Monroe lunged at the younger man with a roar. Townsend dodged the older man's clumsy attack, spinning to the side as Monroe crashed into the wall and tumbled to the floor. When Townsend swung back around, he was holding a revolver.

And he was pointing it at Felicity and Sophie.

CHAPTER 16

Adam got Miss Lemagne her hackney and was able to send her off home without further incident. He breathed a sigh of relief as the cab trundled off down the road, and he turned back to the Monroe house.

Though he was tired of socializing, Adam wasn't about to leave without speaking to Sophie again. Especially after this most recent incident where she wouldn't even look at him as he left to get Miss Lemagne's hackney.

But they were still no closer to finding Pinebar Tufts's and Billy Morris's murderer. Today hadn't helped much at all—while he couldn't eliminate Mr. Monroe from being the culprit, he wasn't convinced the older man was. Stuart Howard was another possibility, and as Sophie surmised, he had the opportunity to learn about the family secret. But Howard hadn't struck Adam as someone conniving enough to carry out a blackmail plan—especially one as complicated as this seemed to be, with a delivery person in the form of Piney Tufts.

And then there was the fact that whoever killed Tufts had gone through the trouble of making it look like suicide. He'd killed the man, and then strung him up in a public place.

Whoever killed Tufts and Billy Morris had *watched* those men die when he strangled them with a walking stick. He was there, close up to their faces, kneeling over them—and he watched as the life went out of them.

What sort of man would do such a thing? What sort of man would kneel over someone, holding a stick across his throat, and watch him struggle while crushing him so he couldn't breathe? Someone who *hated*.

Adam had the image of Billy Morris in his head, with the killer looming over him, there among the massive marble blocks outside the Capitol, in the shadow of that elegant, significant building, slowly murdering a harmless man.

He stopped suddenly as he came around the back of the Monroe house to join the party.

A thought whisked through his mind, and he needed to capture it. Something someone had said . . . something . . .

He remembered it now. Provest, the marble finisher . . . *I always come home wearing some of it, too—like the way she sparkles. Damned impossible to get out of the clothes, though, no matter how hard my missus washes'em. Them little gritty sparkles make me trousers and coat look like the starry sky.*

The killer had been kneeling among the marble blocks and grit while he killed Billy Morris. Adam had seen the marks in the dust and dirt. The effort that would have gone into kneeling into the ground, holding himself steady as he crushed the life out of Billy Morris . . . the minuscule marble grit would have embedded itself in the fabric of the killer's trousers.

And today, Sophie had seen tiny glittery crystals on the front of a pair of trouser legs.

On the front of Carson Townsend's pants.

CHAPTER 17

"*I*'d hoped to have this conversation in a much more digni-fied fashion, but obviously that's not going to be the case." Carson Townsend's elegant demeanor had given way to one of cruelty and barely restrained violence as he locked the door to the study.

Henry Monroe pulled himself slowly to his feet, out of breath, his face white with shock. "How dare you speak to my daughter—"

"Sit down. You. *There*. Now." Townsend gestured with the re-volver and a defeated and frightened Monroe sank onto a chair in front of the desk. Felicity collapsed into the other one, her face so gray she looked as if she were about to faint. This left Sophie standing next to the desk, which was fine with her. Although her mind was reeling, she was also very aware of the revolver in the top drawer of Mr. Monroe's desk. If she could edge around to the other side . . .

"How dare *you* try and trick me into marrying a nigger," Townsend said. His eyes burned with fury. "I ought to shoot you right now."

"It wasn't a trick—"

"Passing her off as white when her mother was a goddamned slave? That's one hell of a trick, and something I knew you'd pay dearly to keep secret." Townsend's voice was cold and hard.

Sophie smothered a gasp. *Townsend* had been the blackmailer?

"How . . . how did you . . . find out?" Monroe said, licking his lips and struggling to take a breath. Sophie hoped the man wouldn't expire from a weak heart in the middle of all of this. "Wh-when?"

Townsend curled his lip at Felicity. "It was only by accident, but I was ever so glad it happened. Imagine if I'd gone through with the wedding? I'd have been a laughingstock if the truth ever came out!"

"But it would never have come out," Monroe whispered as Felicity sobbed softly, hunched in her chair.

"But it *did*. And if *I* found out, then *anyone* could."

"But how did you find out? I did everything I could to keep that secret for eighteen years. Lived away for more than a year, got new servants twice, moved three times... *how?*" Monroe sounded lost and desperate.

"As I said, it was a lucky accident. When your dear, sweet nanny was dying, remember, Felicity? I sent Deucy over with a home remedy to help with her cough? He overheard the woman telling you that you were *her daughter.*" His eyes blazed with fury. "Deucy, loyal bastard that he was, came home and told me I was marrying a darky. He had a smirk on his face when he did, and I—well." Townsend shrugged. "He got the punishment he deserved, and I made certain no one else would learn the truth. You know how those niggers talk."

As she battled the horror of what she was hearing, Sophie edged around the desk, slowly and carefully while he gave his furious, spittle-flecked speech.

"And then I had to decide what to do about the situation," Townsend said. He shifted, moving the revolver so it was pointed directly at Henry Monroe's forehead. "I wanted to kill you for doing this to me. I nearly came over that night and put a bullet into your head. How *dare* you do such a thing!"

He was breathing heavily, and the gun trembled in his hand. Sophie was afraid he'd accidentally set it off and blow Mr. Monroe's head off right here.

By now, she'd reached the corner of the desk and dropped her hand to close it around the drawer handle. She had no idea whether the revolver inside was loaded, but at least she could try. Carefully, she began to ease the drawer open as Carson Townsend continued on his diatribe.

But Townsend got himself under control and continued.

"Then I thought—why make it so easy on the bastard? If I kill him, it's all over with. Instead, I decided I'd make you pay. *Literally.* I'd make you pay for me to keep the secret—that is, until the time was right for me to divulge it to the world. Then I could reasonably break off the wedding—everyone would understand why I wouldn't want to marry a darky, I'd be richer for it—and you'd be ruined.

"But of course, I didn't want to take the chance you'd discover it was me—you're a smart enough gent, Henry, that you'd probably watch for whoever was picking up the money. And so I hired Pinebar Tufts to be my messenger boy. I knew you and Stuart knew him—the better to throw off suspicion onto someone else—and I'd met him when we filed a patent for a new milling grinder earlier this year. He was eager to find a way to make some extra money.

"But then Piney thought he should get more money after he realized what was going on. And that made me angry. He was trying to blackmail *me?*" His mouth was wet with saliva, and it spewed everywhere as he talked. "That bastard deserved to be lynched. He was just as bad as you—trying to fool me into marrying a nigger."

Townsend fell into silence for a moment, and Sophie tensed as his harsh breathing filled the room. He looked as if he were ready to act—what else could he do? He'd just confessed to murdering Pinebar Tufts.

She slipped her fingers into the drawer and closed them around the revolver, praying she was holding it in the right direction, that she could get it out easily, that it was loaded.

"I think it's time for you to pay for what you did—what you tried to do," Townsend said, moving closer to Henry Monroe, holding the revolver aimed at the man's forehead. "And you"—he looked at Felicity, who cowered in her chair—"I'll take you with me. Not as my wife. But you can fulfill other duties in my household." His smile was so cold and lecherous that Sophie felt ill. "After all, you're a very lovely woman."

Suddenly, the study door rattled in its hinges as someone knocked. "Sophie? Mr. Monroe? Are you in there?"

It was Adam.

When Townsend spun to look, Sophie yanked the revolver out of the drawer.

"A private meeting," Townsend called through the door. "Go away."

"Sophie, are you in there?"

"Yes!" she cried, as Townsend whirled back, fury on his face. She pulled the trigger on the revolver as he spun, his gun lifted, and the kick and boom shocked her so hard she stumbled back.

Blessedly, the revolver had been loaded.

CHAPTER 18

"Sophie!"

The door creaked in its hinges as Adam slammed his shoulder and the entire force of his body against it.

One of the servants came running as he slammed against it again, and the man helped as he rammed into the door a third time.

It splintered from its hinges and Adam stumbled into the room, his own revolver in hand, his false arm lifted in front of him like a slender shield. He took in the scene in an instant as the servant rushed past him to Henry Monroe, who was gasping for air in his seat.

Carson Townsend was on the ground, holding the side of his belly, which appeared to be bleeding from a bullet wound. He was gasping for breath and his face was gray.

Sophie and Felicity were clinging to each other—or, more accurately, Felicity was clinging to Sophie, who was standing there with a revolver in her hand and a shocked expression on her face. Felicity was sobbing and Sophie, for once, seemed to have nothing to say until she saw him.

"Adam."

He went to her, but all he could do was place a hand between her shoulder blades, for she was still attached to a sagging Felicity as if the poor girl would never let her go.

"It was him," Sophie said. Her gray eyes were huge in her face, and she still gripped the revolver. "He did it . . . all."

"I know," Adam said. "I reckon you can give me that now." He gently uncurled her fingers from the death grip on the firearm.

"I s-shot him. Is he g-going to die? I didn't mean to kill him, b-but . . ."

"I don't think he's going to die," Adam replied honestly. But at the moment he wasn't certain he'd care if the man did expire on the ground.

He'd heard enough outside the window of the study to know what a cold, amoral man Carson Townsend was.

The moment Constance settled back in her seat in the hackney, she burst into tears. Thank Heaven Adam Quinn had already walked away.

She sat in the carriage, silently furious, tears rolling down her cheeks.

She hated herself.

Hated what she'd done—hated that she'd caused that noble Adam Quinn to look at her as if she were a leper.

Hated that she'd used her fury toward Jelly as a way to hurt Sophie Gates.

Hated that she'd teased and exaggerated and made sly comments meant to drive Sophie Gates—who'd been nothing but kind to her—from Adam Quinn, when anyone could see the two were besotted with each other. And that they would make a wonderful match.

She hated that she grieved for Jelly, who'd *left* her. Who, after more than twenty years of mothering her, holding her, loving her, had simply *left*. Run away.

How could she?

Didn't she care about her, Constance? Didn't she *care* that she had no mother, no one who loved her?

Didn't anyone care that her world was about to be turned upside down in this horrible war?

Didn't anyone care that she'd nearly lost her father, and that a black man had had to save his life?

And that she'd shot a white man in order to save a black man?

Constance sobbed and grieved and loathed all the way home,

and was grateful that Mr. Quinn had given the hackney driver directions so that all she had to do was get out of the carriage and pay.

And then when she found out he'd already paid the fare, she began to sob even harder. She'd been so awful to people today, and over the last several days since Jelly had left and she'd turned into a spy.

She hated what she'd done, how she'd acted, the things she'd spoken.

Constance stumbled into the quiet house, miserable, angry, bereaved, confused.

It took her a moment to realize, through her tears and fury, that she wasn't alone.

"Miss? Are you all right?"

It was George Hilton, coming from the parlor where her father's snores could be heard. He'd been here nearly every day to check on his patient's progress.

Why did he have to be here *now?*

Constance dragged a hand across her face, sniveling and stumbling and bedraggled.

She was so tired. So grieved. So *angry.*

"Come on, miss. Sit down here." He took her arm and gently led her to a sofa in the front sitting room. "Are you hurt? Did someone hurt you?"

"N-no." *Yes.* "Yes. J-Jelly," she managed to whisper. "She left me. I hate her. I *hate* her for leaving me." She dissolved into deep, wracking sobs again—grief that she'd tucked away beneath a brittle exterior for the last few days.

Someone—George—thrust a handkerchief into her hand and she mopped her face with it. She didn't even care that she was a sopping, watery mess.

"Why did she leave me?" she moaned. Her head hurt and she felt as dry and parched as she imagined a desert would be. "I was good to her. I *loved* her. I never"—sob—"hurt her."

He said nothing, merely sat there on the edge of a chair across from her as she bawled and moaned and railed.

"Why?" she demanded, glaring at him through puffy, teary eyes. "How could she?"

"Because, Constance," he said in a low, deep voice, "she didn't have a choice. She ran away because she *couldn't* leave if she wanted to. So she took her freedom and she ran."

"Damn her," she cried as his words pierced her. "Damn her. Damn *you*."

And the next thing she knew, she'd erupted from her seat. He stood, catching her before she threw herself across the room in the violent tantrum she intended. Suddenly, she was in his arms, sobbing as if her heart was breaking.

She needed love, needed comfort. Needed to be held.

George was a physician. He was trained to help and to heal.

At least, that was what he told himself when his arms went around the shaking, sobbing, soft, lovely woman.

He thought: *Dear God, help me.*

It was after dark by the time Sophie and Adam were able to leave the Monroe house. He insisted on getting a hack to drive her back to the Castle, and for once she didn't feel like walking and so didn't argue.

"May I ride with you?" he asked.

"Of course, Mr. Quinn," she replied haughtily. "You're quite handy at arranging for hackneys, after all, and so therefore you should enjoy the convenience."

She moved her legs out of the way as he folded then unfolded his long body to climb in and settle into the seat across from her. His long limbs stretched out in the space between the benches but remained far enough away so they didn't tangle with her skirts.

With a sigh, she untied the ribbon under her chin and pulled off the bonnet with a groan of relief. It felt so good to let her head and hair breathe. "I hope you don't mind my informality, Mr. Quinn, but I just couldn't wear this thing any longer."

She set the bonnet on the seat next to her, and barely managed to refrain from pulling the pins from her sticky, plastered hair. That would have to wait until she was home.

In the dim light, she looked at him from across the carriage. "How did you know? Was it the flour bags?"

"The flour bags?"

"At the Capitol Bakery. I didn't put it together until it was too late, but I remembered seeing all the flour bags with the name of the mill stamped on them. Townsend Mills. It didn't mean anything to me at the time, but I realized that was why Mr. Townsend was roaming around the basement of the Capitol and frightened the Lincoln boys. His family mill in Baltimore was supplying some of the flour for the bakery. I didn't connect the two until it was too late. But how did you know?"

"It was the sparkling on his trousers," he replied, and went on to explain. "If you hadn't noticed that, I probably wouldn't have made the connection and come looking for you. When I realized you were missing—and so was Miss Monroe, Mr. Monroe, and Townsend, I knew something was wrong. I heard some of what he said from outside the study window on my way to the party in the back, but there was no way I could come in through the window without Townsend seeing me—and putting a bullet in me. So"— his broad shoulders shrugged in the shadows—"I came in the other way."

"Thank goodness you did."

"When I heard the shot . . . Damn it, Sophie, I didn't know what to do. I didn't know it was you—I thought one of you had been shot."

"If I hadn't been snooping around earlier, I wouldn't have known about the revolver in the drawer."

"Thank God for that." She saw his mouth twitch in the dim light. "Although I reckoned that your little drawstring bag might have had a derringer in it, from the way it looked so heavy, dangling from your wrist."

She gave a short, surprised laugh. "A candle, a magnifying glass, and a penknife—but I had recently thought I should get a derringer to keep on hand for such occasions. I suppose I'd better do that, now that this is the second time I've come face-to-face with a killer." She shivered a little. "Thank you again, Mr. Quinn. If you hadn't come along—"

"Sophie."

"What?"

"My name is Adam."

He sounded angry, and she looked across at him. "Yes, of course. I just . . . well, drat it, Adam, I didn't realize you were courting Constance Lemagne." She managed to leave off the *too*, but just barely. How mortifying. She didn't want him to think she cared, but, blast it all, she discovered that she did. Or had, anyway.

And of course, her big mouth had to actually *say* it.

Adam's eyes flew open wide as he looked across at her in the drassy light. "Courting Miss Lemagne? How . . . did you come to that conclusion? Surely not simply because I helped her to get a hackney?"

"Of course not. But when a man escorts a woman to her house at almost eleven o'clock at night, it seems quite obvious that he's courting her."

Sophie's heart sank a little when he didn't seem to know how to respond. But his hesitation lasted only a moment. "In fact, that is something I wanted to talk to you about. I did bring Miss Lemagne home very late on Tuesday night because she was crossing the Chain Bridge back into Washington—not because I'm courting her. When I accidentally saw her at the bridge, I discovered she'd given her name as Wisteria Jones in order to cross over."

"Wisteria Jones—what on earth? Why would she lie about her name?" Despite the fact that she was bone-tired, Sophie sat upright in her seat.

"I happened to recognize her, and of course when she saw me, she knew she'd been caught. But I wasn't certain what she'd been *caught* doing. She claimed she was meeting someone, and she made it clear that it was a—uh—a man that she was meeting in secret, and she'd gotten a ride in a tanner's cart."

"Oh." Sophie clamped her mouth closed after that single syllable. A myriad of thoughts raced through her mind, but for once she decided to be like Adam and wait for the other person to say all there was to say.

"I don't know whether to believe her, or—well, I reckoned because of what you'd told me about Mrs. Greenhow, and from what I know about Miss Lemagne, she might have been bringing secrets to the Confederates."

"You think she might be a spy?" Sophie sat back in her seat and thought about that.

She could see it. Oh, she could *definitely* see Constance Lemagne as a Confederate spy.

"I don't know. That was the first thing I thought when I saw her and heard her giving out a wrong name."

Sophie nodded, leaning forward a little. "So she wanted you to think she was meeting a man, in secret, across the river in Virginia? I doubt that very much, to be honest. Constance wouldn't meet a man who wasn't—well, a city man. And there are plenty of places to meet someone in the city. Tell me, what was she wearing?"

Adam blinked at her. "A bonnet. A dress. A cloak?"

She sighed. "Were there any flowers on the bonnet? Was it fancy?" He shook his head, and she went on, "What about the dress? Was it lacy, fancy, wide?" She gave an exasperated sigh, "You must have helped her down from whatever she was riding in. . . . Were there a lot of skirts and fabric that got in the way? Or was it . . . simpler?"

"There wasn't a lot—not like what she was wearing today. Or even you, now." He gestured vaguely at her skirts.

Sophie smiled complacently and settled back. "Then she wasn't meeting a man. Constance Lemagne wouldn't go to a romantic clandestine meeting dressed in a simple gown and a plain bonnet. Absolutely not. I think you're safe in your initial assessment that she is—or was—a spy."

And then, as she spoke those words, Sophie realized what they meant. What they could portend. She could be sentencing a woman—an almost friend—for something she wasn't certain of. What did they do to spies, anyway? "But of course, that's just my opinion."

"I'll make note of that, Miss Gates. Your opinion." He smiled at her from across the way as the hackney rolled to a stop in front of the Smithsonian Castle.

"Thank you so much for seeing me home, Mr. Quinn. Adam," she corrected herself. "Adam."

He climbed out of the carriage and helped her down. "I reckon I should clarify one thing."

"And that is . . . ?"

"Since it's after eleven o'clock—and apparently that's the criteria for whether a man's courting a woman—I confess there is a woman I'm intending to be courting."

Sophie's heart did that funny little trip as she looked up at him, bonnet in hand. "Oh?"

He gazed down at her and took both of her hands in his large warm one. "I hope she'll agree to it. Since it's after eleven o'clock and all."

She couldn't seem to look away from his dark, sober, waiting gaze, and smiled. "She'd be a fool not to."

AFTERWORD

*O*ne week later, on Sunday, July 21, 1861, all of the shops in Washington were crowded and busy.

People were ordering hampers filled with food, and the shopkeepers and French cooks could hardly keep up with them. They tripled their prices for wine, oysters, meat pies, pastries, and other delicacies, packing the baskets full of rich meals and fine linens—and collecting hefty fees for doing so.

Every carriage, wagon, gig, and cart available for rent in the city had been spoken for at increased rates, and loaded up with enthusiastic congressmen, businessmen, and even a few bold women, along with their meals, spyglasses, fans, and firearms.

Carriages and wagons rolled nonstop over the bridges into Virginia, and excitement pervaded conversation of everyone in the city.

Today was the day! Today the Big Battle would be fought—the Union troops and the Confederate army were meeting near a small creek named Bull Run, just outside of Manassas—barely thirty miles from the city.

General McDowell's men had been leaving the city in stages over the last week, and at last they would meet in a decisive battle that would crush the Confederates once and for all.

Spectators—for that was who'd leased the carriages and ordered elegant luncheons—drove their carriages to Centreville, where a small rise of hillocks overlooked the clearing near Bull

Run Creek. They jockeyed their vehicles about, lining up along the rise in order to get the best view possible. Even as they approached, dressed in their Sunday best with spyglasses at the ready, they could hear the distant sound of artillery in the distance. Clouds of smoke and stirred-up dirt filled the air, obstructing their view.

But they knew a battle was going on, and they ate and drank merrily as the troops slaughtered each other below.

Matthew Brady, a photographer, had the idea that he could be the first man to ever photograph a battlefield. He loaded up his carriage with equipment and trundled out of town with the rest of the city, riding over the Long Bridge into Virginia.

Henry Wilson, the senator in charge of the Military Affairs Committee and particular friend of Rose Greenhow, was also one of the audience who rode out to Centreville to watch the battle. Unbeknownst to him, days earlier General Beauregard had received a copy of the committee's map that showed the Union troops' route to Manassas, thanks to Rose Greenhow and her spy network.

Back in Washington, telegrams came in to the War Department throughout the day, assuring Lincoln and his cabinet of great success for the Federals. Their troops were moving forward, pressing on, and all was well. The news was all good.

But at six o'clock the final message came in: *The battle is lost. McDowell is in full retreat and General Scott must save the capital.*

As the inexperienced, green Union army retreated, blind with terror and the realities of a war they'd never imagined, their disorganized, pell-mell flight caught up with the spectators in their carriages. It was a mess of dust, terror, smashing and spilling wagons, carts, carriages, sutlers' teams, and panicked soldiers. Some of the spectators' vehicles crashed; others were commandeered to transport the wounded.

Overnight and through the next day, soldiers, vehicles, spectators, and the wounded straggled into the city—exhausted, terrified, and shocked.

The tide had turned, and it was clear the war would not be over soon.

* * *

In the first battle of Bull Run, over sixty thousand forces were engaged. The Union army boasted over twenty-eight thousand troops, and the Confederates had thirty-two thousand. Nearly five thousand casualties resulted from the "big battle."

The Confederates would hang on, fighting for their way of life, for another four years.

A NOTE FROM
THE AUTHOR

As I research more deeply into this time period, I find more and more fascinating things that simply have to find their way into my books.

For the most part, any historical detail that appears in the Lincoln White House Mysteries is as accurate as I can make it. The only true fictional elements are those around the specific crime and my fictional characters, like Adam, Sophie, George, Constance, and Brian.

Thus, the description of how the Capitol Dome was being built and the mess in and around the building is true. The destruction by the troops in both the Capitol and the Patent Office, as well as throughout the city, is accurate as well.

Yes, there was really a slaughterhouse built on the National Mall, and yes, a herd of cattle really did fall into the Canal and needed to be fished out.

The bakery in the basement of the Capitol remained there until the summer of 1862, despite complaints from members of Congress about the smell, the noise, and the destruction from the chimneys. In fact, someone had the brilliant idea of connecting the basement bakery chimneys to those running up into the Library of Congress . . . which resulted in a significant amount of destruction from smoke and soot to many documents.

And yes, the Lincoln boys and their cohorts, Bud and Holly Taft, really did go missing one day and really were found late in the evening in the Capitol basement bakery. Tad and Willie Lincoln were just as boisterous and wild as I've portrayed them in this book, and their father just as indulgent and loving toward them.

Finally, the story about Rose Greenhow and her spy network is quite true. The description of how Constance brought the map to the Confederates is how Bettie Duvall and other real-life members carried such documents, which were often written in a special code that Rose used. The packets were rolled up and bundled in her hair as she sneaked across the lines to the Rebels.

Whether Rose Greenhow and Senator Wilson had a love affair is a question that may never be answered; there are arguments both for and against it and it's clear she did obtain confidential information available only to his Committee on Military Affairs.

Rose's spy network was cut off when she was arrested on August 23, 1861, after months of being watched by the Pinkertons (in my mind, this was ultimately because of the suspicions Sophie shared with Adam). Rose Greenhow was subsequently imprisoned as a spy, and eventually she was allowed to exile herself to London until the war was over.

I hope you enjoyed these historical details as much as I did, and I look forward to sharing more fascinating information in future books.

—C.M. Gleason
February 2020

ACKNOWLEDGMENTS

With this third book in the Lincoln's White House Mystery Series, I have an ever-growing list of people to thank for their support and efforts in bringing the story to life, and the books to the stores!

The team at Kensington—especially my editor Wendy McCurdy and her brilliant assistant Norma Perez-Hernandez—has been a pleasure to work with, and I'm grateful to be in such expert hands. Larissa Ackerman and Michelle Ado round out a great team of thoughtful, savvy, and enthusiastic publicity professionals. And the new cover design is absolutely brilliant—I was so delighted to see that the actual crane for the Capitol Dome was incorporated in the illustration—and I'm forever grateful to the Kensington Art Department for such a great cover.

My fantastic, patient agent, Maura Kye-Casella, has, as always, been a firm guide as well as an energetic and savvy advocate for me, my books, and my career overall.

Gary March, D.O., continues to be my number-one go-to for all things medical. Any errors are mine alone, for he's spent far too much time helping me to determine just how a leg could be broken—but not really broken, so that George Hilton could save the day. Dr. March is not only creative but detailed in helping me with all the medical questions and issues in these books.

I am so very grateful to my friends, family, and readers who've supported this series from the very first book—especially Mark Clark, Susan Judd, and Denise Phillips (owner of a the fantastic indie bookstore Gathering Volumes in Ohio)—and the gals from the 12TTRT who helped promote the books at Malice Domestic: MaryAlice, Diane, Erin, Darlene, and Donna.

I wouldn't be where I am today without the love, support, and guidance of my mother, Joyce, and my stepfather Larry. Thank you for the infinite ways you've supported me and my career over the years.

And finally, as always, my thanks and infinite gratitude to my husband Steve and my three amazing children—all of whom have been subjected to the various requirements of being close to a working author: last-minute pizza-delivery meals (if that), acting out the choreography of crimes, dinner discussions over the distribution of clues, listening to me ramble on about fascinating (at least to me!) historical facts, and so on. I love you all!

—C.M. Gleason, February 2020